The Bullet Collection

the bullet collection

Patricia Sarrafian Ward

Graywolf Press
SAINT PAUL, MINNESOTA

Publication of this volume is made possible in part by a grant provided by the Minnesota State Arts Board, through an appropriation by the Minnesota State Legislature; a grant from the Wells Fargo Foundation Minnesota; and a grant from the National Endowment for the Arts. Significant support has also been provided by the Bush Foundation; Marshall Field's Project Imagine with support from the Target Foundation; the McKnight Foundation; and other generous contributions from foundations, corporations, and individuals. To these organizations and individuals we offer our heartfelt thanks.

An earlier version of this novel won a Hopwood Award at the University of Michigan in 1995. Excerpts have appeared in *Jusoor: Post Gibran Anthology of New Arab American Writing,* edited by Munir Akash and Khaled Mattawa (1999), and in *Ararat,* in the special supplement *Scenes from Childhood,* edited by Leo Hamalian and Nancy Kricorian (1999). Vermont Studio Center and Virginia Center for the Creative Arts provided time and support.

Published by Graywolf Press
2402 University Avenue, Suite 203
Saint Paul, Minnesota 55114

www.graywolfpress.org

Printed in Canada
Published in the United States of America

ISBN 1-55597-376-0

2   4   6   8   9   7   5   3   1
First Graywolf Printing, 2003

Library of Congress Control Number: 2002111741

Cover design: Julie Metz
Cover art: Zeina Barakeh, *Witness* and *Abandoned Beirut*

∽

In loving memory
Jerome Badanes

 *Autumn*

Before the war was real, I climbed the dry, rocky hill with the neighbor's daughter Salia, we stung our bare legs on the pricker bushes, the blood welling up like tiny bugs. We gathered thyme, carried armfuls of the long, fragrant stalks to her mother, who plucked the leaves and stored them in jars on the peeling blue shelves in their kitchen. We sat at the small table and licked our fingers to dip them in the salt bowl; we ate egg sandwiches with tomatoes; we competed to see how high we could hold the abriq, the water jug, as we poured the water into our mouths. Fadi came in from hunting and I sneaked looks at his gun and the dead birds swinging from his belt so he winked at me and stroked my fine blond hair. I pretended he would take me hunting one day, but he disappeared later in the war; his family waited but he never came home.

Before the war was real, the world went on forever and we were allowed to think of going places. The world meant taxi rides to Damascus to visit the souqs, and day trips to Shtaura, the Barouk Mountains, Trablos, Saida, Sour. The world meant Baalbak, where Alaine and I sat cross-legged on pedestals and sketched the fallen columns. We wanted to ride the tourist camel but Daddy said it was flea-bitten and Mummy said we weren't tourists anyway.

In winter, Beirut meant chestnuts singeing our tongues, it meant unrolling the carpets and chasing the naphthalene balls that sprinkled out all over the floor, it meant bowls of lentil soup and the fire crackling as Mummy dressed us for school. Christmas meant Téta lighting candles in the pine tree and Jiddo singing in Armenian, the smell of sweet wine boiling on the stove. In summer, Shemlan meant the low hills tumbling away into terraces with grapevines and fig trees and olive groves, and the roads winding to distant villages white and spare in the sun. At night Mummy wandered outside, smelling the ghostly jasmine in the dark, and Daddy opened another old book under a lamp, a magnifying glass by his side.

On summer days, we harvested the lavender humming with bees and sewed it into small bags that we hid among our underwear. We wound our way along the bottom terrace near the road, carrying baskets for figs, and we stood in the shade of the tree and opened the figs to eat them as we picked. I sucked on the ripe skins until they were clean and smooth, and Mummy told me that if I touched my eyes the juice would make me blind, so I held my hands stiffly away from my body, like walking on a tightrope.

Before the war was real, stone steps led up between the terraces to a field swaying with red poppies and daisies and heather. Our water tank stood on stilts at the end of this field, and Jiddo taught me to find the water level with my palms flat against the metal. A dirt path sloped up to the main road of the village, and beyond, there lay an old mansion owned by a Macedonian family. They had six daughters, all with straight, long black hair, who sat in rows when we visited, and it was like being in a room full of mirrors. Farther up the hill, Mummy's uncle Ara built his house, decorating the wall along the road with stone heads of ancient gods and goddesses from Jiddo's collection, and they gazed down on us with eroded eyes.

✽

Again: I wake up with my hands reaching for shining sea, cracked summer road, falling away of hills. I'm a child standing at the lower gate to our cottage in the mountains, I look down at my scratched, tan legs, feel the sun-heated road beneath my bare feet. The low hum of summer afternoon fills my ears, the trees brimming with cicadas sway above me. In these moments between sleep and wakefulness, I squeeze shut my eyes, push my face into the pillow to create the darkness against my eyelids that might bring back my dreams. But I am in this room again, this place.

Alaine's bed is next to mine, unmade, her pajamas tossed on the pillow. The closet door stands open, the mirror at an angle reflecting the window. Autumn has come. Damp leaves gust across the empty parking lot beyond the garden. Yesterday, I saw the sky turn to slate midmorning, as if night were coming, but for the strange yellow light filtered between the trees. I have never seen such rich colors, such reds and yellows and browns, the colors of photographs. I never knew what it is to say, *Autumn*.

I turn away, closing my eyes again: nothing here can be beautiful. I look inward to the night, to my dream self who had promised that this time I really had gone back home to my true life. The lingering images grow stronger at my insistence: the sea burns silver in the sun, and Amer teases me for fearing a silly dream, his laughter infecting me with a raggedy hopefulness. *You're here, not there!* he cries, stamping his feet. His arms are dark, it is the end of summer, and his sideways looks show affectionate tolerance for me, me still trembling in the effort to believe. The landscape shimmers and rifts, yielding faint confusion, *Am I really home?* I want to trust him. He smiles, pointing at the sea.

I sense my body's shape, its weight on this mattress beneath the weight of the dark morning. I lie still for a time, listening to the television's low hum through the wall.

My name called for the third time, Mummy's voice snagged with impatience. I do not see the urgency; none of us has anything to do here. I pull the blanket over my head. The door, which is kept ajar, squeaks all the way open.

—Marianna. It's almost noon.

My father's tired, gentle voice I obey. He nods as I sit up.

—Good, he says, confirmation of some inside hope, or final punctuation to the long morning's struggle to raise me from bed.

He retreats. I feel my feet flat on the cold floor, hands in fists on my thighs. *Move,* my fists say, grinding at my legs.

The kitchen has the atmosphere of recent activity. A pot on the stove, towel crumpled on the counter, dishes piled in the sink. Mummy is just starting on them, her face barring conversation. She's wearing a blue skirt and frilly blouse, the kind that embarrasses me because it looks as if it should be on an old person. I don't know why she's dressed up like this. I can tell she has been crying again. Guilt transforms my body into a stiff wooden thing with burned eyes. It fills the kettle, sets it on the stove. It spoons instant coffee into its favorite mug. Then it stares out the window. Noon. The sky is dark silver, roiling with clouds. Trees bend this way and that, spinnning off their brilliant dead leaves. No world is truly this.

—Your water's boiling, Mummy says. She dries her hands, keeping her eye on the kettle as if it might explode.

I turn off the flame. I want to say, *I'm sorry.* I want to say, *I thought it was around eight, and look how dark the sky can become in October.* Instead I pour water and noisily stir in sugar, and she goes into the bedroom adjoining the kitchen, pulls the door closed. Daddy glances up at me from his chair in the living room.

—Why don't you help Alaine in the garden, honey?

His suggestion is tentative, a hand reaching into a wild animal's cage. I don't answer. His hopeful expression shifts to resignation; he settles back to reading as if I am not there. Dull pain in my chest, trudging through the rest of my body. I am amazed by this, that the mind can infect the flesh. I sit at the table beneath the kitchen window, palm resting on my coffee mug's rim for warmth. The noises from the bedroom indicate that Mummy is once again tidying an already tidy, threadbare space. There isn't much one can do with a single closet, an old bed, and a bedside table with a missing drawer.

After a time, I hear chair legs scrape the floor, the creaky release of weight from the sagging cushion. I can picture Daddy's slow, deliberate motions, like those of a sick old man. He chooses the hall instead of the kitchen to get to their bedroom. I listen to their voices, the words indistinguishable. I had wanted to say sorry as he walked by, but he chose the hall, and now the briefly happy intent is mud in my mouth. I am a gargoyle, crouched on the kitchen chair.

We have been in America for eight months. First Daddy fled because of the kidnappings, then we followed, and now the vision with which we comforted ourselves, *Just a little while and then we'll go home,* has evaporated. Mummy intends to return after Christmas to pack the rest of our belongings and ship them here. I argue that we can't possibly live here forever, we have to go back when it's safe, but they shush at me, they turn away.

Daddy likes to say, so sadly, America is your home, too. You are of two countries. They tell me I look towards the past too much. But I know what's going to happen. Daddy's childhood here is photographs in black and white, signifying *long ago,* nothing to do with this place around me nor the places I have come from. He himself crossed the ocean to Lebanon as a young man and did not return for thirty years. In his absence, his parents died, his friends moved away. The landmarks of his youth have been razed to parking lots, the roads no longer lead to the same places. He left it all behind, and now he does not belong here.

—The cars don't drive the same, he says with regret, or, You can't find an honest business anywhere.

He accepts equally all the areas of our new life in the manner of someone who has come to know disappointment. I want him to fight. He storms outside and heaves up the roads and telephone poles and shops and cars that don't drive the same, and from this destruction, my huge Daddy reshapes the place he left behind, all in black and white, and we live there.

It isn't so. The world is furious color signifying an alien winter coming. We huddle in a falling-down house that is not ours.

He has discovered an old, smelly shop downtown, owned by honest men who greet him when he enters and wave good-bye when he leaves, and in between they mention the New England damp. My father loves this place; he will take a bus there just to buy a box of nails. He asks if I want to go along and I pretend not to hear. Everything he says to me is transparent, a scared stitching of words trying to cover up his worn-down heart.

Ever since I almost died, we, this family, circle each other like shadows. We are lit from behind by fear, our shapes moving behind veils, the veils brushed by hand, knee. There is no speaking when I enter a room. I hear their voices, low and cautious behind walls, their steps tiptoeing closer, checking on me. I listen, but I don't care what they say. I already know, from when we talked like this about Alaine and Alaine lay in her room, like me, listening and not caring.

No matter how often I tell myself, *Don't look,* my eye is drawn across the street to the gas station's dirty windows. I part the curtain slightly, peek one-eyed at the tall, thin shape of the young man, Walter, who came running when he saw us. The father in the open door, begging for his daughter, who lay curled at his feet, asleep. The gray light of the day. I cannot endure the pictures in my mind. I brush black over the pictures. Push them down into dark, where they lie down again, slow their breathing. They wait inside me. They will never go away.

Walter watches our house: first he was in love with the older sister, who stopped speaking to him, and then he found the younger one, dying. Our mouths closed to him. His mouth close to me, saying, *There, there,* and my Daddy crying.

I see Daddy pause at the gas-station office now and then, on his way back from errands.

At night before he goes to bed, Daddy mixes a whiskey and sits in the pantry reading news magazines. He sits there so the ice clinking in his drink doesn't disturb our sleep, the walls are that thin. The pantry is narrow and his chair just fits; when he looks up, startled by whoever has come upon him, the confined space and lightbulb above his head suggest an interrogation room.

There is no order to nostalgia. Images assault me, the hungry one. *I have waited and waited,* the stranger says gleefully, and Ziad stares back, not understanding. There is also Muna, many years before I was born, smiling at the sky. And the decomposing body rolling off my sister's hands into the shallow hole she dug herself. Paul cries in the hospital bed, Marko leans the speeding bike away from the truck, too late, and Amer sings to me, the smell of molten silver in the air. There is how we came here, and why we had to. Not only the dead and the missing haunt me: every step, I long for my country that is not mine, where the sea draws back over the mossy rocks, the mountains soar away from the valley, the rivers rush from their source.

In this house, the blotched, exhausted wood floors yield beneath our weight. There are no secrets here; all our desires echo in our creaking footsteps. The wood smells, too, of warm, damp summers, of old food. The linoleum floors in the kitchen and bathroom have their own sound; footsteps thump hollowly, reminding us of the rejected floor beneath. Where the linoleum meets the walls and the shower stall in the bathroom, it curls away, a narrow nest for grit and damp dust balls, an old toothpaste cap, bobby pins. This at first appalled me, but now I recognize it as a necessary facet of our new life, a sign of all we have lost.

I miss the quiet, cold tiles of Beirut, which bore no trace of dirt when cleaned, and which smoothly joined the walls so that the apartment was of one smooth piece, a whole thing. The missing runs through my body, translates into journeys through the rooms until someone gets annoyed, shouts, Stop it! and for a moment silence comes, silence works through me. I have to control my feet, which are always trying to escape the unfamiliar surfaces beneath them. It is as if there is a hidden law created in moving from one country to another, a law against remembering, and I am breaking it.

I have been asking questions. I ask my mother if she knew about the spy and the skeleton and Ziad, and also the other stories, and she says no. I ask my father if he knew, and he says no. Now they're murmuring behind the door, ajar so that I will not be alone, the condition of my release from hospital. I get up. My eye, drawn to the sliver of space between door and jamb, finds them caught in fearful silence, watching. Every motion I make threatens to lift me away, up through the ceiling, beyond their frail powers.

I sit on the corner of Alaine's trunk in the bedroom, place my mug on the windowsill. The sill is dusty, tracked with rainmarks from the last downpour when we forgot to close the window all the way. I rub them with my finger, watching Alaine work in the garden. My whole childhood I watched Alaine through windows or from the balcony. I recognize this, the familiarity of sitting here, spying, mingled with the utter foreignness of where we are. I would watch her and plan what to say and never say it, not really, and here I've been wanting to tell her, *No one remembers anything,* but she is hunched over the hard ground, our American garden, frowning at whatever task she set herself. She follows her private schedules like a soldier. After years of being our family's sorrow, she is determined to help us settle here. Most recently, she has decided to transform this house within and without. She has learned about wallpaper, paint, sanding and staining wood. My father helps her, revealing capabilities we never suspected he had and which date from his youth here. A list on the refrigerator suggests what they each need to do. I have not been on it for weeks.

She kneels in a striped T-shirt and shorts, her face set to a grim sort of stubbornness, as if she is prepared to defeat any resistance on the part of the ground. Two books lie in the grass, the pages held down by stones. Seed packets and bulbs wrapped in clear plastic are piled up next to them. She does not yet know what she is doing. She examines a page, frowning, holding the book in both hands. Her wiry brown hair is long, halfway down her back, and she has it tied in a rubber band. The hair must be tangled in the band, and I know that later she will be furious and impatient while Mummy works at the knots.

She glances up, finds me in the window. Come help, she says.

I want to, but I can't. My body is tired, uninterested in such activities. I am in this dark wooden room, a coffin, looking out onto a bright-colored world of leaves and grass, and onto my sister, who has always been kind to me no matter her troubles. She sees the look on my face, shrugs, returns to her digging. I try to call out that I am on my way, that I want to help, but my mouth remains firmly closed, locking me inside my body, a prison. Anger fills the empty place of my failed intentions.

I ask my parents about the spy and the skeleton and Ziad, and also the other stories, and they say no. I never ask Alaine anything. I think she always knew we would never go back. In summer, not long after the hospital released me, she burned up everything she owned. Then she changed. Like those Russian soldiers burning the land when they retreated, that's what Alaine was doing. She will talk only about this wooden house and how to fix it, as if that's possible, and whatever pitfalls our lost family must watch out for.

Such as, *Be careful of the tomatoes here, they're sprayed red to look ripe and then trucked across the country.* How does one beware of a tomato? By placing it on the windowsill, watching to see how long it takes to rot. Too long, is the answer. You beware by sniffing with suspicion, buying only from the roadside stands, if there's enough money in your pocket. You spend time discussing it all as if it's the key to survival.

Don't you remember? I shout, making no sound. She unwraps one of the bulbs, holds it up for examination. Then she sets upon the rest with swift, efficient motions.

I am small and Daddy says, Go see if your big sister is all right, and I felt special, because I was the only one blessed with passage into Alaine's world, and without me they would know nothing. This was long after the war began, in the time of the dead soldier in the mountains. We ate supper on the terrace, looking down at *poor Beirut* as the grown-ups called it, sparsely lit, swaths of black where the electricity was gone. I felt Uncle Ara wanting us to leave, to go back to the city, taking away our secrets and Alaine's collection of shrapnel and bullets and other things from the war. I walked one foot in front of the other on the periphery of the rose garden, scared to go among the bushes because the ashes of Téta and Jiddo and Auntie Lupsi were scattered there, or I wandered the road, looking for bullets and fossils. The grown-ups' voices drifted in and out of earshot, saying the war would end soon, arguing about why and how, details that held no interest for me, and I counted the stone heads of gods looking out of the wall along the road and stroked their foreheads and lips. Alaine regularly went upstairs early, leaving her food barely touched, and no one said anything, but if I tried to leave anything on my plate I was chastised. Then someone would say, We should check on Alaine, and I imagined her in our bedroom, lying on her back with her usual sullen glare, listening to the voices floating up to the balcony, through the glass doors and into the room.

There is another memory of something different, of climbing slowly with everyone's eyes on me, Go see what's happened, because of the sound of glass breaking a few moments before. The door to our bedroom is ajar, and it is quiet within. All the while, the soft wind blew through the trees, the cicadas hummed. From far away the occasional dull thuds of gunfire reached us through the night, unlikely there, noises made by ghosts.

The wind here is a wind of leaves and branches, the ghostly clanging of chimes. I lie in my bed. The sound of me, breathing, floats out the window, out into that big world.

It happened at the end of summer. That day, the air was damp. Water covered everything. The door opened onto that watery world, the gray light. My father's hands held my head so it would not knock against the floor when my body seized up against the work of my heart. I do not remember this. We do not speak of it.

My eyelids feel so heavy, swollen. Cheeks gritty with dried tears. Was I loud, crying as I slept? No one came. Alaine calls again; the noise that woke me. It is lunchtime, two o'clock. We still eat lunch as our main meal, though in America, it's supposed to be dinner.

Everyone is in the kitchen making last-minute preparations. Anxious merriment, a family on the brink of collapse, striving for normalcy. Napkins, a missing fork, trays, where's the salt. I gather my tray to my chest, rocking on my heels. Mummy smiles into the pot on the stove, poking the meal with a wooden spoon. She's brushed her shoulder-length hair back into barrettes, and her thin neck and profile remind me momentarily of the girl in her albums. I know from the lemony mint smell that she's made my favorite, *malfouf mehsheh,* stuffed cabbage. It's the first time we've had it here. My face stiffens under the skin, a coagulation of hard planes, full of pain. I want to close up, shut out this gift she's so proud of.

—Oh my, honey! Daddy exclaims, breathing in the smell. That looks great! Alaine murmurs the same.

They let me fill my plate first. I cannot believe I didn't notice the signs of this meal earlier, so I could be prepared for everyone waiting, everyone expecting. My mouth waters against my will and I take more than usual. Then my hunger fades under the awkward, poorly hidden pleasure of my parents, who have been worried their daughter will starve herself. I can't bear to please them when the promise is so empty. I put several of the *malfoufs* back.

—Oh, take them! Mummy says. Disappointment crumbles her smile.

I follow Alaine to the living room. She's already turned on *One Life to Live.* We each have our own piece of furniture, staked out the day we brought it home. We never sit in a different arrangement, and we almost always arrive in the same order, like the same code tapped out day after day, *Save us, help us, teach us to sit at a table again and talk like normal people.* But no soul in the universe is listening, so we eat with trays on our laps, hunched so as not to spill between plate and mouth, and we concentrate on the unfolding lives of soap-opera characters. During commercials, whoever has the remote mutes the sound, or else Mummy groans, Oh, why are they so loud? Or, So silly! as if the program we watch in between has substance by comparison.

—Mmmm, Daddy says, nodding as he chews. But the *malfouf* hasn't softened, and there's something off about the filling. Mummy looks tired as she eats, she's eating wood, she chews doggedly on.

—The *malfouf* is different here, she says, her eyes on the soundless commercial.

—It's fine, says Alaine, and takes a big bite to prove it.

They're all waiting for me to speak but I can't, the *malfouf* is awful. It's hard and tastes almost like it should, but only almost, not enough, like everything else here. Each mouthful tastes like failure, the taste of this house and furniture and Mummy's pale face staring at the TV when she used to sit at the table, wise and laughing, and everyone loved every meal.

—If you don't like it, Mummy says with that new ice in her voice, the way she learned to talk when we moved here, then throw it in the toilet.

I eat. The show winds on, drugging our spurt of conversation to numbness. Alaine and Mummy leave, taking my plate as well. Daddy mutes the sound.

—Did you ask Mummy about her interview?

I had forgotten all about this. The frilly blouse, the skirt. That was why. I stare in the direction of the kitchen, the sound of Mummy putting dishes away.

—Go ask, he encourages, but this is impossible. My body is lead, molten guilt. After a moment, he yields, saying, It went well. The library is small, but the people are quite nice.

He gives no information on his own job search and I don't ask. *Too old,* he has realized, seeing the piteous thought hidden behind smiles. But he keeps looking, Mummy keeps looking, Alaine keeps making repairs to this house that is not even ours. They don't understand. Even with a friendly library on our side, this country does not want us.

Down the road a horse walks about a field. It is magical to me that this horse lives in a town, so close to shops and cars and stoplights. Eveningtime, Alaine follows me at a distance, watching me as the doctor ordered; it is a relief to move through each day with my body given over to the care of others. The horse comes when I call. It is plump and gray and old, and it seems to like the sound of Arabic. I have always spoken Arabic with horses, which belong to villages, to stablemen who know no English or French. I call the horse *Ahsan,* and it responds by walking towards me. This simple word for *horse,* so far away from its country, sounds precious and full of meaning, like a real name.

The horse's nostrils flare, exhale warm, damp breath on my hands, a sign of love. I touch the big-boned face, breathe in the musky scent of the animal's muzzle, a dark smell like dough, like water-soaked cracked wheat, bringing back the wood bowls hung in the kitchen and Mummy's hands shaping bread, Alaine and I poking it with our fingers to make decoration. Alaine leans on the fence nearby, cheekbone on her fists, looking the other way. I don't know when the war began. There is so little from before, but I invent how it must have been. There are the memories that became stories, and there are also the things I cannot possibly remember but do, and these are the stories that have become memories. I press my face into the horse's neck, closing my eyes, and the leaves tear away into the wind.

The war started on a Sunday. Amer told me this, and he knew it with such certainty because his family was in the mountains on a traditional Sunday outing the day the fighting started, a trip I now recall as if it were mine. Alaine and I rode in the backseat and squealed when the taxi driver let go of the steering wheel. The car wound higher and higher until the land that stretched away from the road was empty but for white rocks and brittle, humming grass. It was a time of beauty, of earth and rock and the sweetness of summer, and the hills were quiet under the sky. We spread the blanket under lofty pine trees, the blanket a soft bed on the thick brown needles carpeting the ground, and Uncle Ara built a fire and prepared one of his famous meals with Daddy's help. Astrig and Mummy reclined in the shade, smoking cigarettes, and Alaine and I chased each other in the woods, and our pockets bulged with acorn shells for whistling. I have photographs of such picnics. But in the late afternoon as we drove back to the city, dazed with food and sun, soldiers paced at blockades that had not been there before, and the traffic moved along cautiously, bumper-to-bumper, taut with fear. Amer said there was a certain mood of innocent excitement that everyone slipped into that day, thinking it was only temporary.

In Beirut, before the war was real, Mummy took me to the butcher and I hung back shyly by the door, and his son who was in my class at school swept the floor grinning cheekily at me; I thought I would marry him, but later Mummy and Daddy put me in a different school because of the bombing. On our way home we came to a stone house with a staircase to the front door and I asked to visit a friend, but Mummy gave me another bag to carry and said it was impossible. I whined, dragging my feet, until Mummy stopped and said, His father disappeared, he disappeared and he won't come back, so there's no playing, and after that I carried the bags without complaint and kept my eyes in front of me, walking with my toes turned slightly out as I had learned in ballet.

The grown-ups kept saying the war would end the next week, but it did not, and one night a bomb exploded. It was the loudest, most terrifying sound the war had made so far. It undid sleep instantly, as if I had always been awake with the bomb in my arms and legs and eyes, all of me rigid and aftersound trickling down from the sky. I moved without moving, I peeked over the edge of the mattress to the lower bunk. It was empty. I did not know this part of the night. The night crackled fire, swelling like thunder. Men shouted in the streets. I made my body move and the numbness crawled from my legs.

Through the living-room window I saw Mummy and Daddy on the balcony and Mummy's arm was shielding her face, her body bent backwards a little. Orange and yellow light opened and closed the darkness, washing over their faces. I came out and slipped between them, but I could not see over the concrete ledge. Holding my breath, I pulled myself up and glimpsed men running on the street, but then I dropped back to the floor. Uncle Ara and Auntie Lupsi's store was on fire, I had seen that much. No one was paying attention to me. When I jumped again, this time I saw the smoke rolling out of itself in giant balls, like cotton, and I saw that the apartment windows above the store were engulfed. I started to cry, thinking my great-uncle and aunt were dead in their little house with the long hallway and the piano Daddy was always asked to play. They were stumbling around through the smoke, suffocating, falling over. Then Mummy's hands lifted me and she whispered in my ear, They're not dead, Marianna, as she carried me back to my room.

I waited on the edge of my bed for Mummy or Daddy to come back and hug me but only Alaine appeared. She beckoned from the doorway, her thick, tangled hair giving her head an eerie shape against the lights from outside. I crept after her because she was nine and I was seven, and she always knew the right thing to do. She led me to the front door, which was open, and she said, Look. I did not know what I was supposed to see but when I turned to ask she was gone.

I took two steps onto the landing and stared down the winding staircase banisters, down into the black basement where the janitor lived. The air was thick with soot, and I cupped my hands over my nose and mouth. Our building felt so empty and quiet compared to the thundering noise outside. I wondered where everyone was. The windows along the stairwell had shattered and glass slivers pricked my bare feet so I stopped moving. I was too nervous to be frightened, waiting to see what Alaine had seen, straining my eyes through the weird lights. A massive bursting sound came from the store as it collapsed inward, and I could not move for fear that the whole building would fall across the street onto me. Through the broken window I saw the fire, not the flames high up that disappeared in sparks, but the real fire close to the earth, and its voice was different. It was deep and powerful and deadly so that I did not hear Mummy come up behind me. She pulled me back inside and I felt its heat reach for my face before the door closed us into cool darkness.

The next day, Auntie Lupsi stood on the opposite corner and watched the workmen clear out the remains of her store. Her real name was Lusapet, which she herself had mangled into Lupsi as a child and it stuck, even though apparently she had tried hard to undo the mistake once she grew up. In her black wool suit and pillbox hat, she looked like someone at a funeral. It was one of the few things she could wear; the smoke had infiltrated all of her clothes but this had been packed away. She was too heavy for the outfit and it strained at her sagging waist and breasts, but her signature shoes were the best and most expensive as always. Her head moved slightly from side to side as she followed the activities. When I went to say hello because I thought she might need to be comforted, she looked down at me with such fury that I backed away, guilty for things I could not name.

In the meantime Uncle Ara was marching up and down the street shouting at the workers, not in anger but because he was already going deaf. He was the oldest one of our family, Jiddo's older brother. His white hair had turned yellow near his forehead from the cigarettes he was not supposed to smoke, but today nobody tried to stop him and he trailed clouds everywhere he went. His old Citroën, spattered with bullet holes, was blocking the street and the taxi drivers finally threatened to heave it aside themselves if he did not move it.

—How can you think about working today? he shouted at them, as if they should stand about and mourn the store with the rest of us. He tossed his keys to one of the delivery boys. Move it so they can go enjoy themselves while we suffer!

—*Tais-toi alors, Ara!* Auntie Lupsi retorted. Should they go hungry for us now?

Mummy and their daughter Astrig, who smelled of the secret spice combination in her henna and wore silver rings on every finger, walked up and down the sidewalk surveying the damage. I fretted at their heels for a time, until I saw other children carrying goods out of the store and ran to join them. We dragged and carried until a pile was formed on one side of the store, and the stench of burned things made my eyes and nose runny. We competed with one another and I lost because I was the smallest and could not carry as much. Alaine, however, carried loads that were too much for her, I could tell, and she was grim and driven, barely speaking to anyone, as if she were involved in something personal.

Feeling inessential, I found my way to some of the workmen taking a break on the opposite curb, and they praised me for my blond hair and blue eyes, calling me an angel. My baba's American,

I said proudly. I sat with them, noting the quick jealous glances from the other children as I took bites from sandwiches and even sipped a Pepsi when Mummy was not looking. They asked questions in Arabic, testing me, and I answered without mistakes even though we always spoke English at home, so they gave me sweets as a reward.

When most of the store had been cleared, the workmen sent everyone outside, and then they carried the unburned shelves to the middle of the street and tipped them. The heat had curled the paint away from the wood, and a yellowish liquid poured from these shelves, splashing onto the street. The stench caused everyone to cover their mouths and noses, it was so rancid and pungent, worse than anything, even the garbage that rotted all over the city because there was no one to clear it. The horrible liquid streamed across the road, dribbled into the gutters. Auntie Lupsi didn't try to avoid the stench. She kept her hands clenched at her sides, and her eyes followed this trail and they never strayed or blinked and her feet in those shining black shoes were rock still. Water couldn't be wasted to wash the street, and the liquid stagnated in pools for days.

The gutted store stank up the neighborhood with a thick, charred odor that we could taste on our tongues and that got into everything, clothes and hair and furniture. For months we ate out of blackened cans that had lost their labels in the fire. Mummy said we had to help Ara and Lupsi's store because money should always be kept in the family, and it became a surprise game to see what we would be eating when the can was pried open. We could be happy because we had love, Daddy explained. This was why we could play these games and smile and laugh. I knew he had let us in on an essential truth, one that made us unique. I saw the strips of light that encircled us on winter mornings in front of the fireplace, and the light that warmed the water-filled tubs on the balcony in summer. The light was with us at Christmas, as it had been with Téta and Jiddo before they died, and on Easter and birthdays. It protected me when I cried because the jets were flying so low, and when we

looked out the window and saw the burning tires blockading the
street, and the soldiers patrolled the sidewalks.

It was especially sad that the store had exploded because Auntie
Lupsi and Uncle Ara were Armenian. The grown-ups always said,
How terrible to suffer so much at the beginning of their lives, and
now this! What I knew about being Armenian was that Jiddo had
had to travel in a suitcase when he was a child fleeing the Turks,
and that Alaine had *white Armenian skin* just like Mummy, which
made me feel left out. When I told Astrig I wished I looked like an
Armenian, she said I was crazy. Astrig had no patience for things
she could not touch or see, Daddy explained, which was unset-
tling because I had not known such things existed. But it was true
Astrig had no patience. In the rebuilt store, her desk formed a T
with Auntie Lupsi's, and she could not tolerate her mother's worries. Auntie Lupsi had always been vigilant about thieves, but now
she was becoming paranoid. When I was old enough to be trusted,
she clawed at my arm as I walked by.

—Watch for them, watch. They're everywhere, she muttered,
her chair creaking from side to side. If you see anyone taking anything, tell me.

I agreed solemnly, filled with dread.

—Leave her alone, Mama, Astrig complained.

Mummy paused during shopping to smoke a cigarette with them.
She pretended to take over the vigil so that Auntie Lupsi could rest
awhile. But she never rested.

—Is there anyone, Ani? she would say, after a few minutes.

—No, Auntie Lupsi.

—Uf, Mama, next you'll be looking for Turks!

Any comment about the Turks silenced Auntie Lupsi at once.
Her face went pale and rigid, and Mummy gave Astrig a *how could
you* look. I did not know what was so terrible in Astrig's words,
but in these times she no longer seemed merry and exotic with her
throaty voice and flashing rings; instead, she sat back in her chair

with the bitter expression of someone wronged. I told Mummy I did not like Auntie Lupsi asking me to watch, but she said, She's just an old woman, Marianna. Indulge her. But I feared the Turkish thieves. I kept my eyes down so I would not find one. My fear was not alleviated by the arguments that erupted between Astrig and Mummy.

—But Ani, you don't live with her! Astrig moaned. The Turks this, the Turks that! And she was not even there! It was Papi's family that suffered, and do you hear a word from him?

—She didn't have to be there, Mummy pronounced. She can see the ghosts living inside her husband.

I was petrified. When Uncle Ara came to visit, I stayed in my room, I pulled on as many clothes as possible so it would be harder for the ghosts to get in.

—Anna? What on earth is the matter with you? Daddy exclaimed. I lay in a heap on the floor, overheated and faint. He pulled off shirt after shirt, fanning my face.

—It's a figure of speech, he explained, and this phrase delighted me. *A figure of speech,* I thought to myself, over and over, something lighthearted and innocent, and the Turkish ghosts fled.

Later that year, Auntie Lupsi died of a heart attack, and the grown-ups said, *Yeeh,* how sad she did not get to enjoy the new shop for long! I did not feel sad about Auntie Lupsi, not until I saw Uncle Ara sitting in his crumpled black suit staring at his shoes. Then I felt the strangeness of grief, like light passing through my flesh. I offered him marzipan, his favorite, and he took one and stroked my hair, making me sorry I had ever run away from him.

Astrig insisted on selling the shop to fulfill her dream, which was to be in the *haute couture* business. It didn't matter that there was a war. She rented a first-floor space on a busy street, found reliable seamstresses, and set about making designs. Mummy was pressed into service as a model, and we spent long afternoons fidgeting while Astrig, her mouth full of pins, exhorted Mummy to be patient. Uncle Ara sat in the doorway on a wooden chair, urging passersby to come in and engaging them in arguments about the war. Sometimes the shop filled up with people who got in on the arguing, and coffee had to be ordered from down the street and cigarettes were passed around. Even though these crowds often departed without having purchased a thing, Astrig's business stayed afloat because, as she claimed, it was founded in the unshakeable concept that *people like to dress well even with death all around them.*

The war did not save us from having to go to school, though we often missed weeks at a time. Before we switched to another school that was in walking distance, our school bus, a Volkswagen van, pulled up to the sidewalk every morning and the door slid open with a crash. Mummy waved good-bye, beautiful smile, brown hair curling under her ears. She was tall and slender in a short-sleeved sweater and brown pants, and I was certain that everybody loved her; the bus driver, the teacher who rode with us, and all the children.

In the back of the van someone fired an imaginary machine gun at the car behind us. The woman driving the car smiled at first and looked away. A few more of us joined in: Ratatatata-ta-ta! we shouted. She rolled her eyes. Brrratata-brrrratata! Suddenly she fired back and we all screamed, pretending we had been shot. She lifted her hands as if to say, *What was I to do?*

Then I forgot about her because Sawsan said, We had to drink peepee when there was no water.

The toilet in our apartment was dry, and next to it stood the bucket of water for flushing and the wastebasket for toilet paper. I imagined peeing into a cup.

—You could have bought Bonjus, I argued.

—There was no Bonjus, only peepee. She folded her arms, challenging me with her eyes.

—I'm sorry, I said.

She shrugged. Everyone stared at her in awe, and later I confronted Mummy. I wanted to suffer, too.

—Why do we never have to drink peepee?

She did not understand.

—Instead of water, I explained impatiently. Sawsan said!

—Oh, Marianna! Is this what you want, to drink your peepee?

I didn't have to drink peepee but I couldn't play alone downstairs without a long discussion between the grown-ups, and Alaine and I could no longer go on the terrace or the roof anytime we wanted. We roller skated up and down the hallway until Mummy begged us to stop, and then we colored or played board games or read, tucked into spaces without windows, while they listened to the war. If it was quiet, we might be allowed on the terrace, but not for long, as if our hysterical laughter and the noise of the spinning rubber wheels tempted fate. On those days when Mummy said, No going outside, the terrace changed into an empty place of danger, and we peeked uneasily through the shutter slats at the white tiles burning under the sun.

The war began and sometime later we went downtown to see what was left of Téta and Jiddo's apartment. We climbed over debris and glass littering the stairs until we came to their landing on the top floor, which used to be decorated with plants and Greek columns and parts of ancient statues. Everything was smashed to pieces. The ceiling had caved in, and the railing was splayed and broken. The front door hung on its hinges. Mummy stepped inside, stood stiffly in the wreckage of the living room. Her arms came up slowly to hold herself, and then Daddy reached her side and laid his hand on her shoulder. The apartment had been empty since they died, but Uncle Ara and Mummy had kept everything as it was and continued with the rent, perhaps intending for someone to move in at some later date. But now the wall was gone, and the old papers that no one had wanted to remove from Jiddo's desk were strewn about, and the torn curtains wafted this way and that. The house had been looted during the battles and soldiers had even fought from here, firing at the hotels on the shore that had become military strongholds. Pieces from a puzzle of a majestic American mountain, which I had been working on with Daddy on our brief visits to check on the house, were scattered all over the floor, and the green felt card table lay on its side.

—Thank God they did not live to see this, Daddy said, but this did not soothe Mummy at all. She said nothing, just looked around with a stricken expression. I helped Daddy to gather the puzzle pieces and return them to the box, even though I could see that this bit of tidying up was just a way to keep moving.

Mummy walked through the rooms, picking up things that had been left behind, examining them and then putting them down. She did not make an attempt to pack, but Daddy followed her with a box for the smaller objects. Standing in the living room I felt naked: the crumbled wall bared the room to the outside, and the buildings across the street, the bright sea beyond had never been so crisp. People wandered on and off balconies, pointing. A child waved and I turned around. Alaine was picking grimly through the mess for shrapnel and bullets, as if it were her duty.

I stood in the dining room at the foot of the stairs leading to the roof. Jiddo had had a garden there. He would water the plants in diaphanous undershorts, his scrawny legs white in the sun, bald head bronzed, while Téta read Egyptian magazines in bed, trapped by her illness.

I overheard Mummy and Daddy arguing on the roof. Mummy was saying, A woman has them, in the old *souq*. She bought them on the black market.

—You can't go, Daddy said. It's too dangerous.

—These are my belongings!

I climbed the first few stairs and listened for more, but there was nothing. The dining room was empty and littered with trash, even the remains of a fire in a tin, and the old smell of wood and silver polish was absent.

The next day Mummy disappeared until late evening. When she came back, she had a torn plastic bag that held four books, and she cried on and off for days. The books ended up on the shelf in their bedroom. I tried to read them but they were written in a language I did not recognize. Daddy explained that it was dead.

In the afternoons Mummy held me on her lap and told me about Téta and Jiddo, who had died and gone to Heaven just in time, before the war began. She told me about their secret wedding that defied the family, who didn't want Jiddo to marry an Egyptian, and how poor they had been, and how love sustained them. This was especially proven by how Téta had been engaged to a rich man in Marseilles, but instead of getting on the ship at Haifa bound for France, she met Jiddo and got on a train with him to Beirut. In this time before Mummy was born, Jiddo was a commando for the British, and so Téta had to wait for him in Beirut while he went on missions; Mummy had a piece of his silk parachute that she kept in her jewelry box. After the war, Téta and Jiddo founded their antiquities business, traveling all over Asia for carpets and amulets and beads and statues. Téta, who had what Daddy called Crusader blood, smiled at customs officials, enchanting them with her brilliant blue eyes while Jiddo walked away with the luggage. This was acceptable in those days. But they remained poor because Jiddo never wanted to sell the pieces he loved, and many of those ancient objects now lay strewn about our own house.

They spent every summer in the mountains, and one autumn, the rains started and did not stop. The rainwater poured down the stone steps that led from the university campus to 'Ain Mreise and flooded their house, so they stayed on in the village and did not move back to Beirut for nine years. They lived in a small house that I saw as a child, but which is probably gone now along with everything else in the mountains. Mummy grew up there, and their big gray dog tore at the earth, and the donkey Saisaban, memorialized in a photo that shows him in the living room, pulled down the neighbor's laundry with his teeth and brayed at the sky.

These stories I knew intimately from the time I could understand language. I wanted more than anything to live in the mountains like Mummy did and have a donkey and a big dog, so every year I stared hard at the clouds to make them obey my command to flood our apartment, which would have been miraculous since we lived on the fourth floor. You don't really want to live in a village, Marianna, the grown-ups chided me, laughing; but they were wrong.

The best story of all was about Saisaban—not the donkey, who was merely a namesake, but the legendary winged horse who flew through the sky and landed on our balcony. Marianna, he said, Jump on my back, and I would, and Saisaban was strong and beautiful with hide white as stone, eyes black as *mazoot,* and hooves sharp as the tips of bullets. He carried me far away to the Beqaa Valley where the fields were lush and moist and the flowers swayed in the breeze. I picked poppies and daisies and lavender and violets and the fragrance of Mummy's breath in my hair, of her arms around my body, was the scent of the flowers in my mind. I gazed at the sky and Saisaban filled it; he galloped through the air, my fingers tangled in his mane and the warm sweat of his horse-skin dampening my legs, and when he gently deposited me on the balcony I gave my bouquets to Mummy who sorted them and filled vases around the house. On the corner below, rows of blazing tires blocked the street and black smoke rolled away into the sky. Saisaban flew far above, invisible to the soldiers lounging on the sidewalks, and Mummy carried me in for a nap.

Daddy's past, unlike Mummy's that we could visit and touch and hear, was a tantalizing mystery. When I was small, what I knew about Daddy was that he came from America, he had sliced off the end of his pinkie when he was twelve, he was a professor of history at the university, and he had so many books that I could not count them even though I tried. I knew also that Daddy had a younger brother called Jesse who died before I was born, and that his mother had punished him once for losing a minuscule amount of money.

—But this was during the Depression, he would say sadly, and I pictured all of America as a land of people with sad faces, drooping shoulders, and thin, greasy hair. This had been such a serious time that his father, my *Granpa* as Daddy called him, had to give up his dreams of being an inventor for the steady job of garage attendant. It was also when the terrible accident happened.

—How did you do it? Alaine and I cried, even though we already knew.

Daddy held up an imaginary knife over the kitchen counter of his impossibly distant youth. I was chopping too fast, he said, and *woop!*

Then we all scrambled around the floor looking for the imaginary lost piece of his finger.

Later he joined the American army, and for two years he played jokes on generals. In the photographs from this time, his long, pensive face, sloping eyes, and large ears looked out of place beneath the army cap; Alaine said this was because he was actually meant to be a scholar wearing a robe. His brother, on the other hand, had stayed in the army and died in Korea, not from the war but from what the grown-ups called complications with his lungs. I missed Uncle Jesse even though I'd never known him. Daddy hardly talked about him, it was just too sad. Mummy chastened me, Don't ask so many questions! but Uncle Jesse forgave me, grinning from behind the wheel of an army jeep, one boot on the ground, cigarette stuck behind his ear. I fell in love with Uncle Jesse, who died too young. I became a nurse in Korea with special insight. I discovered the complications at the last minute and administered the medicine he needed. My imagination tumbled image after image, always culminating in that exquisite moment when I attached the IV against the other doctors' orders, risking my job for the sake of doing right, while Uncle Jesse gazed up gratefully, one hand reaching out in supplication.

Whenever Alaine and I fought, Mummy got impatient and said, You don't know how lucky you are to have each other! which meant that we might have been an only child, like her, or one of us could have died, like Uncle Jesse. Sometimes Alaine and I felt the gravity of our luck; we huddled together in a makeshift tent in our room, creating elaborate vows not to fight ever again. The vows frittered to pieces over a broken toy or torn drawing, and the cycle resumed.

Daddy told stories at bedtime, when Alaine and I got into our beds and closed our eyes and became heroines, distant and American and brash, in adventures that made us giggle and throw our bedcovers off in protest. Daddy sat in a chair in pajamas, legs crossed, gazing off into the fictions he had spent the day creating, while Alaine and I spoke with squirrels and possums and storks, animals we had never seen but that he described so vividly they sat on the bookshelf, perched on the windowsill, indented the pillow next to my head, chattering and squawking. These were our familiars, our allies in deception and intrigue as we explored the landscape of America, as we entered houses in forests with strange trees and ran through streets that were clean and shiny, and in this way Daddy explained his far-off childhood.

—Tell us a story, I commanded in the morning, and for the rest of the day Daddy paused in the examination of ancient texts to invent his own, his long face fixed in a frown, pen scribbling notes on the plot that was to unfold. What will happen? I begged, and Alaine chastised me because I refused to learn that Daddy kept these things to himself, and the day continued, tensed with the possibilities that lay ahead for our American doubles.

Daddy was a patient man, and he humored our teasing him for his big ears with a shake of the head and a resigned smile. We always knew to ask Daddy first if we wanted something, because he couldn't bear to say no, while Mummy would weigh the request, her calculating gaze pinning us in place while she considered the options. She's the one in charge, Daddy would admit, spreading his hands in happy defeat. When Daddy played his *grand old songs* on the upright piano, he bobbed and rocked to the music while we danced, and then he broke into songs with mystical words about America, about summertime and love and leaving. But he didn't play very much; he said he'd lost interest over the years, and now there was the war. He wore tweed suits and leather shoes with laces, and his watch was one of those old-fashioned ones, the kind that is kept in one's pocket. My favorite game was to steal this watch and hide while he pretended not to know where I was, singing out my name, but then, when he finally came upon me in the closet or under their beds, he would say gently, I have to read now.

I envied the books that were as tall as I, the paper dry and brittle and yellowish, the languages mysterious scratchings and swirls. This is Aramaic, he explained. This is Hebrew, and this is Greek. The sound of the pages being separated and then one slowly lifting over would become one of the sounds of nostalgia, but for now was fodder for my jealousy, and so one day I spread Daddy's favorite American food, peanut butter, all over one of the pages.

—Oh my God, he said softly, shaking his head, his blue eyes sadder than anything I had ever seen, and he did not spank me or shout, he simply rejected my presence entirely, even the tearful apologies urged by Mummy, and he spent the whole day with a knife and a damp cloth, cleaning his precious tome.

—Stephen, you can't do this to her, Mummy kept begging, and finally, in the late evening, Daddy sat on the edge of my bed and explained how one must love books, especially old ones, with a depth that is immeasurable; that books are the essence of history, of mankind; that to violate the printed page is to violate the self and the integrity of the human soul. I did not know what he was saying. My body curled around itself, tense as a bullet, eyes fixed on his long, gentle hands as they unfolded the words he was speaking, giving them shape and magnificence. It was only when he kissed my forehead that the tautness of my frame collapsed and I cried against his chest until his shirt was soaked through. I knew that he still loved me because he kept saying, Marianna, Marianna, as if surprised by this lengthy display.

The day when Mummy came home with Jiddo's books in the plastic bag, Daddy rose from behind his great oak desk; he tapped his pipe in the ashtray while Mummy set the bag down and tugged at clumps of tissue in her purse, searching for a clean one. Then he came from behind the desk to hold Mummy as she wept, and when she had calmed down he took the bag and rummaged through it. He opened a book and peered at it with his scholar's face, as if he had alighted upon some discovery, but Mummy cried, It's not for reading! and wrenched the book from his hands. Daddy hurried after her with an expression of such apology that I remained still for a time, listening to their urgent voices from the bedroom.

Téta and Jiddo died before the war even began, when I was very small, and I cried until my head felt swollen and heavy but Alaine just sat stiffly on the edge of the bed, watching Mummy dress for the service. There is only one memory, shared by both deaths that occurred less than a year apart. Alaine is wearing a dark green T-shirt and corduroy shorts, and she has scuffed knees from playing with the boys in the street. Her white face has closed up, black eyes staring like a cat, her way of begging to be allowed to go to the church, too, but we're too young, someone said. We know it's not that, it's Mummy, who won't even look our way because whenever she does, her face crumples up as if we're part of the reason for her misery. I cry more, realizing Mummy doesn't want us, and the maid from upstairs who's supposed to watch us for the afternoon hesitates on the periphery, then settles between us, cradling me but leaving Alaine alone. Daddy comes to the doorway looking sorry as can be and says, It's time to go, and that is when I understand Jiddo, and then Téta, are gone.

Before the war, summer meant staying in the stone cottage where Jiddo watered the garden while Téta flipped magazines in a chaise lounge, and Daddy built a tree house for me and Alaine to curl up and read under the sweet-smelling leaves. None of it could be any different; this was our life, the rest of it enticing us forward in time, smiling and beckoning. Summer meant uncharted hiding places on the *jels,* the wild-growing terraces above and below the house, it meant feeding stray dogs and breaking pine nuts with rocks. Our best summer friends, Habib and Salia, lived next door; their father owned the apartment building so they lived in the village year round, which seemed marvelous to me. Jiddo said, The mailman came, and Alaine and I ran to the mailbox under the oleander tree and pawed about inside looking for the Smarties or Toblerone bars. The mailbox never had mail in it; it was a mystical object, one that belonged in England or America, and yet somehow, here it was. It had been installed by the owners of the cottage, and perhaps at one time the postman had been attracted to it there at the edge of the courtyard, but when Jiddo and Téta lived it was empty but for the sweets, and when the war started, there was no longer any mail at all.

Jiddo collected stone heads of gods and nymphs and regular citizens of the Roman Empire, and these lined the gardens outside as decoration. Their faces had been smashed, their paint long ago scraped away, but under my hands they breathed and spoke to me: *Marianna, you must save Bacchus,* or, *Marianna, fly to warn Athene about the Palestinians,* and off I went as the heroine of another adventure. Jiddo's world invited fantasy: he had parchments and inscribed stones, vases, figurines, ancient glass beads that sparkled when held to the light. He also had a red *tarbooshe,* a fez, from the time of the Ottomans; he liked to put it on and dance with a horse-hair whip, and from this we understood the Turks were fools.

He tied empty sardine cans to the oleander tree, and whenever he heard the hunters he pulled the string so the cans banged together and birds burst out of the trees and flew away to safety. Then Téta and Jiddo laughed together as if they had only just played this joke for the first time, but I knew what they were doing was noble. I started pulling the string any chance I got so that finally Jiddo said, Marianna, stop scaring the birds! and then I hid by the gate, watching the road for hunters and ready to spring up the four *jels* to the oleander to sound the warning.

None of this could be any different; this was the meaning of summer, the fresh rich scent of watered earth, our family's laughter and the clanging of sardine cans, the war not yet arrived. And even after Téta and Jiddo died, the horsehair whip still hung on the wall and the cans rusted in the tree, so it was as if things had altered only a fraction, as if a shading of light might reveal us all together, still trailing Jiddo as he sprayed a glorious arc of water over his garden, still cuddled up by Téta learning the strange consonants and vowels of Egyptian words. Uncle Ara built a house up the hill, and he transported the gods to the stone wall along the road, and on weekend visits we smoothed their crumbled faces, we trailed the flutes of columns with our fingertips, we cupped the weight of ancient coins in our hands, and I learned that time, even thousands of years, can be made to vanish.

Mummy goes to find the things that were stolen. She walks through Beirut bearing roses, crosses streets that none of us ever see; she picks her way through the rubble of downtown to the red-light district, where tired prostitutes lean in doorways and sit on the curb. This is a story that is not to be comprehended. She walks with her face to the sky, she is imagining the moment of transference, the second when her hand will touch the objects that will undo the memory of the house that was destroyed, or of a father lying bewildered and stricken in a hospital room, his final sorrows imprisoned by paralysis. Mummy carries the rage of books in stores marked with price tags over her father's name, of urine sprayed in the corner of what was once her bedroom, of vomit in the kitchen sink. The city already does not care: the ruined buildings watch her passage with gaping mouths and empty, crumbling spaces for eyes.

The war went on and on, and Mummy experimented with American bread that rose up over the pans and made my mouth water for the hot wheaty taste. We only had such exotic bread because there was no regular bread to buy, and some people had no bread at all, so we were not to enjoy it too much, which was hard. The flour caked on Mummy's apron and arms and forehead where she wiped sweat with the back of her hand. Alaine and I waited in our places opposite each other at the kitchen table, and I leaned my elbows on either side of my coloring book, jealously watching Alaine organize her bullet collection. Outside, the shooting burst on and off, but today it was on the south side of Beirut so we didn't have to go to the hallway. The doors to the balcony were open, allowing in a warm breeze and the soft clucking of the three half-grown chickens on the balcony below ours. I was plotting to buy some as a present for Mummy, whose birthday was coming, and then they would not be able to refuse. Daddy had said, Chickens belong in the country, not on balconies, but Mummy had had a donkey called Saisaban when she was a child in the village, and the donkey actually went into their living room: there was a photograph in the album that proved this.

Chicks were being sold in cardboard boxes all over the city, and people built pens on their balconies to raise them. When the chickens survived and grew old enough to fly, they jumped over the railings, spinning feathers into the air, and crashed into the sidewalks below, and on that day, as Mummy delicately inserted a knitting needle into the bread in the oven, one of the three chickens downstairs finally made it over the top of the flimsy wire fence and fell the three stories to the restaurant patio below. The waiter shouted obscenities, and our neighbor ran onto her balcony.

—Give me my chicken! You save my chicken, you idiot! she screamed, but the waiter waved the chicken by one leg. Its wings flapped weakly and I started to cry.

The waiter laughed, It's ours now! You come eat it later at a discount, and you get a salad, too!

—Mummy, I cried. Will it go to Heaven?

—Of course, Marianna, she said, as if I shouldn't worry about these things. She pushed me back inside and showed me how to hold the bread pans upside down so the loaves would fall out, then helped me turn them onto the metal racks to cool.

Alaine, having broken her concentration to frown at the rest of the world for a moment, returned to her bullet collection. It was arranged in rows of descending height, the bullets grouped according to whether or not they had exploded. On the far right stood the tail of a small rocket grenade, and on top of this was the American G.I. Joe. She had shaved him with a knife, so his face was a craggy mess of plastic planes and grooves, like a rock formation.

I leaned across the table and touched my fingertip to the point of each bullet, singing, Do, re, mi, fa. Let me have one?

I watched Alaine give in to this idea. She exhaled slowly, lips pinched together. She could never resist me.

—Just a little one, I added.

—You should come out when we look for them, she complained.

Alaine should have known I would never go out with her again. Other children always teased me for my blond hair, and the last time, for whatever reason, they had taken to calling me *katiouchka*, a garbled word for shell casing, and I had run home crying. Alaine had laughed with them, not *meanly* she explained later, but I still wanted her to pay.

—Do you want some bread now or later? Mummy prodded the rich golden loaves with her fingers. Daddy had told us this was the kind of bread he had eaten through all his childhood in America, which amazed me, except for during the Depression, which, he said, had been far worse than our having to eat the same thing every day for weeks at a time.

—I like it warm, Mummy said, slicing the bread. I was torn between the delicious aroma and Alaine being so close to her decision. I remained silent, so that my voice would not shatter Alaine's delicate concentration. Her hand inched through the air above the bullets like a fortune teller's, pausing now and then, and I held my breath.

She stopped over the last and shortest bullet. Its tip was pounded in and bent and it looked ugly. Her eyes lifted to meet mine. My disappointment must have been evident, because she looked back down, sighing, and seized another one. A medium-sized, gloriously pointed bullet lay in her palm.

—Can I have two? I said.

—It's that or nothing. Alaine did not even look up.

—Stop being so greedy, Anna.

Mummy said this in a strange voice, glancing down the row of bullets before returning her attention to buttering a slice of bread. I curled my new bullet into my palm; it fit smooth and cold, and I thought, *I'm not greedy,* but it wasn't true, I wanted them, I wanted them all and I was jealous.

Alaine by the age of ten was transmitting signs of the sorrows that would torture her for years. Her dark hair was tangled and she refused to brush or cut it, so that Mummy would have to shout at her to stand still while the brush tore through the knots, and Alaine's black, wet eyes shone like stars, making me feel terrible. This mass of hair offered some sort of defense; it reached her waist, it covered her eyes, it hid her face from everyone. I envied Alaine's hair, her ability to resist our parents' wishes for at least two or three days before finally being overcome, and so my alliance with her was tainted by satisfaction when Mummy transformed the hair into an orderly braid, and Alaine's thin, tight face was bared to us, scaring me. Still, I was indebted to Alaine for many things and I would put my arm around her when she was sad, but she always remained limp and inconsolable in those times, under her own spell.

I did not understand Alaine, but I respected her for the bullets and shrapnel she collected, the way she would take my hand when the shooting started, the way she unrolled the sleeping bag for me when we had to sleep in the back bathroom. Alaine could play soccer as well as any boy, she rode a bicycle at top speed, and she always went first if something was happening, ready to sacrifice her life for me. When the soldiers came some nights to our building she told me where to hide my money and held me as I cried because I knew our sallow, tired concierge was no match for the men shouting up and down the stairwell. When we lay in our sleeping bags squeezed between the sink and the toilet, warm and safe, Alaine sang to me and the bombs sounded like beasts roaring from beneath the earth, popping my ears, shivering my eyelids, lifting the skin from my flesh, and Alaine sang and we were warm and the window, open so that it would not shatter from the noise, allowed in the night air of gunpowder and hot things, metal things whose heat and smells drifted to our faces; tanks, the engines of jeeps, the barrels of Dushkas, shells of bullets spinning down pavements, fiery shrapnel gouging walls and arms and trees, and we clapped our hands and sang and we were warm there on the tiles with the window half-open. When songs were finished, and when Mummy and Daddy had visited again from the hallway, kissing our faces and hands and lips, Alaine stared into the dark the way we both would for years, the insomnia of a lifetime beginning now, her hands behind her head, hair unbraided and tousled, and her stillness as a person was unlike anyone else's, so pure, as if she had slowed her heart and the pace of her blood so that even the space around her was affected.

When the battles edged into our part of the city, Mummy and Daddy became nervous about staying in our top-floor apartment, so vulnerable to stray bullets and shells, so we moved to the second floor, sometimes staying there for several days in a row. Only an old maid called Sabha lived in this apartment, the family having fled to Paris right at the beginning of the war, so there was plenty of room for us. Sometimes we knew in advance to make the move with all our blankets and toys and other necessities; at other times, the fighting erupted unexpectedly, and we had to abandon whatever we were doing or tumble from sleep, dazed and terrified, in order to run downstairs. The open windows along the stairwell invited in a particular malevolence I had heard about at school, missiles that could find their way into buildings and negotiate circular staircases to hunt down their target. Just at the moment when terror threatened to overwhelm me, my body broke free of paralysis, hurtled down the steps to my parents. What is the matter, Marianna? they cried out, hugging my trembling body. I was just running, I told them and squirmed away, the danger past.

This second-floor apartment was dark and furnished with a clutter of chairs and sofas and tables, From the Ottoman Empire, Daddy said grandly, a distance that sounded so exotic I revelled in touching these things. When the bombing was close, we curled up together in the windowless hallway or the bathroom, Mummy playing solitaire, Daddy smoking and thinking and not speaking, but the maid Sabha never hid: for some reason she was exempt, and she journeyed to the kitchen and living room, even to the balcony to shake out the rugs. Mummy never asked her to spend the night on the makeshift beds, and this seemed unjust to me. But when I complained, Mummy said, She doesn't believe there's a war, Anna. She thinks we're just visiting.

I had never heard of such a thing. I watched Sabha for signs of madness, but she was not mad, so I searched for signs of stupidity, but she seemed to know a lot of things. She told me about different ingredients for dishes she cooked, about how to prevent a wart from getting bigger, and why birds fly in formation. Sabha was happy; this was evident because she smiled constantly, so much that I thought her cheeks must hurt, and she shuffled all over the house to fetch things we had not even asked for: pillows, blankets, books, gas lamps. The faded velvet cushions she unearthed were embroidered with fine, colored threads and I handled them with great reservation because they might be from the Empire, too. I secretly examined them for imprints or stains, evidence left by sultans.

Mummy would say, Sit down, Sabha, your feet must be tired, but Sabha only tsk-tsked, How can you suggest such a thing? and then the napkins and plates and forks arrived, the food prepared swiftly and deliciously, and Mummy watched her with tenderness and Daddy praised her cooking. When we woke to the eerie, laden quiet of these mornings, Sabha might be asleep on a chair with her bare feet resting on a padded stool, wispy gray hair sticking up, hands twitching. Or she might be awake already, sitting at the table in the dim kitchen, the air musty and warm from boiling chickpeas or beans.

One day the radio announcer said the war was truly over. The man across the street fired a machine gun into the air, and his son excitedly darted about behind him, collecting the empty shells raining onto the balcony. People ran down the street shooting in celebration. Everyone was laughing, but I was frightened of Mummy's smile, which seemed to have been pulled across her face and pinned there. Oh, look at him, they laughed. Look! Seeing Mummy's smile and Daddy's hands clapping, I thought it strange that they should approve of this man shooting his gun. What if someone was hurt? Then Sabha arrived with pastries and coffee in the expensive set of porcelain, and I allowed myself to be caught up in the celebratory mood.

When we stayed in our own apartment on the top floor, Mummy still made a point of stopping in on Sabha to see if she needed anything, and Alaine and I would go along now and then. They spoke about the places and incidents Sabha remembered from childhood, which was her favorite subject, until finally I understood that this was what kept Sabha from seeing the war: her gaze was turned backwards and inwards. She told stories about a place called Palestine again and again, each time differently, and at first I argued with her.

—We went to the well, she explained, and the rope was so frayed that finally it broke. That was the day my little sister Amina died.

—But Sabha, Amina died later, after the well-story.

In the well-story, someone, an uncle or cousin, fell in and had to be rescued. Amina had died years later, closer to a story about a lemon tree.

—No, I remember clearly. By the time I came home with water she was dead from the fever.

When I complained to Daddy, who was a professor of history, he said sadly, The past is a code that may or may not be broken, which did not explain anything. It was Mummy who taught me to be silent in those moments when the stories changed. She said, How do you know for sure, Marianna? You can't argue with the way someone remembers things.

I would never know the truth, not the real truth, because it had become so altered by the telling. But I understood that what was most true would never change. Amina had died, this was the central life of the story, and over time Sabha walked to the well and back, she carved words into the lemon tree, she packed her few belongings and moved north. Sabha wandered around and around Amina's death, which seemed to have been the most important event of her life, and each time the story changed so that the truth was stronger.

The day came that I caught sight of Sabha traveling down the street with a canvas Adidas bag.

—Look, I pointed, and Mummy came to the window. Sabha shuffled around the corner and Mummy said, But where is she going? a question that it seemed I should answer, and then she ran out of the kitchen. The front door banged open and I heard her footsteps on the stairs. As the onions continued to fry, and the boiling lentils and rice for the *mujeddara* slipped past that delicate moment and began to burn in the pot, I watched Mummy run down the street calling, Sabha, Sabha! People stopped and stared, and I was embarrassed for Mummy, who looked wild and strange in her slippers and apron with her hair undone. I waited and waited and forgot the burning food on the stove. Alaine appeared saying, What's that smell? and turned off the fire. She was disinterested in the commotion, as always. Despite this, I told her what was happening and she said to me, Mummy will find her, and went back to our bedroom. I wanted to be like Alaine: I wanted to be calm and wise. Instead my heart drummed my body to shaking, I did not breathe, waiting at the window forever, until finally I saw them. I watched Mummy lead Sabha slowly back up the street and into the building. She did not come back upstairs for some time.

—Why can't you just take her where she wants? I demanded at once. We could go in a taxi!

She looked as if my question had passed right through her, so I retreated to the kitchen to sit on a chair and wait. She would have to make new food, I thought, and then I wished Alaine would come out of the bedroom but she was working on a model airplane, the pieces and brushes and glue and stickers laid in rows on her work-table. I looked down the hallway and saw Mummy at the living-room window, which had a better view of the street. She had to be worried Sabha might try and leave again. She leaned against the wall and stared down, absently picking at the masking tape that crisscrossed the windowpane to prevent it from shattering.

I counted to forty-two tiles on the kitchen floor before Mummy finally came in. She did not say anything, she just threw away the *mujeddara* and started a new pot, and she scraped away the black curled-up onions and chopped another. As she started the frying all over again, she said, You keep watch, Marianna, and I'll cook, so I took my chair to the living-room window and fixed my gaze on the street, though I secretly wanted Sabha to make a getaway.

In the late afternoon when Daddy returned from the university, Mummy's rigid control fell apart. For this, Alaine came out of the bedroom.

—How can she go to Palestine? She wants to go to Palestine! Mummy ranted. It was by chance that I caught her!

Daddy just stood still and I was proud at how tall and dignified he was. He said, Ani, Ani, as if saying her name would bring her to her senses.

Pretending I knew where Palestine was, I tugged Alaine's hand and whispered, What's wrong with Palestine?

—Everyone's dead there and all the houses are occupied.

I pictured a village of dead people propped in chairs, against walls, at the well, under lemon trees. Who killed them? I asked.

—Jewish people, she said.

Alaine always seemed to know what was happening, even though she never spoke with anyone or read the newspaper. I resolved to listen more carefully. The headlines and gossip and announcements on the radio had passed by me daily without meaning, and I had not thought it was important; until now, it really had nothing to do with us.

After that, if one of us saw Sabha wandering off, Mummy shouted, Watch the eggplant! if it needed to be turned on the fire, or, Watch the rice! if it was coming to a boil, and then she would be off, slippers slapping the stairs all the way to the street, because Sabha would have once again decided to find her way back to Palestine instead of just telling everyone about it, because she did not believe the truth, that it was occupied by dead people.

A proud secret burned in me until I could no longer contain it. I came to Daddy when he was writing at his desk, stood on tiptoe and whispered in his ear, I *hate* Jewish people.

He settled me on his lap and said, Well, you shouldn't hate anyone. After a silence, he asked, Why do you hate them?

—Because they killed Sabha's family. I was on fire with righteousness. I had a part in things now.

Daddy squeezed me, kissed the top of my head.

—You don't know the whole story, Marianna. You should always know the whole story before you form an opinion.

Shame deflated me.

—Everyone is a person just like you, Daddy added as I slipped away. So if you hate them you hate yourself.

Sabha pretended nothing had happened, I concluded, because she could not bear to hate herself.

Later I asked Alaine, What are Jews, exactly?

—The people who left Egypt, she said with finality, and this seemed enough.

Every summer we left Beirut for the same mountain cottage Jiddo and Téta had rented when they were alive. We played next door from morning to dusk, but because of the war there were new sorts of games from which I was invariably excluded. Alaine was the oldest of the players and taller than most of them as well, so she had authority. She took to organizing Habib and other children from the village into scouting parties that she proclaimed were too dangerous for me. I watched from the window as they separated going up the hill, bellying along with wooden guns strapped to their backs. My boring duty was to report their camouflage skills, and I took satisfaction in their vulnerability: I reported flailing arms and legs, a lost gun tumbling down a path, kicked-up dirt. Alaine berated her troops, sent them out again. When dusk fell and the troops abandoned training for food, Alaine and Habib guarded the road, standing in front of a checkpoint made from a pile of wooden fruit crates painted with the command in red, STOP FOR IDENTIFICATION. While I watched from the steps, they waved cars to a stop and leaned in the driver's window, demanding papers. Some people refused to stop, others became angry. I liked it when that happened since I was not allowed to play unless I made my own gun, which I knew I could not do as well as they did. Alaine and Habib talked about building antiaircraft and Katyusha rockets, too. They sawed and hammered and sanded, and the tenants complained about the racket, saying it was bad enough there was bombing echoing up from Beirut, now this?

My days unwound without such excitement. Salia, Habib's sister, found me teary-eyed for not being allowed to hammer, and she led me on the path between their *jels* where she was gardening. She sank her hands into manure and carried it in small amounts to the wheelbarrow. Let me help, I said. I wanted to feel what it was like, to be touching this manure, but she warned me away. Your mother would be angry! I did not understand. I looked back at the house, no one was watching. Salia said, This is not your work, and then I felt a quick relief because I did not want to touch the manure after all, and I left the *jels* for the cool inside rooms and the chance to be with Fadi, their older brother. He played cards with me, and sometimes chess, but if he went hunting he took Alaine, saying I was too small.

One day Alaine came back alone, and after that she did not go with him again. When he would knock on the door with his rifle, Alaine opened it a fraction to say no, and then I would watch him walk up the road, a lonely figure with his rifle resting on his shoulder. I was furious with Alaine, and with him for not asking me instead. But Alaine was resolute in her coldness; if he came onto the balcony when we were reading or playing checkers, or if he waved from the road and held up the thong of dead sparrows so we could see how many he had killed, she looked away without speaking.

—What's wrong with you? I demanded, but she refused to tell me what he had done to deserve this treatment. I decided that probably she had tried to shoot and missed, or the gun had kicked back and she had fallen down. Alaine hated to do things wrong. Fadi came out after hunting and removed his shirt, rinsed his arms and face with the hose. He grinned over at us as the water splashed all over him. The droplets glistened on his skin, and Alaine bent over her book, whispering to herself.

Little birds of many colors fluttered in rickety wooden cages all over their balcony. Their father, who was infirm, lay on a couch watching the birds and smoking the *argileh*. He was a *hajji* and always wore the white robe that meant he had made the pilgrimage to Mecca, except for the few occasions I saw him rise and put on a suit to go to Beirut. Then he wore funereal black, as if presaging his own death, also marked by the sad, downward slopes of his frame and eyes. When he found the energy he beat his children with a cane, swooping down on them in rage, and they meekly bowed their heads. Then he would fall back exhausted and wheezing, and they would run for cold water, coffee, a sandwich, anything he demanded. He cursed the war from his reclining position; he threw the shells from *bizir* and pistachios at the birdcages and the birds sang all day. Fadi stood out of range of the beatings: instead he watched his father calmly and I was proud of him. The birds beat their wings and chirped; they flew into the bars and fell back dazed.

Alaine passed this balcony where I sat licking salt from my fingers and watching the birds with pity, and when Fadi said hello, she did not even look at him but stopped to stare at me, slowly rocking her soccer ball with her heel.

—Come with me, Marianna, she commanded.

I swung my legs, licking the tips of my fingers one by one. The birds chirped and fluttered.

—Why does she have to go? Fadi gestured lazily for me to stay, and I felt older, important. The afternoon was bright and calm and maybe he would take me for a walk the way he used to take Alaine. A dog sniffed its way along the side of the road, its sides heaving in and out in the heat, paws dragging.

Alaine looked up and down the road, shoulders hunched slightly inwards, chest still flat at eleven. Her jeans were loose and dirty, like a boy. Come *on*, Marianna, she said.

Fadi clucked his tongue disapprovingly and held out a palmful of seeds to me. Have some more *bizir,* he said, and I stared at his black eyes, the faint acne on his chin, and I knew I should go with Alaine because she so wanted me to, but instead my fingers gathered the seeds. I hated the house where she was going anyway, because the summer before, the boy had drowned a whole litter of puppies. *Not enough food,* he had said when I screamed for him to stop. I chewed the *bizir,* shaking my head.

Alaine pinched up her face and left without another word. I

watched her grow smaller and smaller half-running towards the house on the side of the hill, her thin white arms thrown out for balance as she kicked the soccer ball up the road.

Fadi disappeared later in the war; he went to visit someone in the neighboring village and did not come back. I said to Mummy, But he must be somewhere, and she said, Yes, with a sad expression. I did not understand why searching had yielded nothing, no *clues* like in the mystery books I read, no *witnesses*. It's not like that in real life, Mummy said. I could not imagine the balcony without him, and it made me cry to remember all the chess games he had let me win, how he would feign awe at my transparent maneuvers. Alaine was lying on her bed when Mummy gave her the news, me sobbing behind her, and she barely responded at all. She just nodded at the ceiling, and I knew she had never stopped hating him. She was thirteen, no longer speaking to anyone but me, and her left hand was in plaster, broken from punching a wall. She had written all over the cast in black ink pen, but the writing was encoded. *Not even Daddy can decipher it,* she had told me.

—Alaine, did you hear?

Mummy took some steps forward, and Alaine turned her head, this smallest of motions forbidding further entry into the room. Mummy looked back at me, the messenger.

—Aren't you sad? I obediently asked through my tears. Alaine's eyes shifted to mine. There was no sorrow there. I remembered sunlight, a white road. My hand reaching to knock over his defeated king, giggling with embarrassed pride.

—Why don't you get up? Mummy blurted. Come have something to eat?

I gripped Mummy's arm so she wouldn't go on. There was no possible response in Alaine's motionless body, the writing on the cast, the smell of dirty clothes she wouldn't let Mummy wash. Alaine had left us for another world, and in that world, there was no recourse other than staying absolutely still. If she moved, her skin tore open, her head and fists propelled into walls, her legs ran fast as rockets. There was danger in rousing her from bed. I pulled Mummy out and closed the door, but only halfway, as she was not to be left alone.

Our summers in the cottage came to an end when the owner returned from abroad. Astrig at once set about decorating rooms for us in Uncle Ara's house up the hill, where we would stay from now on. But the excitement over all living together was overshadowed by the grown-ups' concern for the owner, who was old and unused to the ups and downs of the war. She had returned due to *misguided nostalgia,* they called it. Mummy was extremely worried about her and visited several times. One day she took me along. No going through Jiddo's desk, Mummy cautioned me. No dismantling of couch pillows, and no going by yourself to the kitchen. When we arrived, we had to knock instead of just walking in. The owner, an old Lebanese lady who had spent most of her life in France, drank sherry from a tiny glass and swayed around the room, speaking incessantly while Mummy sat calmly in her chair, also drinking sherry and smoking. Jiddo had told me long ago that this lady was so rich that she used to be carried about on velvet pillows. She verified this by talking about her palace in Persia, the silent eunuchs, and the poetry read by attendants in gold slippers. She spoke bitterly and with great nostalgic sighs. Furrows appeared in her makeup. She was like a tall, rolled-up piece of paper, crackling and shedding powder.

—Where is Persia? I whispered.

Mummy ignored me. She told the lady, Please consider going back. It's different here now. The war isn't ending.

—Why do you keep telling me to leave my house?

—I want you to be safe, Mummy repeated. I could tell she was being infinitely patient, which was how Daddy described her efforts on behalf of others. I resented the old lady for not appreciating Mummy. A Syrian colonel had even tried to take the cottage, and

Mummy had prevented him, but who could say that he or some-one else would not come back? I did not know the details of the story, but Daddy had brought it up the day before so I knew it was important. I looked around the living room, only now feeling the glumness of sitting in a house no longer yours. I had sniffed the double-size drawer where Jiddo used to keep licorice, but it was full of papers that smelled dry. The lady sat down and slammed a shaky fist on the chair arm.

—This is my house! I will die here!

I pictured her shot dead on the floor, fingers stripped of the precious rings, feet without shoes, because it seemed that most of the dead people in newspaper photographs had no shoes. Mummy always whispered when we saw one on the road, There is nothing worse than a single shoe.

After that we stayed with Uncle Ara and Astrig when we went to the mountains. Behind Uncle Ara's house lay several terraces, beyond which was the barren, rocky expanse we called Crystal Mountain, a treasure trove of fossils, bits of flint we pretended were ancient arrowheads, animal skulls and bones. There was a soldier's camp at the top, surrounded by empty land where later Alaine found the dead Syrian. Sometimes we glimpsed the soldier on watch sitting on a boulder or leaning against a tree, smoking. This camp was in a pine forest, and when we sneaked closer our feet made no sound on the pine-needle floor, and the great stone wall around the occupied mansion closed in the soldiers and hid everything from us, so that all we saw were the tops of tents and the smoke from fires. The ter-ror of being discovered fed our legs and arms and we raced down the rocky slopes, screaming with laughter, scattering the goats who hopped away and stared at us with their peculiar eyes. At sunset, we watched *poor Beirut* through the living-room window, far away along the shore, a city of dark spaces and bursts of flame. The grown-ups measured the motion of the war by what neighbor-hoods had electricity, and sometimes in a matter of minutes, whole

areas suddenly went black. We watched from our haven, and between the olive trees the sea shone under the moon. In the deepest
hours of the night, stray dogs howled down the hills and roosters
crowed, and the clock tick-ticked between our beds.

The war would end, the grown-ups assured one another, leaning
back in their chairs after a meal. I could not imagine the sky silent,
blue and silent. In Beirut we were never to move about in the open,
but had to stay close to walls, keep our ears alert. After days of shooting, when that thick, dreamy quiet would descend upon us, the
grown-ups peered cautiously out the windows, measuring the sky
as if it might give them a sign. Then they said, Go, but slowly. We
were not to burst out of shelter laughing. We emerged with care,
stepping like people avoiding ants, as if our very caution would
protect us. Sometimes, the silence held. Then we searched the walls
of our apartment for holes, and we dug out crumbled concrete with
our fingers to touch the bullet lodged deep inside. We shouted anxious stories from room to room about how this one would have, that
one almost. But at other times, the grown-ups felt something in the
air. They turned around, they said, Get back inside, now.

We almost left Lebanon at the beginning of the war, but at the last
minute Mummy and Daddy changed their minds. An American
journalist visited us in Beirut to ask why. He was wonderfully
tall and smelled of shaving cream and general cleanliness. He sat
on our terrace with a microphone and a notebook. Another man
arranged a video camera on a tripod, and the young Lebanese
woman with them smiled and asked questions and fiddled with
the recording machine. Mummy and Daddy talked with them about
things of no interest, the war and the militias and the politicians,
while I stared from the safety of the space behind Mummy's chair.
The journalist was friendly, and his face broke open every few
moments in smiles that tempered the seriousness with which he
listened. He asked Alaine and me if we were afraid of the shooting

and we shrugged at the silliness of that, but still, he was hand-some and I fell in love.

—People in America will watch this, Marianna, Daddy explained, and I felt important.

—Do you like living here? the journalist asked me.

I darted a look at Alaine to see what the right answer should be. She was scowling at him. I said nothing.

—Don't you ever want to go to the States?

I pictured green grass and a sprinkler, which was exciting com-pared to the regular hoses in our mountain cottage. I pictured white houses and black roads with yellow lines. The journalist wore glasses with thin silver rims and had a mustache. I saw us living together in a big house, and he was wearing a cowboy hat. I saw horses and sheep. A dog herded the sheep. I longed for this. I nodded yes, I wanted to go to America with him, and for the first time felt the gnawed-out hole of wishing for other places, other things. I knew I was trapped. Here we were, on a balcony in Beirut, which was so normal and boring.

—Maybe one day you'll go there, he said comfortingly.

—I don't want to go, Alaine snapped. She glared at me. I was crushed with embarrassment for wanting the wrong thing.

For this American journalist we slammed shut the elevator gate and pressed the button for him to show how nothing would hap-pen, and we turned the faucets on and off so he could hear the rumble and see how nothing happened. I frightened him with sto-ries about the missiles that entered buildings and shot up circular stairwells to find their target. Alaine and I strapped on our new roller skates and flew around the terrace so he could record how smooth the surface was, how brightly the strap buckles shone, how pleasantly the rubber wheels hummed. For him, we had to carry water from the basement more than usual. He followed us down-stairs with his cameraman and his assistant, who was beautiful and who Mummy suspected was his girlfriend. I tried not to look bored at having to carry so much water, even though my arms hurt. The concierge, who lived in the basement and supervised the amount of water that was taken, peered out from the shadows of his tiny room with the smelly blankets and the gas lamp, the long black cockroaches crawling on the walls, and he did not get involved. I felt important compared to him; the journalist asked questions as we filled the plastic gallons with water and then, with the camera- man backing up the stairs before us, we slowly went up, the black circle of the lens recording our toil. After that, when Mummy sent me downstairs with empty gallons, I took pleasure in knowing that what I was doing was of interest to America and the rest of the world.

In the evening, the grown-ups had a drink on the terrace.

—I wish I didn't have to go back so soon, the journalist sighed. Everyone nodded understandingly. He said, It's magical here.

The Lebanese assistant replied, Every foreigner experiences this. It's how Lebanon is.

This sort of talk was dull so I urged Alaine to bring out our guns. We had built a tent on the corner of the terrace to play militia. This was our headquarters, and the rest of the terrace was land to be conquered and then the population had to pay protection money. Mummy and Daddy and the journalists sat in ignorance in the green plastic chairs surrounded by fragrant plants, smoking cigarettes and drinking wine, and their laughter was clear and pleasant and con- stant. Daddy was eating peanuts and speaking about his past life in America, and Mummy shelled *bizir* between her front teeth, smiling her smile, legs crossed daintily and one foot moving as was her habit. Alaine and I crouched down and approached along the wall. We burst into their gathering.

—Ten piasters, commanded Alaine, and the journalist complied because I had a gun trained on him and he had best be calm and obey.

I didn't care about the war. I had Mummy and Daddy and Alaine, and we existed apart from the world outside. They enclosed me between them when the bombing came and they covered my ears and eyes with their palms, which delighted me. It was a grand game to see how long we stayed in the hall or in the bathroom, how many days of school we could miss, how late we could stay up listening to the war before sleep's soft hands enfolded us in quiet.

I kept the coins the journalist gave us in a special silver box, and over time the box became something usual, part of the things I had always owned, and I stopped looking inside it. It found its way with me to America without my noticing, and in early summer, when we still believed we would go back home soon, Daddy called me to the living room and waved at the TV, Look! Mummy and Alaine were already standing side by side, tall as bamboo stalks, as Daddy liked to say. Alaine had the posture of someone ready for a fight and Mummy's arms were folded, and she swayed slightly, her face pale and downward turning. Only my father was delighted by what he'd discovered: our journalist, a desert behind him, his graying hair blown this way and that. I couldn't hear his words for the pounding in my ears.

—Isn't this incredible? After all these years? Daddy said.

—He looks well, Mummy commented blankly. Alaine shrugged and headed outside again. My father's smile went a little stiff, and he directed intense focus at the TV as if to prove he did not care if no one else was interested. After a moment, Mummy said, I've got Comet drying on the counters.

Daddy and I were left listening to the journalist's report, not to the words he spoke, but to his voice itself, a rich, deep timbre, the wide vowels the first real sound of America Alaine and I had ever heard, aside from our father. His hair blew in the wind, he gripped the microphone and told his news, and I was amazed by this, that someone could persist in living, in going from place to place, while the memory of him on our terrace in Beirut remained static, full of possibility, edging open what had been so ordinary. We were not going back after all; he was sealing our fate, speaking to us across the span of time, asking that same bemused question, *Why do you stay?* and here we were, in America, staring mutely at his confident, bobbing head. *We didn't,* I addressed him bitterly, willing the message to wherever he was. *A whole war,* I told him. *And now this.*

In the summer of 1976 Daddy sits in the dimness of the entrée, shoes shining, suit jacket folded over his knees. Three large suit-cases stand side by side next to the door, which is ajar, and his fingers tap-tap the telephone on the little bookshelf next to him, as if he wants to make a telephone call but of course there is no line. Mummy's address book, a marvelous metal pop-up contraption that has kept me occupied on many afternoons, is missing. Across from him is the small bathroom where Alaine and I have slept many nights, and it is extraordinarily clean and the bath mat has been washed and lies folded on the toilet seat.

We are on the verge of going to America: the war has spilled over to include foreign diplomats, whose corpses were found at Ramlet al-Baida, and all over the city foreigners are thumbing through passports and identity papers, zipping shut suitcases, say-ing good-bye.

Mummy explores the rooms, and they seem bright and stunned from her work with the cleaning woman the day before. Her finger moves down the list of instructions left for the neighbor, but they are useless, they mean nothing, for what is there to maintaining an empty apartment. She walks through each room, she smoothes the bedcovers and adjusts the spines of books so that they are even on the shelves; she opens and closes the wardrobe doors in the event that something has been forgotten. The sheets draped over furniture make the rooms look like echoes of themselves; she finds herself thinking of her life here as if across the distance of time, as if she herself is an echo, wandering back in sorrow. On the balcony, her fingers slip through the metal grid that has protected Alaine and me from falling over the railing, and she stares at the city through the fragmentation of squares. It is quiet today. The dead are dead and the living are fleeing and Mummy is surprised to find herself here, among the living, her eyes strained from filling out documents that will admit her into her husband's country. On the corner she glimpses Abu Taleb, whose bald head reflects the sun and whose shoes are full of holes, and she imagines walking to his store to buy flowers and to chat about the fighting. About fifteen minutes later, she leaves the store with the flowers wrapped in paper, and walks to Hamra street to visit Astrig's seamstress Sitt Munira and her spinster daughter Jehan, whose shop is warm with the sounds of whirring sewing machines and the piles of richly colored material on every table and chair. There she has a coffee, and the large grimy windows are ajar, the noise of Hamra Street filling the rooms. Sitt Munira's hands are arthritic but she sews as they talk, and Jehan, who is strong and dark and sorrowful, hurries to fetch pastries from the shop against Mummy's protests. When she returns, the opened box gives off the scent of flaky croissants still warm from the oven and of *baqlawa* dripping with honey and nuts, and Mummy licks her fingers and laughs. The people crowd the streets and tinny music blares from cassette recorders and children race by on wooden boards with wheels, imitating the cripples that populate the city. Then Mummy kisses Sitt Munira and Jehan good-bye and wanders home, buying lemons and bananas on the way, and the war does not matter, it comes and goes, and maybe this weekend we will go to the mountains if Mummy and Daddy decide it is safe enough. Mummy walks, her purse hanging from her forearm, heels clicking on the pavement, and far above, beyond the rooftops and antennas and laundry lines, beyond the height of the mountains in the distance, Saisaban's wings lift and fall and his hide shines the shine of the sea as he circles all of Lebanon, snorting and galloping, his mane and tail white as the stones on the beaches, eyes black as the *mazoot* that burns in houses, hooves sharp as the tips of bullets.

Daddy waits in the entrée, and when Mummy comes in from

the balcony, he jumps up to hold her. They remain standing for a
few minutes, her face in his neck, and then Daddy gently releases
her and closes the door. The suitcases remain in the entrée until
evening, when all of us begin to unpack and Mummy complains
about the wrinkles in everything and how unnecessary they were
in the end. One day soon, the journalist will come to ask us why,
and the answer is obvious. Mummy takes command of her home
again, and Daddy chases Alaine and me, pretending to be a great
American monster called Bigfoot, and his stomping feet indeed are
huge so we squeal and run and run.

∽

We live in a green wood house on a lump of hill, patchy grass falling away on either side. The house sags in the center, as if the earth wants to reclaim it from the surface. The inside smells of the wet autumn ground, the hissing furnace downstairs. Alaine smacks spackle all over our bedroom walls, then smoothes it with a knife. She is going to paint next, a light blue that I chose. I could tell she didn't really like it, but she heaved up the can anyway and carried it to the cashier, and Daddy counted out the bills. Every day they work in concert and in silence to rebuild my world. I watch them, a tangle of remorse and fear; I am glass spidering fissures like a windshield struck by bullets; one push and everything will disintegrate. Alaine digs spackle, smoothes, digs and smoothes, shoves the rickety stepladder along. My job is to make sure she doesn't miss any cracks, and I lie on the bed, pointing without speaking. There. Over there. Lower.

In Beirut our apartment with its smooth white walls waits unoccupied, the furniture under sheets and the verandah doors pulled shut. Mummy will clear it out soon, in January. Once a week our neighbor Mrs. Awad goes there to air out the rooms and make sure everything is in order, but by now even she must know we won't be back, at least not to live, so she's probably skipping a week here, a week there. I picture opening the door, dragging my suitcases into the front hall. Check for water, electricity. Pull the sheets off of everything, dust a little, make a Nescafé, make a plan.

—Not bad, Alaine remarks, surveying the patches of spackle. I stare from the bed, obediently following her gaze around the room. She says, I can start painting in a few hours.

I nod when she looks at me, because it seems some answer is required. She packs up the things she's been using—a rubber bucket of spackle, various tools, stepladder, cloths and newspapers. Her easy handling of these things makes me feel even more alone. When she is gone, the walls look forlorn, abandoned too soon by their maker. The bookshelves stand in front of the two beds under an old white sheet; Alaine has left out my framed photograph of my friend Amer to make me feel better, or maybe just to hold the sheet in place. The closet door is closed, our clothes and shoes neatly organized within. There is a new smell in the air.

The time we came to America was, briefly, a time of spending and jokes about our ugly house, grand references to our exile, what we would eat first when we finally went back. I existed in a state of euphoria brought on by the allure of a new life, but the euphoria faded within weeks. It was the end of winter, and a cold only Daddy had ever experienced seeped under the doors and through the shabby windows. I got up later and later, and one day I did not get out of bed at all. The months following blended dark afternoons of drawn curtains, me on the couch with the television low, the burned feel of eyes staring without blinking. Spring came and went. I turned eighteen. There was the new, strong Alaine, a stranger, shaking my shoulder in concern. Mummy whispering, Please don't do this, her palm on my forehead as if maybe it is just a fever, maybe there is something I can give her. There is the day when Daddy convinced me to leave the house, my mission to help choose flowers for their anniversary, but there was so much color, dank smell of flower water, stalks uneven under my shoes, and I cried so hard he had to lead me out stumbling and he got no flowers.

Later, the warm gray day in summer, but my body, its insides, curl in on themselves like something sick. The day is not to be spoken. It cannot be understood.

Look ahead, they say, but I can't face repeating my whole senior year like Alaine did, and even if I wanted to plan for college, there is not enough money, so there doesn't seem to be any point. We had all assumed Daddy would have work by now. My old principal wrote two letters in spring: the first asking why I hadn't finished up the year at public school, and the second suggesting I take the GED and apply for college scholarships based on my refugee status.

—We aren't refugees, Alaine said, enraged.

—I think we might be. I said it more to annoy her. I did not know for sure.

We turned to Daddy for answers. He was typing at the dining-room table, wearing his pajama top and shorts. When Alaine asked our question, he slowly placed his cigarette in the ashtray and folded his hands. He said, I suppose we are, honey. His face had grown too thin, grown deep lines around the mouth, across the forehead, and now he looked to the side, tapping his cigarette on the ashtray with nothing more to say. I wanted to take it back, to hold his broken face and tell him we didn't mind that he couldn't find a job because he was old. The teller at the Cumberland Farms convenience store across the street had offered him an application because the manager's position was vacant. The application was on his desk, in full view, next to his books. He had filled half of it before realizing the obvious, that thirty years of scholarship would not fit.

We are, Mummy explained, a quintessential American family, come here from strife and ready to make a new future. I did not care about this. I watched my father the historian crossing the street to thank the teller for her kindness. His shorts made his legs look like Popsicle sticks.

My face in the bathroom mirror: blotchy, pale skin. Dry and chafed red around the nose and between the eyebrows, a skin condition that worsens in this American cold. I pick at the flakes of skin to clean up my face but it does no good, only makes the red more vivid. My hair is thin and straggly. I try to relax my face. I smoothe on cream and massage, like in the advertisements. I comb my hair into a ponytail. My face has changed. It is narrower, harder. My eyes should be bigger; they are plain-shaped, without uniqueness. Just eyes. I want to cut my cheeks, cut lines everywhere. I could draw a map. When she was thirteen Alaine drew a map, an escape route from Lebanon. She had secret plans to leave us all. Lines going northwards, across the Syrian border, through Turkey, or across the sea itself. She thought she might go live in Greece. My hands make fists, I'm trembling. I jam my fists into my cheeks, my neck, my temples. On my temples the pain is cold metal; it runs around the inside of my skull, stopping me. I open my eyes. I am standing at the sink in the quiet bathroom. I feel my awful heart beating in my feet, drumming through the linoleum floor, down into the foundations, it's going to break this house.

I want to go home, a stupid set of words, over and over. Not even true, because home does not miss me, this blotchy pale skin, this half-breed not belonging anywhere, and here, people's eyes pass over me believing I am one of them. *Nowhere is home,* I tell myself. *There is no such thing.*

I still think of dying and it astonishes me, that this feeling can persist across continents and oceans, that the dismay at things, the despair, can live inside a person like a tiny dark heart, no matter how bright and noisy and fascinating the world is.

The spackle takes time to dry, and Alaine reads the newspaper, imparts the day's advice. She tells Daddy, Don't worry, we won't put you in an old people's home. She tells Mummy, You can't invite people with deliveries inside, they're usually robbers and they'll see things to take later.

—There is nothing to take, our mother says flatly, and this is true. Most of our belongings are still in Lebanon. There was some furniture here when we moved in, and the rest is from the Salvation Army.

Daddy says, I'm going down to the museum. Anyone want to come? and he ends up going alone. He strides up the sidewalk

swinging his arms, to all appearances a content man with an afternoon in front of him. He nods to the worker in each shop opposite
our house; I let the curtain drop back into place before Walter looks.
What does he see? A shadow, retreating slowly until the curtain returns to its own dull orange color. The curtain moves in the breeze.
The door remains closed.

Our street is a space between mirror and mirror, two worlds
reflecting each other into infinity. The gas station and its lonely
occupant are the outside world. He is the only one watching, the
only one who knows we exist. I do not know what he sees.

Sometimes, listening to the house creak in the dark, I think of
Walter settling in for the night in his own creaking house in some
other part of this city. He has to stoop through doorways he's so
tall, and in his pajamas he looks scrawny and sad. Maybe he drinks
whiskey before getting into bed, or a beer, and watches TV for a
while. Then he folds his thick glasses on the nightstand and lies
awake, his big young heart adoring Alaine, who pays no attention
to him.

—But honey, Daddy tells her. You can't just ignore someone who
says hello to you!

—What do you want me to do? Marry him?

—Oh, for Heaven's sake, Daddy sighs. He's a nice young man.

Daddy refers to Walter's act of goodness on that day as if it were
as simple as bringing over pie or changing a lightbulb. Walter sits
at the register, moves back and forth behind the posters decorating
the grimy windows. He is waiting for me to push open the door,
lean my head in, say thank you at long last. Or maybe he doesn't
think about me at all, only Alaine. He must have fallen in love with
her as soon as we arrived, bewitched by her tousled curly hair and
dark, sad eyes. It took only a few weeks for him to start crossing the
street under our family's wary gaze, bearing information about our
new country. The street-cleaning schedule is different this week.
Garbage collection is a day late after Independence Day. The bus
fares have gone up. He focused on telling Alaine these important

facts. I was jealous, even though it was only Walter reeking of car oil, big dirty hands fumbling for purchase, seizing the rail, the lamp-post, his own legs like he might fall over during those few tortured advances before Alaine's chill rejection pinned him in place across the street.

Now, from his exile, he seeks news of her. How is Magdalaine? he asks Daddy every chance he gets. Daddy mentioned her full name once, and Walter uses it as if to emphasize their bond. Just fine, Daddy says, withholding out of pity that Alaine hates this name. When she was young, too young for me to remember, she demanded that she be called Alaine instead of Magdalaine. She even wanted the "e" to be dropped so that she would become Alain, but she had to compromise.

—And how is Marianna? Walter asks.

—Just fine, is the answer, untrue, an apology.

Why don't you let Walter know you're all right? Daddy suggested after the hospital, and the ghost of these words lives on, scared up by an opening door, a car horn, the slam of the metal grille across the gas station's windows late at night. The ghost flits hopefully between those who live in this house, a troubled, disjointed rush through the rooms before encountering me, the obstacle. The words dissolve inside me, leaving only quiet.

Alaine says, It's time to paint, but some men are trudging past the window, heading for the backyard. Their arrival seizes all of our attention. They've come to trim the bushes, which in the last few months have risen above the wire fence and now block the view of the road. The landlord, who has forgiven us the fire Alaine made in summer, is also having them do the yard as a favor since we don't own a lawn mower. They circle the house once, then get to work.

Alaine abandons the painting for later. She and Mummy sit in the living room with the tight, nervous expressions of those expecting a calamity, while I follow the workers from window to window as discreetly as possible. They are young, probably college students. I imagine them catching sight of me, a thin, sad girl, wild hair about her face, smoking. I could tell them my stories. Their voices are so loud, foreign. They probably wouldn't like me, anyway. They seem easygoing, free of thought, so far from Amer's dark, serious eyes, the low sound of his voice describing when he fought in the militia. I met Amer the summer before leaving, and we spent every day together, right up until we left. *The sea misses you,* he wrote. *It is empty without you.* I received one letter from him; the others, like all of mine, were probably lost in the mail, and now I no longer have the will to try. This is what happens to people who take their things and go.

—I don't want them to cut the bushes, Mummy says. Our privacy will be gone.

The bushes are so high they darken the living room. I sense the desperation Mummy is feeling; her family, crowded in these small rooms, protected from the outside world by these bushes, about to be exposed. I don't like her this way.

—Why don't you tell them? I snap.

She shakes her head, too distraught to comment on my tone. Daddy is still at the museum, or maybe he would handle this dialogue with the workers. Alaine sucks in her breath and stomps out to the backyard, slamming the screen door. I cannot tell if she is angry with our hesitancy, or trying to work up her own courage. We hear her saying, Hey! over the sound of the mower. The sound abruptly cuts. Silence.

Mummy and I sneak towards the door, but she is already coming back.

—They have to cut the bushes, she says. I can tell from her eyes that she feels like a failure.

—But everyone will look in!

—No one looks in America, Alaine retorts.

Mummy is resolute in her despair. She sits in the living room, watching the young men shear away the bushes. The room fills with sunlight. Mummy smokes, watching. The young men laugh and talk with one another.

—We should offer them water or lemonade, she announces.

Alaine is troubled by this. You can't do that here.

—Why not?

—You just can't.

We sit in silence, waiting for the young men to finish and go away, leave our little ugly house in peace.

Daddy comes back and paces the yard with care, as if it belongs to him. He stands in its center, hands on his hips. He says, Isn't it nice to have a yard? apologetically, as if the love he finds he still has for the country of his birth is betraying us all. I don't answer his question. He says dejectedly, Things have changed so much here. I wish we were still in Beirut.

I just look away, ashamed without knowing why, the way I always feel when he talks like this. He pulls up some weeds the college boys missed. My father is a kind, soft-spoken man who is tired all the time. His application is on file at the Cumberland Farms. They said once they have all the applications in, they will call for an interview.

Alaine stirs the paint with a stick, like slowly swirling blue molasses. I want to put my hand in it. My hands hold my elbows, which feel like stones poking my palms. I imagine a body made of stones, knocking sounds when the body walks, no pain when it falls, but people point and whisper, *Poor thing, she's got no flesh, she's just a sorry pile of stones.* Alaine tilts the can, pours into the tray. She shows me how to load the roller with paint, smoothly go up and down. Against my will, I find solace in the swaths of blue. I push the roller along, going sideways, at angles, trying a circle. When I glance at Alaine, I find her face puckered with concern, her dark eyes examining the many flaws. She offers a falsely encouraging smile, and I am taken backwards, Beirut, nighttime, Alaine making a clay bowl and us all smiling the same frozen smile, reading salvation in her work.

But Alaine doesn't urge me to go on. She accepts the roller with obvious relief, her attention already turned to correcting my mistakes. I wander to the living room.

—I thought you were painting, Daddy says brightly, and I shake my head no, go to the kitchen. The brief hurt on his face at my dismissive gesture burns my eyes; for a second I can't see, I touch the door frame to keep my balance. Our house is a board game, each of us moving from room to room, searching, searching. My family trails me sadly with their eyes, or they tread carefully into my presence on some fictional errand, glancing me over to check for cracks. I move in slow motion, looking down, my whole body conveying the warning that they shouldn't hope.

I sit knees to chest on a kitchen chair, open Mummy's album on the table. It is all I want to look at, what I read now instead of words. The album pages are heavy and old, they shed dusty lavender as I turn them. The images of Mummy's childhood in the mountains fill me with longing. The photos are grainy and full of sun: my baby mother sitting on a blanket in a stone doorway, the shadows of afternoon, her hand resting on her pet hedgehog; growing up with an elfin face and brown curled hair, peeking over the shoulder of her best friend Muna; in a bikini, long-armed and grinning, caught writing a letter at a table in Mukhtara; the delighted look on a young man's face because she is smiling at him, a dumb man who tried to woo her and failed. I would have been just like her, surrounded by admirers at parties, dancing to Arabic music so beautifully that everyone stops and stares. I stare. It is how things should have been.

The sucking sound of Alaine working the roller intrudes on my sorrow. We live in a wood house instead of stone: this one fact occupies me more and more. I cannot shake away the longing for concrete walls painted white, or the mountain walls, big solid stones laid one upon the other, sunken into the ground, the weight of them steadfast, as deep and true as if they had always lain there. The air is different inside a stone house in the mountains. In summer the doors stand open, and a breeze brushes along cool surfaces, and stone melds with pine, earth, our bodies breathing stone-pure air. Here, the air surfaces from porous, warm wood that's rotting away from damp, warped from years of heat to cold to heat. We breathe the air of all the people who ever lived here.

I hear Mummy's slippers crossing the kitchen, then she's next to me trying to close the album, but I hold the pages open with my fists.

—Why do you keep looking at this, Marianna?

Mummy is pleading in that way she gets sometimes, broken-hearted but at the same time afire with new resolve to make things right. I hold my silence.

—What do you see? she begs. What are you looking for?

Words I've been hoarding for weeks find my voice, drag it out from the bitter pit of my stomach. I tell her, If there hadn't been a war, my life would have been like yours.

Mummy stands very still, looking out the window. She asks, And how is my life?

I've already spoken too much, my mouth dries up and I bend my head so I no longer have to look at her sorry eyes. She doesn't understand that I meant before the war, certainly before now. I get ready to argue, but her hand cups my chin, tilting my face so I am forced to look. In the past few years Mummy has started to age, each grim event of our lives marking lines around her eyes and mouth, the face of someone almost out of strength and angry for it. She never was like this. I shrug out of her grip, I can't bear to look so closely at her, and she just shakes her head at me as if I'm deaf to some song everyone else can hear, and it's the saddest thing in the world.

She says, One life is like any other.

I don't know what she means. The words smack of a lie. No life is like another. She got to live in another world, one that I longed for my whole childhood. I see the Corniche the way it used to be before the war, wide sunlit road, palm trees swaying in the wind blowing off the sea. *Before the war.* The words mean something else for Mummy, a whole other life, whereas mine was a speck of time, a baby grinning dumbly at a serene world. First she had a beautiful childhood in the village, and then as a teenager she lived in Beirut, *Paris of the Middle East.* There was no war. Nothing bad ever happened to her. My eyes scream this in absolute silence. I want to kick the table to pieces, smash the windows. I will make her see.

But Mummy doesn't see. She sinks down opposite me and stares out at the fresh-mowed yard. In the brief time since the college boys left, more leaves have blown in, settled on the now squared-off hedges and stiff grass. She says, I know we have made mistakes with you and your sister, Marianna.

—You don't know anything, I retort, my customary answer. *You don't you don't you don't,* and now I'm thinking of everything at once, of Michel the spy, Alaine running in the night. Of Alaine's hand unfurling, bullets nestled in her palm, her dark eyes locking me to secrecy. I want to blurt something out, anything, some truth about us. The first time I cut my wrists for example, long before she ever knew about it.

I'm about to speak when I realize Mummy isn't thinking about any of that. She is staring at the open album, at the photograph of Muna in a windblown field, wearing a checkered skirt and white blouse. It is a long-ago picture, creased and torn. The landscape looks washed out by time, black and white and gray, as if the photograph recorded not that moment but what was coming, the smiling girl torn out of the world, the place eroded into another. I want to say sorry but I can't even open my mouth, my teeth jammed together, hurting. Mummy touches her friend's face, then gently pushes my fists out of the way to close the album. I don't look up; I hear in her hesitation the desire to ask me to clean something, or put things away, take part in the general work of the house. She does not. She goes outside. The screen door squeaks on its hinges,

back and forth. It is too big for the uneven door frame of our sagging house; the landlord has failed in his promise to do something,
and Alaine and Daddy now and then gravely examine it like uncertain surgeons.

I bend my forehead to the album cover, push, push so it hurts,
to make the pictures go away. Muna died so many years before I was
born, but I've known the story all my life: I can see her standing
by the car, the hot summer afternoon, the man who said he loved
her lifting the shotgun from the trunk. I cannot bear thinking of
Mummy as a little girl, her arm entwined with Muna's. They used
to collect pine nuts and drink lemonade in the afternoons, playing
cards in the courtyard shade of Muna's house in the mountains.
They grew up together, like sisters. In winters Mummy was so jealous that Muna got to live in Beirut; she was fourteen when Téta
and Jiddo finally moved back and rented an apartment in the Minet
el-Hosn quarter. From there Mummy would walk one hour to visit
Muna, and at that time the sea was clean and fresh and the sky
was clear of the smoke from fires. She trailed her fingers along the
rail, gazing at the sea that tumbled on the rocks; she smelled the
kaak that ten years later she would buy for me, wiping the crumbs
from my chin as we walked to visit Téta and Jiddo; perhaps when
money could be spared, she rode in a taxi, delighting the driver
with her beauty. At Muna's house, oblivious to what was coming,
they curled their hair and dreamed of lovers while the city ran its
course, driving towards the future.

A gust of wind and the screen swings all the way open, slams
the countertop. I jerk upright. The cold autumn air raises bumps
up and down my arms; after a minute, I go to the doorway to see
if Mummy is finished with whatever she's doing. She isn't doing
anything, though. She is wandering the back end of our small garden, picking dead leaves off the hedge and rubbing them between
her palms, letting go cloud after cloud of crushed leaf. The pieces
blow about, cling to her skirt, her pantyhose. I catch a whiff of

paint from Alaine's work on the other side of the house. I want to go outside to Mummy but I don't know how.

Nighttime, the sharp smell of paint pervades the house even though Alaine has closed the door and opened all the windows in our room. We have makeshift beds on the living-room floor. Daddy's snores drift down the hallway and the occasional passing car sweeps light over Alaine turned towards the wall, me flat on my back staring up. We are lit up like targets. Windows all around, and only flimsy curtains and weak little locks between us and the outside. *Robbers won't come in if they see a light,* Alaine has instructed us. The requisite lamp burns in the dining room, casting a thread across my blankets. Still, I can't loosen my chest, I'm stiff, a stick figure on the floor with a middle of iron, so heavy I can't move, so sorry I can't breathe. I stare at Alaine's pale foot sticking out from the tangled sheet. I will never sleep, even with Alaine next to me. Here, in this wood house when sleep begins its creep through my limbs, my limbs remember summertime, another kind of sinking down, the weight of eye and skin and mouth, the whole body known, dying. Then I fly awake, breathing, breathing.

One night in the mountains, I woke to men's voices outside the window, the terror of Mummy's hand over my mouth. Alaine sat upright against the wall, her profile etched in the lights from parked trucks. I press my hand to my mouth, eyes wide open, remembering. Daddy shouted, Who are you? What do you want? Even then I knew the futility of this. The shout just to shout something, because there was no hiding from the thieves, not with towels drying on the cane chairs outside the door, an open book, Alaine's G.I. Joe perched on the ledge. I heard men's voices, speaking low. The engines rumbled, tires crushed gravel. Silence. I don't know why they let us be. Alaine did not say a word, just tucked herself in again, glaring at the window. She made me feel safe.

∽∾

Alaine came back one day from Crystal Mountain carrying a dirty rag and a canteen with a hole in it. A gas mask hung from her shoulder and she was bent beneath its weight, the big goggle eyes swinging against her back.

—I found a body, she said, and smiled.

—Like Bella?

A few weeks before, we had heard that someone's dog had been killed. They said its eyes had been gouged out.

—No, stupid. Not a dog.

I didn't know if I should believe her or not. I followed her around, mystified, while she soaked the rag in the water and played with the canteen. Our bright clean room in Uncle Ara's house, decorated especially for us by Astrig, transformed under Alaine's hand. She lined bullets on the shelf. She propped the canteen next to them. She hung the gas mask above her bed and the streaked, muddy lenses frightened me, because the person who had looked through them was now dead and his dead eyes were watching me. I heard the grown-ups whispering in the living room. I felt left out, I wanted to find a body, too.

I looked at her in confused satisfaction when the grown-ups said she must be lying. I looked for a hint that what they said was true, but her face was still and white, eyes dark with secrets.

Later she said, I buried the body, too.

I thought of the body with the bullet hole in its throat—she said that the soldier had been drinking when he died, that was why there was a hole in the canteen—and I thought of her pushing dirt over this dead soldier.

—Did you hurt your hands when you buried him?

I needed proof. There had to be holes in the ground around the soldier, made by my sister to cover the huge body. I saw her scratching at the earth and tearing her fingernails.

—No, not really. I did it slowly.

—Was he Syrian?

—I think so, but it doesn't matter, she said, irritated.

There he was, the dead Syrian with Alaine beside him, taking away his canteen and his shirt that was bloody and now soaking in a tub in our bedroom. I went to check on it even though it made me sick, and the water was cloudy with dark flecks floating on the surface. I reported that it was probably time to change the water.

She lifted the shirt out of the tub and it hung down long and heavy and dripping. I reached for it and she hesitated but then let me have it. I grasped the shirt by the shoulders and held it against me, measuring. It reached below my knees.

—Won't fit you, stupid, she said.

I blushed with shame. I blurted, You neither, but this didn't matter to her. It was her shirt, and I knew she would wear it no matter how big it was.

Later I sat hunched on the steps out of sight and listened to Mummy and Uncle Ara arguing in the living room. Mummy kept repeating, How could you? You went with her, where did she get those things? and Uncle Ara paced with his scotch and ice, shrugging. *She must have run ahead,* I thought, *and by the time you caught up it was all over.*

I couldn't understand why they didn't go and look for the Syrian. He wasn't going to move, after all. I wanted to suggest a search party, but I knew I wasn't really supposed to know what was going on. They were passing me by as if I wasn't there, talking as if I didn't know.

That night I waited until Alaine was asleep. I crept out of bed and went to the shelf where she had placed the canteen. She slept on. I lifted the canteen with the tips of my fingers and sniffed at the jagged hole. There was only the tangy smell of metal, nothing left of the soldier. The gas mask, suspended like some prehistoric fish on the wall over Alaine's curled body, watched me with its black glass eyes, the ribbed tube snaking down the wall towards her. I pictured the soldier standing in the sun, thirsty. Where had we been when he was shot? There were so many shots, every day, and one of them had been him dying. He had been standing, and then he was shot and he fell, and when he stopped moving he lay in the position Alaine would first see, as if this was the plan, his destiny.

Try as I might, I could not picture him, not precisely. I envied Alaine's eyes, her hands. She lay in a heap beneath the sheets, lit by the moon, one hand cupping her cheek. I knew what dead soldiers were supposed to look like. After all, I could see them in pictures or read about them anywhere. But I knew these pictures were nothing compared to Alaine's soldier; they did not show anything personal, the uniqueness that must belong to each cadaver and that announces it was once a certain person. This could be a shaving scar or a bracelet, anything. I had heard that looking at a corpse reminded you that everyone must die, but I could not imagine looking at a dead soldier and thinking, *I'll die one day, too.* Such a corpse would be nothing like me.

After Alaine buried the soldier, Uncle Ara decided we should know how to fire a gun, and I thought it might be because if a dead soldier was so near, live ones might come even closer. He showed us where the guns were kept in the liquor cabinet, how to load the bullets, how to release the safety. I took to this new task with great excitement, though I tried to be grave, like Alaine, who weighed the gun in her palm and did not concern herself with Mummy and Daddy's admonitions that she be careful. Ara, she's only twelve! Mummy fumed, as if I, the ten-year-old, did not need to be discussed. We're in a war! Uncle Ara retorted, and Astrig backed him up, pooh-poohing the harm a few lessons might do. On those bright summer days, we stood with our feet apart and arms extended, one eye shut to focus on our target. We started with a rusting, upturned jeep on the side of the road and worked our way to cans; then one day Alaine shot the thinnest branch of an olive tree and everyone praised her, but she just acted as if she was bound to hit it sometime. I never hit it once and no one was surprised. The day I thought I might, the shepherd who kept his sheep on Uncle Ara's land surprised us with a gift of fresh milk and my practise session was forgotten.

—What happened to the pistol? Uncle Ara asked later in amazement. It was right here!

Everyone searched and searched, but it was gone. Alaine became indignant when the grown-ups questioned her one too many times. She tried to head off in her usual way, and Daddy grabbed her.

—Not so fast, young lady, he said in his cowboy-movie accent. Not after that business last week.

He made it sound as if she'd been caught kissing a boy rather than burying a dead soldier. Somehow, Alaine was allowed to keep the soldier's things. She displayed them in her room in Beirut with the rest of her collection, the gas mask at the center of it all. I started to hate my own room, which was decorated with dumb posters of horses and actors, plants, stuffed animals. I wanted to find a dead soldier, I wanted to wear his shirt and remember his face. At night I lay awake, listening to the shooting, imagining. I walked the mountain under the moon in a flowing white nightgown. Something was keeping me awake, but I did not know what. A *malaise*. My hair was long and lustrous. I walked barefoot, my step so light I couldn't feel the stones or brambles. I heard the shot, ran to save the soldier who lay bleeding on the ground. He begged me for one last kiss, which I gave him, weeping. I wept, wide awake, beating my stomach with my fists for the stupidity of my dreams, while outside my door, the grown-ups went back and forth, all day, all night, whispering, Alaine, Alaine.

Alaine climbs Crystal Mountain. In the telling of this story, I am eighteen years old and it happened long ago, but in my dreams she is still so thin, so angry, and me struggling in my sleep, awakened by nothing with the sheets on the floor, exhausted. Mummy brings me coffee in the morning. I hardly eat and my hips jut like Alaine's always have.

One day in the fall Alaine did not go to school, and after this everything was different. This was the beginning of everything, of blood on her arms and face, of the psychiatrists and the pills she would be forced to take, of her running in the night, pursued by those who loved her. She sat on the living-room floor surrounded by piles of dirt and clay pots. I could not believe that this was allowed, this dirt everywhere. She filled the pots with a trowel without looking up and without stopping. She scooped the dirt and it was under her fingernails and smeared on her arms with sweat. I could see that it was important to fill the pots, and I was afraid because there were not that many and what would she do when they were all filled? Mummy kept an eye on Alaine, and she kept encouraging her, praising her work. I wanted to stay and help, but I had to go to school.

Alaine no longer talked. Her lips looked thinner and harder than usual, and her sad black-brown eyes looked lost. In the photographs of us at the beginning of this time, I am chubby-faced and still grinning, while she gazes into the camera with the knowing eyes of an adult. Her memories eventually would be erased by the fog of medicines, but how could we know that yet? So even at my age I sensed that we needed to treat her delicately, as someone who would forever be haunted by memory. Years would pass before we realized that she had never remembered what we had been trying to help her forget.

I was standing in the hallway and I looked across the living room and through the kitchen doorway. She was sitting at the table that stood against the wall, eating cereal in that grubby childish way we always did, hunched over and absorbed. She wore her favorite brown pants and the checked shirt and her torn tennis shoes, and was no longer slender in that athletic way, but somehow wilted, soft. I felt an ugly surge of pleasure because I had always been the plump one in the family, the youngest with the limp blond hair and wild temper, and she was always more special with her white Armenian skin. Guilty, dutiful, I reported back to Mummy, She's stopped moving, and Mummy answered, I know, but there was little anyone could do. In the evenings Alaine would stare at the pills in Mummy's palm, and Mummy had to beg her to take them. Alaine would not let my arms go all the way around her anymore, and I could not really make her into the person I remembered from before.

This was the beginning, when the grown-ups still sought solutions. Uncle Bernie, who was not a real uncle but one of Daddy's good friends from the university, bought Alaine a trumpet and a music stand. After five lessons she quit and decided to learn on her own. She sat on a stool in her room with the music before her and played the same tunes furiously, for hours.

—This was not such a good idea, Mummy said, but they were too afraid to stop her because she was finally *showing an interest in things,* as Daddy kept saying.

Alaine played with all her concentration and kept her back straight and her feet planted on the floor. Her fierce eyes examined each note and then her whole body expelled it through the trumpet, each blast a direct expression of her soul that had little to do with the song. The cat was the only one who stayed at that end of the house when she played. He crouched on the bookshelf and closed his eyes as if he enjoyed the racket. Alaine played Three Blind Mice and Mary Had a Little Lamb for two weeks. Then she leaped to the Lebanese National Anthem, the Marseillaise, and Silent Night. I wanted a trumpet, too, but Daddy said, One trumpet is enough, and found me a xylophone. I hated the xylophone. Within a month the house fell silent, and the only music we heard was Daddy's, when he felt like playing some of his grand old songs on the piano.

Alaine's classmates gossiped about her, and I was ashamed, because when I told them she was sick with a cold, just as Mummy had instructed me, I sensed they knew I was lying. Mummy or Daddy wrote notes to the principal that I read on the way to school: *Alaine hasn't recovered from the flu,* or, *Alaine has a bad stomach-ache.* The principal looked at me pityingly when I handed him these notes across the expanse of his desk, as if he knew the truth, that Alaine was curled up in bed with her wrists bandaged and warm, Mummy nearby doing cross-stitch or reading.

On the days she was able to come to school, she walked in the halls with her chin to her chest and a deep frown, as if should she make one mistake, step a single pace out of line, she would break into pieces. Her skin was pale and looked sticky. Her new body, swollen from the medications, hindered and embarrassed her and she shrank away from anyone who spoke to her. When she passed me she would smile a little, but I pretended I hadn't seen her. What's the matter with her, my friends asked, and I said, She's depressed, and the word traveled around the school, *depressed, depressed,* until everyone had learned it and stared at my sister in fascination. Stupid, I heard. Trying to get attention, Faker. My friends retreated from me as if I were the diseased one. I sat alone at lunch, choking on my own shame, starved for companionship. Alaine tried to sit with me and I moved away; I spent the break crying in the bathroom.

After school Alaine came out of the building and started across the courtyard, looking at the ground, hands clenched around her books, and everyone was watching from the bench under the tree. I was there, too, by some brilliant chance included in the group for those few hours. There was silence as everyone absorbed Alaine's passage. It was a game the bench sitters played, staring at a student who dared to cross alone in front of the crowd. The goal, to reduce the student to blushing misery. I stared, too, smugly perched amongst the others, on the winning side of the game. At the gate Alaine turned around. She asked, Will you walk home with me?

My voice said no, and a quick, nauseating self-importance welled in me as I told her to let Mummy know I was staying after school, which was forbidden.

She did not say a word, just lowered her chin again and turned around. Then she was gone.

—She's such a freak, someone said.

—Crazy. *Majnouneh.*

—Hey, Marianna, how do you live with such a freak?

I shrugged, like you do what you have to do, like I didn't choose this sister. *You will still love me,* I thought fiercely. They laughed approvingly, me sick and shriveled up inside, legs not budging for all my desperation, not crossing that empty space in self-sacrifice for my sister. *You will forgive me,* I told her, *you will.*

In the night I woke to the slightest sound, I leaped from bed as if I had never fallen asleep. I learned words. I learned *sulfa powder, gauze, pressure, cold washcloth.* I learned *dilated pupils* and *speed.* I learned how to tell if a cut needs stitches or just a butterfly, which Uncle Bernie, who had been a doctor once, showed me how to make, step by step. I learned to make tea for Mummy when she cried and whiskey on ice for Daddy. My tongue tasted the fiery liquid and the fire raced guilt and greed to the tips of my fingers and toes. I drank a little every time, just a sip, a ritual.

—Alaine needs notebooks, Mummy said, and I ran to the stationery store. Notebooks with lines not squares, blue pens, HB#2 pencils, the brown eraser not the green one. I came home with the wrong thing. Alaine stared and stared at the eraser sitting in my palm. She rocked forward and back, staring. Her distress made my fingers slowly curl inward until the eraser was hidden. I put it in my pocket. Brown, she whispered, and off I went, running, running. You're a good little sister, said Daddy, and I ran even faster.

Fadi disappeared and Alaine did not care, she wrote in code on her cast and when the cast was full, she continued on the walls. We'll have to paint them, Mummy said in despair, but Daddy said, Let's not worry about it until we move, so the walls stayed as they were, covered with dizzying spirals of signs that the cat pawed lightly, thinking insects.

Then Alaine herself disappeared. I came home from school, found Mummy white-faced and trembling, police in the living room. Daddy was out with Uncle Ara hunting for her. The day fragmented to cold slivers of terror: check the telephone to make sure there is a line. Look out the window. Look down the hall. Look, look, in case she materializes, tangible, hunched over some book or drawing. Mummy sobbed and caressed the clothes Alaine had left behind as if she had died. Uncle Bernie called; when Mummy realized it was only him she crumpled onto the kitchen chair and started shuddering. I took the telephone from her. Hi, Uncle Bernie, I said. He came over at once, cradled Mummy while she cried.

I compiled evidence. When she was last seen: sometime late morning. What she took: the small brown suitcase that belonged to Jiddo, some shirts, her notebooks, the G.I. Joe. I went to Alaine's room with an index card marked Facts & Theories. It was time to decipher the signs, solve the crime. The hideous walls mocked me. I climbed onto the bed, but the cat snarled at me from Alaine's pillow, all its fur on end and eyes sparkling ferocity.

The telephone rang. It was Fadi's mother, calling from the mountains. Alaine is here, she said, eating olives and *labneh*. She wants to live with us.

But of course she could not, and Daddy got in a taxi to fetch her back home. The incident now transformed to almost amusing, the grown-ups laughed in relief, regaled one another with their own enjoyment of the mountains before the war. I wanted to run away, too. Take me with you, I demanded of Alaine, but she told me I was crazy. Mummy and Daddy said, She's very smart, Marianna, don't worry. You see how she ran to somewhere safe?

Running away. This is what the grown-ups called it, and I pictured Alaine on a wide road, running, hair streaming in the wind created by her pumping legs.

Alaine ran and ran, until one night she was not in the mountains, nor in our old neighborhood, nor at Uncle Ara's. The policeman yelled from the street that he was waiting. I'm going with you this time! I insisted, almost screaming, my whole body rigid with contained hysteria. They did not argue.

I sat in the backseat with Mummy, while Daddy got in next to the policeman. The policeman talked about the fighting as he drove.

—This cease-fire won't last long, he said. We can't stay out all night.

We came closer to the front line. This part of the city was empty. Shrubbery grew through the ruins and barbed wire strung between buildings blocked off streets. A wooden sign painted with a red skull warned that this was a sniper zone. It was after ten o'clock at night and the buildings were blacker and the streets full of shadows. No one lived here anymore, except the guerrillas, who could be anywhere. Whole walls had caved in and I peered into the ruins, perhaps Alaine was inside, but I could not see in far enough. I imagined fighters slipping through the darkness, following us. Then the rat-ta-tat of gunfire burst through the neighborhood. It was only for a moment, but the policeman said, We can't go farther than this. We turned a corner and he stopped the car.

—That's it, he said.

We had reached the latest border between the militias and no-man's-land opened before us, a wide road covered with barbed wire and debris. One of the old seaside hotels, its white sides blackened and its balconies shorn off, loomed on the right. The entrance was sandbagged and an eerie light filled the street from the lanterns, and some soldiers emerged and jogged towards us through the rubble. They surrounded the car.

—What do you want? They beamed a flashlight briefly across our faces then switched it off.

The policeman asked if they had seen Alaine. One of them leaned into the car and asked, She ran off again?

Mummy nodded. I was amazed that they knew who she was.

—We haven't seen her. He pulled out his walkie-talkie, and they started to check with other soldiers who were somewhere in this black city, their voices crackling through to us, and I thought this was crazy, these soldiers were fighting a war and looking for my sister, as if they cared. One of them tapped on the window next to me and when I looked up he waved and grinned. He twisted his hair, then pointed at mine and kissed the tips of his fingers in appreciation of its blond color. I wanted to disappear.

Finally: Yes, she was seen earlier. Not here, farther back, closer to the shore. We'll keep an eye out for her. You better find her, the ceasefire isn't going to last. We can't help if we're fighting, you know.

I did not even know who these soldiers were. They all looked alike. They could have been fighting for anything. Mummy entered into a state of hope as we drove towards the shore. You see? She said, over and over. They don't hurt her. People understand, even now, see?

I had a picture of Alaine trudging down these dead streets, arriving at a checkpoint, being offered coffee, being told, *You should go home*. I sensed the improbability of this, despite Mummy's words, despite the soldiers. I knew none of it was true, and that whether or not she was hurt by them did not depend on their goodwill, but on Alaine's intelligence, her ability to steer clear of these hideouts, or maybe just on luck. They had seemed helpful, but the way they had leaned into the car, their eyes half-closed with exhaustion, it seemed this was a novelty for them, a distraction. I was the only one in the car who knew this, I thought. Mummy and Daddy were only believing in the kindness of these guerrillas because they did not have the strength not to.

—Where do you go? I begged Alaine when we were alone, but she would not tell me. Do you talk to soldiers? Do they give you tea?

She scowled at me. Go away, she said, Leave me alone.

Mummy and Daddy decided we should move. We packed our things in boxes and Alaine spent days copying her walls into notebooks. We were still cleaning out some rooms when the men came to paint. They stared in awe, and Mummy apologized, She's an artist. I could tell they did not believe this as there were no pictures, only the spiraled writing of a crazy person, and I was embarrassed that Mummy hadn't come up with something more convincing. Alaine lingered in the doorway and drank in her walls for the last time, oblivious to the workmen, who gave one another looks.

Our new apartment was freshly painted and full of sun though it was on the second floor. It was larger, lit by university generators, and when we turned on the faucets water came out, a miracle I tested until Daddy said, Stop wasting the water, Marianna! Mrs. Awad from the third floor brought down a steaming pot of *kousa mehsheh*. She lit a cigarette, she eyed Alaine from across the room and said, Hello, you must be the older sister. Alaine retreated with her cat like a jinn sniffed out by a man of God.

Right away Mrs. Awad knew everything. It was because of her cousin Huda, she explained, and then she brought Huda for a visit to prove her point. Huda dribbled spit and smiled, she dabbed her face with tissue and slurped her tea. She was fat and smelled sweaty and sick, and often she drifted into herself mumbling things that made no sense. The only similarity between her and Alaine existed in their arms and necks, scarred from trying to die.

—She's not the same, I whispered urgently to Daddy. He obviously agreed, and then I felt guilty for being mean about Huda, who was thirty-two and would never be cured. Huda had gone off many times at the beginning of the war, but unlike Alaine she had remained missing for days at a time, which was what had driven her mad. Now, steered by medication, she stuck to her paths between her parents, her cousin Mrs. Awad, and other friends who soon included us. Mummy gave her tea and talked with her for long periods of time. I lingered in the living room, longing to help, to say something curative and wise, but searching for the right thing to say was like peering through a dense cloud. Sometimes Huda sobbed and told stories I did not understand, and I was sent for a box of tissues, a fresh tea, a Kit Kat candy bar, Huda's favorite. Fix Huda's hair, Mummy suggested, and I combed out the unwashed tangle, experimented with barrettes while Mummy admonished Huda to remain still. You're being very good to her, Daddy praised, but I wanted to do more. Where does she go? I asked Daddy. What does she do when there's fighting? Why is she like this? If I discovered the answers to these things, I would solve the mystery of her madness. Perhaps she was seeking something and I could find it.

You don't need to worry about her was the only answer I got. She had pocket money, a home, friends to visit. No one would harm her, Mrs. Awad explained, because in Lebanon, no one bothered crazy people, whereas in the rest of the world they were feared and maligned. I believed Mrs. Awad when she said these things, nodding wisely as she spoke, because after all, I had seen it for myself. Once, when Alaine took off in a rage, Daddy chased her down the street and caught her up over his shoulder. I watched from the balcony. She was biting and kicking and screaming. People stopped and looked, and I worried that they might try to help, not knowing that Daddy was rescuing her. But even from the balcony I had seen the pity in their faces, as if they actually knew what was going on, that things had just been too much for her to bear. So it was true that Huda could walk all over the city and no one would touch her, protected by this communal respect for madness, as if it transcended the commonplace war.

—That's crap, said Alaine. She had started cursing without any remorse. No one could stop her. You want to know why she's crazy?

I didn't want to know anymore.

—She was raped, Alaine told me bluntly. That's why. It's crap.

Huda transformed. The shape of her, clumsy, overweight, filled

me with desperation. I could not bear to look at the body bobbing
on the couch, the hands holding her teacup with childlike care.
Huda smiled, dribbling anguish. Mummy's eyes narrowed my way,
knowing I knew without a word. I stared her down. *Do something,*
I insisted just by passing through the living room when Huda visited, *Fix her, help her.*

The doorbell rang. I settled Huda on the couch, gave her a glass
of water. I was proud that I knew what to do, but Huda rubbed
her thighs unceasingly, rubbing the skin raw. Come *on,* I begged
Mummy. She's waiting.

Mummy covered her face, shaking her head no. She said, I can't
manage, I just can't.

—You have to! I pulled at Mummy's arms.

The toneless voice shouted Mummy's name from the living room,
a question mark at the end. We heard her stumbling down the hall
and Mummy leaped out of bed. She gently greeted Huda, guided
her back to the living room. I had never once imagined that Mummy
could tire of helping people. I felt terrible for Huda, because she
could not possibly know that we did not want her here today, and
maybe everyone else, the friends Daddy said she visited, never wanted
her to arrive at all. I pictured walking everywhere with her, being
her only real friend and for a while these images comforted me, until
I realized I was still in the bedroom, wrapped away in myself, and it
was Mummy who was out there with her, not me.

—There's nothing you can do for her, Daddy comforted me.
She's living her life. At least no one will harm her.

Everyone knew the truth but nobody spoke it. I hid on the balcony, crouched like a frog in the dark, staring at the empty street.
I thought of Alaine skulking along walls, beaming her flashlight
down alleys, searching, searching. She wasn't so thin anymore because of the medication, but her pale skin and large black-brown
eyes drew men's gazes; I always noticed this when we walked on
the street. She wasn't safe. Please don't go away again, I begged her,

but she said, I'm smarter than Huda, or, You don't understand. I have things to do.

Alaine sought me out. She found me in the kitchen, in my room, on the balcony, lured me with the promise of unveiled secrets. Come into my room, she whispered, her sweaty hands cupped around my ear. We passed our parents, who pretended not to see us, but communicated to me in swift, discreet glances their joy that Alaine was speaking to me. Their hope made me sick. I was not worthy; I would never learn what was necessary to cure my sister, and still they believed, they smiled with unwavering faith. Are you coming? Alaine said, and I followed carefully because her cat might be lying in wait to claw my legs. I hated Alaine's dark little room at the other end of the house. She said monsters came up from the crack between the wall and the bed at night and she could never scream for help because the room was too far away. And sometimes she did shout and no one came. Maybe this was why she had started running away. No matter how hard we tried to keep an eye on her, she slipped away in a breath, leaving only a note, *You can have everything,* or *I hate you.* We waited, watching food grow cold, twilight creeping through the sky. Daddy's searches with policemen began with promises and hope and ended with the door opening quietly, signifying his return alone, and the drop of his shoes one by one in the entryway. Then we sat on the balcony in the dim light cast from inside. Mummy hush-hushed my questions that had no answers, and their cigarettes burned long ashes as they held each other, very still, their arms entwined about their frames, weaving the fragile, complex knot of safety and reassurance.

But Alaine wasn't running like they said. She was walking, eyes down, methodically searching for bodies. This was what I knew, the secret I had divined from the objects strewn about her room. What else would she be doing? After one, she had to find more. The things she brought home I knew belonged to dead soldiers, maybe even civilians. Alaine whispered, Come into my room, and she put whatever she had found into my hands—a sock, a bloodstained tie, eyeglasses—and gave me warnings. Don't go out alone. Don't talk to anyone you don't know. Don't argue with anyone. Where's it from? I asked, but she said it didn't matter and took it back.

Alaine climbs Crystal Mountain. She grapples with stones and dirt with the agility she has always had, winding her way through the clumps of prickly bushes and climbing higher and higher. We called it Crystal Mountain for the small muddy fossils and pieces of flint which waited there for us during the millennia after the oceans receded, now company to soldiers' cigarette butts and spent shells from machine guns and shrapnel near small craters where someone might have died. Alaine climbs grimly, leaving us behind, leaving us in the white house where we throw stones at stray sheep and practice shooting at the branches of the olive tree. At the top of the hill lies the soldiers' camp, and just below, a flat area where she likes to hide and think and turn in on herself like an imploding device. Alaine's face is flushed with this voyage, dark eyes livid with sorrows we do not understand. She carries a knapsack with paper and pens, the G.I. Joe with the shaven face, a few bullets from her collection for good luck.

When she finds the soldier's corpse, at first she remains still, and then she looks back towards us, as if we might have disappeared in that second when her eyes first careened across the features of the dead. Sitting next to the corpse after it is buried, knees tucked under her chin and the spoils of his death ready to carry away, the story of the country is caught in the dirt on her hands and legs, that history of a place abandoned by a retreating sea that should never have left, that should have preserved the land in silence.

This room is clean, blue-walled, smelling of now. There are two beds, a wooden table between, bookshelves only half-full, and Alaine's emptied-out trunk under the window. The wind blows cold rain, rattling the glass, sound of pebbles. Everything Alaine had from the Syrian and the others she never talked about, even the gas mask, burned up in the fire. She owns nothing but some clothes and shoes, the shrapnel and bullets she keeps in a plastic bag in the closet, and those few books that survived the merciless scale of her palms on that summer day.

I found my voice in the fire. I ask Mummy about Ziad and the dead soldier and Michel the spy and she says she does not know. I ask Daddy and he does not know, either. I don't dare ask Alaine anything. Her whole life burned right up, taking a tree and half the fence with it, and the fireman asked sternly, What possessed you to do this, young lady? as if Alaine were a prankster.

Mummy is concentrating on opening the childproof cap, her mouth screwed up in frustration. The cap pops off, bounces onto the floor. My mouth closes. The pills push down my throat, dissolve into my blood; I try to feel my blood change but I can't. Give it time, the doctors say. Mummy takes the glass when I have finished drinking, says, All right? with her eyes on my throat as if checking in with the pills themselves. I nod on their behalf.

I never saw a corpse like Alaine did, and now it is too late; I will never know what she knows. The people I mourn are strangers, even Ziad, whose thoughts went undisturbed by me, a child on the fringes of his vision. I watched him from the same kind of distance

I do now, the space between our lives ever increasing, as if from the very first moment I laid eyes on him outside the stone cottage in the mountains, he began to die. I have nothing of his, nothing to burn. His is a story, a memory that is not mine, like all the rest. I walk up the road with Fadi, looking back without knowing what I see; I am Muna reaching for my gift; I am a French colonel dying in a hospital bed, begging the girl for water-soaked cotton, taste of the stars, of life almost gone in a country that doesn't care. I am Jamil laughing in the sun.

—Nothing really happened to me, I tell the counselor, and she stares back with the eyes of the Sphinx. She refuses to tell me what she's thinking; it is not for me to know. We sit in silent stalemate. This happens every week when Mummy and I ride the bus to the mental health center, where I have been assigned a new counselor for the third time. Third time lucky, Daddy says, but nothing can grow between me and these people. We walk three blocks to the bus stop, and Mummy checks her watch frequently, to measure how late the bus is, and then she makes one of her comments.

—The bus is always late. You would think in America, it would be on time.

She includes whoever is waiting next to us in her comment, forcing that person to nod, or make a comment of his or her own. The way she says it, *America,* is designed to entice the person to ask where we are from. Sometimes they do, sometimes they don't. Usually, the closest person is several feet away, because we both smoke while waiting for the bus. If we meet another smoker, Mummy says sympathetically, Another smoker, and that person usually slides closer to us so that we become a group.

—This is my daughter, she says proudly, as if we are normal.

I would go alone to the center, but being alone is still forbidden. The ride takes twelve minutes. At our stop crazy people get off the bus from the back while crazy people get on in the front. I never see anyone who looks like me. They are disheveled, they carry crumpled coffee cups from fast-food chains, their hair is dirty and dyed ugly colors. They teeter on the edge of their medication. They all smoke, so when we pass the clusters of people outside the building, Mummy is always able to say, So this is the smoking section, or, Someone to smoke with.

Mummy waits in the sitting area with other parents, relatives, friends. She sits down while I check in at the desk. She holds her purse on her lap and she tucks her feet delicately under the seat, one over the other, like the Queen. No one in the room looks like her. No one has any idea where we have come from.

My heart freezes up when my name is called. This is when I long to push my head into my mother's lap, to beg her to set me free from this. I can see the anxiety in her eyes, but she smiles encouragingly.

—It will be all right, Anna, she says.

So I go, and I spend fifty minutes in a room somewhere else in the building, then we leave, and we have a cigarette while we wait for the bus. On the last block walking home from the bus stop, I keep my eyes straight ahead so the gas station doesn't exist. Walter is tall and skeletal, the lenses of his glasses are as thick as my finger. Through those lenses I appear distorted, a grotesque shape moving swiftly down the sidewalk, part of the shadows. The door closes. The shape moves behind curtains. The shape tries not to look, crouching on the couch.

—How was your session? Daddy asks as he does every time, trusting that one day I will answer. I shrink away from his hand on my shoulder, and the warm pressure withdraws, leaving cold. I cannot bear his affection, which he gives no matter what I do, as if I deserve it. He has never once mourned that day out loud. He bears his second daughter the way he did the first, an old horse clopping uphill, pulling its burden without complaint. I wish he would shout at me, accuse me of being awful and selfish. Instead, he says gently, Want to come with us? We're getting pumpkins.

Halloween is coming. The gas station is strung with paper

jack-o'-lanterns and merry ghosts. Walter ducks amongst them, filling tanks, taking money, waving good-bye.

I shake my head no. I want to give an excuse, say I'm tired or have a stomachache, but I cannot bring myself to make even this small offering. I hear the possible words in my head while Daddy and Alaine fetch their coats and button them up. They leave.

Alaine has been working on a costume in the basement that she swears is going to surprise us all. You're too old to trick-or-treat, Daddy told her, but she insists. No one has asked me what I would be, were I to venture out on such an idiotic expedition. Witch, skeleton, ghost. Amer said Jamil's ghost used to visit him. *Amer,* Jamil said, *fly with me.* Jamil had wanted to be a pilot for Middle East Airlines, what Amer called a modest dream destroyed by a war. Amer told me about Jamil, and then his ghost came to me, too.

Maybe I will go forth as him. *Fly with me,* I whisper to the children in the streets. They run screaming to their bewildered parents, who try to calm them, too far gone in years to sense the presence of a real dead man in their midst.

I met Amer the summer before we left Lebanon. At first, we met infrequently, a day at the beach, a walk on the university campus. Then, at the beginning of winter, Daddy fled to America and wrote sad letters: *It's so different here,* and, *Nobody wants to hire me.* Mummy wandered the house stricken by not knowing what the future would bring. That was when Amer and I started spending every day together. The winter cold set in, and he arrived wearing a jacket I had not seen before. It's ugly, I teased because of the elbow patches, but he showed me a name written inside under the collar and after that I couldn't touch it enough. I wore Jamil's jacket when it was cold and the sleeves hung below my hands, remembering someone else. I let my arms go loose and long, I closed my eyes, remembering, and Amer stroked my hair and the sea spray floated onto our faces. I was seventeen and skipping school, and we would find the only coffee vendor on the Corniche, drink from the tiny plastic cups with our feet on the rail. Then we would go back to my room or his to while away the day.

Amer said, A boy suddenly showed up at the other end of the hallway. The shooting was so loud I thought my head would crack. We just stared at each other. He could have been me. Neither of us could shoot.

He paced my room, tall and hunched, because his body still fought the year of captivity in his own bedroom, when his father would console him through the door but left the bolt in place. I turned the key in my own door against Mummy and Alaine, I listened to Amer with my eyes closed, curled on my pillow. Beneath his story was the sound of the sea, the Corniche wide and threateningly empty, occasional rumble of jeep or truck.

Amer said, Then we both just moved back, as if we'd never seen each other. I thought, *Finish, the war is over for me.* I had such a brilliant feeling! I was going to quit. After this fight, I'd quit! But war doesn't let a man choose his fate. Later in the day, Jamil stood up when he shouldn't have, he started running. I don't know why he did it. We were all shouting at him, Stop! Stop! But he kept going. I think he wanted to die. It was hot, and everybody was crazy. He ran right into the middle of the road, and they shot him. My comrades tried to hold me back, but I broke free, I ran after him. I didn't care if I died, too. But no one shot me. I think they pitied me. I was with him while he died. I dragged him back behind the sandbags, and then the fighting started all over again.

Mummy knocked, accusation in every rap. Amer ignored my irate miming and unlocked the door. She saw me curled up on the bed, Amer still in his coat, a cigarette in his hand. Amer looked sadly at her and said, We are only telling stories. This was when she began to trust him.

I held his friend Jamil in my lap, weeping over the eyes draining light. I hold myself, so angry I can't risk moving my limbs, but in this house there are no keys, and if there were, no Amer to open the door, say, We are only talking. I used a chair to barricade the door that day but Daddy broke through, calling my name, *Anna?* like someone lost. I cover my ears with my hands but it's no use, the sound comes from inside me, sound of sorrow and guilt, haunting the body that tried to take itself out of the world, breaking hearts. After Jamil died, Amer went mad for fighting. He carried guns all over his body, he spent nights sandbagged with comrades in bombed-out buildings. His father and uncle caught him. They beat him till he slept, and when he woke, the room was dark and the door bolted from the outside. Let me out! he screamed, for days. He lived ten months in that room. When the door opened at last, he was frightened of the sun, he kept his shoulder to walls in case the wide bright world snatched him, tossed him into the sky, a speck floating away forever. He wanted to die; he did not have the courage.

We live in a clean blue room that's missing things; the air of filthy streets and clackety-clack of chestnut vendors, beeping cars, old horse clopping misery under a whip; it's missing tile floors and metal-framed windows, a clanking radiator; it's missing things burned up and swept into garbage bags, heaved to the side of the road. My own presence, breathing, moving through air, cannot replace them. I am the ghost of everything we lost. I speak, but no one hears. I close my eyes when I look out windows. The hollow rat-tat of guns echoes between empty buildings, trees grow between the stones, breaking a city already broken. The wild dogs starve. They roam in packs, subtle, gnarled shadows flitting across walls.

᠅

Michel the spy moved into our building during a miraculously long cease-fire, when the grown-ups had get-togethers late into the night and became so easygoing that they yielded to my demands to stay up even though I was only eleven. We sat in the living room eating *fondue* and playing canasta, and people dropped by to eat and laugh, and everyone was merry with hope that the war would end shortly. Uncle Bernie heard a joke at the video store, and after that he told it any chance he got, waving his soft, pale scholar's hands about as he spoke.

—One night in a cease-fire, the neighborhood woke up to the sound of shooting. They ran to their windows and looked out. What did they see? A man shooting his gun. Shut up! someone shouted. Don't you know there's a cease-fire? And do you know what the man said?

Uncle Bernie looked around, delighted with what was coming, and I screamed, It's too quiet! My wife can't sleep! and the guests clapped and laughed.

The grown-ups discussed this cease-fire with new excitement, rehashing memories from a time that had nothing to do with me.

—You were just a baby! exclaimed Mrs. Awad, who, we had learned, was a little mad herself because she insisted that one day her husband Najib would return even though he had disappeared years before. She was very excited by the cease-fire. Do you know your parents took you all over Lebanon before the war? And then, with a sympathetic smile, But you don't remember.

This talk of a past in which I had no part frustrated me, but now, apparently, that unimaginable way of life was coming back. We would go to movies anytime I wanted. Yes, we would visit Baalbak again. Maybe we would buy a car. I discovered that Daddy knew how to drive and that he had even owned a car in America. I had fantasies of riding past people we knew and waving (he knew how to drive!), and of going to the mountains every afternoon. Uncle Bernie came over often, bearing tins of Danish cookies, Mummy's favorite, and candy for Alaine and me. After tea or coffee in the living room, he and Daddy would retire to the study. They sat side by side examining books, making notes on catalogue cards, and they laughed now and then, drawing me to the doorway where I loitered until they invited me in. I sat on the floor or curled under Daddy's desk, reading, and the air blew clean and quiet through the house.

Another promise Mrs. Awad made was that we would be constantly surprised in this new world: surprise trips, surprise walks, surprise visits. This I could not believe. I grilled her, over and over: We could go, just like that?

She glared at me, as if I were just pretending to misunderstand. Yes, and you will have to go to school every day, too! There is a price to pay! she announced, implying with a wave of her hand that this price was nothing compared to the life we would lead.

But I could not abandon myself to these alien visions, even though Mummy broke away from her habitual remarks about the war being endless; she began to smile, to kiss Daddy playfully on the forehead when he was trying to write his articles. Coffee shops magically appeared and people sat at the sidewalk tables listening to radios and eating ice cream. We waved at the Syrians, who were keeping the peace, though it was rumored that in Syria no one had toilet paper because the government had spent all its money on the soldiers here, which made me feel guilty. I asked Alaine what she thought, and she shrugged, said she didn't care. She was thin as could be and frowned all the time, as if she had to concentrate hard on her every move. I told her the war was going to end and everything would turn out right.

Then a young man from Europe moved into the ground-floor apartment, confirming all my doubts about our miraculous future of surprises. Having repeatedly refused Mrs. Awad's invitations for coffee, he became the main subject of every gathering, and soon it was suspected that he was a spy. The cease-fire fell to secondary place along with the brilliant but rather vague changes it held; the grown-ups abandoned their memories of a time long gone for the immediate and pressing mystery of the European. That he was reportedly a chemistry graduate student at the university confirmed the threatening possibility that he was involved in the manufacture of weapons. The few words he had spoken had been in English with a North European accent, which Mrs. Awad referred to as *icy*. He was Swedish, they theorized, or Danish, or German. I watched my future slowly fade as I lingered on the edges of these discussions: the Syrians were not doing too well; there was trouble here; a fight had broken out there; and the Scandinavian spy, had anyone seen him today?

He was hardly ever seen and therefore it was assumed he was deliberately hiding himself. He had the fairest hair and, according to Mrs. Awad who had come the closest to him, shallow eyes. His face, she reported, was pleasant enough at first glance, but (and at this point her voice would lower, and she would begin to nod slowly) when he smiled he did not show his teeth. He wore hats, too: berets, caps, fedoras, and most striking of all, straw sun hats. *No* one wore hats.

But the decisive proof that something was afoot came on the day that a purple clothesline appeared between his window grates and the tree at the edge of the garden. This line that stood in such contrast to everyone else's inspired the greatest suspicion in Mrs. Awad, for what sort of personality would choose such an irrational color for a clothesline? Something was wrong with him. He was homosexual, someone suggested. They like bright colors. But Mrs. Awad ignored this; he had more to hide than something as simple as that. This one act, this buying of such a provocative thing, was

perceived by Mrs. Awad first as an error—for it drew attention to
him when it was obvious that he was engaged in secrets—but she
then theorized that a spy would not have made such a mistake, and
in fact this line was a code announcing to his clandestine counter-
parts that he was prepared to enter negotiations, that he was *in the
field,* as Mrs. Awad called it.

Mrs. Awad lived in the apartment above ours and cooked huge meals
only sporadically, otherwise living on a diet of bread, cheese, and
tabbouli. When she cooked the whole building knew because she
opened her front door and all her windows and the aromas swam
along the landings and curled down the stairs. Mrs. Awad is making *laban ummu.* She is stuffing *kousa.* She is charring the *batenjan*
on the stove. On those days Mrs. Awad cooked diligently all day for
her husband Najib, who had been gone for four years. The smells
started at dawn when we heard her thumping feet in the kitchen
above ours as we ate our cereal, and continued late into the afternoon, well after everyone had dropped by to be fed. Later, as night
fell, we heard the metal pans and silverware and glass (she owned
a set of clear glass dinnerware that everyone admired) clattering
in her sink.

Najib always liked to travel, she said to Alaine and me, and for a
long time we believed he was in Africa or America, until we pieced
together the truth, which was that he had gone out one Saturday
and had never come home.

Mrs. Awad, on the days that she cooked enough food for the
whole building, would come to our door holding her steaming glass
dishes with pot holders and then sit with us as we ate. You have
to live your life fully, she said to us. Here, it is only one-half, not
even that, but only maybe one-quarter. She emphasized this with
the microscopic place between her thumb and forefinger. This was
our life, this space that seemed even less than one-quarter. Mrs.
Awad was a little crazy because she thought Najib might reappear,
when even the children in the building knew he was gone forever.

But she was not tormented by doubts like everyone else. When she spoke it was so definitive that silence always followed, as if no one could possibly add anything to the conversation.

—The Phalange will not sign with the Syrians, she would say, or, The Syrian forces will all be gone by the New Year. They have their own battles to fight.

Najib had been almost sixty when he vanished. If he came up in a conversation when Mrs. Awad wasn't around, the grown-ups always lamented, *Yeeh,* so old, he should have been allowed a peaceful old age! Only young men were supposed to disappear, and when they did, it brought about a different kind of grief, weighed down by fatalism. I realized that Fadi's last walk to the neighboring village made sense in some awful way, because young men were dying everywhere, but Najib's absence was a terrible aberration, something that had gone wrong in the mechanism of the war.

Mrs. Awad mentioned Najib often, and everyone was used to it. She especially mentioned him in the context of food. Najib doesn't like that, she said about *baqlawa.* It sticks to his teeth. Of bananas she always said sadly, They give him diarrhea.

Standing among his relics in Mrs. Awad's home, a stranger might think that Najib was out for the afternoon. If she would put his pipe away, if she would burn the rug that used to cover his knees in winter, if she would stop cooking the foods he liked so much, then certainly he would be gone. The space where he had been was now occupied by the vividness of his absence, a slow, burdensome tolling beneath the soundlessness of the artefacts, the photographs, the watercolors he had painted as a hobby. Mrs. Awad lived among his belongings, unaware of the thick cloud, which was what remained of him, hanging low throughout the house. His objects invoked, for her, a sense of the immediate, of his possible footsteps. She was not the only one who waited, though; when a voice on the stairwell would break the silence, or a certain footfall, I caught other grown-ups looking up with a certain expression that I recognized as a waiting look, but a hopeless one. Except for Mrs. Awad, of

course, who waited without hiding it, waited with all of her facul-
ties, which is why she could breathe normally in her house while
anyone else suffocated in the air that was thick and stale with the
corpse of her husband's presence. On days that were abnormally
warm, we could see what grown-ups could not, the dismal gray
cloud that hung low in every room. We dared each other to visit
her to see how long we could breathe in the oppressive, gloomy
good-bye that circled our lungs and hearts and tried to crush them.
Two minutes, three minutes, and whoever it was came stumbling
out, choking, pale as fish and damp-skinned with fear. It was I who
broke the record, paralyzed by the sight of the mist that wrapped
her ankles, the darkening walls, and her eyes turned to me, sad and
luminous in the light from the window. Do you want some iced tea?
she asked.

On the many days that Mrs. Awad was not cooking, she sat in a
chair at her window and put her elbows on the sill, chin in hands,
occasionally waving at people she knew. It was because of this
habit of hers, to sit in the window and wait, that she noticed the
Scandinavian spy's movements. Every Wednesday the spy hung
his laundry in a tidy row on the purple line. This only lent weight
to the rumors Mrs. Awad had started, for what man is so fastidi-
ous without an ulterior motive? In a city with no electricity, no
telephones, no public transportation, the arrangement of washed
clothing on a line would be enough to transmit a message. His fresh
clothes idled in the breeze, the jeans, white shirts, and undershorts
speaking a hidden language that Mrs. Awad, no matter what code
she devised, could not understand. To me, his laundry seemed normal. He could have been a businessman or a teacher, except that no
one could confirm whether or not he owned a suit. The rumor that
he was a chemistry student had faded without proof.

Then, having detected all his secret means of communication,
Mrs. Awad's original excitement waned to disappointment.

—What are these spies coming to? They can't even hide from

me, a regular person! It's the war, she always concluded. The war has made everyone tired. No one does anything right anymore.

And so, a few weeks after he moved in, the spy ceased to elicit such vigorous speculation; he made his way into the fabric of our existence, and we took the mystery of him for granted. This was the summer that Alaine, on her new medication for depression, was as slender and taut as before, kicking her soccer ball against the garden walls with a violence that consumed her whole body. Her muscles were defined and her breasts so small that they were invisible beneath her T-shirts, and she insisted on having her hair clipped right up against her skull no matter what Mummy said. She was almost fourteen but she looked like a ten-year-old boy. Her eyes were bigger and darker and resisted gazes with a flatness that was unshakable, but still, this was better than the moist, dazed look of the other medicine. No one spoke of what she might be thinking, nor about the dead Syrian. Daddy had asked her to pack away his canteen and gas mask, but she did not, and the under-shirt was still folded with her other T-shirts. The dead Syrian lay beneath any conversation Mummy and Daddy had with Alaine, in our living room, in Alaine's bedroom, in the kitchen. He lay there with his arms by his sides and his wide-open eyes full of dirt, and Mummy spoke over him, Have some cereal, Alaine, or, Please take your medicine, Alaine. Alaine never answered, and the regularity of her silence was dependable, just as the end of the cease-fire was bound to come, just as the spy's clothes appeared on the purple line every Wednesday.

In the morning the news crackling on the radio determined the day's course, and nightfall's curfew brought everyone indoors. The outside world kept a gentle, firm hold on all of us. There were no surprises.

From the roof where Mummy hung the laundry the top of Beirut spread out around us, a world of antennas and laundry lines, and the *keshash hamam*'s cries echoed over the rooftops as his flock of pigeons circled below the gray clouds. The mountains beyond shimmered in the dazed morning light, and the sea streaked silver all the way to the horizon, *dolphin fins* I liked to pretend.

The damp white sheets stretched on the line, and Mummy's back arched as she stood on her toes, wavering slightly, her slender fingers deftly manipulating the clothespins. She liked to hang the laundry. She wore a slight, calm smile, and when she heaved the laden basket a few feet farther, she seemed to take joy in the act of bending, picking up, moving along. She carried the clothespins in a bag around her waist, and her right hand dipped into it while her left held the laundry in place. Our laundry was not hung at random; first the sheets and pillowcases, then our clothes, which were grouped together according to kind: underwear, shirts, T-shirts, jeans. I would run between the lines and the damp material slapped my arms and face and Mummy laughed.

One night we heard on the radio that the cease-fire was almost over. Mummy joked that there was order to this war because the combatants politely warned each other when the fighting was about to resume.

I crouched on the balcony to watch Alaine in the garden. I had become accustomed to doing this, to keeping an eye on her, even though Mummy and Daddy seemed to have relaxed their vigilance. She had stopped kicking the soccer ball and now stood at the gate, the ball lodged between her feet. It was warm and silent. She was picking up and dropping the latch, and I heard the faint clang of metal, over and over. Was she going somewhere? It was almost curfew. This was different, wrong, this standing at the gate, the way she seemed to be about to do something. She never did anything but kick the ball and sometimes she climbed a tree.

The odors of the city were always present, especially in such silence when people were waiting for the cease-fire to end: the rotting garbage heaped on street corners, the lamb roasted on spits, garlic, the grainy black coffee, gasoline and gunpowder, and, faintly hovering beneath, the salty tinge of the sea. In the solid heat that would not break until the first rains, the smells thickened and hung in the air without a breeze to dispel them. Alaine's form grew blurry as the evening inched into darkness and the sky slowly turned to deep blue without a single cloud, bare and clear.

The door to the spy's apartment opened and he emerged, hands in his jeans pockets. I gripped the rails and stared. He was not wearing a hat. He stood on the darkened path behind Alaine. There was no one on the street, the balconies were empty. The world receded except for the distance between them. The spy walked slowly towards her, and for an instant he seemed malevolent again, not one of the people in this building. My throat strangled on warnings. His hands touched her shoulders, and then in one movement she turned and he wrapped her against him, her head disappearing beneath his shoulders.

I pressed my face between the balcony rails until it hurt. Watching them sway together by the gate, as he rocked her, my thoughts scattered, fell apart, and with surprise I saw that it was like a story: Alaine, the waiting woman, the tepid air, the dark path, and then the mysterious man. The vision of them through the balcony rails was fictional, summoned by the forces of a paralyzed city, the quiet, treacherous streets.

Now I heard whispers and some words about her friend, whose name was Michel. I saw that everyone knew about him except me, even that he was a graduate student in botany. Where had I been? Mummy said, It's good she has someone to talk to.

She evidently did not know what I had seen, that he hugged her, too.

—Is he a boyfriend? I asked Alaine slyly. I wanted to know if she was kissing him.

—No. She was smiling, but I was scared because it didn't look right on her face. He's my friend.

—Is he Russian? This was my secret theory, which I had been mulling over for some time now. It made the most sense because the grown-ups always said the Russians were supplying militias here with guns.

—He's Swedish, she said.

A little deflated, I asked, Is he nice?

—I trust him.

—Don't you trust anyone else?

—No one, except you.

—Why me? I was trying to be fair, but I was proud.

—Because you're innocent. She waited a moment, and looked as if she knew something I would not understand. You're just my baby sister.

From that moment on I was infused with a sense of protective duty. I would explain her to the grown-ups from now on. I would be her messenger.

—Where did you meet Michel? I asked without fear. I needed facts.

—In the garden. He spoke to me first.

It became clear that Alaine was locked in an alliance with Michel, that she had finally separated herself from us, from me, in a way that could never be changed. The vision of her lifting and dropping the latch on that warm evening, of her body turning to greet him, now replaced my sister, and I could not see her any other way. Within her was another Alaine who lived in secret from our house, who had slipped into the outside world while we were not watching. How had she done it? The evenings of canasta, the neighborly visits, the pleasant ritual of Mummy pouring milk into our cereal; all of this was now insufficient. I envied her double life. What did he say to her? Did he tell her all about botany? That we had thought he was a spy embarrassed me; he was just a student who lived in our building, the young man Alaine knew in secret, and she must have laughed at Mrs. Awad, our parents, me. Still, in my head I knew him as *the spy*, I could not unname him. *The spy, Alaine.* The words were tantalizing. *Alaine:* even the word of her name was different.

I stopped sleeping. Night became familiar as I lay awake and listened for the inevitable click of the front door opening. I kept watch, heart stopped, sheets tangled around my feet, the sharp scent of the mosquito coil burning my nostrils.

This was a time of looking from windows, from around corners, of listening in secret. It was a time of decipherment and mystery, of hidden codes, of breath-caught watching. Every window and door, every wall and corridor, the rails on the balcony, became a hiding place from which to watch Alaine. On the outside she was the same, but I knew the other Alaine, the Alaine of the evening, of the waiting, of the secrets. I knew of the alliance that had spirited her away. I carried this secret with mixed trepidation and pride. I was lying to Mummy and Daddy. I closed my eyes at night, alone in my room, and invented conversations between them; he whispered to her, *I love you.*

I kept her secret. I knew it was a secret, that everyone else was missing something. I became a part of it, treasured it. No one knew that I, of all people, Marianna, could keep a secret after all *(Anna, you're so loudmouthed, we can't tell you anything).*

—Where's Alaine? Mummy would ask, and I did not hesitate:
—Outside.

Outside. She could not know the subtlety of this, she was blind to it. Alaine was outside in the garden, inside the ground-floor apartment, outside of us. I was with her, but still here, like a magic protector. I took her place during her absences. I stole our parents' attention, became both of us for hours at a time so that they would not notice how long she was gone. Play Scrabble with me, I said. Let's bake something. Let's do something, I'm bored, I'm bored.

When I passed his apartment during those few months that this secret was mine, I deliberately did not look at his windows. Did he notice? Did he respect my determination? He silently thanked me every day for helping their love. I knew this love needed protection; I recognized its nature at once, that grown-ups would not accept it. He was older, and Alaine only thirteen. Any true love, I knew, was forbidden.

Alaine screamed, No! over and over, and Mummy shouted back, What has he done with you? Her words were lost in Alaine's keening. I sneaked out of my room and hid in the medicine closet in the corridor, my head muddled with sleep and the scent of Band-Aids, Mercurochrome, gauze. I peered through the crack of the door. Alaine was struggling, her hand grabbing for the front-door handle, and Mummy, I could not believe it, was fighting her, pulling her away. I had never seen Mummy like this, as if some madness had possessed her, face grim and locked. Daddy hovered nearby. It was Mummy who had taken over, and I knew Alaine would not get away; she was no match for this rage.

——You will never see him again! Mummy screamed, and for some reason those words brought everything to a halt and Alaine's body simply stopped moving. She became a dead weight, an object on the floor. Time warped to the year before, and Alaine's blank, empty face returned, like a sad doll. I knew that I had just seen her go back into the other Alaine. It was clear that she could no longer hear anything, that she could not move. At times like that she simply ceased to exist. Mummy knew this, knew Alaine would not make a sudden break. Alaine the non-person did not move. I stared at her small, empty face and far back in my mind I was aware that she was not saying, *But I love him.* She seemed almost relieved. Mummy gathered her up.

The secret was shattered into the open. Alaine's world collided with ours. How had they found out? It must have been just a matter of time. Alaine was locked in a torpor. She did not leave her room. She refused to eat. She refused her medication. Daddy had to force open her jaws like a dog, place the pills on her tongue, and pour water down her throat. He did this apologetically, clumsily, but with all his strength. He never quite seemed to know how to behave with her. His emotions were all over his face; anger, sadness, impatience, hatred, love. Her brown-black eyes glared over the powerful hands that smothered her face. When she finally swallowed she looked ready to kill him. Everyone said, If you just take your medicine. I almost believed it, that if she just did this one thing for all of us, everything would be fine.

Mummy and Daddy interrogated Alaine until one day she finally spoke, and then Daddy went down to see Michel. My chest hurt with wanting to go and kill him, too. I hoped he would kill him. It seemed all wrong now. I was caught by everyone's fury and the sensation of injustice. He had to be killed, the way men were always killed for these things. I had heard a story once about a boy who attacked a girl in the mountains, and his own father killed him. I pictured Michel lying in the garden with blue eyes wide open, blood all over him, and I knew he would never do anything to Alaine again. I waited anxiously with Mummy, but when Daddy came back he looked confused and sheepish.

—He kept saying nothing happened. He said she's a friend.

Mummy inherited from Téta and Jiddo a powerful dignity that now took command of the story of the spy and Alaine and banished it to the past. This dignified quiet was not something to be argued with. I could see its roots in the photographs of Téta and Jiddo, whose faces were always collected and wise, and Mummy's silence mirrored this. We, too, had inherited this quality, and it held Alaine's tongue. She would not give in. I fell into step. Maybe they truly loved each other after all, for her to be able to maintain such a silence.

Late at night I eavesdropped before going to bed. Mummy and Daddy had consulted a psychiatrist, who confirmed that Alaine was probably making up tales. Daddy said, I want to believe nothing happened. But she's different. What's wrong with her?

After a moment, during which I heard Mummy breathe in, breathe out, she said softly, She's dying inside.

I watched the spy's windows but never saw him. One day soon he would climb the four flights of stairs to our apartment and knock on the door. He had to do this. It was only right. What he would say to Mummy and Daddy, to their unrelenting silence, was vague. But I had confidence in him. One day soon he would walk into these rooms, among the photographs of Téta and Jiddo, among our furniture, and everyone would see he was normal. He could come for tea and canasta. He would be acceptable, and Alaine would eventually marry him. I did not dwell on his absences or the darkened windows at night, instead taking comfort in the inevitable laundry on Wednesdays, proof that he still might come up the stairs. Over and over I pictured him at our door, experienced the delicious surprise of his appearance, the sunshine streaming through the house, on Alaine's face when she emerged from her room with a dazed smile, as if from a long, disordered sleep. I did not understand what was taking him so long. Didn't he know what floor we lived on?

My need for the spy to redeem his love was counterbalanced by evil pleasure that he did not, for I was jealous of what Mummy had said about Alaine. I wanted to be the one dying inside. I would lie in bed with one arm hanging off the mattress, my eyes focusing on nothing. At these times, a weight spread through my chest and limbs, and my vision darkened until just that moment when I was certain it was about to happen. Then, nothing, just me, being stupid. I resented Alaine's pale skin and dark-ringed eyes, and I was glad when I caught her looking at his door from the balcony. Then, guilty, I would return to plotting how to explain the situation to Michel. Maybe he just didn't know. Maybe he thought Alaine had stopped loving him and was in misery. But at the crucial moments when I just might have gone to the door, opened it, and set out on my mission, I failed: I could not perform this one necessary act of courage to rescue my sister. I felt acutely my youth, the weakness of my promises. I stared harder at his windows. He would feel my gaze.

No one spoke about him. There was no more talk of the clothesline, nothing. None of the neighbors, even Mrs. Awad, realized that the subject of him was forbidden in our house: Mummy was that skilled in the steering of conversation.

Then one day he was gone. Someone looked into his windows

and reported that there was nothing left, not a single piece of furniture. I peeked into his apartment late that afternoon. The living room was smaller than ours, and dust covered the tile floor. In the kitchen beyond, I saw a few tin cans on the counter. The door to what must have been the bedroom was closed. I tried to evoke him and Alaine on a couch, but the empty rooms swallowed these visions, made them impossible. It was just a place waiting to be occupied, without any residue of his presence. His betrayal sank into me deeply. When I mentioned to Alaine that he was gone, she turned away.

The clothesline remained suspended between the windows and the tree, taut as ever, its deep purple shade the only color in the garden, until one day Mrs. Awad marched over to it with great gusto and snipped it down with her garden scissors.

Michel left Alaine, and then the first rains of winter arrived, pouring over the city for two days. Cars crept through the rivered streets and the rain fell in the glow of headlamps. We discovered Alaine was gone only because her cat was wandering about meowing in despair. By then it was already dusk, darker than usual for the rainy sky. Daddy left for the police station. I lingered at the edge of the living room, anxious because I had homework; I had a test in two days, and this could go on all night. Mummy was smoking and drinking a glass of wine. I waited, kicking the wall, one, two, one. The cat darted out from behind the hallway door, snarling. Its malevolent eyes knew me, what I was thinking, that I hated Alaine. It fled past, loped towards her room, and vanished inside.

Mummy's eyes followed the cat. She said, We need to search her things.

They had done this before. Whatever they found, they refused to tell me, as if telling me would only magnify their wrongdoing. I guessed letters to boys, parts of corpses, even drugs. They would not tell me. You don't need to know everything, they said. Whatever they discovered never helped them. This time, I decided, I would find out everything and then Alaine would be cured. I would be like the stars of my favorite books, the courageous groups of children who investigated mysteries and solved them.

—I'll do it, I offered.

In that moment my mother's face changed; it made me uncomfortable to stand there for so long trapped by her strange gaze. She turned her eyes away after a time, and drew on her cigarette deeply. Her lips trembled as she did so, and her eyes closed. When she had finished blowing out all the smoke, she whispered, You shouldn't, and I knew she meant that I could.

I came to the doorway and searched warily for the cat. It was on the bookshelf, its favorite place, staring. I crept in, ready to kick if it attacked. It did not move. The room had one lamp, a rickety metal desk lamp Daddy had brought from his office at the university the year before. He had attached it to the side of Alaine's bed, and it could be turned over the mattress or the floor, depending on where Alaine was sitting. The day he had arranged this lamp for her, Alaine was in bed, buried under too many blankets and blank as an emptied bowl, her skin clayish, warm. She had broken the old lamp to bits and used the shards to carve her skin. Her bandaged arms lay over the blankets, the gauze thickly bound and heavy, like wasp nests weighing down branches. I watched from the doorway while Daddy said, There, now you have light, and switched on the new lamp, but the spread of light over her sad face only illuminated the inconsequence of this poor gift, just metal and wire and a worn-out spring, the failure of a parent. He switched it off right away.

I pressed the switch but even with that small movement the lamp creaked, sagged downwards. The spring was broken. I wrestled with it, holding it in place again and again, but it kept falling and finally I left it the way it was, with the bulb shining a hot circle on the floor. I knew where to look, in the ammunition box she kept under her bed. The box contained bullet casings, shrapnel, and the empty magazine she had taken from the dead soldier. I knew

Mummy and Daddy never even bothered to check this box because they did not know about the secret compartment Alaine had made; she'd shown it to me and made me promise to burn everything if she was shot.

I slid all the war things to one end and lifted the piece of wood, felt underneath. My hands moved through papers. Rain tapped and dribbled the small, high-up windowpane. I dragged the box closer to the light, glimpsed words, phrases, and I already knew there was nothing here, no *clue,* the magic word from my adventure books. Alaine left no clues. Alaine scribbled in the dark and then ran. I saw words from the nightmares she had, the ones that came out of her head and lived between the bed and the wall. My hands moved through the papers and I was thinking of water: I imagined this box of water and my hands in it, and Alaine's face floating, a reflection, always sad. The cat came down from the shelf and it did not bite me, but instead moved its body sideways against my thigh, pressed there a moment, then left a space of cold on my skin. Alaine was always whispering to the cat. Maybe she told it everything. *Hsss,* I whispered, and the cat looked full of mysteries like Alaine, so that I imagined it knew the truth of where she had gone, was trying to communicate it to me.

My fingers touched hard corners, folds, a different sort of surface. I bent closer, saw the faint lines of Daddy's grid paper, folded over and over into a tiny square. This was the truth, then, this square of paper, heavy and thick, and the crinkle of it opening made the cat move backwards, wary. It was as perfect and beautiful as any of Alaine's projects, those she found precious, and in the first moment of spreading open the paper, I was enchanted by the complexity of lines, colors. Then from within all this the shape of Lebanon emerged, and Syria and its deserts, the jagged coast of Turkey and the islands. The map was covered in lines of different colors, I thought *borders,* then *roads.* I looked closer. In tiny handwriting, she had written half-thoughts, or maybe they were deliberately obscure.

Taxi to mountains, walk. Cross border north. Or at sea? The map was beautiful, it even showed all the mountains, rows of conical forms shaded just so, and the minuscule squiggles to denote rivers and the sea. I traced with both hands the many lines, purple, blue, green, and all followed the same direction, west, north, west, sometimes through the Bekaa, another from north of Beirut trailing into the sea, another hiding amongst the inlets of Turkey to sneak across the straits, all petering out in various parts of Greece, where her fine-pointed pen had so carefully etched hill, river, lake, ruin.

She was leaving me, she was on her way to Greece. A sob pared a circle in my throat. She could be on any one of the lines now. I traced the thickest line she'd drawn, guessing *this one,* and I saw her trudging in the dark beneath the weight of her army bag and her trumpet case, her small head bent, her legs like a machine. She did not know Greek. She had only been there once, when we all went as a family, so long ago I couldn't even remember it, just the murky imprint of blue stairs, white stone, a goat. She had to have seen something there that was luring her back, even at the age of, what had she been, five? Six?

Then the sorrow of what this meant: she had left her map so that if she were captured, no one would know her ultimate plan, but this was in the trust that here it would stay in its dark place. Alaine could not know how readily we broke into her boxes and books and notes and hiding places, seeking a sign, seeking her. These things became her when she was gone; the scrap of paper her eye, the shell casing her empty hand, the jacket she had found full of pockets, full of her secrets, opened inside out, all of it, so many times. She had no idea, and this security she carried inside her like a little fragile mirror that showed her sad face, it was broken now, by my own hands.

I folded the map but the creases were all backwards and I had to open it again, try another way. The paper lumped up wrong, and now my tears blurred everything. I made myself go slower. I knew

Mummy would not follow me, that she had lost me, lost some battle I did not even understand yet, but she would not come, that I recognized. I felt ashamed of her sitting in her chair, waiting for me to discover what she was supposed to know. I examined the creases, folded. The map slid into itself, hiding, the bland grid paper nothing on the other side, a bit of garbage. I pushed it under the wood. She could be on the blue line now, or the red one that went north along the base of the mountains. She could be in a taxi, she could be running up a rocky hill, and I wanted her to run and run, so she would be free and I would be free and everything would end, definitely, and I would be able to do my homework and go to school without being scared of what anyone said, ever.

The noise of someone crying woke me. I hadn't even realized I was asleep. My side was numb from lying on the hard sofa. I blinked. Lamplight streamed into the living room from the entryway. The front door was open but no one was there. The crying came from inside the house. I sat up, surprised by the dawn sky, the faint sound of birds, no rain. A blanket lay bundled at my feet; Mummy or Daddy must have covered me, and I had kicked it off in my sleep.

I trailed the sound of the crying down the hallway and stopped just outside the bathroom. From here I could see but not be seen, and Alaine was sitting on the edge of the tub staring at the floor. Mummy dabbed at her face with gauze. It was Daddy, out of sight, who was crying. Even from here I could see the gashes on her forehead, her neck, her arms. Blood was still welling up. Her shirt was stained red down the front, like the photos of the emergency workers, and the tiles were speckled. I couldn't believe no one had woken me up when Alaine came back bleeding, drenched from the storms. Had the police brought her, or did she choose to come back on her own? She stood in the doorway covered in blood, and everyone rushed to her, and during all this I was asleep, dreaming about waiting for her while she walked by, and now I looked back and saw the blood tracked down the hall. She hadn't tried to go to Greece after all. She had just done what she always did, cut herself up and wander around till someone found her.

Mummy caught sight of me and said, She's home, darling. Go back to sleep, and Alaine didn't even blink. Her head moved slightly under each dab of the gauze, and Mummy kept a hand on her shoulder for support.

Alaine climbed Crystal Mountain and found the dead Syrian, she buried him with her hands and stole his things for herself, and time passed, one year, two, three, gnawing at the dead man's flesh until he became part of the earth. So quickly? I pressed Daddy, who answered my scientific questions with reluctance. Is there absolutely nothing left? I can't say for sure, Daddy told me.

We did not know this would be our last summer in the mountains, and we whiled it away in ignorance. We broke pinecones for the nuts and slept through entire afternoons; we tossed stones at goats that strayed too close to the garden, and their hooves made a scattery sound as they fled back to the herd. Alaine kept herself home, not for being held captive but of her own accord, brooding in corners, reading books on the Great War procured from Uncle Ara's shelves. She wandered the rooms with a half-read book under her arm, hardly eating, speaking only if necessary, and I knew she had to be missing Michel the spy. Nobody spoke about him, as if the months he had been in our lives had never occurred, and so he joined the dead soldier in this way. The grown-ups revolved around her as if she were a small, powerful planet. She went to the kitchen, the bathroom, the garden, and they raised their eyes, they shifted about in silent concord to keep her in view. She ignored them not willfully, but with the disinterest of the one in control, and she did not notice their hurt when they made their futile queries designed to trick her back into our world, if she would like some *labneh* or a Pepsi or to go for a drive in the village.

I longed to make them stop worrying. I smiled and cooked and swept the floors; I read adventure books and went looking for the clam fossils that Uncle Ara liked to put around his potted plants, and I truly did set out on these missions with goodness in my heart,

but after a time, I found myself looking for the Syrian who had rotted away. There had to be evidence of him in the earth. I imagined a
hand-shape just visible through weeds and flowers. I walked with
detective eyes to the ground, one step at a time, and perhaps it was
my desire to unearth something, anything, that led me on a path
around the mountain, where on the other side I discovered a stone
cottage surrounded by trees. I came home changed. I withdrew the
delicate fossils from my pockets, proof of my innocence, astonished
at the grown-ups' blindness to my secrets.

The small stone house was visible from many different hiding
places. A foreign woman lived there, no one knew who she was
or what she did, but she read a lot; I saw through her window on
summer evenings, and many times she would look out as if she were
waiting. It happened on that first day that as I watched her stare out
the window with her palms on the open pages of her book, the sound
of hooves galloping on the road below the trees startled me and she
must have heard them, too, because she stood up, book sliding to the
floor. She did not leave the room, but remained quite still, listening,
and within moments a man on a white horse appeared at her door.
Her house was swimming in long twilight shadows and the ghostlike
horse pawed the ground as the man leaned down and knocked on the
door. I held my breath, I had never seen anything so beautiful, and
when she appeared I heard her laugh drifting through the silence as
he bent down and kissed her. I felt ashamed for watching them; lying
there behind the trees in the soft pine needles, I had no part in this.

The grown-ups smiled cheerily and waved good-bye, trusting
me, trusting my sweetness, and I went searching for fossils carrying the ones I'd already found, secure that no one really examined
them. I spied and dreamed and craved, and the hills bloomed with
poppies and thyme and *ah-ya-seedi,* which I tapped on the back of
my hand to read my future in the yellow pollen, dying for love.

On Sundays Uncle Ara blasted Russian martial songs for Daddy's
musical ear, and they smoked and argued while Mummy and Astrig

prepared feasts. Guests came for the day; friends of Astrig's from Beirut, Uncle Bernie, and others. The food I relished the most was *bayd ghanam,* sheep testicles, grilled in lemon juice and garnished with parsley. The men shook their heads and made jokes about how I was starting so young, and Mummy said, Never mind, you don't need to understand everything. We set the table on the west terrace, overlooking the garden and hills all the way down to Beirut. Astrig sliced the sweetmeats with a sharp knife and tossed them onto the grill, squirted lemon juice to make them sizzle. The fire sputtered and for a moment ashes were held aloft by the heat. As we set the table, we saw in the distance beyond the slope of the hill a cloud of yellow dust that signaled a car, and then a small Renault appeared, blue, all the windows rolled down, and as it charged up the road Uncle Ara shouted, It's Ziad, at last!

When the young man stepped out of the car and slammed the door, my face burned as it did when I bent over the grill, and I turned away to hide the memory of him leaning down to kiss the foreign woman a few days before. He marched towards us, he disrupted everything with his tallness and his big white smile, and my frail fantasies were crushed by the reality of his presence. This moment would never leave my memory: it would return again and again, long after he mysteriously died and long after I thought had found the truth of that death and the lies it had bred. Daddy rose from his chair and even Alaine stirred, her broody eyes following the activity, and then Ziad arrived, came to a standstill with his feet apart and hands on his hips, like a hero coming home.

I maneuvered so that my back was against the wall. Ziad threw himself at Uncle Ara and they hugged and shook hands and slapped each other's backs. Astrig he held at arm's length for a moment, admiring her waist-length hair and heavy-lidded gaze. *Petit coucou,* she flirted mockingly, offering her ringed hand for a kiss that he gave with utmost attention. When my hand, for an instant, touched his during our introduction, the shuddering in my belly started and I did not eat well for weeks afterwards, and that was how I lost the last bit of plumpness I had been carrying from childhood.

As they ate and I tried to quell my nausea, Ziad spoke about how he would build a disco in his barn that once had been filled with horses. He leaned over his plate and waved his fork, describing the lights, the dance floor, and his presence was abnormal in our usually quiet gathering. He spoke of things that happened elsewhere, in other worlds and with other kinds of people, and Astrig waved his talk aside as frivolous, laying her hand on his arm frequently or patting his cheek. Mummy and Daddy were obviously taken aback. Mummy kept looking down, embarrassed by this talk of dancing and drinking, parties that lasted all night. Alaine toyed with her food, her curly hair jumbled around her face. I noticed with increasing anxiety that Ziad glanced at her too often; he had to sense the experiences she had had with Michel, she wore them in the movement of her hands, the tilt of her shoulders, and I felt inadequate being only twelve. I willed her to leave the table early the way she always did. She did not. He talked and talked, and when his plate was empty Uncle Ara filled it up again.

His eyes were black like jewels, I thought. Like opals. *What color is an opal?* Words jammed each other in my head. A fleeting, shameful image of touching his face, kissing! almost destroyed my show of calm. Everyone could see. Could they see? I crossed my legs and tried to look demure, a word that meant something mysterious but necessary right then. I smiled. In the middle of this rapid, excited talk, he invited everyone to come look at the barn, So why don't you come down? Anytime you want. Just come see.

He waved his arm at the circle, grinning. And in the moment of silence after this invitation, without thinking, I said very politely, That would be nice.

Then I realized I was the only one who had spoken and Mummy was smiling crookedly, that certain look of indulgence that I loathed and admired at the same time, and my insides shriveled.

—Yes, tomorrow? he said, and I was so surprised I said noth-

ing, but he was off again on another subject now, some story about
gunmen stealing his friend's car, and I kept my eyes away from him
and pretended to be only vaguely interested.

When the food was gone and Ziad had finished his third beer,
he leaned back and stretched, yawning. His belt buckle, a cowboy
twirling a lasso on a galloping horse, was huge. Where did he get
such a buckle? It was exotic. Ziad did not shake our hands again. He
treated us like old friends. He shaped his hand into a pistol, pointed
it at me, See you tomorrow, kiddo! and my thoughts lurched. *Kiddo.*

As the Renault sped away, Daddy said words I did not yet understand.

—Ziad's dreaming big dreams for this place. Too big for a war.
He thinks he can rein it in to suit him.

Mummy nodded with characteristic solemnity, but Uncle Ara
grew impatient.

—Leave him alone! Can't a young man have plans?

Astrig laughed. Papa, don't be silly! Who will go dance there,
in the middle of a war?

I did not care about the war. I worried that my breasts, knobs
poking at my T-shirt, were too small to be of consequence, that I
had only had my period a total of four times now, and that if I said
anything at all on my visit he would think I was silly. Maybe he
didn't mean it, that I should go visit. It was just a comment. I was
simultaneously relieved and terrorized by the thought that this
might be true. Uncle Ara was still arguing with Astrig.

—You can support him by going when it opens!

—He doesn't want to dance with *me*, Papa!

A glorious image came of Ziad twirling me under spinning lights.
I was in a black outfit like the one Sandy wore at the end of *Grease.*
My hair was not flat and blond but fell in magical auburn curls
down my back. Alaine's eyes found me. She cocked her head, hiding half her face behind the tangled hair, and her mouth tilted a
knowing smile.

—You're in love, she accused me.

—No, I'm not! I retorted. I couldn't believe that this was how she chose to break her silence.

—Alaine, you are being cruel, Astrig admonished.

—Who's in love? Daddy said, and his bewilderment made everyone laugh. I laughed, too, so that they would think it wasn't that exciting for me, to go see Ziad, indeed, that I might not go at all.

—He's a madman, Astrig mused fondly of Ziad the next afternoon while I tied my shoes. He's heading straight for the madhouse.

I felt I should protect him. I said, There's no madhouse.

—What do you mean? Of course there is!

—Mummy said they've all escaped in the war.

—Who?

—The crazy people.

She ignored me as I knew she would, because she didn't like to contradict Mummy; together, they formed a front, whether against the men in protracted arguments, or against Alaine and me when we made an irrational demand. Uncle Ara handed me a large Tupperware container of fried meat and rice. Ziad's favorite, he said. And don't forget to steal some tomatoes; I want to compare them to mine!

—Don't encourage her to steal, Daddy called from the living room.

His house was about twenty minutes away and I walked slowly, as if this were a usual walk and should anyone see me they would think I was always doing this, walking along. Ziad had spoken by CB to Uncle Ara early in the morning and had said he expected me around one or two *if possible,* as if I might have an agenda, which pleased me. I had pretended to mull it over.

I left the main road and made my way down the rocky dirt path to Ziad's home. The bell echoed melodiously inside the huge, red-roofed house. I heard rapid footsteps and then the door flew open and there he was, in jeans and a black T-shirt.

—Good afternoon, Anna! he said dramatically, and I gave a

little smile, my whole body conspiring to mask my delight at this greeting. He waved me in as if I were a regular visitor. He took the Tupperware and guided me through the opulent house to the kitchen, where the cook, an old woman who was even shorter than me, launched into questions about Astrig and Ara's health, and whether we needed any vegetables from the garden, and, when she saw what I had brought, whether Ara believed she didn't feed Ziad enough. Ziad shifted about in the doorway, which gave onto a lush garden, gravel snaking towards the barn. He rolled his eyes as the cook talked, and the secret signal elated me.

—*Yallah,* come on, he broke in, and we headed out into the sun. I realized he might be a little drunk because his steps were just off, a little too bouncy. The rich, velvety scent of tomatoes permeated the air. A longing swept up in me to be amongst the rows of plants, gently harvesting the day's yield while Ziad waited on the verandah with a drink. The sun would drop slowly in the sky, and while the cook prepared a tomato dish, Ziad and I would bask in the orangey light—

—There! he exclaimed, and I stared at the dilapidated barn. Its roof sagged in the center and all the windows were broken. Grass grew tall and yellow, and vines crept halfway up the walls. An old white car was parked next to the door, the tarp bunched on its hood. The car had no wheels. The scene was draped in warm silence, with the hum of insects rising and falling, and then I knew that whatever Daddy had said was true.

—Come see, he said merrily, waving me foward.

—Where's your horse? I asked, and he explained over his shoulder that he boarded it at a neighbor's stable. I was disappointed; I had imagined touching the animal, stroking its warm, soft muzzle, even riding in a circle. But the fence around the paddock was falling apart and the grass had grown high, and now it seemed his horse did not belong here, had never lived here.

The interior of the barn was dim and smelled of air that had traveled for centuries through rotting wood and dry earth. Beyond the eight stalls, stacked against the wall where the tack should have been, were tables and chairs with velvet upholstery and several boxes of different-shaped glasses. Toeing a box with his foot, Ziad announced, I got all this for a bargain price from a hotel downtown. I pictured a burned-out, shelled hotel, any of those in the city, and then Ziad hauling these boxes and furniture into his Renault. Impossible. He must have rented a truck.

—The bar will go there, he said, pointing. The stalls will be booths, and the front will be the dance area.

After every gesture he glanced at me, sometimes with a wink, and his black hair kept falling over his eyes so he pushed it back. I noticed the marks on his wrist from the copper bracelet rubbing damp skin; perhaps he never took it off, and I wanted to ask about this but couldn't. I dug small holes in the dirt with my shoe, hands behind my back. This dim, gray place, it seemed to me, would never become a disco, because where would people park, first of all, and how would he ever be rid of the smell of animals living in the rafters, and then one cigarette thrown aside and the whole place would burst into flames.

—You seem to have lost interest.

I shook my head. He rummaged about in a cooler, pulled out a beer, held it up with a questioning look.

—No thanks, I said, and this made me feel foolish so I said, Who's going to come dance in the middle of a war? This sounded important, adult. It was a good question. These are big dreams, I added.

Immediately I knew I had said the wrong thing. He raised his eyebrows and then started to laugh. He leaned back against the wall and took a long drink from his beer.

—What is needed is a revolution, he said. This, he waved at the expanse of the barn, will be a revolution.

I was relieved he was still talking to me, but I did not know what he meant. To my surprise he came towards me. Let me show you something, he said. His hand encircled my arm, and the feel of his skin on mine burned pride and pleasure through my whole body. He guided me to the back of a stall, to the window.

—Imagine the view, he said. Imagine!

I imagined. The mountain dropped towards the sea under the big moon, the floor throbbing with disco music, cars coming and going. He described the uniqueness of summer nights in the mountains, how people were dying to escape the filthy, depressing city. Standing there with the joyous weight of his hand on my shoulder, I felt guilty for the thoughts I'd had walking in. It wasn't such a bad idea, was it? I pushed my mind beyond the doubts expressed by all the grown-ups. I could see it, the lights, the floor swept clean, noise of music and laughter drifting down the mountainside late into the night. It was possible!

—You could have a mirror ball, I suggested, and he seemed pleased with this idea. When his eyes met mine, my skin went brittle with the most acute nervousness I had ever felt in my life, and yet, despite its horribleness, I wanted it over and over. I couldn't bear when he looked at me, but it was worse when he did not.

—What color would you paint the walls? I asked, and he told me dark blue, or red, and I stared up at him, but nothing more was happening. He had taken his hand from my arm, even moved some feet away. In this lull of quiet, I became aware of my face, the open feel of it staring up with all my romantic desires laid bare, wanting things I could not even identify. In the whirl of this increasing anguish that I recognized as the downside of love, I sensed that he knew exactly what I was feeling, how nervous I was and why. I stood there, stupid with hope.

—You're sweet, he said, and touched my cheek.

He wandered to the doorway, leaned against the post. His moving away felt like something closing; all my excitement dropped out of me, leaving a residue of shame. I remained immobile, my mind populated with absurd thoughts, the swirl of vines on the outside of the barn and the humming of cicadas in trees and the forlorn and naked sight of a car without wheels.

He smiled a little tiredly at the interior of the barn, said, Maybe you're right. Who'll come here in the middle of a war?

—Someone could come, I said dumbly.

He acknowledged this with a sideways conspiratorial grin, as if to say, *Now you're indulging me.* He finished his beer and tossed the bottle at the metal garbage bin, missed. He headed over to pick it up.

—*Yallah,* he said. You'd better get going. Don't forget to pick tomatoes for Ara, he added cheerfully.

My legs moved, and when I reached the door I looked back, found him slouching on a bench between stalls. He gave a friendly wave, called out that I should come visit any time I wanted. I nodded. Standing there in the sun, squinting at him from this distance, I forgot my embarrassment. He was rubbing his face now, tired, and the long shadows made him seem small inside the cavernous barn. I wanted to believe in it, his revolution of wine-colored leather and women wearing feather dresses and gold shoes. I felt I had betrayed him. I turned away before he looked up again.

For the last weeks of summer I lay on the hill smoking cigarettes and imagining Ziad on his white horse, Ziad in his breeches, Ziad in a suit coming to seize me in his arms, asking me to elope. He visited us two or three more times, and once he let me listen to his Walkman so that the rest of the day I touched my ears, which had in a way touched his, until Astrig tried to check them for a rash. Uncle Ara went to see him now and then, and reported that the disco was coming along, but it was always with sadness that he said this, and later, as everyone had always predicted, the project was subsumed by the war that even then was moving to the mountains. Sometimes I heard the clopping of hooves on the asphalt road through the village, but the firs obscured the road, and it was too far to run to catch a glimpse of him.

The foreign woman was hardly to be seen and I pretended they had fought, that their love affair was irrevocably finished and that it was only a matter of waiting on this hill, waiting in the car as everyone went into the shop to buy ice cream (Marianna, what's the matter with you? Come inside!), waiting on the side of the road as Alaine scrambled though the thorns to pick thyme, her face determined and perspiring, waiting until he found me, by chance, on his way somewhere.

I sat on the hill and smoked cigarettes and watched the stone house. He arrived twice: once in a jeep and the second time on the horse. He stayed with her a long time, too long for me to wait, my head throbbing and places beneath my skin driving me away in confusion. There is nothing more to remember, not in this summer: no image of Ziad turning his head at the sound of a doorbell ringing, of Ziad opening the door and greeting someone, of the surprise on his sunburned face at the discovery that he has been shot.

Or: Ziad sits at a table, swallowing the despair of plans undone by circumstance, of land that has been lost and of houses torn down by soldiers, sold stone by stone to profiteers, and the spinning chamber of a revolver the only sound in the room.

At the end of summer we packed our bags and things and brought them down from the mountains, innocently believing we would go back the following year. All my thoughts were now focused on one thing, my love for Ziad. I leaned over the balcony rail, craning to glimpse the mountains where he lived on without us. I dreamed of being old enough to take a taxi there, dressed in something velvety, maybe feathers in my hat, how he would greet me with such joy and twirl me about to music in his disco. No one believed in him, but I did; whatever doubts I had felt about his revolution were swept aside by my agonized pining for him, my certainty that I was the only one in the whole world who could understand his dreams.

I knew all about the difficulties of bearing secret love, because of Alaine and Michel; I was prepared for the giddy pleasure of not answering my parents' worried questions, or offering sweet lies to deflect them from the truth. What are you doing, Marianna? I'm thinking up stories, I said dreamily, which they approved of; or, I'm teaching myself to meditate, which made them laugh. I lay about in my room while Alaine lay about in hers, and I thought I understood what had happened with Michel, and there was delicious complicity in this invisible link. We were doomed, Alaine and I, lovers struck down by fate, swooning and moping, awaiting our stories' magnificent ends.

—We could all go to Africa, I said. I described our hacienda (I had been reading a novel set in Spain), the giraffes wandering the yard, the panther in our kitchen. Michel and Ziad would draw water from the well while we languished in the hot shade.

—We're not going to Africa, Alaine said.

Her disinterest impressed me, made her love seem more sublime. My problem was that I had not suffered a real loss as she had. I imagined an accident, Ziad trampled by buffalo, me sobbing beneath a dark umbrella. Mummy swooped in on me. It's bad luck inside a house! she cried, seizing the umbrella and collapsing it shut with a rush of air, while I, exposed on the floor surrounded by tissues, scrambled to my feet. Alaine never found herself in such situations. Her despair remained steadily secret no matter how much the grown-ups tried to wear her down with their poorly calculated questions. I so wanted to be like her, melancholic and silent, but I failed at every turn.

I went to Alaine's room, found her scribbling on pieces of paper. I understood what was going on; was I not now dying from love myself? I would drag the truth into the open, break the silence that lay between this end of the house and the other. I would stop Alaine from locking her door and carving up her arms; I would stop her from running.

I asked, Did you love Michel?

Alaine's mouth tightened and she stared at the wall. She said, Just forget it.

—I will, I lied. I'm sorry.

Bloated with duty I curled beside Mummy in her bed. You should apologize to Alaine, I said, softly and wisely, prepared.

I could tell she knew that I was talking about the spy Michel even though so much time had gone by, because she closed her eyes and her mouth crumpled.

—Marianna, she said, you are only twelve. There are things you do not understand.

This was what Mummy and Daddy told me all the time. I thought of all those things I did not understand, of how many there were and what I would do about this, and I became more and more upset. Mummy lit a cigarette and explained that indeed I might never understand everything, which angered me.

—You have to pick a few things, she explained. Just a few, and work on them a long time.

And because of the way she said that, eyes glittering with tears and staring beyond the open balcony door as if something were there in the sky, I knew she was working on Alaine and Michel, and that I was missing something essential, and no, I could not understand. I sat beside her for a time, listening to the street until the clopping of hooves drew me to the balcony to watch the *mazoot* man's sad horse pull the great barrel on wheels down the street.

Alaine told me she went everywhere, she had seen everything. Mummy and Daddy had no clue how often she left us. She slipped out when everyone was asleep, came back before dawn. She didn't always hurt herself; she just went and came back. It seemed as if she had no place here anymore, in this clean apartment lit by university generators, full of polished antiques, books, all the things that seemed normal. She had become a stranger who had severed all the threads connecting her to the photographs from years before, the person I used to play with. That person was gone. I wanted to go with her.

Mummy and Daddy said, Keep an eye on her, and so I followed Alaine to school, I followed her back. Alaine slowed down without looking till I was just behind her, our feet moving the same. Did they tell you to watch me? she asked. Yes, I said, and we kept walking like that with me behind, watching her knapsack. Is she all right? they whispered to me, frowning down the hallway, and I said, She's fine.

I followed Alaine to keep an eye on her, and then the Israelis came, they roared circles above the city, keeping an eye on us. They won't dare, the grown-ups said, and we went about our days as if the sky were empty. I dreamed of someone following me, saving me, Ziad, Fadi, Michel (returned to confess weakness, to prove some kind of love). I dreamed of a stone house in the mountains, dreaming at night with my begging hands caught between my knees. *One day, when the girl is watching from up the hill, I am reading and I hear hooves galloping on the road beyond the trees. I feel something about to happen. I stand up suddenly, my book sliding to the floor. I remain that way, listening, and within moments Ziad appears at the door. My house swims in long twilight shadows; I sense myself in it, a beautiful, solitary, mysterious woman in a flowing gray dress, and already I feel the longing I will have one day, looking back, because of the quality of this light, predestiner of nostalgia. Through the arched window in the door I can see his ghostlike horse stamping, and Ziad leans down to knock.* Then the commotion, the noise of voices and crying and doors. Marianna, why did you get up? I want to help. Cut the gauze. Now press down. The blood seeped through to my fingertips, warm and cold at the same time. There was no electricity and the generator was down. Alaine looked at me with bloodshot eyes, the grim exhausted eyes of a soldier. Once I whispered, Did you fight? and she said, I tried, and I said, Did they do it? and she said, No, I did, I'm sorry. Alaine cried in Daddy's arms, sitting on the bathtub rim, and together they made a flickering candle shadow on porcelain and tile. Go back to sleep, honey. I went back. I wrapped the sheet around myself, over my head. *Ziad knocks on my door, leaning down from the saddle. I hold my breath, I've never seen anything so beautiful, and then I open the door, laughing, and Ziad takes my face in his hands and kisses me.*

Mummy scours the pots and clangs them one atop the other. She cleans the forks and knives and spoons one by one, and I don't say a word, just dry what she hands me. It is raining. The old white horse down the street plods the fence, nosing for new grass in a field already gone over to the coming winter. I can just see him through the trees, the almost leafless branches a shimmering puzzle on the hide, the suggestion of wings. I ask about Ziad and the spy and the dead soldier, but Mummy says there is no need to talk about the past. She says the word *past* like it is a place full of things. I see a long narrow hall, locked at both ends. Cobwebs hang from lofty ceilings, the light dim, from an unknown source.

I say, Don't you care?

Mummy rejects my words. Her whole body ignores them, turning this way and that, checking the pantry, the fridge. She says, Get your coat. We're late.

—Did you *ever* know what was going on?

—We have to eat, Marianna.

Mummy sinks onto the edge of a kitchen chair. She stares at the envelope filled with coupons she cuts out so carefully every Sunday. They are organized by category, marked by dividers. I hate the slips of colored paper, signifiers of poverty, indignity. The pathetic concentration of someone once proud and laughing. I want to tear the envelope out of her hands and rip it all up. When we first came to America, all of us went shopping together. We were like a small, lost group of soldiers cut off by the enemy, huddled together and looking this way and that. We came to the giant supermarket, and awe overcame our fear so we laughed and called to one another from different aisles and ran to show what we had found. Then we grew bored with the novelty and started managing the shopping in threes, then twos, until now, when Mummy more often than not sets off alone on the twenty-minute journey, the two-wheeled grocery cart bouncing behind her.

Mummy slides the envelope into her purse, pressing it down as if it might fly out on the walk. She says tiredly, We never knew. Not until it was too late.

I stand there, a hollowed-out thing, the inside part of me raw and raggedy. I focus on the floor. After a while, Mummy gets up. She puts on her coat and ties the belt, hangs the purse from her shoulder. She doesn't ask me if I will pull the metal cart and I don't offer. We set off under two umbrellas. Mummy walks with her back straight, full of purpose. She's staved off tears, I can tell, and all her effort is going into keeping it that way. By the time we arrive our legs are wet from the blowing rain. Mummy shakes her umbrella before carefully looping the button and snapping it in place. I imitate her, trying to get her to notice me, but she keeps her eyes on the coupons, the cart, the grocery list.

I pause at the beginning of an aisle, overwhelmed by the rows of colors and shapes yawning away towards the frozen meats in the distance, smooth yellow-white floor. Mummy disappears, intent on her coupons' requirement of this can of peas, that brand of pasta. I wait, but she doesn't come back soon enough. I feel a lost child's panic, the threat of tears. I retreat to the outside, sit down against the wall next to the rows of grocery carts. I stare at my ankles and feet through my hair, listening for the approach of strangers, but no one comes. I want a stranger to say, *What's wrong?* Someone who will turn the object of me to the light, to discover how it is made. No one speaks to me. Everything stays the same. After some time, Mummy emerges, dragging behind her the metal cart packed with groceries. The rain has stopped.

—I saw you through the window, she tells me, explaining why she did not worry at my absence.

We walk the twenty minutes home, the cart rattling and banging behind us. It shames me, this cart, which is all we have in a land of cars. Mummy is tired, but I don't offer to pull the cart. I want to, but I can't. I can't yield up this simple generosity, the words, *Let me*. I walk, despising myself, and she walks beside me, slowly pulling, her body leaning forward to bear the weight and her arm stretched straight behind her, the cart like a malignant, rattling creature that insists on being fed and dragged everywhere.

I tell myself it doesn't matter if I don't help, that she will understand.

The cart folds into a flat version of itself and stands on its two rubber wheels behind the kitchen door. It loses its balance and falls over, pushing the door closed. I kick it. I kick it all over the floor and into the wall, until my father runs in and rescues it like a bent and bruised pet. I hate the way he examines it with such worry. Sun streaks the dirty linoleum floor where Daddy kneels. He shakes a wheel, frowns. Mummy stands in the doorway, gripping the knob. She watches me until I make an impatient face, *What?*

—We didn't know, she says, her anger spilling out. Was that our crime?

—Maybe it was! I snap back, though what I really want to say is, *I don't know*. I cringe at her expression. Mummy slapped Alaine once, when Alaine first said the word fuck. Alaine laughed to show she didn't care, and I get ready to do the same. But Mummy's anger has dissolved. She despairs of me; I can see it all over her face. She clamps her mouth shut, retreats back into the bedroom.

Daddy folds up the cart and leans it behind the door. He says, What's going on here?

He sounds so tired and confused. I look at the closed door. I say, She hates me.

—That isn't true.

Daddy begs with his whole being for me to open the door, make amends. But I can't. The muffled sound of Mummy crying follows me to my room. Smell of new paint, afternoon sun. Alaine is in the garden again, digging up the sodden earth; I crawl into bed, staying low so that she won't glimpse me through the window. I wrap the pillow around my head and rock, I hate myself so much I could smash my head right through the wall. Alaine tried that once. She broke Daddy's grip and ran with her head tilted like a bull, straight into the wall. Then she just crumpled down like she'd been shot.

I rock, my head gripped inside the pillow. I spin up my anger to wipe out the image of Mummy's despairing face. They never knew anything. I ask about Ziad, and they say, Why, he died cleaning his gun. I ask about the dead soldier, and they say, What dead soldier? because they think Alaine made it up. They didn't know about Alaine, and then they didn't know about me. There are scars on my body they have never seen. Amer saw them. In those days after Daddy left us for America, I would head off without a word, I would make Mummy crazy with worry. She waited late into the night, terrified. Where were you, Marianna? she shouted. I was with Amer. Why? We were talking. It was Alaine who comforted her while I retreated to my room, evil, sometimes drunk, so angry that every breath threatened a scream.

Amer knew. I told him about the dead Syrian and the spy and also Ziad, who was like Keats, so full of dreams and passion and then dying young. *Darkling I listen and for a time have been half in love with easeful death to cease upon the midnight with no pain while thou art pouring forth thy soul in ecstasy.* It was Amer who gave me that book; the words garbled in constant silent recitation, shedding all but what was most important.

—That isn't the poem I meant for you to latch onto, Amer laughed when I spoke the words into his chest, his skin the smell of lemon and cigrettes and sweat. I don't know what poem he meant. He didn't mark the page, and I have forgotten the title he told me.

The story of Ziad angered him. He did not like loose ends. Someone must know what really happened, he muttered. I felt his impatience, ear pressed to his chest. Inside his ribs, the noise of something trying to batter its way out. His thumb ceased stroking my shoulder blade, now tapped, tap-tapped. Let's go, I said, and he agreed. Amer could not bear the confinement of rooms, even in the afternoon with the windows open, the sunny cold air all over us, let alone at night. People think I'm crazy, he said, but it's nothing compared to before. He held Jamil's jacket for me to slip in my arms, one by one. We went out into the cold gray winter.

—I'm sorry, Amer told Mummy when we came home too late. She was waiting in her chair, cigarette burning to the filter in the ashtray. I'm sorry, I'm sorry. She is safe with me.

—No one is ever safe! Mummy screamed, and Amer looked down, contrite, acknowledging truth.

At night Alaine doesn't stir, breaths so calm I cannot hear them. I do not understand how she became someone who sleeps, leaving me alone. I flip through the book Daddy was reading in the pantry, finish what is left of his whiskey. Daddy snores and Mummy speaks her dreams. She never used to do this. Her voice is desperate, guttural. It hurts to hear this sound, but I force myself to sit there in the dark, listening. Behind me, four pumpkins sit in a row on the kitchen table, witness to my nighttime movements. We are supposed to have what Daddy calls a *carving party* tomorrow. I light a cigarette. I bring it closer and closer to my foot, I will push it into skin, to the bone. The tiny circle of heat is terrifying. My hand trembles. Amer's arms were scarred like this, from the time in his room. Why didn't you try to get out? I asked. They added an iron bolt to the outside, Amer said, and anyway the door was solid. But what about your family? What about friends? Somehow they did it. They kept me inside, away from the war, but I went crazy. You're not crazy anymore, I comforted him, and he teased me, No, but you are.

I can't do it, I am a coward. I tuck my head between my knees, listening to my parents sleep. When I was small I dreamed of fire and woke screaming. Fire encircling Mummy and Daddy's bed while they slept, and me on the edge, crying out warnings that went unheard. Now they sleep but I'm awake and the fire's around me. There is no one who can save me. Not Walter who came running, not the counselor with her silk shirts and interlaced fingers, not my parents, not Alaine. Sometimes I think I succeeded that day, that I am still in that moment before Daddy finds me, sinking into sleep, head cushioned on my arms and knees tucked close. Time is spinning forward, offering up how things might have been, the hospital, Alaine's fire, me sitting here remembering while the ash grows long on my cigarette.

I grip my knees, hard bone in my hands, the body all bone but frail, a breakable thing. My body, the spine shuddering against the floor. I cannot bear it. I cannot.

It is not the idea itself. The idea of dying attached itself to my mind years ago, a microscopic, glimmering question gliding through my daily thoughts. The question asked itself during the first changing of Alaine's bandages when I saw the puckered, pale skin edging the wounds, so soft and apologetic-seeming, failures at hiding the awful thing. I looked into her eyes, but they were flat, impermeable, yielding none of her new secrets. There was something she had, now, that I did not. I wanted it. Then the years of waiting, between the mind's first alighting on the thought and the body, that drone, yielding for its own good, waiting until that day, at last, when I felt the popping open of skin, the red surprise of bubbles in a row and pain like light pouring out.

It is not the idea, which has always been with me and suggests itself daily, familiar as my own hands. It is my father's voice begging my name, the sound drawn through a darkness like earth, my legs and arms the earth and my voice gone. My father, his hands so weakened by terror that he fumbled, dropped me back onto the wooden floor.

I heave up one of the pumpkins, open the front door, and place it on the stoop. I have a notion of a gift, a surprise for when they wake up in the morning. Me finally doing something good. I imagine their delight. I imagine Daddy lighting a candle inside my pumpkin.

The knife point scores the surface, possible designs. I only did this once, at a party hosted by the American Embassy. It was Uncle Bernie who took us. I was so excited, holding his hand, the festivities so breathtaking, the foreignness of it all. I remember Uncle Bernie's brown suede shoe with cranberry sauce all over the toe. He loved his old shoes. When they found him, his feet were bare.

At that party he showed me things, how to string popcorn, how to carve a gaping one-toothed grin. But I want to carve a real face. I don't know whose. The knife slides in more easily than I expected, slicing across the place where the eyes were to be. I try to cut the shape out anyway, but the knife slips again. There is a moment of me breathing, pausing. I stare at the mistakes, telling myself I can fix them, I just have to be patient. But my eyes are already stinging and my whole body's stiffening up with rage.

A noise from behind, then Alaine comes onto the doorstep beside me, looks warily up and down the empty street. What are you doing?

—Nothing.

—Is that supposed to be a face?

I shove the knife into the pumpkin, drag it this way and that. The pumpkin splashes onto my feet. I wipe the blobs with my finger, flick them through the stairway rails.

—It's a bomb, I tell her.

—You're making a mess.

—So?

—We'll have to get you a new one.

—I don't want a new one.

—You'll be the only one without a pumpkin.

—Who cares?

I toe the remains of the pumpkin until it rolls off the stairs. The seeds will settle into the earth, grow a pumpkin tree. The tree will get so big the house will have to hold it up. People will come from all over the world to gawk, but I will stay modestly inside though everyone begs for interviews.

Alaine is watching the knife in my hand. After a moment, I wipe the pumpkin from the blade, hand it to her. She goes back inside, shuffling, her pajamas too long and tripping up her feet.

My arms wrap my knees, I bend my head. Alaine was eleven the first time she cut herself. Daddy ran through the apartment with her in his arms, shouting, Ani! Ani! Such panic for that minor scratch, their minds full of *It will be fine, It's not so bad,* no inkling of the years ahead. Eventually they transferred all the knives to one drawer, and I helped, serious and careful, protecting my sister. A locksmith came by and fashioned a lock for the drawer, a combination so there would be no keys to hunt for. I wasn't told the numbers, Alaine had too much power over me. Mummy, I need to chop an onion. Daddy, I need to cut my clay, it's too hard. And now, nine, ten years later, in another world on another night, my sister takes a knife from me. Her stillness at night is trickery; she probably hasn't slept for months. If I sneak up on her, I might find her crouched beneath the window, listening for something gone wrong. She was always more disciplined. I used to beg the body, *Don't sleep,* in case of fire, bomb, guns, and also Alaine, to watch Alaine breathe, make sure she was alive, but the body sighed helplessly, pulling me down with it, fading out moon and trees swaying outside the window. Night after night I failed to keep watch. But Alaine, she was always ready.

∽

One night I woke to the hiss and whine of an old truck braking. What's going on, I complained to Alaine, rubbing sleep from my eyes. She didn't say anything, just gripped the balcony rail, focusing on the other side of the street. A truck was parked on the sidewalk in front of the main door. I made out a soldier lounging against the wall, the tip of his cigarette glowing, a woman next to him. I said, Who are they? The woman let out a thin wail, a streaming wail of words. She pulled at his jacket, and he shoved her away. I saw shapes in windows, on balconies. The note of her crying rose, wavered, and two more soldiers emerged from the building, pulling a man between them.

Alaine leaned forward a little. She said in a voice full of hatred, They're taking away the Palestinians.

How did she know? I squinted through the darkness at the unfolding scene. The man was blindfolded and his hands were tied behind his back. They pulled him by the elbows so his knees dragged on the ground. His legs flailed in an effort to stand, but he was being dragged too low. I could hear the slight sound of his knees and feet banging against the pavement. The woman's crying rose to a shriek, but she did not try to rescue him; she huddled against the wall and just screamed, My husband, my husband. I could tell Alaine was enraged at her own helplessness. I pictured her storming the truck with a machine gun. I wanted her to attack the soldiers, to tear at their eyes and mouths. The man was lifted into the back of the truck in one motion so his limbs crashed in a heap onto the metal, and he moaned then, a low keen that rose and immediately fell away.

The doors slammed and the truck screeched and whined, rolled off the sidewalk and up the street going the wrong way. In only a few minutes the street fell back to quiet. Shapes retreated from windows and balconies. The woman leaned against the wall, sobbing, but now someone else emerged from the building, guided her inside.

Alaine said, It's over. She said it in such a flat, dismissive way that I knew she must have seen such things before. She went inside, but I couldn't move. The man was gone. The man was still living, and I was breathing in-out quickly, my spine rigid and curved, in half-pretense of being him. There was only the man, and my knowing that he was going to die. The pale limbs in the truck, the back curved weakly over the tucked-in legs, he was a finished thing, each breath superfluous, not to do with living, the possibility of *future, life, age,* but just breaths, the body's dumb work.

No one really believed the Israelis would invade. The jets were visible now and then, slivers high up in the sky trailing plumes of white, and they lazily circled the country, their presence signaled by a distant, muffled rumble. Then they began to appear without warning. I would be drawing at the kitchen table or reading in bed. The household would be moving quietly through the day when the faint rumble edged into our silence. Pens were dropped, dishes left on the counter, books earmarked and closed. Moments later, the jets broke the sound barrier. The explosion dissolved the walls and floors, hurled us into empty space for an instant, like being inside the noise itself, the noise dividing the body into so many fragments. Alaine's cat hid stupidly under the kitchen table, head low and eyes widened into circles, and the roar intensified while we stared upwards, leaning out windows. Then they arrived, racing above the rooftops in formation, so low that the windowpanes shook, and one day after they had come and gone, the silent sky was flooded with paper falling gently down onto the city. The paper settled everywhere, swept through streets by cars, flapping in the breeze against pedestrians and walls and antennas, and children ran this way and that catching armfuls. When someone finally read the message, we learned that Beirut would be bombed; the Palestinians would finally be defeated and for this civilians should temporarily leave.

School closed to wait for the invasion. I stood in a field with some other students. It was early afternoon, quiet and hot. One of the boys was trying to knock bottles off a ledge, and the stones sounded pleasant when they hit the glass, and the bottles dropped, rolled in place on the pavement. I toed my bag, reluctant to go home, the day's boredom stretching before me. A roar under the quiet, and we froze, looking up. We breathed once, twice. Our hearts beat. Two jets exploded into the sky and the grass lost its color, the buildings looked like clay models, and for that second all that existed was the silver, the black hole of the cockpit, the immense sound. They were gone instantly, leaving behind a torn, altered sky, and in the southern suburbs the bombs started falling, and black smoke billowed above the rooftops. We did not run, too young and vain for fear. We wandered around the empty school yard, listening, smoking from a stolen pack of cigarettes until one of us said casually, I'm going home.

In that time of waiting, the streets turned strange and ominous. Cars stopped moving, people stayed indoors. Hooves clattered down the road, a panicked trot then gallop then trot. I ran to the balcony, saw a boy riding bareback, and the horse chomped and frothed, its chest and sides white with sweat. It sidestepped onto the sidewalk, and some people yelled insults, jumped out of the way. The boy hunched over the horse's neck to keep from falling. The horse was beautiful, thin-legged and terrified. It was one of the racehorses from the track that was no longer used. I do not know where he took the horse. There was nowhere to go.

Every corner belonged to some militia. They wore cowboy hats and smoked Marlboros, which Mummy called terrorist cigarettes. She switched to Dunhills, more civilized. Some of the soldiers also wore cowboy boots. They were young, and they crossed their wrists over the barrels of their machine guns, guarding this corner or that street. Alaine tracked the Israelis' approach with newspaper clippings pasted into notebooks. When they bombed, she turned the music up and cradled her cat, glaring. She let me in her room so I wouldn't have to sit on the landing with the grown-ups, and we waited there in our own shelter, the tiny high-up window ajar and crisscrossed with masking tape.

The Israelis circled above, and Mummy and Daddy implored, Be very careful. They gripped my face and arms and told me, She cannot run away again, not now, not with the streets so empty, each footstep on the sidewalk ringing fear. We waited inside, suspended between two dangers, Alaine's bedroom door and the sky. The Israelis would never dare take Beirut. The world would stop them. This is what the grown-ups said, but every day the Israeli army came closer.

Then Sitt Julie came to live with us. She arrived with Mummy wearing only a nightgown. She had wild gray hair and glasses and her feet were bare.

—This is Sitt Julie, Mummy said. She has nowhere else to go.

I wondered if she would take my room, then felt guilty for worrying about that. In fact, Sitt Julie needed a small, dark space and so Alaine was forced to move into the larger empty bedroom. Mummy had been calling it the *sewing room,* which apparently was a traditional room in American houses, and where none of us ever sat because we didn't need it. This was when we finally got to see what Alaine had been hoarding. Previously piled in boxes that only she was allowed to open and dig through, pieces of shrapnel none of us had seen before emerged. She could barely lift them; she stood them on end and rocked them into the corner or up against the wall, and I was astonished by the effort it must have taken to bring them home at all. She also had an unexploded grenade, a pair of army boots, a switchblade. Mummy and Daddy watched with dismay as these things came to light and lined the shelves with her books and the now ordinary bullets and casings. I never found such objects: I never disappeared for long enough because I was tied to home and Mummy and Daddy, cooking in the kitchen, and the stories about Téta and Jiddo, whom I could barely remember.

—The grenade has to go, Daddy commanded, and the next day it was gone, but no one knew where, and I started to live in fear of Alaine getting angry and exploding all of us.

Sitt Julie came from Téta and Jiddo's neighborhood, this was how Mummy recognized her on the street. Her house had been destroyed and she had nowhere to go.

—Now we have a maid, I said to Mummy, and I was punished for having what Daddy called *delusions of grandeur.*

Sitt Julie was willing to cook only three things: baked chicken with potatoes, stuffed eggplant, and rice with curry. If she was not cooking, she dusted and washed the floors, she carried the rugs to the balcony and slung them over the rail to beat them. She wore a blue housedress and slippers, and she had been married eleven times.

—Eleven times, I told Mummy. And they were all British.

—She's teasing you, Marianna.

If that were true, it didn't matter. Sitt Julie's presence in our house distracted me. It was a relief when she asked me to help her fold sheets, or when I dried the dishes she handed to me. Alaine's strange music drifted from her room, melancholy, threatening. Sitt Julie learned on her own to listen at Alaine's door, to knock with bright questions about nothing. I followed Sitt Julie around, asking questions. How long did you live in India? Did you love him? Did you ride elephants? India had been a sweltering place of misery, she explained, but she had learned tricks there. Every night she placed a brick on the toilet lid in her bathroom so the rats would not come up from the sewers. She said it didn't matter that we were all the way up on the second floor, and so I worried about our toilet, but she said it was safe at the other end of the house. Her legs were very thin and pale, and deep blue veins stood up from her hands, like the mountain ranges on the plaster maps at school. I watched her cut goat cheese and insert it in pieces of bread, chew slowly and thoughtfully, thinking about her husbands, no doubt, and the long, steaming voyages to India. I have a love, too, I whispered to her, and she listened all about Ziad without question, even accepting the parts I made up in which Ziad had come to Beirut to confess his love, but was waiting till I was old enough to marry. Oh, Sitt Julie said, titillated. You'd better be careful! I was glad Mummy had saved her. I wanted to save people myself, when I was old enough; my own inadequacy in the face of the looming Israelis tortured me. I longed to go out into the streets and bring home refugees, but where would they sleep? I imagined driving truckloads of food to the poor and starving, opening a shelter with beds and music. I was too young. I became furious.

—There are lots of ways to save people, said Uncle Bernie, who had been a doctor for a while before being seduced by history, as he called it. I couldn't imagine Uncle Bernie in anything other than his rumpled corduroy jacket with the leather elbow patches and old brown shoes. He was pale and plump, and he wore black square glasses and sucked on his lip when he was thinking. But he had served as a volunteer emergency doctor for international relief organizations, which was how he came to the Middle East. I picked up the dirt and let it fall through my fingers, he said, describing the beginning of his love affair with Lebanon. Then I met your father, who told me to go back to school.

—But what can I do?

He smiled. You can do anything you want, Anna. Just anything.

—You always say that, I grumbled.

—You could start by cleaning your room, Mummy said.

—It's all right, Anna, Uncle Bernie comforted me. One day you'll be old enough.

Sitt Julie loved Uncle Bernie. She fussed over him as if he was one of her husbands. You must get new shoes! she ordered him, but he loved his old suede shoes and said he wouldn't trade them for the world. She asked after him constantly, and when he was with us, she urged him to leave before dark for safety's sake. The Israeli jets roared over Beirut, and Sitt Julie screamed, *Sharmoota! Kiss ikhtak!* Mummy made a point of visiting the neighbors, who must have heard her through the walls, to explain that it was Sitt Julie and no one else who shouted such obscenities.

Sitt Julie cooked and shouted at the sky, and my parents spoke late at night, their voices too low for me to hear. The Israeli jets raced the sky all day, keeping an eye on us, and I followed Alaine to keep an eye on her.

Mummy and Daddy argued about what to do with us, and one day I screamed, I'm not leaving! which shocked them to silence. They did not raise the topic again, and I thought it was over with until the day Uncle Ara arrived at the door with a cigarette burning dangerously close to his lips and his yellow hair standing on end. He said, Why don't you send them to Vartan?

Mummy explained later, Vartan was my favorite cousin before he went away. You'll like him.

Astrig was not as taken by this idea as everyone else, but she expressed it in jokes. He'll convert them into Armenians! she said, which irritated Uncle Ara.

—What's wrong with being Armenian? Our culture goes back thousands of years!

Astrig sarcastically motioned her hand for him to please continue with this boring story of the millennia. Uncle Ara shook his head, saying, My daughter, nothing disturbs her. He smiled, but not very happily.

It was true that nothing affected Astrig. She always had a joke ready and wiggled her eyebrows at anything serious, especially when people discussed the greatness of Armenians. There was mystery in her behavior, but Mummy only said, Terrible things happened a long time ago, and some people handle them by making jokes.

I thought of Jiddo wearing the fez and smacking imaginary slaves with his horsehair whip. I asked, Was it to do with the Turkish thieves?

—Thieves? I suppose you can look at it that way. Anna, enough, you should be excited to go somewhere different!

—Vartan is a student of his own history, Anna, Daddy explained without really explaining anything. It is a noble thing to do. You'll like him.

I did not want to like Vartan. I didn't want to go anywhere. Sitt Julie commented that Rome was the most beautiful city in the world, but under pressure admitted she had never been there, only seen photographs. Alaine didn't want to go either, but she did not tell Mummy and Daddy, at least not in words. She refused to speak to them anymore. Her whole body said *I hate you* when they so much as looked at her. They told me, She cannot run away again, watch her. I watched, and my palms felt numb, as if I had already lost what I was supposed to hold. She was forbidden from going outside alone—we couldn't go out anyway, because of the Israelis who might show up at any minute—and so I watched her scowling out the window, sometimes at the street, sometimes at the sky, as if daring the Israelis to make their move. The cat, perhaps chafing at Alaine's imprisonment, took up her tricks. It fled the house by windows and doors, it yowled at us from the shadowy street, refusing capture. When it did come back, its ear hung raggedy, or it dragged a mangled leg. In those times it cuddled up to all of us, and we forgave its behavior out of pity. It licked its wounds in Alaine's arms, then took off again.

Alaine caught me pretending not to watch her and said she needed to show me something important. She guided me to a corner of the playground underneath our building. Sitt Julie was chaperoning, though this was for show only; Sitt Julie would never be able to catch Alaine if she started running. But Alaine hadn't been plotting escape. She made Sitt Julie stand by the building's main entrance while we went to the other end of the playground.

She toed a rock with her foot and said, Everything we might need is under here.

I did not know what we might need, so I said, What?

She knelt in the dirt and pushed the rock aside. She poked at the earth as if to test its stability. They're about one foot under, she said. There's enough canned food to last the four of us a week, and grenades and bullets. She frowned, then added, But I don't have a gun yet.

—So you really didn't steal the pistol? I asked, suddenly remembering Uncle Ara searching.

Alaine looked sneaky. Her eyes shifted my way, then down. Of course I did, you dope. But someone took it.

I was relieved to find out where the grenades had gone, but I did not know what would make us run to this corner of dirt and start digging. I pictured a white world, blasted out of existence by the Israelis like in the nuclear war movies, and us huddled here, Alaine in charge. I said, OK, and she pushed the rock back in place and wiped her hands on her jeans. Don't tell anyone, she said, and I obeyed her.

Someone took it. It was only much later that her words formed so many frightening meanings. I imagined Alaine running, then a man grabbing the gun, making off with it. Alaine backed up against a wall, grappling uselessly. Alaine in the doorway, bloody rivulets down her face, neck, arms, legs, the policeman saying, We found her here, we found her there.

Mummy and Daddy always said, She is in a depression, darling. She hurts herself to let out the pain inside. They spoke the words determinedly, a truth told them by doctors and relatives, something to grab onto, but they had no idea where Alaine went, or what actually happened. I understood this now. While we had been stumbling along in our dumb, loving way, flinging our arms out to rescue her from dangers we couldn't even name, trying to keep her inside the illusory safety of *home,* she had been doing the real work of saving. She'd been stockpiling weapons, measuring our chances.

She knew the whole city, she'd plotted escape routes, she'd made allies amongst militias. Our parents were oblivious. No wonder she despised them so.

—What is the matter with you? Daddy asked me.

—You don't know anything! I accused him, glad someone had noticed my new self. You don't understand!

My father just stood there, shocked, his mouth open a little. It was impossible to take back my poisonous words. So this was what it felt like to be Alaine. I had an inkling of her power then, fathomless, utterly cold, because she never once showed sign of this awful sickness at being so mean. I knew it had to be true, that she did hate Mummy and Daddy. *Sorry sorry sorry* crowded my mind, but I forced myself think of the playground, of her keeping an eye on the invasion. Why couldn't they see Alaine was our only chance?

—I just wanted to tell you about going to Rome, Daddy said tiredly. There's going to be a siege.

Later, the arguments. Why can't you come, too? I demanded.

—We have to stay with Sitt Julie. We can't leave the apartment. You'll be safe.

—What about you?

—We'll be fine.

—Then why do *we* have to leave?

—Stop asking questions, Marianna!

—*Tell* me!

—You will do as you're told!

—Then we'll run away!

This they paid attention to. Marianna, Mummy said warningly. Tell me if you mean it.

My new self crumbled, longing for love. No, I said.

I had no more fight in me. I'm sorry, I told Alaine. I tried.

Alaine refused to pack. She tucked herself into a ball in the corner of her bed, as if she could press herself into the wall and disappear. Mummy held things up, saying, How about this, and musing,

It might rain more there. Alaine paid no attention at all. The day we left, the generator wasn't working and Uncle Ara had to carry her down the stairs because she wouldn't move.

—You're heavy as a Dushka! He shouted at her.

She said nothing. Her curly hair swung back and forth. He carried her stomach-down on his shoulder, gripping her around the thighs. I thought of birds. I thought of a leather hood slipped over her head, calming her, reducing the chance of a breakaway.

Uncle Ara liked his metaphor of the Dushka. Drrrrr-a! he shouted. Drrrr-rrrr-a! He turned Alaine this way then that, firing at the Israelis.

Through Alaine's hair I glimpsed a smile.

Uncle Ara drove us to the Green Line. I had imagined a thick line of green paint, like the faded white lines on the streets, but when Uncle Ara parkcd the car, there was nothing but a wide, empty dirt road lined with destroyed buildings and checkpoints. Uncle Ara struck up a conversation with the Syrian soldier investigating our papers.

—What's your name? he bellowed.

—Abdelnour.

—How do you like Lebanon?

The soldier, who was young and wary, did not answer.

—It used to be more beautiful, Uncle Ara told him. When I was nineteen, I would run all the way from the mountains there, you see them? He pointed in the general direction of Broummana with his cigarette. Down to there, he pointed at the Beirut bay. Could you run that far?

—I am not interested in running, said Abdelnour, snapping our passports into Daddy's hands.

Uncle Ara kissed us all good-bye. We watched his Citroën jounce away on the uneven road.

—He could have had us killed, Alaine muttered, heaving up her suitcase.

Daddy was startled by the venom in her voice. But honey, he's always having fun with the soldiers. They know he's just joking.

Alaine could not be bothered to answer and so Daddy shrugged and picked up my suitcase. I glanced at Alaine to show I agreed with her. She accepted this show of loyalty as if it were the norm, and it felt good to be allowed onto her side. I walked beside her, the two of us behind Daddy, who fell back behind Abdelnour, our guide across the Green Line. Abdelnour did not offer to help us with the suitcases. He trudged ahead smoking, gun swinging from his shoulder, and every now and again he stopped with a great show of impatience while we struggled to catch up. Daddy smiled and nodded at him, meek as could be, and his weakness angered me.

—What's wrong, honey? he asked, looking back. Don't be upset. You'll have fun in Rome.

His gentle words broke my anger, leaving me ashamed. Innocent of my thoughts, he touched my shoulder briefly before he picked up my bag and walked on.

We stayed in Uncle Ara's empty apartment in Rabieh. At night the jets flew over West Beirut. Flares lit the targets, and the city was silhouetted against a white glowing sky. Then the white flooded with red and as the smoke lifted, the sound of the bombs reached us, ba-boom, a beautiful, deep sound, and the smoke billowed upwards, thick until it disintegrated high up above the buildings. I counted seconds between the time of the red explosion and the sound of the bomb itself. Daddy said that sound traveled slowly, but I didn't understand that. He sat with his legs crossed, smoking, sipping his whiskey, his face gray in the faint light from the living-room window. The jets came again and again, sharp black streaks in the brightened sky, and Daddy reassured us that Mummy was all right. But I thought of Mummy alone, or running on the road to Astrig's apartment, or in the basement lit with flickering gas lamps. For the first time, I questioned the habit of staying in the basement during bombing. What if the building fell on top of you? It made no sense.

—How do they know they're hitting the right thing?

Daddy said, They don't.

I had heard that hospitals were bombed because the Israelis thought the roofs were occupied by the Palestinian fighters. The city became a maze. I pictured it from high up, the way it would look from the jets. How could they see a single terrorist? Did they have binoculars? I closed my eyes and tried to imagine Mummy, Astrig, and Mrs. Awad from up there in the sky, but this was like trying to find a person in the minuscule lines of a map.

—We don't want to go to Italy, I announced.

—You have to.

—No, we don't, Alaine said sullenly. She squatted on the balcony floor, staring through the rails at the fire and smoke like a small, fierce animal, coiled and ready to spring across the the sea straight into the bombing. I readied myself for Daddy's argument. I felt giddy and strong, on Alaine's side.

Daddy said, Think of your sister.

This was what they always told me. I glared at the floor. Everything was always *Take care of Alaine, Follow Alaine, Speak to Alaine.* Since she was actually talking for once, Alaine could handle this. She would never be forced onto the boat, and I would cling to her. Tomorrow we would be back home. But Alaine didn't say a word, and as the moments passed I felt something in the silence. I looked up. Daddy was examining his cigarette, rolling it back and forth between thumb and forefinger so the smoke shifted in the air. Alaine stared at West Beirut. The bombs blew, smoke roiled into the sky. Nothing had changed, but it was all different. He had been addressing her, not me.

—I don't want to go, I said weakly, pathetically, the sister to be thought of. They did not answer.

I was enraged that Alaine had been enlisted to protect me. As if she herself would not smash a window or run away or try to kill herself. Mummy and Daddy were just as stupid as Alaine had always said. I pictured Rome, a city of medieval stone towers, Italian men in white shirts, fountains. How would I even enjoy myself? Alaine certainly couldn't; she never enjoyed anything. She would run away, then they would see. *I'm sorry, I told you we shouldn't go. You're the ones who thought I needed to be away from the Israelis. Instead you doomed her. We would have been fine, she had grenades saved up.* I sank into the whirl of fantasies, relishing vengeance, the sickness and guilt of it. In the end I would provide comfort, holding back the desire to blame them because it would be cruel in their grief. The flares and bombs fell, lighting up the black expanse of bay usually dotted with fishing-boat lanterns. Daddy went inside to pour another whiskey. I quickly tapped one of his cigarettes out of the box, hid it in my sleeve for later. Alaine signed I should take two, but I didn't, deliberately putting the packet out of her reach. The clink-clink of ice cubes signaled Daddy's return, and I burst into tears.

Daddy took us by boat to Cyprus, and he kissed us good-bye in the airport and we flew to Rome. We'd never been anywhere alone before. I tried not to cry, but I couldn't help it, the tears kept forming no matter how much I scrubbed at my eyes. Alaine told me not to worry, she wouldn't run away and leave me. Then she stopped talking. The whole trip, she sat still and dark and silent. The stewardess said, Want some lemonade? and after that she left Alaine alone. I smiled till my face hurt to make up for things. I unfolded the blanket, contrived to have it fall across Alaine's arm to hide the scars. They embarrassed me. Alaine shrugged the blanket away.

—It's hot, she said, though it was freezing.

I was so upset that she put her arm around me, and I thought of her skin where it touched mine along the back of my neck, her white skin the American-speaking doctors called *pearly* in the emergency room. The cuts had healed in a mishmash of raised, ugly scars, like fake rubber scars glued on but they were real. Alaine never let them use anesthetic because she hated injections. Imagine

that, a doctor told me once, trying to make a joke of Alaine's raggedy arm, stripped to bits by razor blades. I hate injections, too! I
told him, and that shut him up.

—We're here, Alaine said, peering out the window at a gray expanse of city.

As soon as we walked into Cousin Vartan's apartment, I knew that
none of the grown-ups had any idea where they had sent us. Cousin
Vartan's apartment was a palace of wood and silk and mother-of-
pearl, each room illuminated by dim lamps decorated with thousands of dyed beads so that the walls shimmered with color. There
were canopies and curtains and silk floor cushions and the blinds
remained half-shut. Cousin Vartan was tall and thin, he made grace-
ful gestures as he described the objects in his house, and each motion released scents from his silk robe, scents of ancient things, of
turpentine and vegetables. He guided us down a narrow hallway,
he stopped and turned around. Pointing to a curtain on the wall,
he said, Behind this is the door to my secret room! and then he
laughed with his head thrown back before going on. Alaine pushed
me forward because I could not move, the visions of corpses and
heads and weapons in the secret room rooting my feet.

In the room where Alaine and I would sleep, prints of Indian
people making love covered the walls, so my skin became hot and
tremulous. The shelves were crowded with zoo animals made of
wood, plastic, clay, ivory. I could not believe these innocent toys
occupied the same space as the pictures. I sat on the floor, knees
to my chest, trying not to openly stare. Alaine took over settling
in with the brisk efficiency of an older sister, as if she'd been this
way all along.

—I can't believe Mom packed this, she said, holding up a red
sweatshirt. I haven't worn it since I was twelve.

She arranged our clothes in the chest of drawers Cousin Vartan
had provided. She did it slowly and with all her attention, frowning her way through the task. I watched her in fear, thinking at any

moment she would revert to the motionless, unspeaking Alaine and I would have to bring her tea, bring her food, make her take the pills. My fear was increased thousandfold by the world that lay just outside the drawn curtains. I did not know where anything important was, the hospital, pharmacy, police. I could not fathom that I was in another country, that if I were to part the curtains and raise the blinds, I would see a magical place of buses and trams and restaurants, glimpsed on the drive home from the airport. There was the noise of traffic, deep and constant, and the clanging of tram bells, and birds chirping in trees so lush and big; I wondered for the first time why Beirut was so devoid of greenery. I hated it here. I wanted to go home. I conveyed this to Alaine with all my might, without words.

Alaine closed the suitcase and pushed it under one of the beds. She looked at me. Don't worry, she said. He's Mom's favorite cousin.

I clung to this in relief. His resemblance to Mummy was acute, the same brown hair, the round brown eyes. I wished she had come with us. As we drank tea in the tiny kitchen, I confessed I was already homesick, searching for sympathy.

—Home? Vartan said. Armenians have no home.

I glanced at Alaine to see if she understood what he was saying, but she was sucking on a sugar cube, staring at the floor. I waited. I had never thought of myself as Armenian.

—We are exiles, he announced. Do you know nothing of Armenian history?

I shook my head, ashamed. I knew only that Jiddo had served in the British army as a spy, which was much more interesting than being Armenian.

—That is nothing! They were among the first refugees to arrive in Lebanon! Vartan reprimanded me. Your Jiddo spent part of the trip in a suitcase!

This fact did not astonish me as I knew it was meant to; I had known the suitcase story my whole life, and besides, we saw refugees all the time. I shrugged uncertainly. The notion of being homeless, of carrying this in my blood, appealed to me. But it did not make sense. We had a home.

—The past will never be undone. Vartan turned away and began to rinse dishes in the sink, and it seemed that something terrible lay in his words, as if they were a prophecy whose meaning I had failed to read.

Vartan examined our skin and clicked his tongue in disapproval, but did not explain what he had seen. He fed us liver to ward off disease and carrots to make our eyes shine. He strapped on a sugical mask and disappeared into his secret room and we listened to him moving about in there, forbidden from entering lest we *destroy something from the past.*

He had letters from Uncle Ara and Astrig beside his bed, and they were months old but he could not bring himself to read them, he said, because they gave him headaches brought on by nostalgia, and by the fear that his father would die before he saw him again, like Auntie Lupsi had. I sat on his bed, listening to his lectures on history as he lay prone with cucumber slices on his eyelids. While the Armenian kings fought battles and more battles, while the Armenian Church held synods to argue about the dual nature of Christ, the letters looked sad and thin, as if inside there was only a page, a brief hello that would be easy to read. I did not understand what was wrong with Vartan. He said only that if he returned to Lebanon he would be shot, and I thought of Fadi, and I wanted to tell Vartan about him but my mouth clamped shut.

—We, as Armenians, he said, do not belong anywhere. So you should make your home wherever you go and be pleased you are somewhere at all.

I thought of Jiddo and Uncle Ara fleeing the Turks, which had always seemed an adventurous way to grow up. Uncle Ara never talked about it, while Auntie Lupsi used to say, *The church floors ran with blood,* but she hadn't been there so somehow it didn't count. I hadn't been there, and neither had Vartan. His obsession upset me.

I had a home, and I missed it awfully. The room grew dimmer as the afternoon passed, and with the waning of the day, the delicate silk vine and geometric patterns on the curtains and pillows, the ancient prints in their gold-leaf frames seemed to hold a key to the mystery and sorrow of my cousin's words, but the more I looked, the more anxious I became. I could not yet understand that Vartan looked at us through the eyes of an exile, and that he had divined our own from a history of ocean crossings and marriages made with foreigners. I understood nothing. I sat still and waited for Vartan to rise and fix us dinner, and I was homesick and longed for the familiar streets of my childhood, the sky and the sea, as if all of this were mine.

Alaine struggled to read the newspapers with the help of Daddy's English-Italian dictionary. She poured over the articles on Beirut and gave reports on death tolls, numbers of bombs, time lines. Vartan was distressed by her brooding concentration on the news. You cannot do anything, he chastised. You can only wait. You, he said, speaking only to her. I retreated, feigning disinterest. In our first weeks there he took us on field trips. He drove us to a great arch built for a Roman emperor. Your history lies here, he announced, and I stared up at this monstrosity of stone and scaffolding. It was impossible that I had anything to do with this monument. But at the very top, after a long climb up narrow stairs and with many stops so that Vartan could scold young restorers crouched before sections of stone, he showed us a procession of kings, one of whom he said was Armenian, paying tribute to the emperor.

—Do you see? he whispered, and I stared at the blind surfaces of the eyes that had gazed out over Rome for centuries, the flowing robes. I hung back and he placed his hand on Alaine's shoulder, guiding her along the scaffolding, and their hair and skin was so similar, separate from mine. I thought about how Jiddo used to take Alaine out for walks, when I was still a baby, and how he had died before I was old enough to go along, and the envy of this rose bitterly in me now. I did not come from anywhere, not anywhere at all. Daddy had always been happy with my blond hair and green eyes, because I looked just like him, but I did not want this anymore, I wanted to come from somewhere I knew, and these stone figures, so tall and cold and eroded, had nothing to do with me.

The days wound on and on. Our routine changed because Vartan had to go back to work. Breakfast was followed by Vartan driving us to whatever friend had agreed to watch us for the day. The friend, usually a woman, took us sightseeing. The Coliseum. The Pantheon. Fountains. The Forum. One day we drove hours out of Rome to see Hadrian's villa. I did not care about Hadrian or his villa, so she took Alaine in alone. I sat at the café drinking a Pepsi, swatting at bees. A man reading a newspaper caught my eye. His face reminded me of Ziad; I wanted to tell him. I saw myself through his eyes, a waiting woman, perhaps abandoned, sorrowful, mysterious. He could be seeing anything. *Ciao piccola,* he said when he left. I thought *piccola* might mean flute, wasn't there a flute with the same-sounding name? I missed him. I sat there alone, missing the stranger, who might return at any moment to rescue me.

—It means Little One, Vartan's friend told me, and I rode the whole way back in mute embarrassment.

Eventually we were allowed to go on day trips on our own. Alaine was put in charge. She carried the money, the passports, the tickets, and Daddy's English-Italian pocket dictionary. No one bothered us, because the moment anyone approached, and they were usually men, Alaine gave a death-stare. Her eyes went black with rage, and her hair itself seemed to stand on alert. Her whole body said *fuck off,* and they did.

I did not understand why we were going anywhere at all. Alaine said we had to be independent, not become burdens to everyone. I complained, dragging my feet, so angry I sometimes screamed with my mouth closed and teeth clamped together. Stop it, Alaine told me. What are you so mad for? I did not know. My rage was immense and all-consuming. I screamed on. We marched through train stations, churches, fields. People turned to see what this noise was. I walked behind Alaine, relentless, screaming into my closed mouth until my throat was raw. I hated this country of silence and time. White and blue buildings across the tracks; summer-white sky above a vast countryside, green and brown, carved into squares and dabbed with red roofs. There was no war here. The hot and sticky air settled on my skin and the days sank. Trains were late. Alaine walked up and down the platform, T-shirt damp and clinging to her back. Her curly hair dripped at the nape. I smoked and drank water, hating her and this place and everything.

—You have to stay longer, Vartan told us. He folded up the long-awaited telegram into a tiny square and stuffed it into the garbage. I fished it out. I did not recognize the sender's name. A man, someone Mummy and Daddy must have paid to send a message. *Absolutely cannot come home. Will call when they can.* The Israelis were destroying Beirut. I pressed Vartan for details, but he was closemouthed and frantic. At night Alaine whispered to me in the dark. No food, she told me. No electricity, no water, no chance.

—We should go back, I urged her.

—You don't understand, Marianna, Alaine said impatiently. We can't go and they can't leave. They're trapped.

I struggled to accept this, but my head went murky with fear. I wanted to go home. I wanted my own bed and my own things and Mummy and Daddy in the living room. I doubt they're sitting there, Alaine commented, and I turned my thoughts to the basement, equally as familiar, safe. The days came and went in tense silence; even Vartan did not want to give false hope. I do not remember anything more of this time, other than the day Alaine said, Come see, and we watched the blurry footage of the PLO soldiers evacuating Beirut, and Alaine said, We'll be home soon.

Vartan received an invitation to lunch from a Lebanese family, but no matter how he pushed, Alaine refused to go. I don't like eating with strangers, she said, and climbed into bed and held a book up to her face. I was glad, because apparently there was a son who was seventeen, and if Alaine came he would certainly fall in love with her and then no one would talk to me.

—You can't do anything when she gets like this, I warned Vartan. Still, he called around until he found someone to stay with her those few hours.

Alaine absorbed this news without expression. She told Vartan in a bored, you-don't-know-much voice, I wouldn't do anything here.

—Good. But. Nevertheless!

Vartan's concern for us, for our family and his, for all of Lebanon, had robbed him of his ability to speak full sentences. He headed back to his room to prepare for the luncheon. I kept a wary eye on Alaine, who was reading, or pretending to. I saw the stiffness in her face, the grim lines of movement that meant will, only will and not something deep-down and permanent. *Wouldn't do anything here.* Her recovery was all an act. She was doing it for me, for Vartan, for the larger cause of the Israeli invasion and our parents suffering without food or water. I felt small and foolish and afraid. I should have been watching her.

—We won't be long, I told her. Are you sure you want to stay?

She just looked at me, disdaining the concern under my words. I fell back, leaving her to Vartan's friend.

The father of this family had been killed some months before in Beirut, and Vartan cautioned me for the thousandth time to be especially polite for this reason. This offended me; of course I would be careful. I had been fantasizing about this dead man's son for days. I imagined his hand on my arm, I imagined lips, the warmth of his face near mine as I whispered comforting words. You come from the same place, Vartan had told me, which will be good for him. I knew my role, to be good for this poor boy, who was so alone in his grief.

But the boy we met was not the one from my dreams. He was

much taller and stronger, he smiled without kindness and from the moment I walked in, his black eyes latched onto me until I thought I would faint from shame. The atmosphere was subdued after the initial flurry of welcomes. There were aunts and uncles there, and family friends, all of whose names disappeared from my mind as soon as they looked away. Every time the boy spoke, the rest of them flinched. Pass the salt, he commanded, and conversation tripped, lurched back on track. Fear lurked under the table. I felt it on my legs, in my lap. His eyes bored into me. I wanted to leave. I gazed desperately at Vartan, but he was oblivious. When the boy told me to follow him, nobody suggested I do any differently. There was a silence, and finally I stood up, because, astonishingly, it would have been rude not to accept this improper invitation. I felt like a sacrifice, following him so meekly. The house was cavernous. He led me down this hall and that hall and upstairs and downstairs. It was silent but for our footsteps.

He opened a door. My suite, he said, as if he was escorting me to a show. I stood around awkwardly while he flipped through records. What do you want to hear? he asked. Whatever you want, I told him, and he replied curtly, That's stupid. He selected a record and as he was lowering the needle, he added, You should insist on what you like. Me, he continued, sitting down and snapping a Zippo to flame, I like to kill people.

The room filled up with the smell of his cigarette. All I could think of was that Vartan had said he was a kind boy, polite and genuine, and that it would be important for him to speak with someone from his home, someone like him.

—I was just fighting in Beirut, he said.

I nodded courteously.

—You don't believe me.

I made some protest, but his eyes were more furious than ever. I stared at his fists. When he inhaled, he covered half his face with his hand, his eyes watching me through the smoke. I scrambled for truth, alighted on one.

—I found a dead soldier once.

It was good Alaine had stayed home. I waited, not breathing.

—That, he said, is nothing.

I heard Vartan laughing in the garden, and far off in my mind I registered that we had gone in circles through the house, that we were actually above where we had started out from. In the ensuing silence I became aware of how beautiful this house was, the French windows and wide marble balcony, the pine trees in the garden below and the wrought-iron furniture, the fountain of carved dolphins. I tried to imagine what Alaine would say to this boy, but nothing came, there was nothing to save me. He paced the room. I stood very still. He walked behind, bent close to my ear.

—No one knows I've been fighting except you, he whispered.

I waited. His mother had appeared exhausted with her black clothing, dark-ringed eyes. But how could she have let me go upstairs? She could not know her son was a fighter, that he would circle me and say these things. Or, it came to me, she did, and had no strength left to stop him.

He sat on the edge of a chair. He said, I'm supposed to go to Paris to study engineering. But I'm not. I'm going back. To find the people who killed my father.

He crumpled backwards, eyes closed. Vartan had said we would share the same history, but his was nothing like mine. I could not imagine it, not at all, not the way he wanted me to. The memories came and went, pathetically ordinary, of gunmen in jeeps, of bombs falling into the sea, of Mummy's hands on my ears, her body curled around mine.

—Have you ever held a gun? he asked, challenging.

I thought of Uncle Ara's pistol, how we used to fire at the branches of the olive tree, and I said no, I had never held a gun. He smiled at me then, and in that moment I no longer knew where I came from, how to negotiate the shameful space between the rooms where I had hidden and the streets where he had fought. I did not come from the place that Lebanon really was, a place of dark streets, of whatever he had done, of his dead father and Fadi being gone and Alaine's hands scooping dirt over her soldier. I wasn't even truly Lebanese, but part Egyptian, Armenian, American. I wasn't anything. And here we were, sitting in Rome in the warm breeze, the record circling its music, our feet moving a little to the rhythm.

He leaned forward and I smelled his cologne, saw the soft hairs on in chin. He said, You won't tell? and I shook my head, No, I won't.

Back home, Alaine grew irritated by my silent presence in the room.

—What?

—Are they going to die? I asked her. I needed to be strong, too. What will we do if they die?

It was a relief to say *we*. I pictured us trudging away with our suitcase, alone, bereft but courageous. Now I regretted the way I had behaved on our trips.

—We'll go back, she said flatly, and bury them.

The terrible scenes rolled through my imagination. Alaine re-arranged herself, lifted her book. The scars on her arms showed vividly in the lamplight. She held the shovel, set at the hard ground in the garden with all her might. Mummy and Daddy lay dead beside her, wrapped in sheets. There was no *we*. I thought of the night Alaine climbed one of the trees. She climbed so high she was almost level with the balcony. She crouched there, glaring, while we pleaded with her to come down. Hours and hours she stayed nestled amongst the branches, while we shone flashlights from the balcony and the ground, promising food, gifts, then threatening punishments. One of the neighborhood boys volunteered to get her by force, but she vowed to jump and he had to make his way back down and suffer the taunts of his friends. It was Uncle Ara who had had the brilliant idea of ignoring her, and finally she climbed down at sunrise and went to bed. We were all awake; we eavesdropped on her return like thieves.

There was no *we* then, and not now either. I learned something

in Rome, the essential truth of my sister, the fundamental difference between us. Alaine did not exist in this world, but despite it.
I was superfluous, like Mummy and Daddy, like Cousin Vartan and
all the rest. She subsisted on her own nature like a wild animal,
feeding herself, teaching herself what she needed to survive. She
even learned enough Italian to watch the news on TV. She tracked
the killing of Bashir Gemayel and the Israeli invasion of Beirut, the
massacres of the Palestinians who had been left behind, the return
of the multinational peacekeepers. She gauged our moment. One
day she told Vartan, We can go home now, and she emptied the
drawers and packed our things before he'd even agreed.

The day Alaine and I were to leave, Vartan developed a headache
and lay down for an hour while we fidgeted around the house that
was already growing unfamiliar, not home, not where we should be.
When I sneaked into his bedroom his eyes opened, and he looked
through the dim light in my direction. Then he said softly, What
will become of Lebanon? but I sensed he was not really speaking
to me, so I pretended I had not heard him, that I was searching
for something. On the drive to the airport, I planted myself in the
backseat, angry because he was telling Alaine more details of our
history, about how Jiddo's daddy vowed never again to speak the
word *Turk* or any of its forms, and how people tried to trick him
into it and failed, and so he became a legend for what he wouldn't
say. Alaine listened and asked questions. I did not care about what
happened with the Turks, which had nothing to do with me. I
covered my ears, enraged.

I was so beside myself that I barely said good-bye. All I wanted
was to find our plane and get on it. Vartan stood waving for a time
as we waited in line for security, and it embarrassed me that Alaine
waved back. But the moment we passed through the gate, our return now definite, I suddenly loved him and wanted to go back. He
had been so kind to us, Vartan; he had given us gifts, a marionette
for Alaine and a silk jacket that I was supposed to grow into, and

watching Alaine make her marionette jerk across the floor, I had felt foolishly marginal, unappreciated. Longing assaulted me, to stay longer in Rome, to learn the recipes in which he had tried to awaken my interest, to go with him to all the monuments and ask questions. I whirled about, prepared to convey all of this emotion in my waving arms; but he was nowhere to be found. Come *on,* Alaine told me, and after a minute I had to obey, there was nothing left to be done. I turned my back to the crowds, and this movement, so precise it repeats itself under my skin even now, caused a flicker of emotion, a foreshadowing of what his dying would mold inside me permanently, the sense of never having paid attention, of *too late.* But on that day, walking the passage towards the waiting area, my mind and heart drifted from Vartan with the erratic merriment of youth: we were going home at last.

When we arrived, the cat prowled about Alaine resentfully, accusing her with half-closed eyes. Sitt Julie's room was empty, so Alaine at once began to move her things back in. Mummy and Daddy did not stop her, even when she put up a huge poster of Bashir Gemayel, who had been assassinated for being in cahoots with Israel, as Daddy said bitterly. Bashir Gemayel stared into the distance against a clear blue sky, promising a united Lebanon, oblivious to his own fate of dying in a bomb blast; our parents must have understood that Alaine's love for him had more to do with his being dead than with politics. They had no energy to argue anyway. They looked pale and exhausted and sad, and their questions about our trips around Rome did not interest me.

—What happened when we were gone? I demanded.

—Uncle Ara found vegetables when no one else could get them, Mummy said.

I did not see what was so thrilling about this. I knew from Alaine that the Israelis had driven down the street in tanks and crushed the parked cars, and that one of Mummy's friends had died of cancer in the middle of the siege, and that late one evening Mummy was walking home and heard Hebrew, this was how close the Israelis had been to our building. But Mummy did not want to tell me about these things.

—He went to the checkpoints, she continued, and, depending on the militia, he said he was such-and-such, a name common to the religion. Mummy started to laugh. I did not understand what was amusing about Uncle Ara in his Citroën at the checkpoint. He could have been killed.

—So they let him through, she finished. What donkeys.

—You really couldn't just go buy vegetables?

—Marianna, enough with the vegetables. Go clean your room.

—Where is Sitt Julie?

—She left.

—Why?

Mummy shook her head in despair. I don't know, she said. She just left.

—Sometimes people do things we don't understand, Daddy offered, but this wasn't enough. I peeked around Alaine's door. The tiny room was dominated by Bashir Gemayel.

—Where is Sitt Julie?

—She went crazy. Alaine was lying in bed, her thin bony body eliciting envy in me.

—How do you mean, crazy? I said.

—She thought Mummy and Daddy were planning to abandon her. So she left.

—Why would she think that?

—Because she was crazy from the bombs.

I pictured Sitt Julie walking away in her nightgown with a plastic bag, going away the same way she had come to us. No one can find her, Mummy said, and her tone made the words mean something else. But in my imagination, she walked and walked and all around her the bombs fell harmlessly, and her madness drove her to seek a ship to India. She was so crazy that when she reached the port, a ship appeared right there in the sea, and the bombs missed it, too, blasting sea fountains high up all around it. Her madness created a gangway and a steward to take her plastic bag and the ship boomed its sorrowful farewell to our bombarded city, sailed for the Suez Canal.

—In the old days, Mrs. Awad sighed, one might have taken a train to Egypt, then sailed the Red Sea to the Indian Ocean. Trains are so romantic.

—But *now,* I said impatiently. How would a person go now?

—No one goes anywhere now, Marianna. This is why you are a lucky girl, to have gone to Rome!

—We didn't want to go.

Mrs. Awad was stunned. She said, You are luckier than you can ever imagine.

Bit by bit, the stories of what had happened trickled in, from Alaine, from neighbors, from overhearing snippets of conversation late at night. I learned *phosphorus,* bombs that burned a person up on the inside, and *cluster,* bombs that blew tiny pieces everywhere shredding flesh and bone; Like a shawarma, the concierge said blandly, which made me see the commonplace sandwich with new eyes. Most of all, there was the massacre of the Palestinian families who had been left behind in the camps when the PLO soldiers left West Beirut. The grown-ups could not stop talking about this. There would be a lull in conversation, then a gravity would settle over the group. Someone would say, How could it happen, or Do you realize how many died? The shooting had gone two days without stopping. The camps, they called them, and I imagined rows of tents, but Daddy explained that the camps were buildings. I did not understand. Daddy said, They were camping there; it wasn't permanent. He sounded bitter and I felt he had lied to me somehow.

I tried to picture the camps being *closed off,* but how did they do this to an entire neighborhood? They talked and talked, and I saw towering walls built during the night while the Palestinians were sleeping, and when they woke up they were trapped. The Israelis, who had been guarding the camps, allowed in the murderous Phalange and guarded them instead, and by the time journalists and ambulances were allowed in, it was all over.

Mrs. Awad kept saying, If they build a subway, then we will know how many people died. I knew about subways from Rome, and I could see vividly the corpses flashing by, their arms and legs hanging out of the walls, yellow in the weird light. People said there were so few Palestinians left, they would never again be a threat to Israel. This was as unfathomable as the disappearance that night of the man across the street. I could not grasp how so many people could simply disappear, nor that the graves were as large as they said, large enough for subways. What made the least sense was that everyone blamed the Israelis for not stopping the killing, as if they ought to have protected the Palestinians they hated so much.

—There are supposedly laws made in Geneva, Alaine explained. She was cutting out photographs of dead people in Sabra and Chatila from the newspapers Mrs. Awad had saved. I had never heard of these laws. Alaine seemed to find the notion as unlikely as I did. I watched her scissors do their careful work.

—Can I have some? I asked, pointing at the clippings. She selected those she had doubles of and gave them to me. I examined them in the privacy of my own room. They were like the pictures that had been in newspapers ever since I could remember. I mulled them over, trying to see what was different, and I came to the two white horses fallen like dominos against a wall, their eyes closed. They could be just sleeping, but strings crisscrossed their flanks connecting a spattering of black holes, like a map of the constellations. Their legs were entwined, tails spread over the rubble. This was the only part I could really grasp, that the horses had been killed. I imagined being there at the right moment, riding one and leading the other through the gunfire, galloping to safety. The hundreds of people who had died lay strewn about us, intangible, stick figures, not to be understood. When I saw their photographs, the woman lying in the dirt, her hand gripping the identity card that said she was not Palestinian, or the dark photograph of the woman in a doorway's shadow, dress pushed up to her waist and the space below her hips smudged and grainy, as if even the camera could not look, all I could imagine was the feel of a horse galloping, darkness, shooting all around.

Mummy walks home from visiting Astrig. The summer of 1982 is drawing to a close, and the Israeli siege will soon end but she does not know this yet, so for now each day means trying to find vegetables and bread, or sitting in the hospital room mourning her dying friend who sleeps and moans, skin pale and papery. Every day thousands of bombs fall on West Beirut, and Sitt Julie wails in her room, gathering her few belongings into plastic bags, but there is nowhere to run, and when Mummy and Daddy return from the hospital they grip Sitt Julie's chicken-bone arms as she raves about the loneliness of the apartment, about how she is being left behind.

But none of this daily misery can compare to what is about to happen. This evening Mummy hurries with her shopping bags and purse, hurries because it is getting dark in a city under siege, and her heels clack on the pavement. She turns onto our street and sees a group of soldiers in the shadows, farther down. The fear makes her stiff and controlled, she must keep moving forward, ready to say who she is, what she has bought, why she is coming home so late. Their voices become more distinct as she approaches, but no matter how much closer she gets, she cannot understand, she does not know this language. In that moment before Mummy knows what this signifies, she experiences the sensation of having been lifted out of her place in the world, the strange words filling the void she has become like water rushing into an empty bottle. Then she stands before them, the Israelis, and when they ask her questions she only stares, enraged, refusing to understand the interrogation she knows so well and that is common to all soldiers. She stands before the invaders who have finally entered the streets of her city and listens to their language, and each sound, each syllable, has only one meaning.

The Israelis had driven hundreds of thousands of people from their homes, and now they lived in abandoned buildings all over Beirut. Alaine, her wrists bandaged once again, considered them from the balcony for days, sipping tea and staring like she had a plan. The day the bandages came off, she tucked her soccer ball under her arm and went downstairs. The boys watched her assault on the wall until finally she asked their names and divided them into teams. They played every day. Alaine fell into her routine and never strayed from it. She went to school, ignored everyone there, came home and went downstairs immediately, taking cookies or *fatayer* or Popsicles, whatever was on hand. They sat on the wall and ate, and their laughter drifted alluringly up to me, the spy on the balcony. I was too shy to go down with her because I couldn't play as well and because I looked so different from everyone else with my pale hair and eyes.

—They don't care, Alaine said. Don't be stupid.

But I had heard things said when I went around town, and people looked at me differently, accusingly. It was worse for Daddy, because he was a man.

—Everyone hates Americans, I said.

—They don't hate *you*, Alaine corrected. Then she got a sly, teasing look and said, They're all in love with you. They watch you at night when you undress.

This destroyed any chance I would go downstairs with her; I gave up sitting on the balcony as well. I hated them, but at the same time felt terrible because I was hating refugees. They're still boys, Mummy said. Just close your blinds. But all I could think was that they lived in a half-constructed office building without any furniture, not even blinds. This fact consumed me; I could not see them in any other way. I hated my home: the objects we owned were vulgar, and the water running from the taps, provided a few hours a day by the university, was a luxury that should not have been allowed. I felt small and mean and lazy. I wanted to help, but I didn't have money or games or boys' clothes (Alaine had already given away almost all of hers). All I had to give them was an unobstructed view of changing into my pajamas; this was the small and simple role the larger movement of saving refugees had offered me. But every night I lost my courage, I lowered the blinds with sickening self-loathing mixed up with relief. As a form of compromise, I stayed in front the evil blinds, nude, but my body's outline, if visible at all, would be nothing clear like a real woman, just a smudge.

—What can I *do?* I begged the grown-ups.

—You can help by making dolls, Mummy suggested.

Alaine had made some before she met the boys downstairs; there was ample material left over. The dolls were donated to relief organizations and driven to refugee camps. I cut out the pattern, threaded a needle. Within half an hour I gave up, I was so intimidated by Alaine's perfect example doll.

—You aren't selfish, Marianna, Daddy comforted me. Sewing is a skill.

This made me feel even more inadequate. He thought awhile, then came up with, Why don't you draw pictures for the children's wing? This enchanted me. I drew horses, houses in green fields, cedar trees and more horses. Mummy delivered them and said they looked beautiful on the walls and the children enjoyed them. A girl called Rana was brought in from the south and she loved my drawings the most. Both her legs had been blown off when she stepped on a bomb left behind by the Israelis. I lay in bed and willed myself to lose feeling in my legs. I had stepped on the bomb and everyone was feeling sorry for me. Why don't you visit, Mummy prodded me, but I was too shy, I felt stupid and guilty. Rana put in requests. A golden horse. A dog with spots. A house built on a cloud. I imagined the day I would finally visit. We were going to be friends forever, and I would be the one to push her wheelchair, even uphill. I relished these fantasies with all my soul; my selfless love infused every line and every dab of color in the pictures I made for her.

Then Rana died of complications. What complications? I asked, crying. An infection in the blood, they told me. It came on so quickly the doctors didn't even notice before it was too late.

The hospital loomed above our building, a few minutes' walk away, a gleaming white expanse with hundreds of windows, one of them Rana's but not anymore. It had been so easy for me to go, and I had not, I had instead imagined it over and over until it was the same as the act itself.

—You did what you could, said Daddy, cradling me.

—That isn't enough! I cried, and he didn't answer, he didn't try again to make me feel better. He just stared at the floor with a sad, long-ago look, and I knew then he was thinking about Uncle Jesse who had died of complications and nothing had been enough.

—Why didn't you go to Korea? I sobbed, thinking of Uncle Jesse all alone, reaching for me as I attached the miracle IV.

Daddy's face fell apart in surprise. What?

—He was all alone!

Daddy's mouth crumpled a little. He looked at me with his sad blue eyes. They said it was a flu, Marianna. That's all. A flu.

I cried harder, criminal for having awakened Daddy's sorrow. I knew I would never dream again of saving Uncle Jesse, that the craving for that life wasn't mine, but I didn't know why, and once again the awful weight of everything I didn't understand about the world sank into me. I would never grow up, never say the right things, never have any answers to any questions and I hated it, I hated it. Daddy turned my face to his, shushing at me. He waited until my sobs were piled up in my throat and I was trying to breathe, a moment of quiet.

—My brother died, he explained gently. But everybody dies.

This truth, so simple and clear, was meant to provide comfort, but it did not, it horrified me. I felt all of time itself, a hurricane sweeping life away. I saw Daddy's face with its quizzical smile vanish, and me and Alaine, and Mummy, and Uncle Ara and Astrig and everyone else, we were all dying and now other people sat in my bedroom, living and breathing, and then they died, and someone else walked in, dying, and there was no meaning to anything at all.

◈

In my nightmares the mutilated horses pass in an open truck, heaped over each other, their eyes gouged and hooves cut off, leaving only bones with shreds of flesh and the dark circle of marrow. In the second truck the horses are still alive, tied together with rope and their black eyes fixed on me, heads all turned to look back, and I scream and bang on the car windows, making no sound. Far away is a hill where Ziad waits on his white horse, and his robes swirl as the horse tramples circles, neck arched and dark smudges of sweat on its chest and flanks. The trucks draws closer and he throws his arm up, waves circles in the air to signal *Hurry,* and the trucks thunder up the white chalk road in a storm of dust, obscuring him from view.

Alaine makes me go outside with her so we can talk in private while she arranges bricks around her garden. She wants to convince me of what she knows to be true. He died cleaning his gun, she insists. My worrying about the truth is pointless, because she knows it, and all I had to do was ask.

I cannot believe she is talking to me about this. I get suspicious.
—Did they make you?
Alaine has the look of someone found out. She tries to cover it up with irritation. She snaps, Mummy's worried you think he committed suicide.
I flash to the image of Mummy whispering her fears to Alaine. It make me feel important and sad at the same time. He didn't, I say. It was Russian Roulette.
Alaine scoffs, even when she finds out the story came from Astrig.

She is secure in her version, and Ziad sits on the edge of his bed, peering into the barrel of a shotgun, one eye squeezed shut, an oily rag in his hand. The apartment is small, a few rooms, furnished with the same kind of furniture that was in the barn. He pulls the trigger, just to hear the click.

—It's impossible, I repeat. How can someone so experienced make such a stupid mistake?

—And Russian Roulette is what? You can't play Russian Roulette with a clip, anyway, she adds.

Some moments pass as I absorb this illogical resistance. Alaine jams bricks into the dirt. She is dangerously close to upset; for an instant, I glimpse the old Alaine, the pinched-up face and furious eyes. It frightens me, but I don't want to give in.

—He must have had a revolver, I suggest carefully.

—He didn't.

I argue, but she is resolute. She knows what kind of gun he owned. But how? She just knows.

—What's so special about him anyway? she demands. He wasn't that interesting.

She says this terrible thing with simple confidence, a fact as obvious as the temperature or the color of the sky. She tamps down the earth alongside the bricks, and I see Ziad lounging in a chair next to the grill, rewinding his Walkman. He grins when I tell him my favorite band is Supertramp. Supertramp, he agrees, is great, and my love for him balloons with new hope. You want a tape? I ask, but he tells me he already has them all, gives me the Walkman so I can listen. All I hear is my own breathing, staring down at my knees pretending to focus on the lyrics, transported by the feel of earphones that moments ago lay against his ears. My chest hurts remembering.

—What's important is no one knows for sure how he died, I tell her.

She doesn't notice I'm upset, or pretends not to. Well, she says, he didn't have a revolver.

I give in. There is no way to convey how things happened unless one was there. And even then, things get distorted, perhaps even more so. Maybe he did not play this reckless game. Maybe it was as she said, he was cleaning the gun. I rock on my heels, watching her work. In the past weeks I have seen her hands churning through the dark earth, I have had worms thrown at me for being so lazy, I have been amazed by her ability to make this a beautiful place. The rocks and red bricks now almost enclose the flower garden, lodged in so carefully one by one, forming a jagged miniature wall.

—I want to leave America, I say. I could go back to Rome.

I know that Vartan's apartment is still as he left it when he died, that someone is needed to organize his things into boxes for shipping to Beirut.

—Why would Astrig let you?

I have not considered this possibility. The notion of my going back and performing this important task has been with me since we heard he died, and it became so real that I forgot others are involved.

Alaine makes a huffing noise at my disappointment. They'll never let you go now, anyway.

She says *now* with finality, evoking hospital bed, the ride home in the taxi, my face turned to the hot summer wind. She looks up from her patch of American land. A clump of earth sticks to her jeans, and her dark, curly hair is tied into a bun with a piece of cloth.

—Can you just explain your problem? she says.

It takes time for her question to sink in. She looks patient, serious, ready to take on whatever has been haunting me. This is my only chance, here under this gray sky, the cold ground numbing my knees.

—Nobody remembers, I say. And if they do, it's always a different version.

My pronouncement does not have great effect. Alaine purses her lips, considering her garden design. Then she says, Nobody wants to think about that kind of thing.

—Why?

—Because it's not important. Now's important.

—But now is coming from somewhere.

She does not answer. The awful words form inside me, and I speak them before I can help it.

—Nobody believed you about the body. Nobody remembers it.

Her face becomes a mask. It stares at me for a time. Her face says, It was half-decomposed. I buried it with my hands.

—I know. And then I tell her, as if to explain: *I* remember.

—So?

There is nothing to say but *Sorry,* and my mouth can't form the little word, so useless. I stay with her, rocking back on my heels and holding my knees, while my sister's hands clear her garden, tossing out fallen leaves and other debris. Underneath, the tulip bulbs wait in their dark holes. She is counting on them all the way from now, from the end of October. She says they're for me, to see from our window next spring. She can see below the surface, even after the trowels and empty seed packets have all been carried away. To me, the ground looks empty. From my window, this patch of ground looks like a brown rectangle, nothing more, and my footprints trace its rock and brick boundary, single-file.

What matters, I should have told her, is to know exactly what happened, from the first moment of one's life until the present, because without that, a person can't live. There has to be truth, or else we flounder, grasping at air, suspended by nothing and on our way nowhere. It is too late now. I can't explain what I meant. She won't talk again and she won't listen; I know my sister, she's caged herself in silence no one can break.

There is the last time I saw Ziad. It was a summer afternoon, I was watching Alaine from the balcony as she trained with the Civil Defense in the empty lot behind our building. He was a mirage, Ziad, in white shirt and jeans, a cowboy hat on his head, climbing out of the old blue Renault. I could not believe this thrilling fortune, dropped into my life so unexpectedly. I flattened myself on the balcony floor so he wouldn't catch sight of me. He disappeared into our building. I ran to the bathroom and stared desperately at myself in the mirror. My blotched red-skinned face was horrible.

But there was no time to make myself beautiful. Mummy's greeting carried to me: Look at you! she exclaimed. You shouldn't be driving around now!

I peeped at them from the hall. Ziad was handing her a plastic bag. From Ara, he said. He's staying.

—He cannot, Mummy said.

Ziad shrugged. He won't leave the house.

Mummy stared into the bag. She did not take anything out, just tied the handles again. She said, I don't want vegetables. I want him in Beirut. Does Astrig know he won't leave?

—I haven't spoken with her yet.

—When the Israelis go, the mountains will turn to hell.

—The house could be robbed.

—Fuck the house! Mummy shouted.

I had never heard such a word come out of my mother's mouth. Ziad just looked down. She stood there clutching the bag. Then she carried the bag to the kitchen. When she returned, she asked if Ziad wanted anything to drink and he said no, which increased my anxiety because it meant he would leave soon. He filled up our living room like a god. His black hair had grown out to shoulder-length and he was still wearing the same copper bracelet. Who had given him this bracelet?

—Marianna, I see you, he winked in my direction, and I was forced out of hiding. I edged into the room step by tremulous step.

—Hi, I said stupidly. The last word I ever spoke to him, my head tilted shyly away. Scent of aftershave and sweat and cigarettes. For days after I wandered surreptitiously through the space he had occupied, breathing deeply, longing.

—I'm in Beirut for a week, he grinned. Want to come to a party at the beach club?

Mummy frowned. She said, Marianna is too young for such things.

I retorted, No I'm not, but Ziad was already answering her. His words burned up my face and made me want to shrivel to nothing:

—I know, he said. I was only joking.

Then he looked at me, registering my outburst. Well, he said awkwardly, and under Mummy's stern gaze he turned sheepish. I'd better leave.

I do not know if he looked back; I kept my eyes on the floor till I heard the door slam. Then I turned on Mummy

—I hate you!

—Don't be silly, Marianna!

—You'd let Alaine go!

No, I would not! Mummy raised her finger in warning that I hold my tongue.

—You let her with Michel! I screamed, and before she could react at all I tore down the hall to my room, slammed the door, and barricaded it with a chair. Mummy's heels clacked in the hall, then she pounded on the door.

—You come out of there, Marianna!

I was already at the window, though, watching Ziad talk to some of the Civil Defense workers Alaine was training with. He hefted a handgun, examined it this way and that, holding it up. He seemed to approve of it. Alaine stood nearby with her hands on her hips. He touched her shoulder in farewell and she nodded at something he said. I wanted to kill her. I looked for something to throw.

—Marianna, come out NOW!

I shoved the chair aside so hard it fell over with a crash. The door flew open and Mummy tumbled into the room, her weight carrying her straight into my hanging plants. She grasped at the macramé tassel for balance. The whole thing crashed down from the ceiling. Mummy stared at the mess of clay and dirt and vine, the milky roots prodded out into the light.

—We did not know about Michel, she said in a low voice.

—I don't care! I retorted. Get out!

—Get the broom. She made it sound like if I didn't go at once, the building would collapse all around us. She glared down at me, clutching the bottom tassel of the macramé, and I saw a trickle of blood on her hand. Instead of obeying, I hurried to the window. He was getting in his car. I heard the door, the engine. The car pulled out. I saw his legs through the windshield, one hand on the steering wheel, the other tapping a cigarette out of the box. The car went out of my view.

That was it, the last time I ever saw him.

I lie on the floor because that's where I think he died, on a floor, no matter whether he was cleaning the gun or someone rang the bell or the betting table piled up with dirty bills, his friends standing around, waiting. Maybe Alaine is right. Maybe he was not interesting, just a young man dreaming big dreams, none about me. But his long-ago features drift against the surface of memory, sometimes pressing through, a glimpse, swiftly retreated, and it leaves me in tears. I am the one who remembers, and my memory fails me, over and over. Nothing is true. I look for someone, anyone. Amer: if I try hard enough, I can feel his face inside my hands, but my hands go cold in this cold house, they look foolish holding air. He is gone.

It is nighttime in Beirut now. Amer shifts in his sleep, the moonlit sheets kicked off. I close my eyes. He is dreaming of Jamil. If we both dream him, he will return from wherever he went. He will be full of sun, he'll take his jacket, laugh, and shrug it on. Amer will press me forward, *This is Anna,* and Jamil-full-of-sun says, *I remember you from the dreams in which I died.* He squints a smile, amused, bemused, and his hands touch his own body with new uncertainty, looking for the truth.

Daddy comes in, he tells me, We're all going, honey. It's a family outing.

Mummy and Alaine must have decided to use him as bearer of

this bad news because they know I cannot bear to disappoint him. I hear them talking in the living room. Dusk has fallen, and they're exclaiming over the wine Mummy bought as a special treat.

I say, Can I have a drink? Just one?

I am not supposed to drink because of the medication. Daddy struggles with my compromise, decides it isn't too great a price to pay. I get up. Groups of children chatter their way up the street; they are taken out just as dark falls because of the many dangers we have heard warnings of on TV; roaming, mischievous youths, devil-worshippers who kill cats and might be looking to take a child this year. There is danger in the candy, too, and parents have been urged all week by anxious news reporters to check each piece for razor blades or any sort of tampering. Our light is off, signaling no candy here. Mummy said, We cannot afford to feed the world, and yet now she seems to have been swept up by things, drinking wine and waiting excitedly to see her older daughter's costume, which Alaine is putting on in the basement, maintaining secrecy until the last moment. I pour a glass and go back into my room. The old sheet Alaine used as a drop cloth is folded in the closet. I shake it out, snip eyeholes. I drink the wine in one long gulp. The sheet drapes over me, smelling of paint.

—I can't believe you're making me do this, I say to anyone who will listen. My breaths waft the sheet back and forth against my face.

Mummy and Daddy, disguised as themselves, ignore me. They are staring at my sister, who emerges from the basement like some mythical creature, draped in feathers dyed brilliant colors and a feathered mask that floats gently on the air when she walks. She opens her arms in silent, ominous greeting. A feather drifts to the floor.

—What are you? Mummy asks, fear in her voice.

After a moment, Alaine says disappointedly, A bird!

—Oh, yes, Mummy and Daddy say in relief.

What could they have imagined she was? For years Alaine had so many secrets, they dread another sewn into a feather costume, some message about herself they cannot read. The feathers smell of dye and glue, and Alaine's black eyes glare through the mask at my poorly designed sheet. I am a failure before her magnificent effort.

—I didn't want to go anyway.

—I need string, Alaine retorts, and our parents rush to obey the orchestrator of our night out. We wait in the doorway.

—Why a bird? I ask.

—Because I found an old stole at the Salvation Army.

Her lips moving below the mask unnerve me. I look down. Mummy cuts the string and Alaine bunches the sheet, loops the string around me several times like a belt. The heat from my breathing settles on my face, itching. The string is too tight. My parents say, Everyone ready? I hobble forward, part of the sheet caught under one foot. Alaine tugs it up, stuffs it into my string belt. *I can't breathe,* I want to complain, but now I'm thinking of the traitor who was shot on television just a few months before we left Lebanon; he didn't even have eyeholes, and my discomfort shows itself to be frivolous, as usual, poor Marianna. The soldiers dragged a large white bundle tied with rope to a mound and Mummy said, Oh my God, the words welling up from her chest. Don't look, she said, but I had to, and the top of the bundle moved as if the man inside was turning his head from side to side and there was no sound, only static. The man squirmed around weakly then gave up, hunched into the shape of an S for a moment before he jolted from the bullets and toppled, and soldiers rushed forward, filling the screen.

—What's the matter? Mummy asks, poking at the sheet.

—Nothing.

—You can't bring that, Alaine tells Mummy, and Mummy looks down at her glass in disappointment.

—But we aren't going far, she says.

—It's illegal in America. You could go to jail.

—All right, Daddy says cheerily. Off we go!

Alaine closes the door and our family sets out on our quest. I am the ghost of the man who was executed. I move up the sidewalk, showing him America, the glowing faces lighting stairwells, the children squealing as they run. *This is insane,* the man whispers. *I know,* I comfort him.

—Isn't this fun? Daddy inquires, looking back at me.

I nod under the sheet. Ye-ee-ee-sss, I moan, ghost language, and Mummy smiles, too, pleased that I am getting into the spirit of things. We aren't out to trick-or-treat, just to walk, a family outing. She puts her arm through Daddy's, and her smile is fragile under the streetlamp's passing glow. I feel pain in my chest, I am the traitor, a liar poisoning their efforts to enjoy this evening. *Just try,* I tell myself. I keep placing one foot ahead of the other, my eyes on their backs. Alaine leads the way; I pick up a feather, then let it slip from my fingers. One foot, then the other. The night is full of children and proud parents and burning lights. Electronic skeletons cackle and glow, screeching witches teeter on brooms. Alaine's costume is gaining attention. The rest of us stand back while she is admired by children and adults alike. No one looks at me because I am a ghost. They can't see me. I shuddered on the floor, the body battling the spirit's crime like a faithful old engine. There was nothing it could do. The wood spread through with tears. I actually died. This is all fiction, my way of clinging to the life I want after all. Marianna, can't you just decide? Marianna, just pick one and finish! But I hold everything close to my eye, I fall in love with it a little, it tears me up to choose. Clothes, menus, movies, it's always the same and once I have it, I think of what I might have had instead. *I don't think I was meant to die,* I confess, but no one can hear me. My body has gone numb; I grope for a sense of my arms, legs but get only a vague impression. It is true, then. Alaine revolves down the sidewalk, waving her arms in slow arcs to make the children nervous. Mummy and Daddy gaze upon her with pride. Then they catch sight of their younger daughter, the dead one, lagging behind.

—Come on, darling, they urge.

—I can't, my voice whispers. *Because I'm dead and no one told me,* but already the thought is losing power. My feet are chilled inside my shoes because I couldn't be bothered to put on socks; not the dilemma of a ghost. Mummy's smile is gone. I can't, my voice repeats, much louder.

I can't make my body do what it does not want; I know this feeling, helpless, trapped in the body that rushes on its own trajectory, feet full of fire and hatred, I hate myself, I run and run. When Mummy catches up, breathless, I am huddled by the front door under my sheet, looking at white because the eyeholes slipped. She doesn't say a word, just opens up and lets me in. I go straight to my room. *You could have kept going,* I accuse myself, enraged. *Tried harder.* It's too late. The body's melted down now, tired of its own pretenses, so tired and guilty it can barely crawl its way to its favorite place on the floor. Its mother drinks wine in the doorway, one arm folded across her belly, her face white and drained of all emotion, just a person having a drink in a doorway, as if nothing ever happened and nothing ever will.

—I'm sick of this, Alaine mutters. She's throwing my clothes off the bed. The feather costume lies crumpled on the floor. I must have slept. A shirt lands on my face. What's this? How long's it been lying there? She kicks the bed frame. Once. Twice. I remember her kicking the soccer ball downstairs against the wall, over and over. Her whole body taut with rage. Her arms run with blue dye from the feathers. She is angry about everything to do with me: me staying in bed, me never helping, me crying. I know her rage.

—You did this for years! I scream.

This stops her. This brings quiet.

I am tired of causing such silences in my family. As if I alone hold the correct answer, can flip the right card over, can blow open the safe. I am the cause, I realize, of everyone's frustration, because I cannot just shut up. I imagine thread tugging through my lips, looping around until I am sealed. *Shut me up,* I want to say.

—You know, I hardly remember anything, Alaine spits at me. She slumps down on the edge of the bed, holding herself. I don't want to look at her because that would imply I'm listening, but after a time, curiosity gains my stubborness, and I peek through my hands.

She is rocking, rocking the way she used to, her face stretched with anguish, and I stare from the floor, paralyzed by this vision of my grief-stricken sister, so familiar, the face of my childhood, the Alaine I know. I do not want to look. I do not want to know this. She is her old self, still, but in secret. How have I been so blind? It was always like this. Alaine, hiding, full of secrets, while Marianna spun through the days with her arms thrown out and mouth wide open, telling all. Alaine squeezes herself harder, drawing her legs in and up and locking her head so tight between knees and chest that her thin white neck might snap. She is depriving the old self of air and light, suffocating it out of existence. It is almost gone. This is what she has been doing, methodically crushing herself, creating the new Alaine as she did in Rome. I think of all the times she is alone, in the garden, the basement, making things, fixing the house. All that work.

—You used to do this all the time, I tell her, because I don't know what else to say.

—I don't remember, she says viciously through her tangle of arms and legs. And I don't want to.

Alaine's arms, slender, scarred. Her neck, also, scarred under the ears. How can she clothe herself without seeing her own body? How does she look in a mirror and not remember?

—There is no need to, Mummy tells me. Many people go through their whole life just living from one experience to the next, and never putting it all together.

—They must be really stupid, I reply.

Mummy looks wan; she has lost weight and doesn't sleep well. I don't know why I cannot prevent cruelty from edging into anything I say to her. I gaze at her out of my body's prison, begging for forgiveness. She avoids me. She cares for me perfunctorily and with wariness.

I watch Alaine. I cannot stop watching her. I am the carrier of her memories, and they haunt me, they surface from every expression in her eyes or shift of her hands, linking me to her, explaining me, who I have become. I am astonished by her hands. They wind over each other under a stream of water in this aluminum American sink, the dirt from our garden swirling into the drain. She has finished planting and enclosing and clearing. She has finished preparing our garden for spring with the resolute trust that spring will come. Her hands, I understand this now, have always been reaching into the earth and leaving treasures there.

꒜

Alaine played soccer with the refugees, she traded bullets and shrapnel around the neighborhood, she smashed her fists through the bathroom window and tried to climb out. Daddy shouted for help, and I was the one who got there first, hung onto her legs with all my weight while he pried her fists loose from the jaggedy window frame. The doctor said, She will always have trouble with this finger, and he held Alaine's hand aloft like evidence.

But Alaine's hands regained their strength. She stood in front of the mirror and cut off all her hair again so that Mummy had to take her to the barber to have it done right. She trained with the Civil Defense, though at sixteen she was too young to be more than an honorary member. Why don't you take your sister? our parents urged, and I hung my head, said I didn't want to go anyway. Her fellows caught sight of me on the balcony, however, and saw the potential. After that I played their victim, screaming hysterically in windows, clinging to my rescuer as he rappelled down the side of the building, but there were many days when I was not called upon, and I lounged on the balcony, peeking through the rails at Alaine coiling ropes, doing jumping jacks and running, administering CPR.

Then French peacekeeping forces occupied the building behind ours, forcing the Civil Defense to train elsewhere. Alaine kicked her ball around disconsolately for a few days, until the French soldiers joined in, three on three. She darted amongst them like a fly, her hair cropped like a boy's. They gazed at her in admiration, and I imagined my eyes could launch missiles to blow her right up. They paused in the game, wiped their necks and faces with T-shirts. *Mais pourquoi toi tu ne descends pas?* one of them yelled up, grinning. I shrugged disinterest at his invitation, flounced back inside to listen to music. Maybe they would find her stash of food and weapons; they were bivouacked right on top of it, after all. Then she would get into so much trouble. I played the possible scenarios out in my mind, wicked vengeance.

Daddy found an unfamiliar grenade on Alaine's shelf, shaped like a tube. I seized this opportunity to ruin her life. She got it from them, I lied, nodding at the French barracks.

He went up to the two soldiers on duty. Did you give this to my daughter? he fumed in his terrible French.

—No, sir, the soldier said. They looked troubled. One of them held out his hand.

—Now *you* want it? Daddy said irrationally.

—It hasn't exploded.

For a moment they all just stood there. Then Daddy handed over the grenade. Sorry, he said, and I was embarrassed by the way they shook their heads when he turned around.

—Why do you keep interfering? Alaine screamed at Daddy. I hate you!

It was around that time that Alaine took a bottle of pills. I do not know what they were called, but they drove her mad with terror. She stayed awake for three days, because she thought if she slept, she would die, and she kept shouting that she didn't want to, she didn't mean to. The stench of her sweat filled the room, and whenever Alaine allowed it, Mummy cleaned her face and neck and armpits with a washcloth. I'm cold, she kept mumbling. I'm hot. The cat lay beside her, purring obliviously while she trembled and sweated and whispered. Go to sleep, Mummy begged her. It will be all right, the doctor said. But there was no convincing her. Mummy and Daddy divided the watch, and

Uncle Bernie stayed over so he could help. There was no need for me. I retreated to my room.

The idea had lived inside me for so long, through nights of my ear pressed to Alaine's door, through nights of folding sodden bandages into the garbage. It was familiar as my own name. There was the dead soldier, whose gas mask sat on Alaine's shelf; there was Alaine's persistent misery; there was Mummy sobbing in the night and the clinking ice in Daddy's whiskey as he made his way from the kitchen to his chair; there was the question mark made by my fingernail digging into the soft, white place between veins on my wrist.

There was the day the American Embassy blew up. The top windowpane moved. In the heartbeat of time, I saw the glass bulge inward, an optical miracle only just filling me with surprise before the glass yielded to the pressure of sound, shattered into the room. Ba-boom, the bomb roared, and the building shuddered. Minutes passed. I picked up my magazine and held it so the glass slid off. I looked at my bare feet. Blood trickled down my thigh and I touched it with my fingertip. I felt no pain. Perhaps this is how the bright idea beckoned me, that old friend, with the promise that there wouldn't be pain.

Mummy arrived in the doorway, and when she saw me, she collapsed against the doorjamb in relief, hands pressed to her belly. I thought, *What is wrong with me, I should have screamed.* I jumped up, to show fear, because now she was looking at me strangely but she cried out, No, don't walk in the glass! She left me there crinkling my toes, rushed away to find my shoes.

Hours passed. The ambulances came in and out of the hospital down the street, and then there was shooting. A jeep, the driver shooting in the air to make a car move out of the way. In the backseat, two men propped another in between, and his head rolled from side to side, making cries, Aah, aah. Hurry, someone shouted, the out-of-place word in English, so I realized they were American. The jeep reeled around the corner to the hospital entrance. I stood at the window a long time. It was as if everything I had always heard happening outside had just been confirmed, and there was a certain security in that.

Alaine came home several hours later. She had been there. She told me, The bomb was so strong, the bodies flew across the road into the sea.

She was ashamed that the Civil Defense workers had not allowed her to help. I imagined the bodies floating away as rescue workers waded after them, yelling back at Alaine to stay where she was; all this while I had been standing at the window so impotently. I couldn't help feeling glad she had been turned away, that she was in trouble for not having come straight home.

A heavy stillness lay around the ruins of the embassy, the same stillness that could be felt elsewhere in the city, of things meant to be hidden now laid bare. The back of the building stood intact, but in front, the floors drooped in layers down to the ground where the rubble had been partly cleared away. It was like looking through the window of a giant dollhouse, but a desk hung precariously off a shorn floor, a toilet tilted in the shadows, farther in, still attached to the wall, while the sink was lodged on a slab of loose tiles that slithered farther down every time it rained.

The great silver ships of the American soldiers lay offshore, moving imperceptibly through the sea, so that one day they were here, the next day there, and no one knew when they had moved. Smaller boats cut white frothy trails back and forth between the shore and the ships. Beirut waited in this lull, and the foreign soldiers threw flowers at girls, gave them photographs and presents, they marched confidently through the streets.

—They are only containing what is bound to come, Mrs. Awad proclaimed, and Mummy agreed in that way of hers, the wise, slow nodding. I understood from this that Lebanon was like a stunned beast, netted and charmed temporarily by these handsome, pale soldiers, and it was only a matter of time before this beast would awaken. I felt a strange kinship to these men who had no idea what people were saying. I wanted to save them. But I was useless, a small, angry girl with curling blond hair and no courage, not like Alaine. The anger festered inside me, only increased by the long days spent indoors for the bombing and shooting once the Druze and the army started fighting. I sipped Daddy's whiskeys when he wasn't looking, then I made my own and sneaked them into my room. I wrote a serialized novel about myself in which I was a resistance fighter with an army of my own. *You must leave,* I told the foreign soldiers in clandestine meetings punctuated by the scratching of rats in the garbage, the occasional gunshot that made us all pause and concentrate on the sky. *You're only containing what's bound to come,* I informed them, hoisting my machine gun over my shoulder. *Help us,* they begged, and I led them through the myriad dangers of my territory, and they admired me. One of them became my lover, but it was around this time that Ziad came to our house with the news about Uncle Ara. The soldier was killed off in a firefight, and Ziad entered the story as a spy sent to infiltrate my army, but who turned double agent out of love for me.

—What are you writing? Mummy asked, flipping through one of my notebooks. I stared at her in dismay. She caught my mood, gave me the notebook with a smile. I know about being a writer, she said gently, and for the rest of the day she brooded over a small notebook of fairy tales her best friend Muna had written when they were young. I read the stories in secret, gazed at the photograph pasted in the front. She had been tragically killed, and I wanted to be just like her, remembered with sorrow and regret.

The novel twisted in a new direction. *I have to do it,* I shouted, wrenching myself away from Ziad. *No, no!* he cried, but I ran into the hail of bullets, sacrificing myself so that he might live.

Even though there was fighting all the time, school started again, and I skipped classes to write in my notebooks in the café next to the school. School's boring, I told Mummy and Daddy. They tried threats, but they had no ammunition; I had no hobbies to be banned from, and after school I stayed in my room anyway. They cajoled and begged, which worked for a time, because I disliked being the cause of their worries, and then they tried to enlist Alaine's help, but she refused, saying she had no influence over me, and this made me feel good. You hardly have to go anyway because of the fighting, Daddy attempted to reason, but the café lured me from the dreary routine of school and my fellow students. I wasn't the only one who skipped; I had an ally in the senior Marko, who was Greek and older than everyone else, almost twenty, because he had missed a year of school after a motorcycle accident. We did not speak, but acknowledged one another in the café, in the halls, during the numerous detentions that had no effect on our behavior at all. He played pinball while I wrote, and we took cigarettes from each other without asking.

He had the highest scores ever recorded on the pinball machine; he even left free games that he had won for others to play, this was how much he won. He could play for hours without pause. I knew this because I stayed longer and longer, and Ghada, who ran the café, grudgingly let me know if a teacher was coming.

Marko's right hand was almost useless, I supposed because of the accident. The hand dangled against the side of the machine, and he used the heel of his thumb to push the flipper button. The hand was thin and white with a faint scar that began somewhere near the knuckles and traveled up under the cuff of his shirt. I could not understand how the doctors had managed to sew his hand back together and yet leave it so lifeless.

In addition to being older, Marko was taller than any of the other seniors, and he wore round shaded glasses like John Lennon. He did not seem to take care of himself and smelled sickly. He always wore long-sleeved shirts. I had read that people who are depressed wear a lot of clothes, because they are frozen with sadness, and certainly Alaine had hidden under her blankets for years. I suspected that the accident was the root of his sadness, the long-sleeved shirts and pallid skin, because he hadn't been the only one on the bike.

His friend had been riding behind and was killed, and I could not see how someone could recover from that, from killing a friend by going too fast.

A commotion outside stirred my attention from Marko. Two French jeeps had parked across the street, and the soldiers were unloading. Ghada, smoking her *argileh* behind the counter (Have some, she always taunted the younger students, who thought it was hashish), noticed the trucks and hurried to stand in the doorway as enticement. Her fat arms waddled as she patted her dyed hair, then she placed one fist on her hip, and arranged herself into a stance I imagined a prostitute might use. I was ashamed that Ghada shouted so loudly, *Venez! Entrez!* but she was in acute competition with the store across the street.

One of the soldiers smiled at me as they filed in. They seemed a little awkward, and I supposed it would be the same for those American soldiers on duty by the Embassy, if they were trapped here without the protection of their barbed wire and tanks. No matter how friendly everyone appeared, these foreign soldiers could never know who might begin shooting. They bought Pepsis and Mirandas, then grouped around Marko, who nodded at them while he lit a cigarette. I could see his score from my seat, and it was in the hundred thousands. He drew back the exploder, as I called it, slowly, to its maximum tension, and froze, concentrating on the miniature world of lights and pathways and targets under the glass. He went over his plan, looking for trip wires, blinking challenges. The soldiers paused with him, one with his drink halfway to his lips, the other holding a cigarette and lighter, waiting. The long pause grew longer, and it seemed that I was witnessing a pocket of time within the clanging and talking noises of the café, something separate, a sign. I did not breathe, I, all of us, were on the brink of something greater than Marko's free game, and his hesitation was an unwillingness to unleash it, as if he held in his hand the taut bowstring, the almost-there trigger, but it was inevitable, he had to let go, it was a matter of time. And beyond the happening of it, there were those of us who watched it, like me, and those who were a part of it, like the soldiers and Marko, and those who were innocent and continuing about their day, eating, drinking, chatting.

He let go. The ball jettisoned with such force that it cracked into the glass before speeding on into its violent world. The soldiers eased their way around Marko, chuckling, lighting cigarette, drinking, and leaned on the other machine, which was broken again. They stole respectful glances at Marko, and at first I thought it was because he was such a good player, never tilted though he banged that machine around like he could break it, but then I realized they were looking at his scars. They must have thought he had been wounded in the war.

—Why aren't you going to school? Astrig shouted. Do we need this now, at such a time?

—School's stupid, I said, secure that she wouldn't pursue this with the other important matters on her mind. She was furious because Uncle Ara was still in the mountains, and no one could make him come down. The whole world knew the fighting between the Druze and Christians would explode into a war once Israel pulled out, which could happen any day. But Uncle Ara said he wouldn't leave his house and garden unless he was in a coffin. Astrig adjusted the collar of her silk shirt; she had taken to wearing the clothes from her boutique because less and less people were buying things in this endless war. She looked at me with narrowed eyes.

—You can't force me, I cut her off.

—You see how she talks? Mrs. Awad moaned, as if I were her own daughter. She has turned into a *shitaneh!*

—If you fail, it will be your responsibility, said Daddy. This was his latest speech, repeated daily. He had been trying this with Alaine for years, and she was just scraping by, so maybe he thought it would work with me. I shrugged. I wanted to fail. I wanted to get my own apartment and write books and have French lovers.

—Alaine goes to school, said Mrs. Awad.

—She didn't always, I pointed out.

—But that wasn't good.

This was such a weak argument that I did not bother answering. Astrig had lost interest in my behavior, anyway, and the talk returned to Uncle Ara.

—He has an old Kalashnikov, Astrig told Mrs. Awad, who did not yet know all the stories coming to us from Shemlan. The Israelis came and he pointed it at them. What are you doing? the Israeli commander yelled. Are you crazy? Get out of here! We can't protect you! So what does Ara, my stupid father, say?

—What?

—He says, Please, Mr. Commander, don't worry about *me*. Would you like some tomatoes? No? Please, if *you* need anything, you know where I am. The Israelis, they're so stupid, they think he's a crazy old man so they leave him alone. They don't understand that he's mocking them!

—He should leave, though, said Mrs. Awad, dampening everyone's mood.

I did not care about the Druze and the Christians massacring each other, and what Jumblatt said and what Gemayel said. I supposed Uncle Ara would come down to us at the last minute, so I did not think about him, and I persisted in not caring even though my nonchalance tasted false, with a trace of something desperate. But there wasn't anyone to discuss this with. The grown-ups walked about with despair all over their faces, taking Alaine to the doctor, feeding her pills, begging her to speak. She controlled the daily motion of our household, whether Mummy went for her volunteer work or not, whether Daddy went to the library, whether the psychiatrist would come to us or they go to him, escorting her like a prisoner. The Israelis left, the mountain war began, but we still had to go to school. I played Marko's pinball machine when he wasn't there; the times he came in, I ceded my place without complaint, sat on a chair next to the window with my knees drawn up to my chin. At last the principal himself came to punish me. He forced me back to the office, lectured me on attendance and responsibility while I stared resolutely at the carpet.

—Why, Marianna? he asked despairingly. This is your freshman year. Do you want to start it like this?

—Obviously.

—Why are you imitating your sister?

It's not imitating, I snarled in my mind.

It was as if he heard me. He tilted his head, waiting for me to speak. I thought then I might say, *I want to die.* The words popped into my head like a bit of nothing. I did not know what they meant. I felt tiny and tremulous, verging on childhood. A rush of gentle memories assaulted me: Mummy dressing Alaine and me in front of the fireplace; Téta humming as she swept the cottage walkway; the mess of Jiddo's drawer, my hands groping through Persian prints in search of sweets. The noise of bombs interrupted whatever punishment the principal was devising for me. The door opened and one of the teachers poked her head into the room.

—It's too close, in Khaldeh. I've told everyone to go home.

She ran off. Bombs thundered in the distance, mingled with the chatter of students filling the hallways. The principal sighed. He stared at me with his sagging brown eyes, hands folded on his desk. He resembled some hulking creature perched on the edge of extinction and no longer willing to put up a fight. The door rattled, a student evidently fallen against it. Laughter followed. A teacher shouted, There is no need to go home! The fighting won't come here! but the noise grew just the same. I wondered where the Israelis had reached, and who was bombing who. I thought of Uncle Ara in his house, Astrig yelling at him. She had gone up to join him the week before, saying she would not leave her father on his own.

—You had best find your sister, the principal said.

—She could find me, I countered.

He just smiled a little and shook his head. Find each other, he said.

I got up, the good younger sister, the strong one, the happy one.

I left the school without my books. I walked through the university campus and made my way into a bit of wood. A wildness thrashed about inside me; with every step my head hurt more, my limbs ached from some kind of pain whose source lay just below my ribs, right in the center of me, and I walked with my fists jammed against the place like it could explode. I wanted to cry, but I did not. In the thick privacy of the foliage, while the Druze militias shelled the Lebanese army at Khaldeh, I pressed the razor blade to my wrist, gasping at the swift pain. I waited. The pain was followed by something deeper, a hurt deep inside the flesh seeping out in a thin stream of blood. It congealed almost at once, the cut superficial, nothing like the things Alaine did to herself; but it promised more, something craved. Now a calm draped over me, muting the wildness, pushing it farther inside until it was a mere pinpoint of light, and I sat still for a time. Then I made my way home, borne by this awful calm, and my body was weak and powerful at once, laden with guilt and transformed by awe.

At the door I paused to gather my sleeve into my fist, hiding the scratches, but no one looked my way. Hello, I said, and they answered, Good, you're home, and I slipped back into the household without any trouble.

—They're using the ships, Mummy cried out in anger. What right do they have?

—Typical, typical, Mrs. Awad bitterly shook her head. America always wants to crush the East! Look at Vietnam!

—This is hardly Vietnam, said Daddy, but he was embarrassed. The war, as the grown-ups took to saying dispiritedly, had changed its character, as if it were a person that others had grudgingly accepted but was now displaying ugly traits that couldn't be ignored. The Americans were to blame, because they chose to help the Christians, who were fighting the Muslim militias in the moutains, who were being supplied by the Russians. In the middle of it all,

Uncle Ara and Astrig and Ziad were either dead or alive, no one knew. The war shifted, adapted, feeding on the new alliances.

I hated them. I hated the foreign soldiers, the Americans most of all, and I was ashamed of Daddy's American eyes and hair and skin, which had so sickeningly repeated themselves in me. I passed the days indoors, pale as a mouse, my hair long and stringy. Come out, Mummy cajoled, but when I walked on the street, I felt everyone staring at me, despising me for making the bombs falling on the mountains. I am from here, too, I wanted to say. An evil, helpless desire grew in me; maybe Uncle Ara and Astrig would die, to prove me on the Lebanese side once and for all. I could not believe I was thinking such a thing, but I did, and the thought did not go away but pestered me unceasingly with detailed images of hearing the terrible news, the weeping, the funeral, the pity of it all. I asked after them daily to counteract the malignant thoughts, but there was no news from the mountains, they were cut off from the world.

After the bombing of their embassy, the American soldiers onshore had constructed a barricade of sandbags and concertina wire that twisted and turned like a metallic snake along the Corniche from the destroyed building all the way to the British Embassy, which they now shared. They draped a thick sheet of wire from the roof to the street, at an angle, as a shield against any bombs, which would strike it first and explode harmlessly. In my novel they begged me for help, and I turned them away. *Leave,* I commanded. *There is nothing for you here. Please, Carinna* (my heroine name), *you must help us! Go or die,* I told them, which was so dramatic I could not bear to sleep until I had played out the scene over and over to exhaustion.

The Sunday morning of the two bombs, I rolled over and tried to go back to sleep, but Daddy came in and sat on the edge of my bed and told me exactly what had happened. I already knew, though, because the ambulances were starting to echo through the city. It angered me that Daddy seemed so moved. I thought, *No one knew*

what they were all doing here anyway, but then I felt the weight of
my own ignorance, because this wasn't really my opinion, I had
overheard someone say it. I didn't know anything about them, or
the war, or what any of it meant. I don't care, I told Daddy, and he
looked sad and left me alone. I could not go back to sleep, and the
ambulances wailed back and forth. I imagined the hospital lobby,
the people running everywhere, how the beds would be filling up.

At school all anyone could speak about were the attacks and how
awful they were. I sat in my corner, warding other students away
from my table with my cigarettes and foul mood. Ghada smoked
her *argileh,* listening to the news from a grimy radio on top of the
refrigerator. The story was the only thing in the news, too. Ghada
seemed impassive, her face bloated and sticky-looking in the heat.
I wanted to know her opinion, but Ghada and I never spoke about
anything other than the high cost of cigarettes and the quantity
of garlic in her chicken sandwiches. A girl was going on about the
hospital; her father was a doctor and she had stayed up late into the
night, holding one Marine's hand. Her pity angered me. Thousands
of people died all the time in the war, and only now was everyone
talking about it like it mattered. I felt the knotted anger in my
chest, but at the same time I imagined going to the hospital to help,
as some of the students were contemplating. I could tell the nurses
that I was half-Lebanese and that I was born here, just like them.
Then I was jarred by the realization that almost all the nurses were
Filipino; they came here to make money.

  Marko was far away from these stories. He played today just as he
did any other, and he was on his fifth free game; I had been counting
through this jumble. He smiled now and then, a private, scornful
smile. He was the only one in here acting normal, and I wanted to
slide between the two machines, watch his game, but this was an
intimate space, reserved for close friends of his. The floor between us
stretched longer than anything, a place not to be crossed.

He played on, and he didn't care about the bombs and the dying soldiers. It had to be because he already knew about such mysteries, about people dying and how to feel about it and what one is meant to do. I examined his face to see what it must have been like before. There had to have been some change. His forehead and cheek had jaggedy red scars, and another one skewed his lips. He looked tired. Maybe he had nightmares. I had heard that the motorcycle slid right under the truck, came out the other side. I could imagine this, a movie screen in my head of slow-motion screech, roar of metal, the fragility of the human body become pathetically small, gangly, ripped up like paper. Then the quiet, tic-toc, tic-toc, of a place in the world that's transformed from day-to-day noises to crash and scream and stop.

I also could imagine afterwards, when Marko stood up. He got on his knees first, then his feet. He could not feel anything yet, only a heaviness, a numbing. The doctors told him later that it was shock. He saw his friend lying on the street. Now some people were running towards him, shouting. He asked, What happened? They told him the motorcycle hit the truck wheels, which was going too fast, though the bike had been, too, and skidded right under and kept going. They tried to hold him back from going to his friend, but he persevered. Marko, supporting his friend under the shoulders, lifted off the helmet.

The story went that Marko saw the inside of his friend's head. The head, crushed in on the side, collapsed without the helmet to hold it together. Marko saw his friend's brain. Maybe it looked like the lamb brains Ghada displayed on beds of parsley. I knew it couldn't be like that, but it was the only image I had in my head of brains. Then the onlookers tried to pull him away but they had to fight him, because that was when he went crazy, when they pulled him and he lashed out, lost his balance so the body rolled limply off his arm and he heard his friend's ruined head strike the asphalt. That sound had to be what he heard in his dreams, every day, every night, and no wonder he didn't care about the foreign soldiers; but what was it that I had heard, to make me care so little? He knew what it meant to die: he had cradled death in his own hands. I did not have these secrets. Death had always occurred far away from me, in photographs or overheard conversations. I longed to be like Marko, to have a dead friend, despite the part of me that recoiled from my own strange feelings. I couldn't help it. My lack of caring was fraudulent; Marko, though, he had seen everything he needed to see in the broken bone and shimmering juices in his palms, and he did not have to care anymore, he did not have to try.

—*Akh, haram!* Mrs. Awad lamented, shaking her hands at the ceiling. All those poor young men!

Mummy agreed sadly. Their rancor about the foreign soldiers had dissipated, leaving only pity and worry for what would come next, especially with Ara and Astrig still in the mountains. Uncle Bernie and Daddy sat up late into the night, drinking whiskey, talking about America and the lives they used to have, about politics, about the future of the Middle East. Alaine became grimly obsessed by the bombings. She had always collected newspaper photos of the war, but these she decided to paste on her wall, painting abstract images around them. Mummy and Daddy protested this macabre collage, but Alaine retorted, It's art, which for some reason silenced them.

—Why are you upset? I demanded. They deserved it!

She was painting a skull next to the collage, and now she paused to glance at me, contemptuous of my ignorance. No, they didn't, she said. They didn't have anything to do with the war.

I stared at the collage, trying to feel remorse. All I felt was a tautness in my chest, a scream lodged there. I hated Alaine. She always knew everything, did everything. It was she who found a body and buried it, she who had a collection of unexploded bullets and shrapnel, she who knew nighttime streets, gunfire, bombs. And now this. I wanted to tear every photograph of every corpse, every stunned and frightened face, every blast of concrete, arms and legs dangling out. I wanted to rip that collage to bits.

—Get out of here, Alaine said, and I did.

One day passed, two, and then the moment came when I just got up and walked out of class. The teacher followed, reprimanding me, threatening detention, but I continued down the hall. As soon as I reached the street, I started running in the light rain, and I ran all the way from the Corniche to the hospital. No one asked me questions, no one stopped me as I shouldered my way through the crowds swamping the hospital lobby. I rode the elevator with the grieving, the exhausted, a foul-tempered orderly rubbing a rash on his arm. I got out on a floor, I did not know which, and the first door that yielded, I slipped through.

The door sighed shut, muffling the hospital noises. An American soldier was standing next to an empty bed, speaking into a telephone. He glanced at me. What was I doing here? What had I been thinking? But I couldn't bring myself to move, because the soldier gave me a nod and a small smile, as if he accepted my presence. Then he went on talking. He was reading a list, pausing now and then to answer questions. It was a list of the dead, the mutilated, the nameless and the named. There were movie-sounding names like Red and Hammer, and also normal American names, like Roger or Willie. There were men whose dog tags were lost, men who were in comas. I drank the sweat from my lips. I became aware of the bed on the other side of the room, a man's bloodshot eyes peering at me out of bandages.

Then the soldier hung up the telephone. He said, You can be alone with him now, and walked out. I stared at the door closing, my whole body a wire connected to the door, pulled away from the dying man in the bed. *I'm not a relative,* I shouted in my head, but he did not come back. Quiet, only my breathing. I smelled the antiseptic air, the sweat and medicines, and the man in the bed shifted, still staring.

I approached the bed and started to speak about nothing that would be remembered, and then he whispered, *Français.* I seized his hand, saying in French that I was sorry, and he stilled me by closing his eyes. Minutes passed. When he finally spoke, his words crumbled in his mouth, they went only as far as his throat, a hushed talking, so I had to lean closer where the smell of him, antiseptic, sour at the same time, settled inside the cave of my mouth, a taste more than a smell. I listened until he fell asleep, and I held his hand even then, staring, reading the cracked, dry lips, the crusted blood in his nostrils, the measure and hover of lashes on cheekbone.

He is already on the balcony because he was roused by the first bomb, that first one that killed all the Americans, and he is a young French paratrooper looking across this still city that is hot and damp in the morning, and his eyes are blurry with sleep but his mind is alert, watchful. The sergeant stands nearby rubbing his eyes and then lifting the binoculars, searching through the haze of heat already starting to lift through the city, and it is hot and numbing. The mountains form a purple line through the misty morning heat and Paul, looking at them in the moments of silence after the first bomb, is bothered again by dreamed images of village streets, of a father gone and a mother with amber lips and silk kaftans, of the day her hands stuffed his clothes into bags and suitcases to send him to France forever so she could vanish into Africa.

He stands and looks and a spiral of smoke is swelling into rolls like boiling water and he says to the sergeant, because suddenly he pinpoints the source of all this fire and smoke and he is fearful then; *Mais çe sont les Americains!* Then a split second of knowing, as if he feels it before it happens because it is already there in the smoke filling the sky, in the wails of sirens already starting, it will happen to all of them, too. His knees are failing before the roar comes, because his body here on the top floor, tiny on the edge of this building, has sensed the shudder in the walls and floors and windows, through all the sleeping soldiers inside, through the eyes of the soldier on duty downstairs who must have been the first to see the truck aiming like a rocket for the doors. Then he is falling, and behind him inside all his friends and the beds they are in and knapsacks and bags and cups and ashtrays are rolling inwards into each other as the building hollows itself out, a funnel of concrete and wires and tiles and plaster and soldiers slipping into it still stunned with sleep. He crumbles down with the outside of the building, falling with each floor that falls, one balcony onto another, one by one, riding down with the walls of the building, the sky revolving over his head.

The second day in hospital he tries to move his hands but cannot raise his arms with two broken shoulders and a gouged-out chest. The plaster on his nose itches hot then cold and his eyes burn incessantly. A man groans in the bed next to his and then two orderlies carry him out and the sheets are left there all day, rumpled and soiled, but the man is not brought back.

The door opens and closes, again and again. Through bewilderment of drugs and surprise at being here at all, he faintly recognizes, then loses, his general and captain and chaplain who are speaking kindly to him, patting his hand and telling him he is a strong soldier. But Paul keeps losing his place, the pages slip from his fingers, where he is, when: for a time he is in his room at home in France, napping on his blue bedspread, but then he finds himself speeding through wooded trails, his dirt bike jumping like a wild, living thing, and the autumn crush of leaves and mud and motor-oil smell wet and chilled, but afterwards he becomes who he really is again, a paratrooper stepping from the plane, taking pictures of the world as he falls, of the tilting line between sky and earth, the noise of his laughing lost in the roar of wind in his ears, and his skin lifts in slow motion and his mouth opens to swallow the sky. The medics come and go, the nurses rub the crook of his arm with alcohol and pierce him with needles. Outside the tall windows, night inks the sky then recedes, and when his eyes open again to the present, he sees a girl standing on the other side of the room.

—You will never go back there again, Mummy warned me, but I was crying so much I could not answer. I could still taste the smell of him, and it hollowed me out, leaving an agony I had never before experienced. Marianna, Marianna, Mummy cradled me. You mustn't go back. There's no need for you to see such things.

But she was wrong. The next day I hurried home from school, I twisted about in front of the mirror, adjusting my wraparound jean skirt. I brushed my hair, anxious that it was too flat, and despaired of my big mouth that Astrig said was a movie star's mouth. What are you doing? Mummy said, and I said, I'm going to visit Paul, and she stood aside because my whole body threatened kick and scream should she try and stop me. What's going on? Daddy asked, and when he found out all he said was, Don't stay too long, I'm sure he's tired, and I was grateful for the way he held onto Mummy's arm, let me pass.

I had imagined an empty room, Paul gazing at me from his bed. To my horror, the room was full of soldiers who seemed to know about me already, because they winked and asked if I was a new nurse and where was my uniform? Paul told them to leave me alone and I sneaked behind a chair and stared at the floor, willing my cheeks not to be so red. Every so often the soldier who was the captain gave a stern glance, as if I were a child, and I wanted to flee but I could hardly do that, being behind the chair as I was and with all the soldiers blocking the way.

As soon as they left, Paul said, Where were you? I waited all day.

—I had to go to school.

It had not even crossed my mind to skip school altogether, stay at his side. He moved his hand slightly, gesturing me closer. I'm sorry, he said. Of course you need to go to school.

The whites of his eyes were spread through with red and his lips kept sticking together, chalky with dry spit. The smell of this room, of bandages moistened with medicine and blood and pus, of sour mouths slightly opened, of the food left on trays for hours, entered me then and for years, unbidden, far away from this room, they would come back.

The first time I fed him dinner the boiling soup spilled on his legs and he shouted in agony, throwing off the sheets. I was shocked by the sight of his thighs and what lay beyond. Towels! he cried, and I rushed to the bathroom. He could not move for hours afterwards because of the renewed pain in his shoulders, and I was inconsolable until he began to tease me.

—What did you see under the sheets? he asked slyly again and again, until I begged him to stop tormenting me and the mistake of the soup was forgotten.

I fancied becoming a nurse, for I enjoyed spooning food into his mouth and adjusting his blankets, but then his bandages needed to be changed. I want to watch, I said, convinced of my own bravery. The nurse peeled off the outside bandage from his chest and began removing the gauze with tweezers. With every piece of gauze, my stomach turned woozily, for the layers did not end, and the wound went deeper and deeper. The nurse smiled wickedly at me, lifting out the gauze that was now sodden with blood, and Paul laughed.

— You don't have to look, he said.

It was too late; the wound was fresh and glistening as a steak, lined with white threads. I sank down to the floor. Paul gripped my hand. It will be over soon, he comforted, and he and the nurse laughed together at my weakness. After this, I went into the bathroom during this procedure. Is it over? I shouted; the first time, they lied for a joke.

I lied about Mummy and Daddy not caring where I was until one evening they entered the room still wrapped in their coats as if they had no intention of staying. You're coming home, they told me. Paul was beside himself with regret. He tried to sit up in his consternation and fell to the side; I caught him and propped him up, sending my parents death looks over his bent head. They relented, unbuttoning their coats but not taking them off, and sat on the visitors' chairs to talk with him. I loitered in the corner, mortified. But I could see they liked Paul, and then the nurse brought in dinner and greeted them effusively, praising my good nursing skills, and they watched how I fed him so carefully and knew just how much sugar he liked in his yogurt. They lengthened my curfew to ten o'clock at night provided I did my homework here, and Paul said I most certainly would and that he suspected I was a good student, better than he had ever been.

—How could you make your parents into such ogres? Paul asked in amazement.

I agonized that now he would dislike me and send me away, but he held my hand, counting my fingers as if this time there would be more, or less, than five. He told me, You should be grateful they love you so much. I knew then he was thinking about his own parents, for he had been adopted when he was very young and could barely recall his mother and father, who had left him alone like a forgotten piece of luggage.

—The one thing I know is that I'm Lebanese, he confessed, astonishing me, the nurses, everyone. He said, I never thought I would find myself here, in this country.

—Welcome home, the doctor joked.

I spent evenings next to his bed with my notebooks and pens and textbooks and did my homework, smiling shyly when he asked what I was learning. I showed him the math for help and laughed when he did not know the answers. He drew silly cartoons for me next to the equations, and I cupped my hand around them in class so that no one would see.

—Is he decent to you? Alaine asked.

I shrugged that of course he was. I was relieved that her interest did not seem to extend beyond this question, and put aside my worries that she would want to go with me.

The journalists began to arrive. They came in groups carrying stand-up lamps, cameras, tape recorders. Paul could not turn them away. For the families of those who died, he explained, but I was horrified with the questions, the hot lights and microphones pushed up close to his miserable face, and worst of all, the same question, over and over, the demand that he describe exactly what he had heard and seen on the day of the bomb.

It was only a matter of time before the journalists discovered he was actually Lebanese; the coincidence entranced them. To accompany the article on him, they needed a photograph. Hold this telephone to your ear, they said. Yes, just like that. The photograph came out the following day, with the caption saying he had been speaking with his French parents. The fabrication infuriated me.

I stood outside the door and refused to let the journalists in. Papers, I commanded.

—Listen to the little girl, the nurses said, and the journalists confessed they had not obtained permission for the interview from the French Embassy. The third time this happened, Paul shouted from inside the room for me to leave them alone, to let him answer the questions, because who else could comfort the families who had lost their sons? But when they departed, he groped for my hands as he cried because the nightmares had been stirred and the screaming kept echoing in his head. His eyes looked wild over the plaster encasing his nose. He turned his head, shifted his body as he wept, trapped in all his bandages, the blanket pulled to mid-chest and tucked tight so his wounded body was outlined in every detail, frail-seeming, all the way down to the feet pointing up and making little tents of the blanket. Daddy came to find me because it was past ten, and he did not argue when I refused to leave; he sat on a chair in the hallway and waited.

The other bed had been empty for several days but then the nurses wheeled in a gurney and told Paul, You have a roommate now. This soldier was older, a colonel, and he had miraculously survived being thrown from the seventh floor in the explosion. He groaned all day and all night for water, for his wife and children, for the pain to subside.

—I can't sleep, Paul cried. Oh God, make him shut up! but the man kept moaning, unaware of his surroundings.

The nurses taught me how to soak gauze swabs in water and insert them into the colonel's mouth so he could suck them dry. More, he mumbled. More, more. Not all at once, I told him, and his face twisted up in despair. Fix the IV, he cried weakly one afternoon, until a nurse finally arrived. She yanked the plastic curtain, noise of racing metal rings. There was a silence, then a moan, and blood splattered onto the tiles. Shit, said the nurse.

But in the following days the colonel became more alert, so I tried to entertain him with my problems at school and my plans for the future. Math is a difficult subject, he agreed. But you have to finish school if you want to have an apartment and a dog.

—Not necessarily, I argued.

—Finish your homework, Paul said, or your parents will kill me.

The nurse flung open the door. You have visitors! she announced.

A group of men and women filed in, awkward, laden with flowers and boxes of sweets. A journalist followed. They looked at the colonel, whose hand was in mine, then at Paul. He smiled uncertainly. They grouped around his bed. We will be your family in Lebanon, one of the women said in Arabic, since you do not remember yours.

Paul looked to me for translation, but the journalist stepped forward and spoke first. There was a silence as Paul digested this strange offer. *Send them out of here,* I thought, but instead he started to cry, not loudly, but in whispers, not violent, uncontrolled, but just tears that come when nothing can be said, and I ran out of the room because I could not bear the way Paul was just lying there, looking so frail.

After they left I climbed into bed with Paul even though the nurses could walk in at any time. Why did you like them? I asked, and he said, Because they are kind. But they aren't your real cousins, I pointed out, and he knuckled my chin. You're jealous, he told me, which shut me up.

After this, new relatives visited every day. Paul's lost family grew and grew. They brought chocolates and clothing and cards from others who could not come. The magic of Lebanon had brought him back, they exclaimed, which was a captivating idea, that the place where I was born was magical. Any person born here, I learned, and any visitor who stepped onto this land for even just one day was infected by this magic. No one could ever forget Lebanon, nor could one leave without longing to return.

Paul was not convinced. He said, I enlisted in the army. It was chance.

I shook my head, insisting on the truth of the spell that had him in its thrall.

More and more vases of flowers wilted on the room's balcony, left there so they would not suck away Paul's oxygen, and I counted them, delighted by the absurd numbers, by the bright new clothes, the chocolates that gave me stomachaches and that Paul could not bring himself to eat. Paul smiled and laughed with me, and we whispered lying side by side, and the nights passed.

When he was well enough to be taken to a hospital in France, I stood near him on the sidewalk outside the glass wall of the hospital. Soldiers milled about, and jeeps waited in a line for the time everyone would have to leave, and he laughed in my ear, asking for a kiss in front of the captain who had always intimidated me. I finally gave in to his cajoling, and he smiled against my lips. The chaplain came close and whispered, I can marry you two now! Paul looked at me questioningly but I was in a state of alarm, and he pulled my face to his chest. The chaplain touched my hair with the tips of his fingers, saying he had not meant to frighten me.

Paul climbed into the ambulance, leaving me holding the half-empty boxes of sweets. The lights started spinning and he was carried slowly away, face framed by his palms against the window, and now I think about the other soldier in there with him, the colonel, and how everyone knew he was dying, even I knew, but still, it was a secret.

I closed myself away in my room at night with the vodka I had found in the kitchen, easier to steal than Daddy's whiskey. Mummy and Daddy did not notice me, and Alaine lived in her own world, headphones clamped to her ears all day, playing Pink Floyd. An empty space grew around me each night as I scribbled half-drunk letters to Paul, who wanted to marry me; he had promised that when I finished high school he would take me away to France. I sat in the darkness and smoked cigarettes I stole from Mummy. My love affair, unlike Alaine's, would be a success. I dreamed about wearing silk dresses and drinking Campari in France, I became someone else, someone older and quiet and mysterious who had nothing to do with me. If she were to meet me she would ignore me, a pathetic child. I sanitized a safety pin in my lighter's flame, pushed it through my lip. Mummy screamed when she saw me, and the emergency doctor shook his head, lecturing me about the absence of a punk movement in Lebanon and how I would be shunned. My lip ached for days. I settled for safety pins strung together as earrings, drew black around my eyes, dragged a knife through my jeans until they hung in rags around the knees. You look like a beggar, Mrs. Awad criticized in a weak attempt to jolt me back to normal.

At school I noticed I was alone. Like Alaine, I realized, and this seemed acceptable. I sat near her outside, not too close, but in her vicinity. We did not speak, except to ask for part of the other's lunch, or for a book. She took her medication without complaint, she didn't run away anymore, and she was trying hard to pass exams, but I walked right out of classes just as she once had and passed others like a satellite, untouchable. I was the older woman, walking down the street towards Ghada's café, *impenetrable, melancholic,* words from books. I looked out the eyes of stupid Marianna, confident that no one could see this double life. I made up entire histories for myself and revised them as I watched the other students, who were oblivious to me and my complexity. *Before all this, when I was in Bordeaux, and the windy house crumbled around me, a knock at the door; it was the writer who was summering up the beach. He said, Are you all right? I was touched that he noticed something was wrong, but how could he know my terrible story, what brought me here . . . ?* At night, I lay wide

awake while the whole house slept, alive in my made-up world, playing the same scenes over and over.

The Americans wanted revenge. The bombs from the battleship *New
Jersey* were louder than anything we had ever heard; each one shook
the entire country, and the silence after was so full, the air bloated
and sagged with it and its weight held us in place and in silence.
We heard tales of whole mountains being gutted. The size of a foot-
ball field, I heard my father say, as if because the guns belonged to
America their effect could not be measured in meters. Sixteen-inch
guns, they were called, so I stood a ruler on end, measuring the
remaining space with level palm, and it amazed me that something
so small could be the source of the loudest bombs I had ever heard.
Uncle Ara and Astrig came down from the mountains, thin, wild,
full of stories, reporting that Ziad was alive as well. Christmas came
and went, and when the Shi'a fought for West Beirut we retreated
into the darkness of the basement. I chafed with boredom; I missed
the long days at the café with Marko, and I wondered where he lived
or if he was even still in the country. Late into the night, the streets
alive with gunfire and bombs, I snuck to other parts of the building
while everyone slept; I stood near windows, shivering, expecting
death, and Paul sent telegrams, *Come to France, little flea. You must
escape.*

But there was no escape. The months blended, drifting by, one
battle erupting into another with only a few days or hours between to
rest on a sunny balcony or stock up on food. The windows shivered
and broke; I scraped my wrists along the edge to trace destruction, to
say, *The window broke and I did, too,* and this fantasy of being a window giving onto another world occupied me. Why are you so quiet,
Marianna? Because I'm thinking. What are you thinking? About
life. She's thinking about life, so grown-up. This from Astrig. A great
sigh. War eliminates childhood. This from Mrs. Awad, whose sharp
eyes missed nothing but because I was a window they missed me and
looked straight through to Alaine, whose junior year was doomed by

the fighting so she tossed her books on the burning garbage pile up the street. How could you throw away books? Daddy cried, but then he found out they were only about calculus and economics, and the grown-ups laughed at his relief. By the time the peacekeepers finally evacuated, Alaine had managed to regain her footing in school, and our parents invented what they thought would be a more virulent threat to make me work in school, that of not being as courageous and smart as my sister, but this had no effect.

The evacuation of the peacekeepers was played on TV, and we threw a party for it because, said Astrig, any excuse for a party was acceptable at this point. The peacekeepers retreated in jeeps and tanks, they filed onto boats, they looked back. The camera sought the most sorrowful ones to foretell Lebanon's dark future. We marveled once again at the plumage decorating Italian helmets. Mrs. Awad said she didn't know how huge feathers could serve as camouflage, especially in city warfare. She said those words, *city warfare,* as if she was a professor of some kind. They should be in the opera! Uncle Ara chortled, and the Italian banker he had brought as a guest took offense. This is an age-old tradition, he complained, but Uncle Ara said, *Tfih!* and brought up his issues with other idiotic but more sinister headgear, the fez, though it had no real bearing. They argued on. Daddy received word that America would help evacuate him and his family, if he wished. He wrote back, *This is my country,* and we all felt proud and Uncle Ara clapped his shoulder and called him brave as an Armenian.

There was merriment in this war; we laughed at it from the basement or the landing, and our laughter kept the little building safe, though a balcony was lost from the other side, and one night bullets shattered the windows behind Daddy's desk and strafed an arc through his books. Still, there was no escape. Daddy announced he wanted to usher in the Christmas season in style, to celebrate survival. Everyone came at the right time except for Uncle Bernie. We drank cups of hot spiced wine and we waited, but the doorbell did not ring and the streets went black and quiet. When Daddy and Uncle Ara came back from searching, they were alone. The party ended and everyone went home. Daddy sat at the kitchen table, the phone pressed to his ear, but there was only the *khish-khish-khish* of broken lines.

There is the awful day, soon after. I close my eyes, but the day remains. Daddy pushes the button for the elevator. I slouch next to him, all hairspray and cigarettes, my eyes drawn in thick black lines and safety pins dangling from my ears. We hear the elevator making its way down.

His sad blue eyes meet mine, and they seem to be asking something.

—I don't really care, I explain. I can't feel it.

I was speaking the truth. I couldn't feel anything about Uncle Bernie being kidnapped, and what was most important, to me, was to convey that coldness and its terribleness. Daddy just crumpled a little as if he had been slapped on the back, and he lowered his head for a moment. The elevator bell rang its arrival, and Daddy stared at the light inside and he didn't open the door so the light went out and all was silent.

He said, I am going to pretend you didn't say that, and then I wanted to tell him I did care, I did, but it was too late. Daddy held the door open for me, and we rode up in silence, the floors gliding by under the straining clanks of the old elevator. The months went on, carrying us ever farther from the last time we had seen Uncle Bernie. The grown-ups said, He might be here, or, We heard he was there and he is in good health, and Uncle Bernie was moved from place to place, all around the country, and I did not tell Daddy I cared because parents always know, anyway, the truth inside their children. Rumors found our door, slipped through as rumors will, and the grown-ups, starved, fed on them: Did you hear, the kidnappers were kind at heart; did you hear, they brought him medicine when needed. The rumors offered a warm bed and no blindfold,

kindly captors, a ransom about to be paid, and I did not listen, because it did not matter, because I knew with the easy certainty of a
child that Uncle Bernie would be returned to us eventually.

I was a window, and people looked through me and did not see,
and so I moved through the days and nights. I sought the parts
of my body that I could hide, dragged open the skin with knives.
The pain slid out, trailed by that calm I craved, but then it always
returned. I made a path out of the cuts, leading to the place under
my ribs, the seat of my soul. One day, a lover would find me. That
is what I dreamed, and in all this time, Uncle Bernie waited in one
dark room or another, his feet in his shoes and his soft hands folded
in his lap, and now and then I did think to miss him, I did.

In this wood house I dream with my eyes wide open, staring into the dark. I dream of small cold rooms and the feel of a wood floor and the noise of hooves galloping in air, a slight and perfect sound.

My parents learned the truth about their daughters, first one, then the other. The first time I really tried to die, they were so shocked, as if they'd discovered an imposter inhabiting their daughter's skin. But they knew what was coming. Their lives have been spent in terror that we might die, not for a stray bullet like those lodged in Daddy's books in Beirut, not for fiery shrapnel tearing into our flesh, but by our own hands, helpless in their terrible work. It does not matter where we are. It is the truth. Our guilt drives us deeper into silence, the glimmer of thought, the wretched suggestion egging us on, us like drones with teary eyes, unable to resist the drug of dying.

You can't burn thoughts. After the fire, Alaine forged an iron prison in her mind, shoved the winking thought inside and slammed shut the door. She hangs her head, the prison weighing it down like an anchor, her whole body bending with it. She lets this happen when she thinks no one is looking, but it doesn't matter, she means it, the thought won't escape again. I like to believe it's about will, and she always had more will than me.

Ziad died when I was sixteen, I think. It does not matter. In this linoleum kitchen, the white pills are like two eyes in my palm waiting to be swallowed so they can see into me, find the places that need numbing. It is cold. Wet leaves blow up against the windowpane. The earth outside is hard and cracked with frost. This amazes

me, that cold can go so deeply into the ground. Mummy says, But
it happens in Faraya, in the Cedars, too. We were hardly ever there
in those times, so for me, it is amazing. I walked circles in the yard
this morning, breaking the frozen grass under my feet.

He was shot in his apartment, they were saying, and I eavesdropped, shivering in the hall. It was just before Christmas. I was
wrapped only in a towel, and the cold winter breeze stroked my
dripping hair, froze my nails, and in this moment the years of sorrow to come made themselves known in my body, opening it like a
soft, ripe thing, penetrating my lungs and settling there.

There are some rooms, a carpet, furniture similar to that in the
barn. He is probably reading, or maybe he is cooking, and then the
doorbell rings.

I knew it was him because they said, God forgive us for saying
this, but he was a dreamer, he spent all his money just for a disco.
How his father loved him too much!

There are some rooms, a window giving onto the sea. He is remembering his plans, the dreams he had. He feels guilt all the time
for not making his parents proud, how they are so disappointed.
The doorbell rings.

I saw parts of their faces through the sliver of space where the
door was almost closed, their eyes half-shut as if in a trance. They
did not look at each other, perhaps out of some shameful respect
for this death. Mummy was slowly nodding, and her face had that
look of things that cannot be changed, of things that are necessary
and destined. I was awed by this expression; I had practiced in front
of the mirror.

Someone said, Yes, God be merciful, God forgive us, but perhaps
it's better that he's dead, his problems are now ended.

I struggled to understand this, that it was better he was dead.

—He was full of plans all the time.

—So many plans.

—Kindhearted. But a dreamer, a big spender.

—He suffered so much. He was confused.

Astrig's voice interrupted, and it was quiet and final. She said, He didn't know when to stop.

He leans back against the stalls and looks at me with a certain kind of sorrow, and the light of the barn is the yellow of summer grass. The doorbell rings.

I closed the memory. I went to my room and dressed. Outside my window a fisherman stood in the shallow water on a rock, pants rolled to his knees. The streets were empty. The palm trees that had been planted in summer to beautify the city were dying from the war, strafed by shrapnel and bullets. I wished there were something to do, other than go find out the truth. I was afraid now that it really was him and not someone else. He was a big spender, but the white horse stands in the shade beside the stone house, and he is leaning over, touching its neck.

They were so calm and I was ashamed of my nervousness. I was not supposed to feel anything, this was the way things happened in a war, after all, where everything is certain and there are no surprises and the only solution is to deaden the heart.

—Who died? I asked, and Mummy said his first name and then his last name, pronouncing the words as if I would not possibly remember. The name looked wrong on her lips. It settled in my ears in the slow syllables that Mummy spoke.

I pretended not to care, like them. I shrugged and said, Oh, him.

Mummy looked at me sharply. She seemed afraid of my voice, the way it was so thin and cold. *Uf,* Astrig sighed, how blasé even the children have become.

They all stared at me, waiting for a response, and it became clear they could not have heard how they sounded. They were simply talking the way people do when someone dies after so many others have died. He had had big plans. He was a dreamer. The war had turned everyone into automatons who accepted the worst, no longer able to truly weep for anything. I could have shown them, no, you have to feel it, even if it happens every day. I could have been true for him, and now it was too late. My betrayal was like quietly sinking below the surface of the sea.

—Anna, Astrig motioned me to come sit down. She looked concerned.

I ignored her. Everyone dies, I said, and I meant it as something true, but my voice was harsh and did not fit.

I went back to my room and curled into bed. The murmur of their voices floated to me. Mummy's face, still like a stone. I had seen someone, known someone dead, and now I was supposed to accept it, but I couldn't, no matter how hard I tried. I was so sad, even though I barely knew him compared to everyone else, and then it came to me that maybe this was why, because I could mourn without any doubts. I thought of how he was alone forever now, but I was there, and maybe the trueness of what I felt would reach him. It was a clear and vibrant sorrow, and I was lost in it.

The stranger walks into his apartment and lifts the gun—perhaps the stranger says, *I've waited a long time for this,* and then, the inevitable act, he kills Ziad.

Everyone had secretly been expecting this, that was how they sounded, but it was wrong. I wanted to rush back and tell them I hadn't meant what I said, people did not just die. It was all wrong. I was pulled into memories of Ziad, so vivid that they stifled me, the way his hair curled to the side, his eyes, the gravel path and garden, and, choking on grief, I held in my tears with such fierceness that it hurt.

The stranger walks into Ziad's apartment and lifts the gun. Ziad looks surprised, he did not expect this, not ever. Perhaps the stranger says: *I've waited a long time for this.*

When he leaves there is only the sound of the city through the open windows.

Later, in stories told at lunch or over a cigarette in the boutique or between the heavy bolts of material in the seamstress shop, Ziad weeps with a pistol in his mouth, or hums as he polishes the metal, pulls the trigger just to hear the click, or stares blankly at the spinning chamber, one fated bullet whirring into place, but in all versions of his death the ending is the same. He leans over the horse's neck, whispering, and its wings unfold, filling out the space between earth and sky and I am crying.

I bent close to Ziad's bleeding head, nudged him for a sign of life. When he did not respond, I sought to join him. I did not want to make mistakes. I took as many as I could, one pill after another. I closed my eyes. I willed the loose, wavy feeling to spread through my body, but I could still move my legs. It disturbed me. I wanted to die, but the world was still about me.

Daddy rolled me over and I pretended I could not move. He called my name, shaking me. He pulled me up to my feet but I made them buckle, so he held me to him and dragged, all along his voice quivering my name, *Anna?*

It cannot be coicidence that he practiced this act, once, years before he had to perform it for real. The practice was nothing, not compared to what was coming.

Mummy had mixed mustard and water and pushed the glass against my lips. Daddy was shaking me, to wake me up, so the glass banged against my teeth. How many did you take? I was embarrassed. I had thought it would be different, all this concern; it would feel the way I had imagined, comforting and warm. Instead there was only shame, failure. She couldn't have taken that many, Mummy said, which made me feel even more ashamed, but still she made me drink the mustard and water so that I would throw up. We stood in silence over the toilet, but all I felt was a winding tightness in my stomach, no nausea. I had heard that taking lots of aspirin could put you in a coma, but I had only taken fifteen, which had seemed a lot, but now I knew it was hardly enough and all I had done was frighten everyone, for no real reason. I started to cry and Mummy rocked me, My poor darling, my baby, and this was what I had wanted but it was too late now, and I felt Daddy's gentle hand on my hair. Alaine watched from the doorway, upset all over her face, and her love for me made me cry harder.

At night Mummy and Daddy talked and talked, anxiously exploring all the possible solutions to us, their daughters. I had hidden in this hallway many times, it was habit to pause before entering a room in case there was something to hear. They wanted to send me back to Vartan. But Vartan was ill. Perhaps they could send me to the American school in Greece. Whatever we do, we have to separate them, Daddy was insisting, as if Alaine and I were criminals. *She's the one you should send away,* I wanted to shout. *Let her go. She's the crazy one.* This held true even though Alaine was working hard at repeating her senior year so she could graduate, and she hadn't actually done anything in a while. But she was still broody and depressed, her very posture threatening imminent relapse, and it was all her fault anyway so they should send her, not me. I backed away and sat on the floor. Mummy said, What happened to her? When? I waited for them to realize, *She's dying inside,* but Mummy's voice just kept asking the same questions that seemed so irrelevent. How can we manage? What started this?

There was no reply from Daddy. I pictured him sitting there, examining the floor and smoking, arms crossed over each other on his knee. That was how I had seen him sitting for years while they spoke about Alaine, and now I was being talked about, too. Eventually he might say something, but calmly. I wished he would talk now. I wished he would hug Mummy, who was so terribly sad and all because of me. I did not know what I wanted. I pressed my cheek to the cold tiles.

My parents learned the truth first about Alaine; they locked cabinets and drawers, they slept on full alert, ready to spring up at the slightest provocation. The war outside was nothing; we slept through whole bombing raids, laughed at our own lassitude, but Alaine, the sound of her stirred even the deepest sleeper. The second daughter broke them to pieces, such a surprise, and quickly they sent her away, as if distance would startle her back to her old self. But there is no answer for the one who has at last posed the question; she mulls over the fragility and uselessness of the body daily, with single-minded determination. She does not get well; she bides her time like an animal in winter, and no one knows and no one sees. The suicide never fails to surprise.

I lie in my favorite space between bed and bookcase, curled on my side cheek to floor. The stories join, not for any reason but just that they do, and afterwards, they cannot be remembered or told without one another. It has been some months since Ziad died. The girl has been sent to school in Greece. She breaks all the rules, gets detentions, breaks the rules again. She discovers the ease of getting love from strangers, but she always runs just in time. She learns bus routes, hitchhiking, how to get on the Acropolis after midnight to scuttle amongst the ruins and avoid the watchman's arcing flashlight. It is spring 1986. Paul flies from Paris all the way to Athens for her seventeenth birthday. She meets him at his hotel, but she is tongue-tied, because the young man standing on his own feet and holding a bouquet of purple flowers seems like a stranger. Only his eyes and mouth are familiar. My nose was in plaster when you knew me, he teases. He is awkward, and she is no longer as she was; she is no longer innocent. The girl wears a beret and a scarf, and he pulls on the scarf so that it unravels from her neck and she blushes. He knows he cannot marry her now after all, she is so young, and this causes a sorrow between them without the words being said aloud. They go up to his room. When there is nothing left to be said, she asks to see his scar, now a shallow indent, a bowl shape like the flesh was scooped out. Her tender fingers slip across the taut, colorless skin, and his face is serious and pale and he does not laugh. When did you become so sad? he asks, but she does not tell him when or how; she tells him nothing of her first love, whose death revealed the passageway where she still walks, guided by the glimmering thought. Her fingers follow the scar, recognizing, and he explains how skin was taken from his thigh to cover the wound.

He leaves his shirt off because this is how she knows him. When he sees the marks on her arms, her belly, he says, I would give you all my skin to heal you. She lies beside him for a long time, holding his hand, and he does not kiss her or move, and her eyes are closed.

Some days later, they decide to eat in a restaurant, and they walk down the springtime streets, laughing.

From those months in Greece I have a photo of Daddy and me in the Agora, Christmastime, when we toured a few days before he left me at my new school. I have a dried-up flower from Paul's bouquet, I have numerous poems about Ziad, a postcard of a fountain that caught my imagination enough to shed blood into from my wrist, discreet, my wish. I have ruminations about the school I attended for one semester, about bars where we drank beer and kissed strangers and about riding the late-night buses in the rain. There is more, from when Paul came, the day in the restaurant, the upside-down face in the newspaper, but there are no words for it. The pages of this old diary run to empty, what I couldn't write that spring, and what reason is there to write a story that cannot be dreamed because it ended from the first moment it began to unfold? It had no other ending than one, and I cannot bear it. *I don't care,* I told my Daddy, and I never took back what I said but that is finished now, and parents always forgive; that is what they tell us.

My Daddy cooks pancakes for his family, humming old *American Bandstand* tunes. He flips them onto our plates, he asks if we want sugar or syrup, he checks the coffee for a burnt taste. My Mummy eats careful bites as if the food might choke her. She stares at nothing, and she doesn't talk. Alaine clears the table and washes up, her soapy hands a dance under the running water, so precious, but we let it run until the last piece of silverware is clean as if to say, We know where we are.

∽

When Daddy first left for America, he was alone. He wrote us letters. *I am too old,* he wrote. *This is not my home.*

Daddy left at the beginning of winter, on a cold day so we rubbed our chilled faces with reddened hands, and jokes were made about this weather being like midsummer compared to what lay ahead in America. Daddy held Mummy a long time and Uncle Ara made noises of impatience because the ferry engine was rumbling. He started off with the suitcases so everyone laughed, and Astrig shouted at him about his lack of romance and tact. But when Daddy's boat pulled away, Uncle Ara had to hold Mummy up by her arms because she went so weak her body couldn't stand. She hadn't given in at all, not until now; not when the bodyguards came to the door, sheepish, searching for Daddy who had given them the slip out of shame; not when Alaine's cat came back from wherever it had gone, trailing blood on the tiles and yowling; not when she found the vodka in my drawer. Even on the day Daddy woke up mumbling his dream, saying he had realized he had to go, Mummy got up and began to pack with the grim efficiency of someone working alongside fate. My Daddy's dream had shown him a closed room, a glowing bullet suspended in the darkness, and Uncle Bernie smiled sadly from the corner saying, *You'd better go to the opera,* and then a light shone in like an arrow and the back part of Uncle Bernie's head was gone and he said in a surprised voice, *I'm tired.* Mummy packed, and Daddy sat with Uncle Bernie's favorite book, reading the marginalia as a way of talking with his old friend, and I couldn't bear to see him sadly nodding at the pages. The soldiers now clustered at the building entrance, relieved to have cornered their charge in this time of foreigners being kidnapped and murdered, and when they heard he planned to leave for good they smiled and thanked God and said it would be wisest. They were young; in their newfound merriment they smiled at me with suggestions in their eyes, seeking praise for bravery that I knew, if tested, would crumble. When I passed them, I kept my eyes down, and Amer teased, At least give them a smile. He put his arms around me in the elevator, breathing in my hair. Why aren't you kind to your father? he asked, and I said, I don't know. I followed my family's preparations with the detachment of an observer. There is a stone in my chest, I told Amer. His palm felt for it, he shook his head, smiling. You should be nicer, he told me, but I couldn't, so he joined them in the living room as my emissary until the day we had to go.

It was decided Daddy should leave by boat from Jounieh, as the airport road would be the route expected of him. At the American Embassy branch in East Beirut, we were guided into a large, bare room. It was dim in there. A fan creaked slowly above and there were some wooden chairs against the wall. The tall American man in charge of us wore dark sunglasses, even inside, and called out orders every few moments. He paced and frequently checked the road as if something terribly urgent was happening, and Mummy whispered, What a donkey, and we laughed into our hands. The day was hot and slow. We wanted to know what was happening; we sent Daddy to ask this American man, imagining them to be comrades of a kind, being both from the same country. Daddy approached and said something, smiling, and the man replied curtly, Have a seat, sir. Daddy looked small and old. He found a chair and sat down. We remained silent, the jokes finished, and I imagined all of Daddy's years here piling up on top of this smart young agent, crushing him, teaching him a lesson about history, and then I thought of exactly what to say as we left, something memorable and cruel that would haunt him the rest of his stupid life, but all that happened was a Marine came in and said, Their ride's here, and we filed out obediently and Daddy said, Thank you, young man.

On the dock Mummy stared after Daddy as if tying part of her gaze to him, her gaze drawn away, farther and farther. Other people milled about, themselves grief-stricken for whomever they had lost to the ferry chugging away in the filthy sea. I headed back to the car before everyone else. I knew he would come back, for it to be any other way was unthinkable.

I was seventeen, the nights were cool, and I lit one cigarette from the stub of another. I made Amer drive his old car down the narrow streets as if he were in the Grand Prix and the guards at the gate stared after us. There was no outside world. I pushed aside the stories about young men who crossed the Green Line from West Beirut and were never heard of again. There was a prison where these people who vanished were taken, but I never quite found out where it was, only that it was in the mountains somewhere. At a party one night, I eavesdropped on a reporter who had just come from an execution. He had thought meeting, statement, a few photographs. But then, he said, they brought the guy out, made him kneel, and bang. I can't believe I'm at this party. I sipped rum, listening without listening. I had nothing to do with these struggles. Amer and I balanced the edge of the war, driving at one hundred kilometers an hour, the windows always down so my hair whipped over my face and the city sped by, broken-down and gloomy and failing to rebuild itself, nothing compared to us. The Syrians had not yet returned, suicide bombers hurled themselves at the Israeli occupation in the south, and I went to school most days just for something to do. The letters came regularly from Daddy, who was living in a two-room apartment in America. He could not find a job because he was overqualified. *They don't want me,* he wrote. *I'm too old.*

I stripped these words from my tongue where they had settled, I unglued them from the lining of my ribs where they clung, I scraped them from under my nails where they trembled, and we went to buy vermouth, which I drank like water and which Amer sipped dubiously. I was unconscious of the hunger with which I would gaze through memory at the dashboard of his car, at the

weight of his arm around my neck. He had agreed to help me pay
for a one-way ticket to Rome; my one semester in Greece had not
enchanted me as much as Rome, which had become the place of
my dreams. I planned to live there and be a haunted writer like
Mummy's friend Muna. I would speak Italian and never come back
to Lebanon again. Amer and I left the house in the evening, and
Mummy no longer tried to stop me, she just looked away without
a word, but one night in a traffic jam on the Corniche the sky filled
with light and shells plummeted into the sea, into the cars, into
the vacant land bordering the road. I stared upwards, tipsy, Amer
shouting to passing cars, Water! Water! because the car had overheated and the white steam was spiraling up into the night.

—Where *were* you? Mummy demanded, huddled on her chair.

I told her we were fine and she shouldn't worry so much, but
Amer sat on the couch in silent apology. I went to the kitchen,
pursued by Mummy's angry words. The bottle of Pepsi I found in
the fridge was almost empty and the remains were flat; I spat out
my mouthful in disgust. The bottle just missed the garbage can,
rolled across the floor spinning liquid everywhere. I did not want
to clean up the mess. Alaine's bedroom door opened. I saw her
reflection in the mirror opposite; she stood there, leaning forward
slightly, listening. Mummy's voice rose and fell, Amer's soothing
baritone accompanying. Alaine emerged from her room, paused
to give me a look that told me how loathsome I was, and then she
went to Mummy. I watched; she squeezed in beside Mummy on the
chair, she cradled her, and after a short time, Amer got up and left.
I wanted to comfort Mummy, too, but I stayed in the kitchen, and
so it was that our family was made into its new self.

I walked close to Amer because the faces on the street had changed,
people looked at me as if I were a trespasser. Don't be afraid, Amer
whispered, and we went to his room, the sun warming the floor,
the silver for his jewelry half-melted, shining and soft and not to
be touched. The outside world disappeared in here, and that was

a relief, for the world no longer wanted me. Mummy spent days wandering the house as if she might happen upon Daddy, in the hall, or in one of the rooms. Alaine had emptied her room of all furniture, because now she was a minimalist, and the hallway closet was stuffed full of all the things she wasn't supposed to need. Her friends from university came to drink tea in the living room and argue about philosophy; Mummy said, Enough with existentialism, do the dishes! but this humor was thin, false, and nobody laughed as much as they should have. I thumbed through the piles of university books in secret, left out and feeling ignorant. I would never make it to university, not on my current trajectory. Come sit with us, said one of Alaine's friends. I said no, headed for the door.

—Come back here, Alaine warned, but I was running.

It was a better place, Amer's apartment. He and his friends traveled to India once a year, which seemed an exotic, essential journey, one I wanted to make, even though Amer had said the weeks spent on a filthy bus would change my point of view. I waited at the small table in the kitchen while he made coffee and poured it into porcelain cups, then we went to his room. I sat on the bed, shoes off, under the open window. Amer smiled, then he held his arms out.

—Why? I said.

—I want to hug you.

I shook my head. He laughed at me and asked, Are you going to cry again?

I nodded and swirled my forefinger in the grains at the bottom of my cup, destroying my fortune.

I met Amer in the summer before Daddy left. You don't remember me, said a young man with black curly hair about his face.

I regarded him with suspicion. His long wool coat smelled of mold. He blocked my path. I was in the museum, on my way to visit Daddy in his office.

—Are you afraid?

—No.

He laughed. His name was Amer, he told me. He had been in our old school, before we transferred. He was older, twenty-three. Of course I would not remember him, he said forgivingly, because I had been so small. How is your sister, he asked, but I could tell it was me he wanted to know.

—How did you recognize me?

His fingers touched my hair, tugging out a strand. The color of your hair, he said, smiling. Open your hand. He held out his fist, promising a gift inside.

After a long moment during which I heard the secretaries burst into laughter in the next room, and the sound of footsteps in the hall and the rustle of papers, the whispers of the ancient objects that had been numbered and catalogued and saved from the annihilation of time and wars and civilizations, and during which I realized he would not harm me and that he smelled of must and beard and coffee, I finally held out my hand. His fist rested in my palm for an instant before unfolding, and I saw a tiny elephant.

He said, Open it.

I pulled the pouch off the elephant's legs and a cloud of minuscule elephants fell onto my skin.

—Ivory, he explained, smiling. From India.

I heard my father say my name, and I turned quickly, blushing. But Amer was the nephew of one of the secretaries, his face was known, and Daddy merely waved hello. There is a clarity to this memory, Daddy smiling in the doorway, a sheaf of papers tucked under his arm, the smell of Amer's coat and the feel of the tiny elephant gift. I look away in embarrassment, as if I have been up to something more than what is nestled in my hand. I tell Daddy to go on his errands alone after all, dumbly trusting that the days will send me this ordinary chance again, that we will trudge across the campus as I complain about another missed day at the beach; but Daddy's dream is only weeks away, and now, peering back to that moment of him turning around to go off alone, it seems I ought to have known what was coming for the gloomy, high-ceilinged room and the glass cases filled with artefacts, my father's slow footsteps fading away down the hall. But I did not know; Amer invited me to join him on the Corniche for coffee, and I went.

That winter at Amer's house, I felt my life as if it were a tangible thing, the mystery of it all around, on my skin, in the breeze through the window. His room smelled of thick cotton, of his sweat, and faint burning from working silver at a desk, where the tools lay in rows with lumps of the unshaped metal that I could hold in my palm and the silver that came in strips laid neatly in a box. I watched with one eye shut the fire of his soldering, the melting and moving and gluing. Outside, the world fell quiet on these afternoons. Across the street an old woman swept the playground, working up and down the square area methodically, the *hish-hish* of the broom making me sleepy, and he said, I don't know why she bothers, the children come every day and the sand goes everywhere. When I was half-asleep with my head against his chest, my tears finally finished, he asked me why I always felt so sad, and I could not explain that it was not me who cried but some other weaker thing, and that there was a bad place inside me that made me want to die.

—How can you possibly suspend her? Mummy shouted at the principal. Do you know what we have been through?

—We've all been through it, Ani. The principal looked sorrowful about having to destroy our family. But she hasn't been to class in three weeks.

—Please, said Mummy, but it was futile. She bent her head, examining the official letter clenched in her hands. I tried not breathing. I held my breath as long as possible, then expelled it with a desperate noise. They looked at me. I looked away.

—At this rate you'll never go to university like your sister, the principal warned, as if Alaine were the star of the family.

The days I was suspended dragged on with a different feel. Because

I didn't have to go, I started missing school, the talk at the lockers, sitting in the back of class and doodling illegally on the desk surface. Morningtime was strangely void; I was an intruder on routines that were not mine. Alaine went to her university classes, and then Mummy made coffee, settled at Daddy's desk to write her daily letter to him. The letters piled up until they could be sent with a traveler, since the mail system was so undependable. The steam from her coffee and cigarette smoke mingled above, and the apartment was silent but for the pen scratching evenly across the pages. She wrote to him with her whole body, bending into the creation of each letter, her bottom lip sucked under her teeth.

—Did you tell him about me? I asked, and she said, Of course. After a moment, I said, I'm sorry, and she answered bitterly, It's the least of our problems, and then her face fell at her own cruel words, but she didn't say anything more, just gazed down at the desk and things went deeply quiet. I'm sorry, I insisted, paralyzed by the vision of her tilted head and sad, curved-in shoulders, and I wished Alaine were home.

I took Amer to show him our old building across from the store. A new floor had been added, covering the terrace where Alaine and I had once roller skated, but still, I wanted Amer to see. Strange faces peered out from windows where I had stood searching for Ara and Lupsi in the fire. Men sat on the steps in front of the main door, smoking and drinking coffee in paper cups, and I wanted to enter the building, climb the stairs to our apartment, but it was all different, even the concierge was gone, fallen from the fourth-floor landing when he was drunk. When I was a child, his life in the basement had remained outside my curiosity because he had always seemed a little mean. I had been so conceited about the American journalist interviewing us, thinking the concierge would be envious. Now I felt sad for his dark basement room, how he had survived there for so many years, through a whole war, only to die in a fall.

We went up to Uncle Ara's house so I could get some Italian language books. Astrig opened the door and looked me up and down with one raised eyebrow, but there was no humor in her now.

—You are killing your mother, she told me.

—I just want the books, I argued. Amer loitered behind me, and I felt his embarrassment.

—You come here for books, without having even a coffee?

—Who's there? Uncle Ara shouted.

—It's Miss Marianna, come for books without stopping to say hello.

—I need to learn Italian, I said weakly, but Amer pushed me forward and closed the door.

—At least Monsieur Amer is polite. Why do you need to learn Italian? Does this look like Italy to you, Miss Marianna? Astrig waved at the drab, wintery buildings beyond the balcony, drained grays and browns. A truck honked annoyingly on the street below.

—Just to learn, I said, all innocence, my escape plans still secret.

Uncle Ara was going through a box of Vartan's antiques, which he did often. We knew of Vartan's illness and assumed it would pass; the truth was that he was dying, and in that moment there were only months left for him to live. There was no way of keeping in close touch—the telephones did not work, and mail did not come and go as it did in other countries—and besides that, Vartan did not want anyone to worry. In that time, we believed he would recover, and in all my fantasies of moving back to Rome, I helped to nurse him back to health, I sat at his bedside, attentive to his lectures. Now I watched Uncle Ara poking through the antiques, trying to date them for Amer. We waited for the coffee, listening to Astrig crash about the kitchen. I wished we hadn't come at all.

—This is from Sidon, Uncle Ara said. This was in his room when he was only fifteen!

I wanted to believe him, but I suspected these relics might have been found at other moments in their lives, and he was naming them, over and over, pointing towards a past that resisted being recovered, like a house that is boarded up and whose interior furnishings are obscured with fine dust. Uncle Ara had gotten old. In the last time of fighting, he found his new car riddled with bullet holes. Wearing only his bathrobe, he drove it to a more sheltered spot farther up the street, but the fighters there took it over and slept in it. So then he moved the car to the middle of the street, and the tanks rolled by all day, narrowly missing it. It is safest right in the middle! he shouted to anyone who wanted to hear his story. Astrig had watched from the window. Whenever he started up an argument with the soldiers, she screamed down at him, You are mad and crazy! *Fou! Fou! Fou!*

She explained to us, I have to pretend we are completely gaga or else! and she signed her throat being cut. That was the first time I realized Astrig didn't necessarily think her father was crazy.

—When are you getting married? Uncle Ara shouted, pointing at Amer so that he jumped.

—We're just friends, I said, for the thousandth time.

Astrig bore in a tray laden with food and coffee and served Amer, telling me I could fend for myself. I put sugar, she confessed to Amer, and he replied, That is good. Uncle Ara cupped his ear with a huge, gnarled hand yellowed from cigarettes, and commanded, Stop whispering, you stupid people!

—We are not whispering! Astrig yelled.

Uncle Ara measured Amer with his eyes, then said, You should shave so you don't look like a stupid Shi'a.

I cringed, but Amer replied, On the contrary. I look like Jesus Christ.

Uncle Ara shouted to Astrig, Did you hear that? Jesus Christ! Then he leaned closer to Amer. Do you have any Roman coins?

Uncle Ara brought out Vartan's coin collection, and Amer said he could make a great ring for him, a ring with Caesar on it, which would only be worthy of him.

—Caesar was stupid! retorted Uncle Ara. The only great people are the Armenians! Astrig shook her hands at him, berating him for being so rude to a guest. He pushed her hands out of the way, shouting, And our family is the greatest of all!

—*Yeeh* with you and your ancestors!

—They are yours, too!

—What's wrong with them? Amer asked.

—Oh, Astrig said, gesturing the abysmal lengths it would take to explain. Oh, oh, oh.

Amer became more curious, and I was glad, because all this talk distracted Astrig from criticizing me for how I was making Mummy so upset. They think they are so cultured, Astrig began. They think they come from royalty, but so does every Armenian, and I say, *Uf*, Tigran the Great, you had a big *hareem*, the size of a civilization! As she went on, I contemplated the food: *hummus*, leftover *kafta*, chicken and rice. Because I knew Astrig would be offended if I did not eat, I tore the bread and stuffed it into my mouth, forcing the dryness in my throat to tolerate this invasion. Amer watched for the crying that might come, the crying that happened frequently now, without warning. But I controlled it, I focused on the box of artefacts Vartan had collected as a child on trips all over Lebanon, bits of pottery with faded paint, part of a clay lamp, a strange-shaped piece of glass, and I told myself I would be in Rome soon, and I saw myself as I had been one night, my skirt pulled high up my thighs to wade in a fountain, the lights through water rippling on my white skin. I leafed through the Italian books while Uncle Ara educated Amer on his father's lifelong terror of skylines formed by the ominous shapes of domes and minarets. This is the only country, Uncle Ara said triumphantly, where you hear the *muezzin* singing with church bells, and that is a phenomenon! Astrig, yielding to her father's memories, watched me from the other side of the room, the light growing dim as afternoon passed into the early winter night. The way she sat without talking for so long, I knew she was preparing something to tell me, and I chafed at being trapped by her disapproval.

—What? I finally asked, annoyed.

She said, You keep wanting to know what happened to Ziad.

My hand stopped on the page and there was quiet. It was Amer who, tormented by my whispering the many stories of Ziad for months, held up one finger to keep Uncle Ara still and said, Yes.

So she told the story, and we listened without speaking, though Uncle Ara kept shaking his head and mumbling at the pity of it all. Nighttime came while she spoke, and when she reached the end, Amer walked me home and the streets were empty and frightening; we walked swiftly, his hand under my elbow pushing me to go faster.

—You want to go? Go! Mummy dug into her drawer, throwing underwear, jewelry boxes. She found an envelope, tried to tear it open, then simply threw the whole thing in my direction. The bills inside separated, floated to the floor. I pretended indifference.

She stopped moving. She said, Take your things, go. I am so tired, Marianna. I am so tired.

Alaine came to the doorway. You told her about the ticket?

I nodded. I had thought it would be different. It had made sense before. Mummy sank onto the little gold couch from Téta, her hands dropped open on her lap.

—I *miss* him, she said. Each word emerged alone, ragged.

My face remained frozen, nothing on it, pretending not to care.

—So go, Alaine told me, knowing I would not, that I did not have the courage necessary for such a break. There was finishing high school to consider, and how would I make money, and would Vartan love me enough to let me stay. I felt so small and stupid. Alaine approached Mummy, bent to hug her. She had transformed into a new person, taller, her hair uncombed and wild and her thin muscled arms encircling our mother. Mummy leaned into her, Alaine the lifeline, the strong one, the dependable one.

I thought of Daddy, far away in America. Our apartment was an empty place of cool breeze and quiet. Daddy's desk looked almost the same as the day he left us, except for Mummy's letter-writing box, her pen lying on top. The sounds of him were missing: the coffee cup clinking on the saucer as he walked, the snap and hiss of his World War II lighter, the mumbled injunctions at Alaine's cat, which liked to sharpen its claws on the spines of his old books.

He should never have gone, I thought vindictively. He had left us in this mess, it was all his fault. I gave Alaine and Mummy a cold stare while I thought this, so they would understand that I was separate, that I had risen above our situation while they suffered on. They did not pay me any attention. Mummy was just sitting there with her hands open in her lap, eyes sparkling tears, and I remembered Daddy being snubbed by the man at the Embassy and how his shoulders drew in and he looked so old. My Daddy was a sick man, with an aching back and a tremulous heart. And then I understood, *He would have died in a place like they kept Uncle Bernie.*

—Fine, I won't go, I said, which I meant to be a kind of apology but it came out like a threat. They just looked at me with the same weary look. I tried to stay in the doorway, but my body turned around and walked off as if the object of rebuke, and the body went to read a magazine and paint its toenails, sick with inertia.

＄

In this wood house I dream of fire, the silence of ashes. How we would all stand in the morning gloom and I would say, *Now we should go back*. Daddy's sad eyes reproach me. We came here for him, and now his fate is embracing us all.

My Daddy types at the dining-room table; he thumbs through books with the same frown he had in Beirut, as if things are the same. He leaves for the library alone, old and without friends. I squeeze shut my eyes. But memory is relentless; it hunts me down in my hiding place between bookcase and bed. *I don't care,* I tell Daddy, and the elevator clangs its arrival. The light winks out. The words stay, never unsaid.

This I do not dream. Paul and the girl are in Athens, eating strawberries. It is her birthday, and she giggles from too much wine, from him wiping cream off her chin. The man at the next table disapproves of us, even more when Paul reaches for the discarded newspaper. The girl sucks on her spoon, eyeing the man, who is preparing a rebuke. The crinkling paper distracts her, and her eyes alight on the front page, on the blurred photograph of a face she knows so well. It is upside-down, and his eyes are closed, mouth puckered like he's thinking.

Paul kept asking *Quoi, puce, quoi?* through the bathroom door, and then he broke it in even though a woman was yelling at him in Greek. He grabbed my head so I'd stop banging it against the wall and he held me inside his arms despite my struggling. I couldn't see for the tears and the snot and the noise of my own voice, wailing, Uncle Bernie, Uncle Bernie, whose last moments had been spent on an empty road, blindfolded, a pistol to his temple. All I kept think-ing was, *Did he have his shoes,* because they were warm and old and I couldn't imagine him without them, not ever.

Nine months have passed since we left, and Mummy gets a tele-phone call, she has been given a temporary job at the local library. For days this is the only topic in our house. She lays out clothes, discusses when the best hours will be, counts the money she hasn't earned yet. On her third day, she has to take me.

I can tell she's hoping for enthusiasm, for me to want to see this place where she works and be proud of her. I dread going, but Daddy is at the university library, researching his article, and Alaine doesn't want to watch me anymore; I know this from eavesdropping, she is scared of the responsibility. So I am shuffled between my parents, and they refuse to stop playing this game of *Don't leave Marianna alone,* and I hate the game but crave it, too, crave the open door, the person always nearby.

—You can take out as many books as you like, she says encour-agingly, as if this is an opportunity she has created for us.

— So?

Her face, when she hears that. Like my mean little word hooked into it and tugged, so everything fell down.

The walk there is fifteen minutes of strain and quiet, and me all jumbled up inside with *sorry sorry sorry* but no words said.

I expect to see a real library, but it is only a square one-story building, and inside there is just one big room. She introduces me to the librarians, who exclaim over my torn-up jeans and the ink drawings all over them. Now that's like art, one of them says. Then they and Mummy commiserate about their wild children. Mummy behaves as if they are fond acquaintances, not two old women who hired her out of pity.

Mummy's job is to retype all the catalogue cards. Some have new numbers, and these are flagged red. Some have questions associ-ated with them, and these are flagged yellow. Mummy carries one catalogue drawer at a time to the office, a tiny room encased in glass in the corner of the library. She has a wood table, an electric typewriter, and a swivel chair. She sits with her back straight and examines the card, types with two fingers, examines again, types. I can't bear to see her, but I keep looking up, and then it's worse. Every so often, one of the librarians says, You must be getting stiff there, and Mummy nods, showing gratefulness for the sympathy. The librarian who smokes likes to say, Shall we go be naughty? and then they stand outside and smoke together. Most of the people who come in to read the magazines or check out a book greet the librarians by their first names, and have a conversation about the weather or a recipe or the children.

—It's a community, Mummy says happily. What have you found?

I am cross-legged on the floor in the poetry section. I have found Keats, "Ode to a Nightingale." I barely look up, because I don't want my mother to see my poem. I bend closer to the book, ignoring her. Her feet move a little in front of me, I hear her take a book from the shelf, flip the pages, then she replaces it.

—Well, I should get back to work, she says, and her feet walk away.

It doesn't matter, I tell myself.

"Ode to Melancholy." This is a mystical title, this is the poem Amer meant for me, I know it. Reading, I think of Amer, then of Paul. I cannot stand the sight of my mother in the little glass office, or the sight of her in our smelly wooden house, crying in the morning for the spilling of coffee grounds or the dirty spoons in the sink. She always recovers by saying, We are luckier than most. When she was younger, she inspired love everywhere she went; Jiddo took her to the theater, to festivals. Her life was meant to be different. I want to see Keats's grave in Rome; Vartan was too fixated on Armenian things to have shown us that. At the grave, I am in black, my hair is thicker than in real life, curly, reddish. *Oh, I turned around, startled. He looked a little awkward. He said, I've*

seen you here before. Are you all right? I hid my face, I couldn't let him
see what terrible things had happened to me . . .

The square room of the library, whispers, legs in brown pantyhose trotting by. I cannot tolerate it here. I go to the glass-walled
office. Mummy looks up with a surprised smile. She has typed only
a portion of the cards she is meant to finish today.

—Mummy, let's go.

Her expression changes to confusion. We can't, not yet.

I make my face troubled. I make myself sad. I say softly, I have
to go.

She looks at the typewriter, at her hands resting on the keys.
Her eyes move to the cards she has typed and inserted into the
drawer, and she passes her finger over the row. Then she asks in a
tired voice, You're sure?

She knows my deception, but she has no choice; she can't afford
to accuse me in case she is wrong, in case her daughter is speaking
from the heart. Her hand measures the work she has left, and she
looks at her watch briefly. The daughter's heart is sick with grief.
The daughter, a coward, says, Yes.

The walk home strained worse than before. I carry my two books
pressed between my arm and side, hands jammed into coat pockets.
I walk behind Mummy, because I can't stand the idea of her seeing
me, but seeing her is worse. Her back hunches a little, every step
of the walk a reminder that she'll have to come back later, to put in
her second hour, and that the little bit of pleasure she had found
in her routine has been stripped to the dull bone of a job that isn't
enough. Oh, she's feeling sick, Mummy told the librarians, and they
nodded sympathetically with heads tilted, like two birds.

At the corner I come even with her. She's squinting up at the
stoplights as if the moment they change is the most important thing.
My Mummy's face is wrinkled and her hair is going gray too soon;
Armenian genes, she likes to say, as if the marks of suffering can
be passed on.

—Mummy.

She shakes her head just once. I can't, she tells me, without looking my way.

I fall back as she crosses the road. She hates me now, and with good reason. I clutch my books. I'll stop speaking entirely. I'll vanish into books and my secret worlds and never bother anyone again. I trudge behind Mummy, aflame with injustice, *I'm not even allowed to say I'm sorry, I'm the one who almost died, I'm supposed to let you know when I'm feeling "dangerous."* The deception spins me into its cocoon and I am stuck, grimly prepared to defend myself and my cocoon to the last.

—Well, you're home early, Daddy remarks.

Mummy goes straight to the bedroom. I hear her sobs bubbling up before she closes the door, and then the bigger crying, like gashes.

Alaine comes up from the basement. She takes one look at the closed bedroom door and then turns on me.

—What did you do?

—Now, honey, Daddy interjects. He always stands up for me. I can't look at him.

—Nothing, I say.

—Right.

Alaine pushes open the door, slips inside, closes it, all one motion. Murmuring, tears.

—Are you all right? Daddy asks. He's gotten up from the dining-room table where he does his typing. His big face uncertain, hovering around sorrow and exhaustion.

—I'm fine.

He nods, but doesn't move, and I realize he doesn't want to leave me alone in the room, that he's obeying the rules without question, *Don't leave Marianna alone,* but he's staring at the bedroom door.

—Go talk to Mummy, I say, and he nods again, then he moves, like the lock was undone.

I stay where I am, and he leaves the door ajar. Mummy is sitting on the edge of the bed, her face in her hands, crying so her shoulders bob and Alaine pats her back, pressed up close with black eyes fierce and cold, looking at me. Daddy lowers himself next to Mummy, and they become three, huddled together. He says, Honey, what's wrong? and Alaine's mean gaze fixes on me again.

—Why are you so mad at me! I yell at Alaine. You have no right!

Daddy with a look of waking up, the quick examination of one daughter's cold rage and the other's quivering defense. Now my tears start, and I hate them. I fist my eyes, stopping the flow.

—There, there, Daddy says. What's all this about?

—She's mad at me for making Mummy cry!

The fury at Alaine has exploded into fiery spinning trails of hot in my arms and legs like an explosion blew in my chest and the boiling shrapnel's coursing through me, making me hot metal, not human. I am screaming now.

—She did it her whole life, and she doesn't even remember! Oh poor Alaine, oh go check on Alaine, oh don't bother Alaine! Everything's Alaine!

Mummy lifts her head. This simple movement cuts my voice and it ribbons away. Her hands falling from her face, the slow lift of her eyes to mine. The wait for her to speak, and then she does.

—Everything is you, Marianna.

She says it soft and clear and piteous, the way true things come. My feet won't move off the floor, my arms so tight around my books I think they'll break against cover and spine, the spines digging to bone under the strength of my self-hatred. Even my Daddy's looking down, there's nothing he can say to extricate me from myself, make it ignorable and minor. He looks almost embarrassed, his face turned from the spectacle of me, of my selfishness in this time of extremes. My father is a bent-down man, a scholar who was told yesterday that he cannot be hired at the Cumberland Farms because he is too old and too intelligent. The man doing the interviews said, You'd go crazy here, and chuckled.

—I'm sorry, I say, blubbering. I mean it this time, I do. There are pictures in my head at once: Me cooking a dinner for everyone. Me cleaning up my clothes. Me saying brightly, *OK!* about going to the library. I can fix it, I can. Then I realize, *Me,* and I erase it all, one swipe of thought to another, *How does she feel,* about Mummy, but I can't do it, it's like treading into mud and water, the quick pull downwards to drowning. I'm sorry, I say. I'm sorry.

Daddy looks at me as if he is hearing me for the first time. He wears that gentle, surprised expression, so familiar.

—But honey, my Daddy tells me. You don't have to be sorry.

I stare at him. I feel myself crumpling up, the gentleness of his love too much to bear, I'm going to fall over. Alaine gets up, takes my arm. Come on, she says.

We go to our bedroom. I lie on the floor, staring up; the ceiling is dirty compared to the freshly painted walls. Alaine is going through our shoes, putting them in rows with the toes lined up.

—I'm sorry, I tell her.

The time it takes for her to answer is agony. Finally, she nods. She says, Me, too.

Nighttime and I'm wandering, kitchen to living room, living room to bathroom, bathroom to porch. The streetlamps make my arms gray, and in the grayness, strands of white, the scars made over the years. I lift my T-shirt, run my fingertips along my ribs, down my belly. Some of these scars are smoothing out, pale traces, and I feel again Paul's fingertips discovering them, the dismay in his eyes. I lower my shirt.

My parents saw the truth about their daughters; the cunning thought lives inside the mind like a snake, it strikes in moments of calm. Still they fought for us. They fought until they dropped, exhausted, the war finally bigger than all of us put together, and my father's dread fed his dreams such violence that he fell out of bed, crawled on the floor, fleeing the specter of his friend kneeling on a mountain road. There was no laughter, no solution; they huddled together, overcome by the loss of all the futures they must have dreamed up before the war started and then during it, when there was still hope. That is when they became who they are now, and everything they once were is gone.

Today Mummy cried sitting on the edge of the bed, Daddy and Alaine on either side, cradling her shaking body. I can't feel love, she said. What's wrong with me? I have no more love.

—Of course you feel love, said my father, who worships words, but his words did nothing, my Mummy cannot feel love, it is gone.

This is who they once were. During the war, Mummy received a telephone call from a neighbor in Shemlan. The man said he had no choice, that he was frightened for his sons. For this reason, he had not argued with the Syrian colonel stationed in Souq al-Gharb who had noticed the little cottage and found it pleasing. The Syrians had arrived in Lebanon in 1976 in support of the Maronites, and they didn't seem about to leave. In fact, this colonel now intended to bring his family from Syria, the man explained, and would like a tour of the inside.

The caller must have felt relief when Mummy assented, the relief that comes when danger has been passed discreetly from one's own hands to another's with that awful but necessary cowardice. But Mummy did not fault him; we were the ones who had been renting the cottage since Téta and Jiddo died, not he, and it fell to us to negotiate with the colonel. Who knows what she imagined on that day when she dressed for the trip to Shemlan, slender as a match, her brown hair curled beneath her ears? Daddy insisted on accompanying her, so they left us with Mrs. Awad. I, not part of this story, watched them leave from the window.

In Souq al-Gharb, the colonel eyes her carefully, delighted, and confesses to concern for his family's happiness, that he wishes to make them as comfortable as possible in this foreign place. He motions her and Daddy to a waiting jeep, and their taxi driver lights a cigarette and settles outside the Syrian headquarters for the wait. As the jeep winds towards Shemlan, Mummy explains calmly that this cottage probably would not be the best choice. The kitchen is small and dark, she says, and the stove does not work properly and there is, of course, no running water anymore. The colonel nods patiently as she lists the defects of the house, and Daddy's hand covers hers, and the soldier driving them pays no attention.

They stop in front of the cottage and there are sounds of feet scuffing gravel, of the soldier muttering at the beauty of the place. The lavender sighs its scents and the oleander leaves rustle at Mummy who is envisioning Jiddo right there, thumb over the nozzle of a hose, the water spraying in a steady, sweeping arc across his roses. Vines decorate the stone arches that shade the doorway, and the bamboo chairs and table are dusty so she wipes them with her palm, without thinking, as if she has arrived for the weekend.

The beds, she says, shaking her head, are unsuitable. They are too old and sagging. This is not a place that becomes a man of your rank. He smiles at her, enchanted. Daddy hovers on the edge of this vision and the rooms of this house emit their smells of worn carpets from Persia and silk cushions, the pine desk where Jiddo hid our Smarties and his pipe tobacco, and the uneven tiles shift and knock together beneath the colonel's boots.

But this furniture is nice, he counters, and she tsks at him. The wood is rotting with worms; you deserve Formica.

He remains unconvinced until he sees the kitchen, which is truly a dark and terrible place with its odor of damp plaster and the groaning, smelly refrigerator that never quite gets cold. The colonel sighs and admits that this is not such a perfect environment for his wife and two daughters, but his eyes search the objects decorating mantels and shelves. Mummy senses his desire to come away with souvenirs, so she guides him outside, away from the landlady's belongings and towards the downstairs room Alaine and I use for playing, where she has stored things that belonged to her parents.

When Daddy follows, the colonel suggests that Mummy accompany him alone. Daddy has no choice. He comes to a stop next to the soldier who drove them, who grins and offers him a cigarette, but Daddy is listening to the sound of his Ani's footsteps as she and the colonel walk around the corner of the house, down the paved steps and past Alaine's red swing. The key creaks in the lock and the colonel, just behind her shoulder, mentions how pretty the landscape is, and how unfortunate it is about the kitchen, and how did she, such a woman, manage to cook there for so many years?

Mummy gives him our toys for his children, she gives him her parents' glasses and trays and silverware and vases, and he nods, occasionally returning something that is not good enough, until there is nothing more to offer and he sits on the bed and remarks that it is indeed much more firm than those upstairs and perhaps they should test it?

The colonel is a large man, a commander of troops, an occupier of territories and of people, but he is nothing before the wisdom of Mummy, nothing before the stories that are hers, before the startling vision of Jiddo in uniform cradling her infant body with Téta smiling nearby, of the stark white walls of her childhood home, and of the donkey Saisaban, memorialized in a photograph, braying in the living room and stamping his hooves. She replies, This is not a good time.

The colonel must have been surprised at this bold rejection; perhaps he entertained a quick, violent thought, sitting there with one hand on his knee and the other on the basket of our toys and things, but in that silence after she spoke, something changed in the order of occupiers and occupied, and so he rises lethargically, shrugging, You may be right. And as they walk back on the path and up the stairs he chuckles, he asks, Why is it that you are not afraid of me? Everyone is afraid of me. Mummy's bones have drained away and only air sustains her, she might faint here on the wide stone steps. She replies, using Jiddo's excuse for all his eccentricities, Because I am Protestant.

—*Brodesdan?* He does not know what that is or means, thinks it is an insult in dialect, and so she directs him to the stone church in Souq al-Gharb. That, she says, is Protestant, and the lavender hums with bees and gravel tick-ticks onto stone, kicked up by his boots, and Daddy smiles.

Nobody knows where we have come from. Our house is wood not stone, and Mummy scrubs the yellowed shower-stall walls, she cuts coupons on Sunday and marvels at the amount we will save. She reads about polishing wood floors and then for days we all shuffle about on an old sweater *to buff the floors,* but at the end they look no different. Her failures sit inside me like sharp stones. The stones dig and scrape my gut, and her small, tired face draws me towards anger. I want to shout, *Stop,* because it is futile to try and live here, there is no future, but I know, also, that I must be wrong, I must be missing something. Afternoons, she sits in the Salvation Army chair holding her cup of tea. Mummy has tried to make this house our own, and it resists, she cannot protect us from its shabbiness, she cannot erase the years of other people here, living like us. Still, she sits quietly and thinks, and she does not fight. Sometimes, when I want to be near her, I memorize her figure and reproduce it in my room, my legs crossed, my head tilted towards the window. The thin wall, so thin I can hear the lighter snap.

Night. I open the front door. Dark windows across the street, chains, grilles pulled down and locked. The street itself is puddled with dim light from streetlamps; the one next to our house is broken. I go down the four steps, treading carefully in my bare feet. The asphalt is cold. Tiny sharp stones sting my soles, but I keep walking. If I had courage, I would run. In Beirut empty streets signified danger. The heart jammed with fear at the sight, at the deadly quiet. I reach the other side, navigate around stains near the pumps. I stand with my back to the gas-station window, stare at our open door. The autumn cold seeps through my flesh, into bone. I do not move. Up the road the field is empty, the white horse gone in for the night.

 *Summer*

∾

That day, the air filled with damp early in the morning. Water covered everything without it raining. It was as if the wet sky had come down to the earth, and it had no color but the color of the air, gray and warm. The cars moved slowly, tires shiny black and hissing, and I didn't have an umbrella so my hair was sticking to my cheeks and forehead. There is no telling the feel of a small box nestled in one's palm, nor the weight of it. I am feet in shoes, I am wooden legs and socks sagging from wet, the bulk of me working a path through the gray air, now here, now moved along a little, on my way. A finished thing still moving and breathing, doing the work of the body to keep the body alive, but the work's for nothing, poor little body, betrayed.

On the bedroom floor my fingers work at plastic, the pills pop out one after the other, for a long time. Taste of metal. I write till the pen slides away across the page, marks like hairs, and there's comfort in nothing more to compose because the hand can't. There is peace in that.

I hear typing, far, far away. Remorse wails inside me. Daddy typing during, not knowing.

Later, the wandering thoughts, *Why am I here? What?* Then the memory of what I have done. Distance is a weight coming down on me like the top of the world saying no room for you down there and crushing me, no cut-out shape with feet that is you anymore. I try to remember, to tell myself my story before I go. My story goes away, *no time left for that now.* The rough floor intrudes, lifting my palm from below with extraordinary heaviness, and digging into my cheekbone but I am not moving, then the sense of my hand, which lies nearby, *like something out of a box,* and I cannot link myself to it. The approach of dark.

Marianna? Oh, my God. Honey?

I wake to faraway noises, the shush of people bending over me, leaving, returning, and the whiteness hurts my eyes. When I try to move, my body doesn't respond. The faces of Alaine and Mummy and Daddy appear, and they look so drawn and sad, but I do not understand what has happened and who everyone is, but now, some distance away, an insistent beeping pushes through the cotton of my hearing until I see the great machine and the rises and falls that record my heartbeat. I stare down my body that I cannot feel. Gauze binds my wrists to the metal bedframe. A doctor shines light into my eyes and speaks and leaves, then I sleep.

It is darker now, a different room. I move my hands and they obey; they feel my face and neck, annoyed by the scratching of something lodged in my throat. In the dull light that comes from the hallway, I see an old man lying across from me, propped so he curves like a bowl, and his head sags to the side. His half-open eyes seem to be peering in my direction. Tubes enfold him. He looks apologetic, and his mouth droops and he moans at me, as if begging to be released, as if I, the failed suicide who can barely move, will be able to help him. *Beep beep beep,* his machine says softly. *Beep,* says mine, just off center, and all I can hear is the mismatched sound of our pulse, one pulse knocking softly on the door of the living. Mummy and Daddy's absence is sharp now: I cry and cry, pushing the button I find beside my waist.

It is bright morning. The curtains have been drawn around the old man, but if I shift over to the metal rail I can see him. I wonder if he is aware of me, whether he is curious or sad or dying. He looks dead. He and his bed look like a charcoal sketch on white paper, his head and arms shaded dark and dimensionless, the white blanket touched up here and there with gray to show the bony shadow of his body. I talk to him in my mind. I tell him he doesn't look so bad and soon his children will come see him. His half-eyes glisten, the only sign of light still burning inside his charcoal body. I wonder if dead people's eyes still shine, or if they dry up right away. In the middle of our conversation doctors and nurses come in. They surround the bed and smile and talk. A nurse says, When I tell you, exhale. Exhale! and then a column of fire races from my stomach, through my chest, throat, and out my nose. Blood spatters onto the napkins he laid on my chest. He swiftly folds the tubing as I wipe my nostrils and examine the blood on my fingers in wonder.

—That was inside? I say. My throat feels open and dry. The itching is gone, it was a tube. I am glad I didn't know I had a tube inside me.

—In your stomach, sweetie. He is older and has an accent. He moves around the bed doing things I can't see. The doctors ask me questions. They sit me up, cold circle on my back so I think of leeching, this is how it must have felt just before the skin broke. I take my hand from the rail, rub my fingers together, then on the sheets, saying, What's that? and they say, Charcoal, and I ask, Charcoal? thinking of fire. We pumped charcoal into you, they say cryptically. I see black smudges everywhere on the sheets, the rail, my arms. You vomited last night, the nurse tells me in his accent, but I don't remember at first, then an image surfaces of myself crouched over a bedpan in the darkness, emptying my body, everything black and foul and the hands turning me, lifting, the spread of clean white in the air making a crisp new bed. And vomiting, too, leaning over the side. I am so ashamed.

The doctors file out, and the nurse is about to leave but I say, Where are you from? because I know the accent, it is resonant and familiar.

He says, Israel.

The shames of my body recede and my mind encircles this startling answer, closes in. I calculate his age, maybe forty, and picture him in a tank traveling towards Beirut, or maybe a jet, on foot, anything, and there is nothing to talk about except this.

—Were you in the invasion?

—What invasion? He shakes his head at me like I'm getting delirious again but I press him. The invasion of Lebanon, I say. You called it The Lebanon War.

He is amazed. You're from Beirut? he exclaims. You were there?

I hesitate, then, like an admission of crime, We were taken to Rome.

—So you were not there, he says.

The way he says this leaves me bitter, so I say, My parents watched your tanks crush parked cars. How necessary was that? and he becomes a person now, not any old nurse, he lets himself be seen in the way his face closes up, starting with the eyes and working downwards like a shade drawn down. My story is too big, it's ballooning inside me, many faces and hands, all mine, pressing outward from the inside and there is nowhere to begin, to go back-wards or forwards but I don't want him to leave so I say when he's opening the door, The walls here remind me of Cyprus.

He looks around. The walls are light blue and the paint is peel-ing away. He eases slightly, smiles, I never thought of that before.

I ask again, Were you in the invasion? but he shakes his head, maybe this is a *No* or maybe it isn't, and he leaves me alone with charcoal man who hasn't moved at all. Some kind of quiet empties the room, makes the ceiling a sky and the shape of me a planet un-der blankets. We are the charcoal people. *Beep beep,* we say.

For three days, I am safe here, there is nothing for me to do but lie still, dozing with the comforting noises of the hospital staff in the halls. The Israeli nurse doesn't come again. I imagine him telling his superiors, *I upset her,* but others visit me now and then, touch my face, my arms, smile. I have known this kind of time before. I recognize it, as if I was always in Alaine's body looking out, the cat purring on my chest, everyone whispering.

I slept for I don't know how long. I didn't want to wake up but my body could not help its own light, its hunger for *stand up, walk.* The psychiatrist suggested a hospital to keep me safe from myself, but we couldn't afford it. I was there when the subject arose. I lay in the bed and Mummy and Daddy sat in plastic chairs carried in for their visit. They wrapped their arms around themselves and leaned toward the doctor, peering at him with the open, fearful expressions of those ready to obey any command. Their faces changed as the doctor explained the costs. Daddy said, Maybe we could find a loan, but he sounded without hope.

I wanted to go. I wanted to be in the white hospital with the men in white jackets and a schedule. One of the women in my ward had told me you get your own dressing gown. I desperately wanted a white dressing gown. I knew it was absurd, but I wanted it and I cried. The doctor explained that if I was allowed to go home, I could not be left alone. My parents promising gravely, We won't let her out of our sight. Me turning around myself like a snail, shelless and soft, sorrow spilling out of me. The silk leash of fear bound us, it spooled around me until I was immobilized, then tied its ends to my parents' wrists, whispering *don't pull* in case the thread broke, dropped the weight of me out of this light universe.

Later Alaine told me that in any case she had insisted I not be sent away; she had read about these places and didn't trust them. Her hand on mine, patting. Her black eyes like Vartan's, round and shiny, so full of love and sadness.

—I'm sorry, I said, which was all I said for days.

I lay in bed, staring at the shape of me beneath the sheet. I was flat, for the most part. Here and there, parts of me extruded like sharp little rocks, breaking the smooth surface. I wished I could slice away my tiny breasts, my hipbones and knees, my knuckles, my feet. To flatten myself, to become a smooth surface, vanish, *Where did she go? We loved her, we miss her.* Alaine was barely able to speak with me. Her face shed its new calm; she looked even more terrorized by me than she ever had about herself. She brought me food, napkins, cigarettes. She watched as Mummy placed the pills on my tongue. I couldn't bear Mummy's face when she did this. I looked to the side, mouth open, body limp, as if such utter subservience might convey my grief over what I had done to myself, to my family.

I wrote letters. I wrote to Paul, but I couldn't tell him and I couldn't lie, so I stuffed the letter in my diary. I wrote to Amer knowing he might never read my words. I wrote to the Israeli nurse, apologizing for my curiosity but stressing that I needed an answer to my question, for the sake of understanding history, how stories fit together, because it was miraculous to me that he had been there, and was now here, with me. It had to mean something. The different versions of this letter piled in my drawer.

Every morning Alaine got up, made her bed in silence, and she'd never been this tidy, it was a message to me: *There is order in this room.* She cleaned the rest of the house, too. She cooked. That was when she embarked on the garden; she surveyed it from our window like territory to be seized, plotting, consulting books. Why don't you help, honey? But I was a dummy, dumb and crumpled, my button eyes staring at nothing. Deep inside, nestled inside stuffing of straw and cotton and grit, the remorse, and the longing to pour it out. The dummy failed, circled by worry, losing one opportunity after another.

I knew I was a fraud because Alaine, I was sure, never for a moment considered us. She had been self-sufficient, locked inside her solitary dark room. I, however, could not restrain my curiosity about the effect of myself on the world. I could not stop imagining that day, the part when I had been still conscious and the parts after, blending together what I'd been told into a dreamlike film unwinding over and over before my eyes. I had learned that when Daddy opened the door, Walter saw us. The man with his daughter curled at his feet, asleep, the man crying. It was Walter who knew what to do with my shuddering body, my heart stopping for the sullied blood, slowed like muck. My Daddy saying my name with each breath, as if such soft breath and name can ease the monstrous noise inside a body fighting not to die. He cried so much the wood floor soaked tears, left a patch of damp they found late at night, after the hospital when they stared at the place where she almost died. I closed my eyes to his imagined face, not a face anymore but black and white lines, all the ways you can draw fear. The light filled up with Daddy when the door opened. The gray light settling on his white face.

—Your pain is as real as anyone else's, the first counselor told me.

I sensed falsehood, lackluster truth edging through. Seeing things, I knew, is never as bad as being a part of them. She had a goal, to make me feel good about myself. I argued at first, but she wore me down with her stolid goodness, and the room, too, wore me down with its good, soft blues and pinks. The Georgia O'Keeffe print on the wall above her chair served as a hypnotic tool for her patients, I theorized; I spent many sessions entranced by it while trying to think of stories to end her waiting silence. *Nothing happened to me,* I kept thinking, and this seemed clear and sad. *I was a witness. I was the one in the window.*

Then the truth of it, that I lost my hold. She would not let that go. You almost died, she repeated, so gently, like gently prodding a ball forward through thick grass towards an immobile child. You were the one, in the end, who almost died. You were not in the window.

I tried to tell Daddy I was sorry. He had grown so thin, tremulous. He had lost all reserve. You were the strong one, he said.

That day when he found me, he dragged me from my room to the living room, then to the entryway, and from deep inside my dark place I heard him sobbing, *What do I do?*

A venomous thought winked through my dark. *Just do something right.*

What do I do? my Daddy cried.

I watched Walter, imagining again and again this scene of my near death, his role in it and Daddy's crying. I will never remember this part of it, my punishment. I examined the entryway floor, the way the light slants through the curtain in the afternoon, how we, my father and I, must have appeared in the doorway in this kind of light. I estimated where my father's tears soaked into the little patch of wood; by the time I came home from the hospital it was dry. The jumble of it, the arms and legs and faces and the hot strange light of summer rain, and the song of the ambulance. I hate this imagining and thinking that I can't control, I hate all of it, and most of all myself, reasonless, without words to answer *Why,* to answer *How could you.* All I had and all I have, even now, is the feel of the walk to buy the pills, there being no other act than this.

I am ten and Alaine is twelve, and Daddy says, Go see if your sister is all right. I feel special because I am the only one with passage into Alaine's world. I slowly climb the stairs, sensing their eyes on me, the worry in the air.

The bedroom door is ajar and I reach out my arm, push lightly. The door opens. The tile floor is water, pinkish, I realize, *blood.* I see my sister on the floor, she is curled tightly with one arm outstretched, like an offering. Her wrist is cut again, and the blood spills off into the water, and I see the broken glass everywhere, the sound of it what brought me here. Her eyes looking through me. Anger in them, frustration, an animal twisted up in a trap, each movement another failure.

—She's tried to kill herself again, I report to the grown-ups in the stairwell.

They rush past me. Alaine resists, making her body a dead weight, her face grim and white. Daddy drags her to the bathroom, props her on the toilet.

—Fuck you, she says calmly.

He slaps her. Then he crumples. Oh God, he says. He gently shakes her by the shoulders, as if to jar loose whatever has her in its hold, but Alaine's staring at the floor, her body heavy and falling this way, then that, so that finally Daddy hugs her close and her blank eyes look past his arm and out the door. Mummy eases her way towards them, carrying cotton and a bottle of hydrogen peroxide. I will get to bandage her wrist when it is cleaned; that is my special duty, how I help because I want to help, I want to be a part of things.

At night I am afraid Alaine will get up and kill me. I lie awake, listening.

At the end of summer, six months after we came to America, Alaine burned most of what she owned—books, things collected from the war, everything she had ever written. She kept her trumpet though she didn't play it anymore, and she kept what could not be burned, such as her bullet collection and shrapnel, and she kept a basic set of clothes. I don't go anywhere, she said, and at the time it was true, she never left the house but gave Daddy lists of what she needed, if she needed anything at all. It was after the fire that she changed.

Daddy, the only one of us who knew the rules about fires in America, wasn't home at the time or he might have stopped her, and I suppose that is why Alaine did it then. First she spread everything she owned all over the bedroom. I did not know what was happening. I lay on my side, the sheets kicked away in a tangle, my pale body in shorts and a sweatshirt. I was cold and hot and cold, and my voice was locked up inside me. I saw papers covered with her crazy writing, from so many years ago. But the writing, she didn't even look at it, she stuffed it into a garbage bag, all of it. Notebooks, loose paper, journals. All the writing she had done since childhood filled two giant garbage bags. She carried them one at a time to the yard, then came back inside.

I wanted to say, *Don't do this*. This was the kind of event that led to regret. My mouth stayed closed.

She was paying no attention to me. She threw her G.I. Joe into the box. She threw in books, even the Narnia series. She tore down her posters of Lebanon but left the one of Annie Lennox. She threw in the stuffed kangaroo from Uncle Ara, the wooden marionette from Vartan. I had always wanted that marionette. It lay there crookedly on top in its little velvet clothes. I could take this stuff, I realized, all the stuff I'd coveted for years. The scene transformed into an opportunity. My lethargy drained away, leaving me awake, buzzing with purpose.

—Put it back, she said.

—You don't want it.

—It's mine.

—You're throwing it away!

Alaine grabbed the marionette and tossed it into the box. It's all mine, she said darkly.

All yours, I repeated vindictively in my thoughts. You'll regret this, I informed her with malice. Where's the map?

Alaine glanced at me, confused.

—The escape map, I said, but all the puffed-up vengeance had gone out of me.

She did not even ask how I knew about it. She said, I threw that out years ago, and the way she said it, with such disinterest, made me feel small for having intended to upset her.

Alaine kept piling things in boxes and carrying them to the yard. She was tidy in her purging. As she emptied the closet, shelves, walls, she rearranged my things so they filled up the empty spaces, made it look like only my stuff had ever been there. She made everything mine. When she was finished in the room, she worked on creating the bonfire. I followed reluctantly. The first sign in me of curiosity, of seeing outside. The sun burned my eyes. I didn't want anyone to remark on it; I knew that a glance, a pleased word or two would send me running back in. But Alaine wasn't concentrating on anything except her bonfire, and when Mummy came out to investigate, her attention was fixed at once on her older daughter's methodical work. In this way, I reentered the life of my family, without ceremony, a quick shadow slipping through a door.

—What are you doing? Mummy asked.

—Making a fire.

Mummy wondered aloud, Is this against the law?

—It's like cooking hamburgers, Alaine said irritably.

First she emptied the garbage bags of papers and notebooks, shaping them into a round pile. Then, bit by bit, she added her things until they were gone. The empty boxes she tore into strips and threw them on as well.

Mummy circled the bonfire. She pointed at something. You are sure?

Alaine nodded.

—You're crazy! I blurted. My voice, out in the daytime. The past weeks a dream.

—Shut up, Alaine tossed back.

She examined her things with concentration, not as they had been, but in their new function, in terms of how they would burn, whether slow or fast, which way they would fall. She stuffed something in deeper here, arranged something there, as if this were a sculpture. Her things cried out to be saved, to be loved once again. I wanted to save it all, pile it into my own big box. I would never do this to my things. I raged at the loss of the marionette. I could see the little head and a hand. I couldn't believe Mummy wasn't stopping her. She was in her *serene state,* as I thought of it, her movements all deliberate, slow-motion, and her face so peaceful. She got this way. She seemed to like this notion of a fire. Of course, part of it was knowing there was no way to stop this, that Alaine would find a way to pile everything up and set it alight no matter what.

Alaine struck a match. Within minutes, the fire lickings exploded into a conflagration. The little marionette hand disappeared, books curled away then sighed back towards the flames, the G.I. Joe's ugly face finally melted off his head. It was over sooner than any of us expected, and an atmosphere of disappointment then settled upon our group, me because my rage had deflated to an empty sack, and they because the flames' hypnotic dance was finished. The yard boiled from the fire and the sun. I became aware of ants crawling away in the grass, the dead summer quiet underneath the smoldering fire.

—Do you feel better, darling? Mummy said.

This was a mistake our parents seemed incapable of not making with us, this casual inquiry into our feelings. Alaine and I shared a look. Mummy, the odd one out, retreated, and I felt badly, then, watching her slowly go into the house, her shoulders curving inward.

—Well, Alaine said, surveying the wreckage. Smoke drifted in the hot air.

—Is that OK? I pointed. Flames were still licking out. As we watched, they whipped out, touched the leafy tree at the edge of the yard.

—Fuck, Alaine said.

It was too late. We ran for water. The flames sped up the tree in delight while we tossed arcs of water from glasses, bowls. A siren wailed and moments later, a firetruck exploded into the parking lot next door and firemen launched themselves at the yard, bearing a hose like a battering ram.

—What were you doing? the fireman accused us, hands on his hips. The yard stank of wet ashes and the melting G.I. Joe.

—I made a fire, Alaine said unnecessarily.

—But how did you come so quickly? Mummy interrupted, shading her eyes in the sun as she gazed at our savior in astonishment.

—One of your neighbors called. And a good thing, too! Young lady, do you realize what you almost did?

Alaine nodded. She regarded him warily. The fireman lost whatever words he might have said next. He looked at Mummy, who said, We're sorry. It was a mistake.

By the time the air began to cool for autumn, I had written twelve letters to the Israeli nurse so I called the Intensive Care ward at the hospital to find out his last name. I said I wanted to send a Christmas card thanking him for his kindness. There was only one Israeli nurse there, fortunately, so she knew who I meant right away. The woman said, But he's Jewish. Perhaps you'd better send a more general card. I said, That's a good idea.

I folded each letter separately and placed them in order in the envelope. The changes from one to the next were subtle. I hoped he would be able to follow them. He was only a nurse, after all, so my concern grew and I thought of adding a note, explaining how he should read the letters. I took them all out and read them again through his eyes, which made me anxious.

Alaine picked up the envelope. Who is this guy?

—Is there no privacy in this house?

—He's Israeli, she said incredulously. Why do you know an Israeli?

—He was at the hospital, I snapped. I think he was in the invasion.

The word *invasion* was supposed to shut her up, make her see the worth in this, but she retorted, Who cares if he was in the invasion? Do you want an apology or something?

I shrugged. I set about folding my letters again. I hadn't even read them all, but it didn't matter now. I'd just send them.

—Anna, come on.

I kept folding.

—Anna, why are you sending these letters to him?

I pushed the last letter in and licked the glue. My chest hurt from how fast my heart was beating. Black dots appeared before my eyes and I thought I would scream from the rage inside me, it was trickling out from pinprick holes and I'd explode any second.

I said, To make him understand. The words barely scraping past my teeth.

Alaine sat beside me and gently extracted the envelope from my grip. She turned it over, looked at the address.

—You know he won't understand, she said.

I stared at my stupid, fat letter bobbing in her hand as she considered its weight. I wanted to destroy it. I wanted to go to the hospital and stuff it in the nurse's mouth till he choked. You'll need two stamps, Alaine decided. He'll have it in just a few days.

Guilt was already working its way into me, disintegrating the violent images. He had been kind to me, I judged. He had been a good nurse. In the invasion he had simply done what he was told.

Alaine put stamps on the envelope. She said, Let's go, and I was grateful to her for accompanying me to the mailbox when she could have refused, stranding me here with my secret letter, unable to ask Mummy or Daddy. This complicity heartened me, made me light and full of hope, so I said, Let's make a fire for me, too, and she said, Sure. I imagined all my stuff disappearing in a conflagration, and not only the stuff on my shelves but everything that had ever been mine, sweeping through time to the moment of the fire, such as these letters, refolding themselves in an alien drawer and flying to the heat and ash, or the little alphabet shoes of my childhood or the silk scarf I'd lost years ago. I saw a fire roaring up to the heavens, making the blue sky black for days, choking pedestrians so they held hankies to their faces, and everyone said in amazement, *Marianna's burning.*

—You'd never be able to, though, said Alaine.

This was true, so I said nothing. My letter dropped in the mailbox and we stood there for a moment, staring at the blue box.

—Don't start, Alaine warned me. You can't get it back now.

—I want it back.

—He'll never answer anyway.

I let her drag me away. For days after, I pictured my letter reaching him, his look of surprise, the confusion on his face as he read. I saw him at a desk mulling it over. Then I put him in the park downtown mulling it over, and I believed this so deeply that I made Alaine take me there on the bus, on the pretext of wanting an outing. Every noise became the possible noise of him, ready to answer my question. But such questions have no answers. He walks his rounds, administering medications, giving comfort where he can. His eyes were dark, kind, before I pressed the issue. Maybe he cannot bear to speak of it. Maybe, one day, I will stop wanting to know.

 *Winter*

Before the war is real, the girl pauses just inside the butcher shop, re-
moves with care her straw and plastic lavender hat because one should
not wear hats indoors. Damp hair strands lift into her fingers, caught
up in a soft breeze of sweat and cigarettes stirred by the ceiling fan
clanking around. Flies zigzag hulking, shiny cold carcasses draining
in the window from iron hooks. The dead ribs resemble half-built
hulls of fishing boats, broken where the butcher hacked a row of black
marrow eyes. His son, in her class at school and constant toiler of fail-
ing grades and her pity, sweeps long strokes with a feather broom,
and blood mixed with water sloshes a slow wave out the door, over
the one step to sidewalk and curses, hopping feet. Her secret watch-
ing follows the back-and-forth, now with a cleaver, now with a mop,
now with crumpled newspaper, and all the while his resin eyes brush
hers, quick and cheeky. The boy's face is round and flat as a plate
under stiff brown hair; he is her first love, fulfilled across mottled tile
floor littered with bits of fat, cigarette butts, stained newspaper. She
fantasizes marriage and an apron like his, tied twice around, the short
rubber boots.

   It is 1978 Lebanon. The girl's mother and the butcher speak about
grown-up matters; a villa in the mountains where a man was shot; his
wife and daughter, too, curled around their wounds; militias, armies,
elections. They speak cautiously, with silences. Through the streaked
display window the girl sees the butcher carve meat from bone, press
it through the grinder three times to fineness for kibbeh nayyeh. He
wraps the meat in wax paper, seals it with masking tape, and all the
while their conversation continues, occasionally interrupted by a cus-
tomer waiting on a chair and smoking; No, the possibility of outright
civil war is absurd, or, Franjieh was a murderer, too. What he got is

what he gave. This give-and-take is nothing to the girl's interest in the boy, slouched down now and picking his nails, pretending nonchalance, and she is feeling the joy of this, the sensed promise of adulthood.

The girl's mother pulls her away from her love. They cross streets, turn corners, they buy brioches, and also a strawberry tarte when she begs. They go back home. The girl and her sister sleep on the bathroom floor, playing clapping games with their hands and singing, and the fragile walls quake and rock beneath the roaring leaden sky. From now on she will live inside, beneath things, away from windows. There is nothing for her outside. She learns from herself, in the dark.

෨෩

The leaves have all fallen and blown away, and this American landscape is barren and still, in winter's hands. Daddy puts on a suit.
The jacket is an old tweed with brown corduroy patches at the
elbows. It is raining outside. The raindrops are big and heavy and
slow, they drag the dark sky down with them. Cold seeps through
the windows, under the front door, through the floorboards. Me,
Alaine, and Mummy are sitting in the living room watching Daddy
smoke and adjust his shirtsleeves every so often. Nobody speaks
for a time. Daddy's wrists look white and scrawny next to the thick
warmth of his tweed jacket. He has always worn tweed jackets. In
the many months here, though, he has taken to wearing sweatpants
and sweatshirts, clothing that is entirely alien. Now, in his suit, he
looks like Daddy again. *What do I do?* His voice won't leave me. His
voice, breaking from love, is the only sound from that day. He puts
out his cigarette with slow, gentle taps. He is going to the university because they've given him a teaching position, and all morning
our house has been full of awkward affection, encouragement, a
house full of people pretending no difference exists between a man
without work and a man with.

Mummy says, Are you ready?

—Yes. He gets up, smiling his everyone-cheer-up smile.

Alaine is still in pajamas, her hair a mess of tangles down her
back. She has drawn in blue pen all over her feet so they look tat-
tooed, like the *bedu*. She hugs Daddy good-bye.

—How about you? Daddy says.

I let him hug me. I can't bring myself to hug tightly, for the

guilt. My love for my father is torn up and raw. It is something broken; I broke it, I don't deserve it. The tweed scratches my cheek,
smells of long-ago pipes, books. Daddy sitting at his desk in Beirut,
the great window behind him. Once, a flock of geese flew by. I had
never seen them before. Daddy said they were always shot at in the
war, and here they were, a miracle. We stood at the window, Daddy
and I, and the geese flew past towards Egypt.

—Well, then, Daddy says. He picks up his flat leather pouch, in
which he carries legal pads and other papers. I'm off.

Mummy kisses him tenderly on his mouth. Good luck, darling.

Alaine checks for Walter but he isn't there yet, so she is able to
huddle with us in the narrow doorway, waving good-bye. Daddy
pauses on the front steps to open his umbrella, then strides up the
sidewalk. He has not changed at all, he looks just the way he did
in Beirut, walking on campus. He holds his leather pouch by the
corner strap and swings it as he walks.

Alaine is building bookshelves for Daddy in the basement, and
she melts away at once, and soon we hear banging through the floor.
Mummy stares at the rain, smoking. This is who she truly is, how
the thought of her manifests itself in memory, a woman seated in
her chair with a cup of tea, smoking, her face turned to the light.
She lives in an inwardly place, composed and silent. I could never
be that way, even though I've been trying. I want to be quiet. Ever
since the hospital, I've longed for my own voice to shrivel away
for good. It did, briefly, but it came back. I don't want to tell any
secrets, I don't have any left. I see this new me in a black-and-white
setting, light washing over my face and hands, my eyes brimming
with things not told. But it's never that way. My whole family
knows everything I feel. My whole family knows everything except why I wanted to die, because that has no reason, not one that
exists in words.

I press my cheek to the porch screen, try to peer through one tiny
square. In this diminished world I glimpse a pattern encoded within
the mesh, a pattern of ocean crossings and ships deliberately for-

gotten, of Paul, a soldier returning by chance to the land of his birth, of Vartan, who spent a lifetime fearing the return home but never imagining he would die before doing so, and now us, our feet creaking on floorboards, our necks stiff with listening to news about a country that is no longer ours.

The street dissolves. My palms are sore. The grid is imprinted on my skin now, a puzzle, a maze. At night we dream of home, by day we remember the dreams until we no longer know what is real and what is dreamed. This must be the Lebanese magic Paul's pretend relatives explained. It is the magic of a land that has enchanted travelers and those who were born there for centuries: even now, the country in ruins, it has to be that visitors examine their tickets ruefully, fantasize staying on.

America: This is the land where people want to be, that is what Mummy told me once. She said, You're living where half the world dreams of being. But if I like it here, if I accept the black shining streets, the smell of grass early in the morning, the absence of dirt, I will relinquish my hope of going back. I still have my expired membership to the beach club, my university I.D.s, my outdated identity card that says I belong in Lebanon. I kept them in my wallet at first, then in a drawer, and finally, I stuck them in my album next to my photographs. These cards that I once tossed on tables, lost and replaced without a care, are like talismans promising a return one day.

The cold rain falls quickly, heavily, and within minutes it turns to wet snow and the cars pass more slowly. I see the shadow of myself on the porch, looking out, and longing drains my feet, my hands and arms, what is this magic, this country that insists on being remembered even after forcing us to leave? A spell that works in both directions, a palindrome that catches me always looking backwards, enraged.

—You never wanted to come here, I reminded Mummy. You fought against it for years. Even Daddy did, because of the magic.

—What magic?

I explained, and she laughed, told me that this was Lebanese self-aggrandizement.

I ache for the dead stop of my vision: from the crumbling city, look, the purple-gray mountains around Beirut, barred by check-points, and look, the sea goes just so far, the circle of my vision closed and complete, all possibilities contained in it and no more. This was what I had, and the wait to reach it, or for it to reach me. It was only a matter of time before every detail of my dreams had been explored, used up, and there was a sense of knowing the world that came with that. It was simple, and the hatred of it, the rage stayed in one small place.

First the whole country was available, and the sea whispered of other shores, other people. Ships came and went. Airplanes roared over us all day. The mountains between Lebanon and Syria looked like a giant's fingers resting on the lush table of the Bekaa Valley, but we did not travel that road again. I saw a camel at Baalbak, and then the north was closed off. The pale ruins of Tyre were struck by shells and so we did not go there, although the road leading south began at anyone's door. In the Barouk, ancient cedars sagged under the weight of snow, their trunks big enough to house someone, and a soldier waved us back with his gun. We learned to stay in Beirut, and we swam, and just offshore the unmoving tide of the Mediterranean held the garbage and waste from sewers in thick stationary lines, marking the territory of the war. We came back and lay in the sun. They claimed that the dolphins had left never to return; whether this was someone's fancy or truth, I did not know. The world grew smaller, until there was only my room, a quick drive to a friend's house and another room, a walk around campus, the only place in the city with trees. The mountains, the north, the south became places as far off as a foreign country. On a clear day, standing on the Corniche in full sunlight, these places that were only hours away were as distant as Europe or America. The war closed in tighter, winding itself around the city, closing in like a hunter.

I can recall the day I first dreamed of leaving Beirut. It is lucid, bitter, because I can't help thinking I should have known the consequences. I was walking to the beach, too impatient to wait for Amer. The dust caked between my soles and the damp, sticky leather of my sandals. It was so hot, every step was torture, from the heat and the people watching my lonely passage, the occasional appreciative hiss from a man striding past. I was no longer used to walking alone. My throat closed up, I could hardly breathe. Everyone's eyes were on me, the fair one, the foreigner. I stared hard at every crack in the sidewalk, my feet going forward step by step, each footstep saying, *This is my home, I have always walked here.* But then I could not tolerate it anymore. I beckoned a taxi and climbed in. The driver's eyes pinned me in the rearview mirror, and he chastised that I should be careful, I shouldn't get into any old taxi. I didn't answer. I stared out the window, fixing my face to blandness, as if his words had not even registered. Then another passenger got in front. Where is she going? he asked in surprise, assuming I did not know Arabic. The driver said, The beach, and his eyes found me again.

This was when I conceived of leaving, truly and utterly, without looking back, as if such a thing is possible. It was not that I might fall to harm. It was that I had woken up to find myself a stranger dropped into a dream of heat and smoke, tedium of sunlight, the odor of sweat seeping out of ripped leather seats. And in the haze of waking, someone's eyes on me asking, *What are you doing here?*

I opened the door before the car came to a stop. The passenger exclaimed in annoyance, Where is she going so quickly?

Going, going, gone, I thought, and ran.

I spread my towel on a concrete ledge right over the waves. Behind me, the club decks were filled with people on chaise lounges, playing cards or backgammon. None of the people Amer and I usually sat with had arrived yet; it was early in the day. The sun burned a hot glow on my dark lenses so I closed my eyes, and I asked myself what I was doing here, but twenty years ago Mummy was at this very same beach when she found out her best friend Muna had died, shot by a cripple who had loved her. Mummy ran all the way to Daddy's house and he comforted her, and that is when they fell in love. I lay still, in my mother's body, listening. There was the scent of the oil on my skin, the salt in my hair, the sound of dice clacking on backgammon boards and the laughter from card players, music playing on radios, and then farther away, beneath these innocent sounds, the deep booms from the south, where the fighting had intensified recently. The solid concrete beneath my back and feet seemed like nothing now; I floated above it, tremulous, fragile, skin separating from my flesh and arms spread outwards, palms to the sky, and I thought I had gone mad, sitting here in the sun listening to bombs and cards and the waiters shouting orders. I fixed my gaze in the direction of the mountains and the places where I had played as a child and where Muna died years before I was born, and I pretended that I was her, smart, on the verge of my whole life here at the edge of the sea. In her time, the water was clear as glass, the luminous fish darting between moss-covered rocks. Motorboats hummed along the edge, wealthy predators, waiting for the girls to climb down ladders and drop into the water like offerings. Ella blared on radios, the mountains in the distance rose green and sweet against a brilliant sky, and the moments of quiet were real and deep. Not like now, everyone tensed up and staring south for the booms we just heard. Such quiet, such waiting. But this time it was only fishermen dynamiting fish. I hope there aren't any divers down there, someone laughed.

The water rocked, its own motion or the explosions, it didn't matter. A thin border of filth floated some distance away. Dermatologists warned of skin and eye diseases, but we had a certain pride at being immune to sewage, the victory of the civilian in a war. I slid off the ledge, sank below the surface. I began to dream of other places: of Rome, where I had been, of the bars, the piazzas, the noise of trams and tourists and hawkers, and I dreamed also of New York, which was completely mysterious to me, a place of glass buildings and perfect people. I gave myself over to this idea of leaving, yearning for more than this routine of the beach, of *mloukhieh* on Thursdays and of playing trump games I could not master, of eating cheese-and-tomato sandwiches in late afternoon, my skin hot with sun. I dreamed faithlessly of other, more magical worlds, where I would fall in love, I dreamed of foreigners and movie theaters and different kinds of food, blind to the place I was in that I loved as one loves a mother or father, carelessly, without understanding that it will be gone one day. I was so foolish; I did not know how viciously nostalgia can trick a voyager far from home, of how we crave the past for its every sensation, for what has been irretrievably lost.

Cousin Vartan never answered my letters begging him to take me in, and then he died. We found out months after it happened. Mail from Lebanon was a rare and special event for which all of us had to be present. While Mummy carefully opened the precious envelope addressed in Uncle Ara's spidery hand, we made jokes about where it might have traveled in all the months since the postmark date, each trying to outdo the other in inventing Eastern bloc countries. Kakastan. Pissistan. Then Mummy began reading: *Dear Sweet Ani & family.*

I've looked back in my journals; I mailed two letters to Vartan after he was dead. I do not know what happened to them.

I keep dreaming of winding cobbled streets near Piazza Navona. It is Christmastime, the piazza is crowded with kiosks lit up with plastic santas and colorful decorations, people milling about making purchases and eating. A light, cold rain falls. I cannot find Vartan's apartment. I am desperate, I want to say good-bye, say I love him. The streets grow dark with the rain and people hurry by, their faces hidden under black umbrellas. A familiar building looms on a corner, I run, examine the names beside the bells but now I can't remember which one, even the floor we were on. I can't see because of the rain falling on my face. My frozen hands push at the bells, pushing all of them. Voices crackle through to me. Do you know Vartan? I beg, and they click to silence. The door remains closed. I turn around and the street yawns away in the cold dark rain, to the far-off glimmer of lights and joy from the piazza.

Many times I have told myself the story of how things could have been: I serve as Vartan's apprentice, cataloguer of the secret room, breathing through a surgical mask and living on vegetables. I grow rich, lounging about in penthouses, traveling all of Italy. I ride the train to France to marry Paul. Or, I grow old alone; I sink back in velvet chairs, smoke drifting around my sad eyes, saying, *It was all a long time ago.*

But now the fantasy looks backwards, to Lebanon. I board the plane in America, waving good-bye to my family. My belongings fill two suitcases, and I carry my old typewriter on the airplane. In my pocket is the tiny elephant from Amer and some money to tide me over till I find a job. I'm going to live and work in Rome, and when the war ends in Lebanon, I will go back. Maybe one day I will ride a bus to India.

—India? Vartan cries, appalled. What is this new madness?

India is a mystical place, I argue, but he refuses to understand. The fantasy founders on the truth, on what Cousin Vartan actually would tell me.

—Stop this dreaming! he commands. Stop pretending you can have what you had! It is gone.

I find myself alone in a dead man's apartment in winter. The heating and electricity are not connected, and it is so cold that I pull my coat tighter around me and stamp my feet. His friends have been coming by, packing up his belongings. They are stacked floor to ceiling in wooden and cardboard boxes, in trunks dating to the Great War, in inlaid chests and silk scarves. The zoo-animal collection spills over shelves, legs and heads and tails and some with wheels for feet. The Persian carpets lie folded in a small hill against a wall, tied with twine. They emit the smell of naftaline.

I follow Vartan's ghost through the dim rooms. He wears a woolen scarf around his neck and one around his head, tied under the chin like a cartoon of a man with a toothache. His eyes are wet, dark stones deep set into his face. He examines his belongings; he parts cardboard flaps with his fingers and peeks into the darkness of packed books, silk and wool clothing, pottery wrapped in newspapers whose dates elicit a rush of nostalgia as the pages crinkle open.

Now I am in the tiny kitchen decorated with yellow and green tiles and faded gray shelves. I hold my fingers above the stove's heat, waiting for the water to boil. Earl Grey in the metal tea holder, the clink as it drops into the cup. Sunlight, drab as thinned material, settles apologetically along the dusty ledges and chair backs and tabletop. I wash my hands in the weak light, turning them over one another, staring at how my skin looks so young and white and clean compared to his.

Vartan prepares for his nap. He folds down the bedspread and unties his shoes.

—I wish, I begin, but he interrupts.

—You are a dreamer! he accuses, repeating the speech from years before, when Alaine and I visited him. He lists our family's criminals in staccato.

—Your grandfather, with all his antiques that he would not sell, no matter how poor they were! Your grandmother, who could have lived in Paris, living in Souq al-Gharb! My father and sister, selling *haute couture* in the middle of a war! Your mother, aah, your mother—he slows down, for she is his favorite cousin and deserves emphasis—Your *mother,* who studied history and married a historian: Dreamer! And your father, even if he is American, he is one of us! We affected him! You want to be like them, always dreaming?

The day he gave us this tongue-lashing, I was too miserable to answer, upset that I had so disappointed him. I only wanted him to love me, to think me grown up and not a foolish dreamer. But even then I sensed he had to be wrong, and now I think he was; there is realist blood in my veins, after all. Auntie Lupsi, for example, built her store from nothing, and secured the love of three men in her lifetime, possibly more; Uncle Ara told me these stories with pride even though she was his wife. And Daddy's father, my granpa, I never think of him, but it is true that he gave up his dreams in order to support his family during the Depression. Even the dreamers themselves were never truly punished, except by being poor; after all, were Téta and Jiddo not happy? In every photograph, their eyes shine with love and satisfaction. And most of these dreamers, such as my father and Téta, left one country for another.

—I'm going back to Beirut, I tell him, a last-ditch effort. You'll see.

But Vartan has closed his eyes to me. He is already settling into sleep, taking the deep breaths he claims are good for the blood. I stand in the doorway and watch him. The bed is stately as ever, covered with a deep burgundy, gold-fringed bedspread, and the silk pillows billow out around his head. He has pulled his scarf down across his eyes and snores faintly, one hand on his chest, the other by his side, feet slightly apart. The bedside table drawer is ajar, years of letters from his family spilling out. He never went back. He is gone. I acknowledge this now, while he sleeps. Holding in my two hands a steaming cup of tea, leaning in the doorway, I see him dying, and the room is cold and very still but for the wisps of steam and the whisper of his breathing that sounds so precious, each breath finite, one closer to the last, and from between the heavy drapes across the windows, a thin stream of winter sun edges across the tile floor, silently recording the passing afternoon.

∽∾

This is how we had to leave home. The militias went to war for West Beirut; Amal, Hizbullah, PSP, I didn't know who was fighting and I didn't care. Within days, Astrig and Uncle Ara came to stay with us since fighters had occupied their building. We moved a small table and chair into the bathroom. We sat in there and smoked and drank coffee, and the bombs shook the building and each whistle of a rocket snapped us in our places like a photograph, tensed for the explosion. Astrig burst into laughter. What would your father say, in America, about his family and relatives who socialize in bathrooms?

I retreated to my room, away from everyone else. My windows were opened wide to this war, and through a haze of whiskey, which Mummy no longer cared that I drank, I saw how funny it was to have the windows open simply so that they would not shatter but therefore inviting what was outside to come in. It was a valiant and predictable feeling, to lean my head out into the air of the battles and their smells of gunpowder and dirt and metal. Drunk, I sat before my typewriter and wrote about other places. *Listen to this,* I wrote. *The war never meant a thing to me,* and as I wrote this I knew it was true, that the war was other people's business, all this noise had nothing to do with me and I was separate and floating and calm. The militias traveled the streets, and I listened to their boots on the pavements. The sea was heavy with waste, its movements pendulous and slow as breathing on a deathbed. The fighting continued until three, four in the morning, and still I would be typing, crumpled paper all over the floor, and Astrig complained that it was too loud, this clackety-clack, so that Mummy ordered me to sleep. But I could no longer sleep. I lay in bed and stared. I stared at the piano that I could not play well. I stared at the walls covered with posters of rock stars who had no idea I existed. I stared at the lumps of my feet under the sheets, at the still-open windows, at the sliver of movement through the dark that meant Alaine's cat had gotten into my room and would try to scratch me. I returned to planning a new life, the only other one I could imagine: I would go to Rome after all. I would work in a pub and meet a lover and write a book and drink wine. I would do this, I would do that, and as the battles waned at dawn, the rest of the world presented itself to me: I stared, eyes dry and fiery, at the ragged palm trees and the buildings, the concertina wire, the mountains just visible from here, and then at the sea across the Corniche. It was so quiet now. Rome, my only other imaginable world, would soon be ready to wake. The merchants would shout at one another in the markets. The streets would be flooded with precious water to prepare for the customers. The trams would start moving and the population would yawn and stretch and shower and dress in fine clothing. I began to cry, my hands beating at the windowsill, enraged at how there was nothing to do here except wait and think and smoke and stare, dumb to the coming years of nostalgia, dumb to my future self who would cry in the same way in other countries, craving what I had so despised.

The fighting intensified, the shooting and bombing went on without pause, and we gathered blankets and pillows to move to the basement along with all the neighbors. Someone had a gas burner, and tea was passed around. People became ghosts, staring at one another, silently knowing we might die. We felt despair, and it kept each of us in place, seated, separate, a viewer of the self and others. It made it not really matter to die, and acceptable not to. The lifts and falls of hope had no place here.

During these long nights the hallucinations began: the waiting

ghost-eyes in the dim halls were the opened eyes of exploded bullets, they were the vaults in the ground and buildings that had
evicted the population, they were the splattered holes across the
walls of the city, the spillings of shrapnel, or a sniper's mistake.
There were eyes everywhere here, watching and waiting.

I sneaked upstairs, craving solitude. I imagined my room, reading
in my bed. My bed, my walls, mine, mine. But I stepped through
the entryway into a place no longer mine. We had fled the rooms,
taking those few objects that might mean survival, and the war had
moved in: all that dwelled here now was the vast, awful sound of
battle: the trra-trra of machine-gun fire and whistling rockets; the
deep, resonant booms, windows shivering with every explosion.
I hadn't truly heard it before. Our own voices and laughter, the
warm presence of us hiding in the hall or bathroom, running from
room to room to fetch this or that—we had somehow, impossibly,
thinned out the true sound of the war. I wandered through the
rooms, an intruder. I gazed at the furniture layered with dust, the
curtains hanging so still. I gazed at the photographs, the empty
glass next to Mummy's chair, the book left open on the couch. It
was as if we had fled long ago, and I had happened upon a relic of
our lives, or a dream. I did not touch anything, I did not take anything; I was a ghost, floating about from room to room, viewing all
that had been left behind.

—The hospital was hit.

This message, deciphered from the splutter of the radio, reached
our group in the basement against impossible odds. Where was the
announcer? What building contained this person whose voice kept
going, talking, announcing? He should have been in the basement.
What was he doing, in this crazy night, and how did he know what
happened every minute, every hour?

Alaine had told me once that there was an international conven-
tion, rules to maintain order during a war. But no laws governed
this war. The things that break rules happen in secrecy and in darkness, and those who are watching do not see clearly because their

eyes are ghost-eyes, covered with a film that will not be removed, even with surgery, and the world becomes opaque and shadowy, as if a tear has flooded the eye socket and stayed floating across the cornea, and we swim towards the mirage: it is not so violent, not so terrible, it is time to go shopping, there are sales on Hamra.

One morning I woke in the basement to find myself alone with the neighbors' children. They were laughing and pulling the blanket from under me so that I started to roll, and they squealed when I lunged at them. *Sshh,* I whispered, and they knelt on the floor, fingers pressed to their lips. The silence outside was shocking. I sat very still until I heard the faint noise of the sea, and it was as if I had not heard it for a long time. The night before teeming with people and talk was finished, the basement bare and ugly, and there it was again, the sea lapping the rocks, the endless sound of a world gone quiet. I pictured people slipping away, Mummy, Astrig and Uncle Ara, Alaine, gesturing *let them sleep,* as if we were in our rooms.

—Hurry up, I told the children, and we started to fold the blankets, I at one end, they at the other.

Alaine brooded during the weeks of fighting. With Astrig about, she did not need to help Mummy as much. She sat on the floor of her empty minimalist room with paper and pens, her wild dark hair shrouding her face, and she explained that she had invented a new game for mankind, and that for this game one would need at least four or five people, and that it involved each person being hooked by the flesh onto one chain suspended from something strong. They would hang one above the other, and the goal was for each person to unhook himself so the next could do the same, and the ultimate goal was for everyone to survive, which was unlikely. Naturally, she added, there were problems with this, such as the person on the bottom always having the advantage and how would you get people to play to begin with?

—She's crazy, I told Amer, who managed to sneak in visits during lulls.

—Maybe we should just play.

Amer's face was hollow from exhaustion and he smelled rancid. I gave him a towel and some of Daddy's clothes; our building still had water at least. I sat in the hallway while he bathed, and he sang Arabic love songs to me off-key through the door. Alaine's cat seemed to like them; it sat with its tail curled about its paws, listening. Amer was flattered. He promised he would take it to his house if we ever had to leave.

—Maybe we should make the cat play, I told Amer.

—Poor cat.

—I hate it. Look. I showed him scratches on my legs.

—It's just an invention, Alaine said with impatience, because she had remarked on our obsession with the game. Something to pass the time.

—A crazy invention, I pointed out.

—What do you expect? Croquet?

Amer unloaded marbles from his pocket, distracting us.

—It came to me, he said, that the minimalist room is perfect for this. He thumbed a marble across the floor, and we played.

That is how the days went, and then the Syrians arrived. Soon they were everywhere peeking out of sandbag houses on the sidewalks, the gun barrels pointing out at the streets. They stared straight ahead and kept their faces still because they knew no one wanted them here. The old joke resurfaced about Syria having no more money for toilet paper and I measured the gauntness of their faces in the corner of my eye, the rigidness of their backs, trying to imagine the places they were from and what they had to be missing. People walked past these barricades as if they did not exist. No one would speak to them.

I, too, ignored them, although I knew no one seeing me do this would appreciate it, because I looked foreign, and the Syrians

themselves likely did not even notice my coldness. I was not unaware of the irony, that I was bonded to them through this twisted
route, their foreign faces and mine, our separateness, and I despised
them for it.

There was supposed to be peace now, but one day shooting flared
up as Mummy and I were walking back from shopping. It was only
a few blocks away and everyone on the street stopped, and the
Syrians leaped behind the sandbags and cocked their guns, clack-
clack. People ran for the shelter of doorways, jostling for room, but
Mummy seized my hand and we kept walking, hugging the wall. I
saw Mummy's reasoning; the sound of jeeps careening towards us
came from a few blocks away, and if we snuck down this next side
street we would be fine. It was too late. A jeep burst onto the main
road and screeched onto the sidewalk in the turn. There is only
this: the driver's fierce concentration as the jeep tilted onto two
wheels, the mounted machine gun and the soldier behind it laughing, his glance at me and the gun swinging until the black hole of
the barrel immobilized me. Then the moment was gone and the
jeep crashed off the sidewalk and went down the street, the soldier
looking back over his shoulder as if he knew me now.

Alaine told me that once in a parking lot a piece of shrapnel had
whizzed past her, and I also knew that years before, Mummy had
been shot at by a sniper when she was hanging laundry on the roof,
and the hole in the sheet was testament to that near-death. For me,
there was only a look, the fractioned glance into the black eye of
a barrel and the laughing face of the soldier who guided it, and it
might not have happened at all.

I stood on Amer's balcony though voices on loudspeakers were
ordering people to stay inside. You should obey, Amer called out
from bed, but I didn't want to.

The Syrians had surrounded the area, and the building down
the street was being emptied of men. They were being led single
file into the trucks. *Palestinians,* I thought. But the Palestinians had

been taken away like this years ago. Who were these men? I had heard about the Syrian prisons. There was no way out for these fighters, whoever they were. They would be taken across the border and never seen again. Women and children gazed down from the balconies, and the building was wretched with bullet holes and shattered railings, laundry strung everywhere. I could hear crying all around. A soldier looked up, noticed me. His arm waved energetically, but I looked elsewhere, he would think I had not seen him. In the corner of my eye, I saw him look around, wave again. He had come all the way from Syria, and it seemed improbable, that he should be right there on a road he did not know. If he were in college, he would be studying civil engineering. It was a popular subject for young men. When he turned and deliberately lifted the machine gun to his shoulder, I felt Amer's hand on my arm and then he pulled me in.

Soon after, the fighting started, and stray bullets pitter-pattered like rain onto the empty dirt playground across the street.

Amer and I drove to pass the time; we drove from this shop for vermouth to that friend's house to his to mine and back to another shop for eclairs. We turned a corner and there it was, the butcher's where a boy from my childhood had worked with his father. I had not been by here for so long. I looked through the dirty windows past the great cadavers hanging on hooks, and saw him, long-legged and slouching on a tall stool, a box of Lucky Strikes sticking out of his shirt pocket. His round face had narrowed with age, but his hair still looked cartoonish, like fieldbrush tossed flat.

Amer pulled at my arm, You don't speak Arabic, and I was confused, then saw the Hizballah checkpoint ahead.

As I remember this, I see that it is not a coincidence that this area was also where the butcher shop with my silent childhood friend was located; this is how you realize the truth of things, that a road and a person can be the same, that a land and a face can speak the same language. I did not belong here anymore. Even though

I had just as many remembrances of this land, when I walked on the street people stared as if I had dropped in from the sky, as if I were an explorer who was a little nervous and ashamed. My hands held each other in my lap in fear. If I stare hard enough, even now I will see him through the butcher's window, sitting on the stool, older now, smoking, longish stringy hair around the plain face, eyes implacable, and what would he say or think to see my shadow in this car? There is nothing I could say to him, or he to me. Amer touched my arm as we stopped for the checkpoint. The window rolled down and I smelled the smells of the road, the evening heat, and I kept my eyes on the smooth surface of the dashboard, on the scratches in the vinyl and the places where the metal underneath shone through.

I invent now, on the butcher boy's imaginary face that visits me, a scar from eye to ear; I yield that he, like the rest, could not completely dodge the war. How did it happen? What did he do to pass the time of the war, and how was it he lived? I, disguised, drift between ribcage and loins, the soft, washed-out scent of flesh calling back wide broom-sweeps, quick eye-meet and tremble, his sudden thrust of broom handle an act of communion. The cool bloodied water sloshed over my sandaled feet, his startled grin of triumph how I knew he loved me, too.

It was only a matter of time before we would leave; I should have read it in the motion of our car, pulling away from the soldier, him young with a dark close-cropped beard, eyes flat with disdain. I should have read it in the slant of that road, the light on the butcher boy's window and how surprised he looked, lowering the cigarette from his lips and staring.

꒰꒱

The air is silent, cold. The thinnest veil of snow covers things and the postman's boots crunch on the strange ground. The mail drops through the slot. Smell of coffee and Daddy's cigarette. I am in bed, late morning, staring through the window at the empty street. Alaine's hammer bangs in the basement, and Mummy went shopping a short while ago; the metal cart clanging is what woke me. I dress, still unused to the transformation of our bedroom from a dark hovel to this place of blue walls and tidy shelves. The room feels empty without Alaine's things. All she owns takes up one side of a shelf, but I have been trying to make use of it. The rocket ends hold up my books, and the bullets are heaped in a few glass bowls as decoration. She lets me keep the trumpet out, to brighten the room, because she says she'll never play it again anyway. She laid the biggest piece of shrapnel on its outside surface, so that it curves like a boat, and placed in the hollow all the marbles she ever won in contests. We have tried playing on the floor here, but discovered it is not actually flat. Part of the charm, Mummy said.

I check the mail, nothing. I sit in the living room under a blanket, the TV on low, listening to Daddy pour his coffee in the kitchen, then the soft clinking of his cup and saucer as he walks back to the dining-room table. I know just how he looks; his hands rummage through papers, drawing out something written, then he inserts a blank sheet in the typewriter and turns the knob three times swiftly, slowing down to one click at a time until the paper is arranged just so. In the few minutes after this, he sighs, sips his coffee, and lights a cigarette that will burn away in the ashtray, leaving another fallen column of ash. Then the clatter begins. I have not turned around at all in the silence; my Daddy and I live away from each other, surrounded by pockets of empty space. We catch each other looking and turn aside; we share something not to be put into words, or faced. This is what it must be like when a person has an accomplice in murder, or when two people witness something dreadful and cannot bring themselves to speak of it. I have a cruel pain inside me. At night I stand in the entryway and place my finger where Daddy's tears fell, I lay down my hand where my head lay under his two hands. I have heard him crying at night, not the clean, clear tears of sadness, but a heaving sound, like wreckage coming to the surface.

I've realized I never really saw the truth during my childhood. They hid this from me, the apartments in Beirut were big enough for hiding. This is how they must have cried over Alaine, while we slept.

Walter has hung many-colored lights in his garage window, and his forlorn shape moves slowly back and forth beneath these loops of lights. I have been waiting for the courage I need, and now, from the mixture of the lights and his patience and the noise of Daddy's typing, the courage comes. I wrap a scarf twice around my neck and chin, zip myself into a ski jacket Alaine found at a thrift store. I am encased in bulging material, overwarm, but I can't imagine the opposite, me running out in my sweater and jeans as Alaine does if she wants something from the Cumberland Farms. I put on gloves, I pull on a hat.

Daddy stops typing. He turns his frightened face to me. Where are you going?

I say, To see Walter.

A moment passes. Then he nods and resumes his work as if this is the most normal thing in the world, his daughter leaving the house, his daughter speaking.

Bells clink when I push open the glass door, a wave of heat, car-oil smells. Walter looks up and I catch astonishment on his long face.

He is seated on the high stool, his boots hooked through the metal rung. I stop in the doorway with the cold air leaking in around me. There is nowhere to go but closer to Walter, the room is so tiny. I cannot close the door for the heat, and for being closed up inside, in the quiet here.

—Close the door, he says.

—Oh, I just wanted to say thank you.

It sounds terrible. It sounds empty and stupid. Anxiety floods me, he thinks I hate him, he thinks I don't want to be here at all. The little room is full of cold now. I let the door close a little, but stay blocked there, one foot still outside. Walter untangles his big boots from the stool and sets them on the floor. Even half-sitting and slouching, he is extraordinarily tall. His wispy blond hair sticks out from under a Mobil baseball cap. I realize he's young, not much older than me. All this time I thought he was at least thirty.

—Well, he says. That's quite all right.

He is embarrassed. He punches open the cash drawer, fidgets with the bills, squaring them up. Tucked between the wall and the register are two magazines, rolled loosely. A sci-fi magazine and *Newsweek*. A huge muscular woman with windswept purple hair stands on the sci-fi cover, her sword raised, her feet planted on a craggy boulder. I stare at her with interest on my face because I don't know what to stare at, and maybe I will think of a question to ask about the magazine. But I have no questions. The magazine evokes a corridor of anxiety in my mind, me running blindly towards whatever *Walter* means: a house somewhere, a car, a place apart from the gas-station office where Walter dreams, eats, nods off in a big chair reading about his science-fiction world. This same Walter stepping outside in summer, the bells ringing against the glass as he leaves, because he's seen the open door, a man and his daughter.

—Your dad's a good guy, he says. Most professors around here are impolite.

—He is a good man, I answer. I nod, and he nods back.

—Well, he says.

—I like your lights.

He shrugs. We put them up every year after Thanksgiving.

—Oh, OK.

He doesn't look at me because I'm teary now, but he says, You take care of yourself, and in this way he releases me. I let the door close carefully. To make up for my inept apology, I turn and wave as I cross the gas-station area, and he waves, too, the lights winking over his head. In that moment I'm aware of the minutest motion of my body, the way my gloved hand moves through the air, the feel of my face making a smile and how I'm twisting a little, to keep him in sight, then the arm dropping and the one-two-three of the icy steps, my feet groping for a safe place.

I close the door, stamp the carpet. Daddy looks up but he doesn't ask any questions. I concentrate on getting off the gloves and the hat and the coat and the extra sweater. During all this he stays in his place, considering the page he is typing with great attention. I get back under my blanket. In the window, tiny flakes of snow blow about, sticking nowhere, and then my voice speaks for me, rushing out like something scared.

—Isn't today the day you go downtown?

His hands, startled, stop above the typewriter keys. I wanted to, he says. But Mummy's going to work when she gets back.

We consider this truth in awkward silence. I can feel myself going all numb with guilt for having to be guarded so I say abruptly, before it gets too overwhelming, Well, I can go with you.

It sounds angry, the way my efforts do, but Daddy's used to that.

—All right, he says after some thought.

That is how we finally go downtown, a place of desolation for the developing strip malls, and how I meet his old man friends; the moment they nod hello I know they've been told what happened, and there is an atmosphere of tense pleasure at my arrival, at the implied success, however small. They get into conversation and I walk amongst the shelves, dipping my cupped hand into the nails to enjoy the feel of metal pouring between my fingers. Their voices roll through the pipe-smoke air of the shop, quiet for a time then rippling with chuckles, and I watch my Daddy through the peg holes of metal shelving, a man spending some time with friends, talking about nothing but alluding to everything, and the snow falls gently over the abandoned streets.

We're waiting for the bus inside the glass hut but the freezing wind sweeps in. I get closer to Daddy, maneuver so he's blocking the cold, and then I say, I'm sorry about Uncle Bernie.

It's so quiet despite the wind and the men talking on the sidewalk and the rumble of the bus approaching. Daddy says, Me, too, and he frowns down at the ground as if something is there that will help him get things in order, and he just has to find it. That world of Uncle Bernie dying and the way it happened is so far off I don't think it ever existed, but for times like this. I want to take my Daddy's hand but the bus arrives, and his hands are busy searching his jacket for the tickets. I know I had them here, he says, a little frantic, and then he finds them. We board, and we ride the long ride home in silence, Daddy not once turning from the window.

Because we know the story, there is no mystery, no room for dreaming. Uncle Bernie put on his coat, he set out to have drinks with his old friend Stephen, and he never arrived. Fifteen months later, they shot him in the head. My Daddy bent over the table at the morgue, said, That's him, and then he left, and I cannot know what it is to do such a thing, to identify the corpse of my best friend. This I do not dream. My father is a man who did not go to his younger brother because he only had the flu, and now he carries his brother on his back. He was not there when his friend was beaten and gagged and folded into the trunk of a car; he was not there when his friend was made to kneel without shoes. My father is a man whose parents died far away, suddenly, and whose family drifted to different parts of America, proof of their existence only in the occasional card or telegram. His daughters have reached for death in his own arms. At night, his wife dreams beside him, moaning in her sleep.

My father sits in the pantry sipping whiskey and perusing news magazines. The smoke from his cigarettes lifts to the ceiling and hangs there. His legs are crossed, slipper dangling to show a pale, veined foot, the heel dried up and hard like an old orange peel.

I do not remember the last time I saw our cottage in the mountains, and now I know that it is gone. All that is left are the walls. Uncle Ara described it to us; I have seen pictures of such places. The broad reddish floor tiles were stripped but for some scattered broken-off pieces, and the dirt beneath has become the floor, an uneven, rolling surface of broken things, unidentifiable books swollen and dried like puff pastry, shell casings, petrified human excrement. The only things the thieves and soldiers did not steal are the books and the old rotten-smelling refrigerator, which lies on its side in the tiny kitchen. The house blends in with the garden; plants grow along the inner walls, and the sun travels where it does not belong. From any room in the house you can look up to the sky, and the trees bend over the walls to provide spots of shade. Beyond these walls, the property itself has merged with the neighbors' land, whose mansion of dark stone with arches is a ruin. Our best summer friends' building was bombed long ago, the family moved away and lost to us. Building stones have become more valuable over the years, and the soldiers sell them. If I were to go there, I would not find the lower gate, nor any other sign of where the land began and where it ended, and it is the same on Crystal Mountain, where Uncle Ara built his house that was destroyed twice in the war. This is what it means to change a landscape. It is what happens in memory, to those familiar streets that would surprise one with their strange twists and turns that have been erased over the years.

The small house at the end of the road that I would watch because I was so intrigued, the woman reading in her velvet chair, who was she? I close my eyes and see the shutters shut and the door barred and everything dark and silent. It was only by chance that the story of Ziad came to me, the truth of the door opening and the folded white wings of his horse and the spinning chamber of a gun. The night Astrig told me and Amer what she knew, she stretched out her hands as if to show me Ziad's blood, how it felt on her skin, as if he were laid out before us and she had just stroked him.

I know this secret that everyone knew but which was secret, and too many years have gone by to tell again and again what happened. He travels round and round the stone house but it does not let him in. They say he was murdered because of a bad business deal. Someone came in and said, *I have waited for this.* Someone came in and said, *I am going to kill you.* The story fascinates, this stranger killing and disappearing. Over and over the stranger re-enters the apartment. He made his own death. He squandered his father's fortune. He wanted to build a disco.

It does not matter how he died, though it should. The stone house remains closed, more likely destroyed, and I have been told that the landscape has changed forever: there is no place left that can jog truth into clarity. How do you change a landscape? The empty, ruined mountain stands guard over the city on the shore: on the rocky slopes of burnt trees and weak shrubs, there is possibly still a soldier smoking in the hot haze of morning, and it used to be that he would stand in the shade of the pines, behind him the barracks with the antiaircraft lodged firmly in the ground, his eyes waiting for the sky to change, children rustling in the underbrush, *Who can get the closest?* Now that there is nothing left to fight over, still he is ordered to wait and he does, the lot of soldiers.

Uncle Ara sold his house. I expected to return in twenty, thirty years, measure and sight the property, mark the borders once again. There would have been a way. I would be the crazy old part-Armenian lady on top of the mountain, my house a harbor for young travelers passing through on their way to India or Nepal. I would buy fresh goat's milk from the herders, plant roses in the ashes of Téta and Jiddo and Auntie Lupsi. From memory I would have resculpted that side of the mountain that should have been ours. I would have found the god heads lying on the road, ignored by soldiers who did not recognize their value, and I would have placed them in a new wall. In the evenings, I would have curled up in a velvet chair, counting the stars through the open window. Alaine always said we would never go back.

I ask about Ziad, I ask about Muna and the other stories, and I tell myself the stories the way they seem to be. My Daddy's chair is wood, with a thick cushion tied to the chair back. I sit with my fingers on his typewriter keys, tapping them without hitting the ribbon. The keys fly towards the ribbon on their long necks, like sticks beating, many tiny people with sticks beating at one thing, one thought. The sound of half-typing is miniature, an echo of itself.

I am a poet. I will be old and beautiful, revered. My books will be small, delicately bound, light in the hands. Vartan never answered my letters, the ones that I sent before he died. I picture him with cucumber slices on his eyelids, trying to ignore the presence of my ink-sprawled pages, trying to keep his body alive. I want to know where my letters are. Perhaps they piled up in the foyer, or perhaps they were delivered to him in the hospital. *Dear Vartan. I wanted to tell you.* The letters folded, held together with a rubber band by strangers, Vartan dead with his hands at his sides, under the ground. He was already dead when I was writing. Writing to no one, crying and writing, and I am crying now, tears like water, so full they splash on the typewriter keys, the wooden table, my hands.

—Do you still miss Muna? I ask, the question not formed before reaching my mouth. My mouth slightly open. Mummy's shocked eyes and the snow falling steadily, in absolute silence.

I need to know how it is to lose the best-loved one, how it is the years pass afterwards. Vartan's hands restored things to beauty, and his voice admonished me but even now the precise sound slips a notch higher, dips too low, and I don't know how to remember the sound of one who is dead, so I ask and ask, but Mummy does not tell me.

Muna is unlike anyone the young man has ever seen with her short, blond hair, thin like silk, and light brown eyes. She plays records for him and lends him books that he reads avidly, taking notes, finding interesting passages to bring up during their next conversation. She hardly notices his deformity, and for this he is grateful: he was born with one leg shriveled and twisted, and his gait is awkward and strangers pretend not to notice, their curious eyes a source of humiliation for him.

Muna and the young man speak about European poets and novelists, about the mystery of religion, about the creation of the State of Israel. He is Palestinian; his family fled to Lebanon in 1948, when he was four years old, and Muna's sorrow for this shows in her eyes, which lower every time Palestine is mentioned, when the homeless and the lost and abandoned surface, when his father's rage, which has been directed at his only son for years, leaves bruises that she touches with her fingertips. He is not afraid to cry in front of her, and his tears, big and luminous against his dark skin, glisten in the lamplit room where they sit close together, Schubert in the background.

She lives in Ras Beirut and attends the American University; they are both nineteen and in their first year. It is 1963 and young women are restless and toying with abandon, and the city is colorful and wild with foreigners and sailors and festivals and concerts. Muna disobeys her mother: she and the young man walk on the Corniche in secret, they read poetry to each other under the trees on campus, they smile across small round tables at cafés. Their friendship is deep and powerful and new; it occupies all of her time. Muna tells her best friend Ani that she has never felt this way before, so understood, so inspired. She and the young man write poems to each other: he writes a stanza, she the next, and then back to him, and the verses become more and more romantic, until finally one day she reaches the last line of his latest composition and knows that he has finally admitted to loving her, and she cannot think or feel anything except that she may have known this all along.

They are sitting under a Banyan tree on campus, it is early summer. He has been pacing while she reads, and now she hears his foot dragging in the gravel as he approaches. Muna does not love him, but for an instant—perhaps it is the sound of his foot or the ripe smell of summer, the dragonflies hovering above the grass and the tingling insects in the flowers—the possibility throws itself open, vast and piteous, and she looks up in surprise.

He sees this happen, this moment when she might indeed fall in love with him, and he bends down and grasps her hands, pushes his cheek against them. The touch of his skin, the muscles of his hands fiercely binding hers, is shocking. She at once tries to pull away but he holds on, staring stubbornly at something beyond either of them. Frightened now, she pulls harder, and her hands slip out of his so suddenly that she almost loses her balance, and then the moment is finished.

He reaches for the poem, folds it, and pushes it into his pocket. She intuits the source of his fury, the way he looks at her with such disgust. It is rage at her life, at the trips to Europe, the opulent summerhouse in the mountains, the way she has kept him a secret from her family. Muna finds herself gripping the edge of the bench, body tilted away as if he might strike her. She tries to find something to say, because she does love him, of course she loves him, but her love is fractured and wild, more enthralled with his admiration of her than hers of him. Muna works to find something to say and all she can produce is, I'm too young, which her mother tells her all the time. She looks away as he leaves, because the jerky motion of his crippled body as he quickens his pace is embarrassing now.

At night the pain in her limbs is so terrible that she cannot eat or sleep and she lies in her shuttered room and dislocated phrases from the poem will not leave her, and the vision of his anger becomes more and more frightening. In the morning she calls Ani, who comes over immediately, and they lie on the floor and smoke and talk until they conclude that all of this will pass, indeed, there is something romantic about how enraged he became. They listen to Ella Fitzgerald and giggle and sing and begin to recover from this declaration of love as if they both were present at the unfolding of the poem. Ani twists around the room to the music and Muna laughs and the breeze blows their hair across their cheeks.

During the following months, they listen to him singing softly in the night, they gather the flowers he leaves on the steps, they read the poems he slips underneath the door, and Muna meets him occasionally because their past friendship haunts her: she misses being allied to someone forbidden by her parents, she misses him staring at her so intently as she reads out loud. She keeps thinking that if she only waits, he will understand that they can be friends, he will stop begging her to love him. And one day it seems this finally has happened: he calls and says he has a present for her because he is sorry for all the trouble he has caused.

Muna waits for him at the window, chin on her folded arms, and the sun shines and cars pass and she imagines setting things right. It is pleasing to be so optimistic, so when he arrives she is happy and full of plans: she runs down to the street and obediently closes her eyes, shifting from one foot to the other while he fumbles with keys to open the car's trunk, she holds her hands out palms up and smiles, listening to the key in the lock and the gritty sound of the hood being lifted. Just one more second, he says, and she laughs and says, I'm waiting.

—That's not at all how it happened, Mummy says, but she will not tell me the truth, she says it is hers and I can't have everything just because I ask.

Muna reclines on the rocking bench at her house in the mountains, oblivious, reading a book, and any one of us could be on the verge of becoming what she has become. She sits on a bench under the jasmine, oblivious, the whole future of her life resting in the low summer heat, in the hiss of water running through the hose towards the azalea, in the slow swing of the rocking bench, in the smell of the flagstones dripping with water and loose streams of dirt running from the garden plots, in the small African deer nosing the wire fence of their enclosure, and above, beyond the stairs, beyond the black iron gate, the sound of a car coming up the road; Muna, her palms flat on the pages of her book, looks up, thinking about anything, anything other than what will come, and all of the time that's splayed before us fills and unravels with the sorrow of this, and this is what is most true. The car comes to a stop outside the upper gate. *Beep-beep* the car says. *Beep-beep*. Muna's mother glances at her daughter, her writer, her slender olive branch, and she smells the rich earth of the garden that is now full, the water running away over the glistening stones, and it is all there, in the pines and the deer and the creak of the rocking bench, and Muna climbing the stairs two at a time now, tan legs and lemonade dress.

Muna was not nineteen when she died, and it did not all happen how I say, and so it is that stories are told. The cripple who loved her said he had a present, and she waited with her eyes closed, and he shot her and then himself. I turn the page of an album and Muna coyly hides her face from my eyes, and next to her, wearing the same outfit, Mummy grins at the camera as if a trick has just been played. When Mummy was fourteen, she would walk slowly along the Corniche to Muna's house in Ras Beirut, and the walk would take an hour, and it was terribly romantic, to be walking along the shore with the sea moaning around the rocks and the couples hand-in-hand under the sun, and she longed to be met, to be seen and spoken to but nothing ever happened, and she would arrive at Muna's house where they sneaked cigarettes and dreamed about love, as if all the future were theirs. And on the day Muna died Mummy ran from the beach, she ran through the streets to Daddy's house to cry in his arms.

Mummy has all the albums out now, and she's found a photo

of Alaine and me under the Christmas tree. We're in wool stock-
ings, sweaters, and kilts with those big safety pins, Alaine's navy
and mine red, and the green tree is beautiful, full of shining red,
gold, blue balls, strings of Lebanese flags, and candles burning so
everything sparkles color and light.

This photo stops her. Her hands stop and the creaking of the pages
stopping leaves the room so quiet. Then Mummy circles Alaine's
face with her finger, she says wonderingly, But how was she so sad,
even then?

I bend closer, and I see it too, in such contrast to me with my
white blond hair, brimming with *I can't sit still* and grinning. Next
to me the pinched face of my older sister, just ten, kneeling with
her hands on her knees. In all this candlelight she is off-center, in
shadow, and I know she must have yielded the better spot to me,
in her gentle way. She kneels so still, even now the depth of her
obedience is striking and so how could Mummy not have seen? Her
brushed hair pulled back with two blue barrettes leaves her face
exposed, and her white face is all eyes and small, tucked-in mouth,
as if she senses what lies ahead, and the eyes say, *Help me,* reaching
us in time only now, my arm around Mummy who's tucking the
album to her chest, whispering, I'm sorry, my darlings.

I speak of everything. There is a word for everything, for love and its differences, for certain moments, for sex, for a corpse. There are words, and they tumble from me in a waterfall, a fountain that trickles over cold stone sculptures that I carve, the soft white stone, the eternal stone of paper. But of this city there are only images that repeat themselves as if emerging from dreams, over and over, the same images without words, without language, and when they come there is only fear, when they come and I show them, always it is with fear and in a solitude without language, without description, they go nowhere, they are in mirrors lying opposite each other, endlessly repeated, always the same, and the fear takes me, I speak, I write, indecipherable. The images themselves: the poppies, the garbage heaped on the sidewalks, the cripples, the gunmen, the road south, the coast road, the Banyan tree, the people, again and again: Mrs. Awad, who never existed, is framed like the eyeless timeless woman in the window from the Balawat Gates, history repeats itself, she is cut from stone, and her desire to hear Najib's footfall is Sabha's remembrance of Amina, it is the cool water trickling down stone stairs as Muna runs, two stairs at a time, towards the gate, it is Ziad's thumb on the safety, his palm sending the chamber into a metallic spin, it is Alaine's hands on her bleeding knees, toes gripping the earth, it is Mummy's grief and the gentle roll of tears on Daddy's cheeks as he says good-bye to the land that threatens to devour him. The places and the people, endlessly repeating themselves in silence and in fear and in solitude. How can I tell? I tell and I feel nothing. Only the fear, the search for language, a code that does not exist, it cannot, a way to read, to decipher, translate the alphabet of these images, the *s* of the road, the *o* of the sea, the endless *m* of the wave-trails in the sand, the *z* of the crippled body, the *l* of the soldier on the ground, the *u* of Saisaban's wings in the sky, the alphabet of the universe, the colors of the tracers when I was drunk on the roof twirling in my black dress celebrating, the sound of the rockets over my head, in my head, in my hair, that whistle, the bomb, the great bombs that filled my body, you see, no words, only a wish to find and not to find words, to feel and not to feel, to remember and not to remember. Images without language, without code, words without language. There is hatred for feeling and remembering and hatred for not feeling and not remembering, for language that has no strength, its frailty, its innocence on a page that can be torn, crumpled, its susceptibility to violence, for language at all, that it exists, only to hold my tongue, to twist it, to cut it out.

I am fourteen and when a chauffeur arrives to pick me up for Ziad's costume party, Mummy smiles and trusts him and we go, and it is in this way that history might be changed, because in this moment nothing has happened yet, there is still a year or two until his death.

The nightclub is on the sea. The road leading down the hill is decorated on either side with beautifully manicured cacti and white boulders, and palm trees rustle and the lights sparkle over the water and people in costumes push past when I stop to gape at the wonders. A tall woman swathed in white feathers spins by, accompanied by a man in a cape, and more people, so many more, in glittering shoes and gowns and masks and gloves and the chauffeur pulls me, Come on, it's time.

I enter the nightclub through a magnificent arched doorway and the lights reflected off the mirror ball speckle arms and faces and walls, going round and round, and Ziad is there, a drink in one hand and the other resting on a woman's shoulder. How do you describe the handsomeness of someone who will die in so many ways, his story distorted and ridiculed and retold? Possibly his hair is still black and curly, his skin dark from the sun that shines on an irresponsible, capricious lifestyle, and it could be that he is dressed in white since this is his farewell party and he is the prince. His silk shirt reflects the warm glow of the spinning lights, the radiance of his revolution so long in the making.

In the back office, the walls trembling with the beats of music, with the laughter and shouting and dancing outside, Ziad lowers his forehead to the desk, his temples sore with the headache of orchestrating such happiness in the midst of a war. The office smells of leather and cigarettes. I stand in the corner, the princess, waiting to be kissed.

—Do you remember, he says at last, how the horse waited in the shade while I spent whole afternoons in her house? and of course I do, these are not details to be discarded, and the horse's eyes are half-shut, tail slapping at flies, and its great white wings are folded and the feathers flutter in a breeze scented with pine. Ziad stands up, he is more animated now that everything is coming back, that unrepressed joy at having invented a solution to the war. He cannot be restrained: he is destined to live and live and live, and the war means nothing to him nor to me: it is a figment, a kite streamer of contradictions and promises, of cease-fires and gunshots dismantling the sky. So he paces the room and his shirt dampens with sweat as he draws the fantastic images of the future in the air, his hands shaping this new world. He will steal for all this, he tells me, he will steal and steal and he does not care. Ziad is malicious, handsome: he is too much for this war, it will never contain him.

On the beach we slide the kayak into the water. I lie on my back while he paddles, and my head is at the prow and the sea rushes past my ears, sloshing onto our bodies, cold and unforgiving of what will come and of my frail attempt to avert it, and on the shore the party wails on, lighting up the waves and the rocks and the trees. When the sea is deep, when the party has become a flickering parade of lights, Ziad tucks the paddle between us, puts his arms around me, and I think I might have done it now, rescued him from the dying that is coming for him. His breath spreads and fades regularly on my damp cheek and he whispers, There is nothing this country can do to me, and this might have been possible, for him to say such a thing.

The sky is vast. Before us, between our tangled feet, the mountains divide the stars from the earth, and behind us, for we are lying with our heads to the west, the mammoth battleships distort the line of the sea. We float here, Ziad and I, between the fierceness of his living and my memory of it, between the silence of the American fleet and the coming winter bombardment, between lips and hands and ink that is smudged in anger. If we could only stay here long enough.

None of this can be remembered. If it were to fit into history, then the suicide missions against the foreign soldiers and following bombardment of Souq al-Gharb by the American fleet are only months away, and soon the hotel in Dhour al-Shweir where Téta and Jiddo celebrated their wedding, scandalizing the family, will be destroyed by the Syrians, or Phalange, or Israelis, what does it matter, and the roads lined with firs and olive groves will be impassable. People will vanish, and Uncle Ara and Astrig will crawl along the side of Crystal Mountain, shooting chickens, scrounging for food, while Druze fighters fire rockets from the road below. A man from the village will beg these soldiers to arrange themselves elsewhere, and they, surprisingly, will comply. Uncle Ara and Astrig will descend from the mountain in winter, alive as saints, thinner, full of anecdotes about stupid gunmen and vegetables and fruit growing in gardens that are wildly luxuriant, dumb to the war and left to flourish without restraint. In this time Ziad was there, and he, too, grew wild and untended. But now, none of this matters, it is not important: Ziad breathes against my cheek, his arms around me, and the sea that has no illusions rocks beneath us, and the land waits for him to yield with the security of things ordained.

I do not know when the war began. I've read of April 13, 1975, which would be a few days before Téta's birthday and five months after Jiddo's death. Jiddo had died because his brain suddenly started bleeding, Daddy explained, and this left a cold feeling in my head, a terror of faint movements and trickles. Late at night I spoke with Jiddo, my hands waving in the dark, until Mummy came in to rock me back to sleep.

On the weekend before Téta's birthday, Uncle Ara and Auntie Lupsi hosted a party at their house in Shemlan, and all the aunts and uncles and cousins attended, but Mummy stayed home with me because I was sick. I see the party, the cars blocking the dirt road, I hear the chatter ringing down the hillside. Téta sits on the verandah, smiling and nodding politely; no one is truly merry, not so soon after Jiddo's passing, but they all make the effort. The day winds on, and at dusk when the revelers head for Beirut, they find themselves ensnared in traffic, cars backed up for miles in response to the busload of Palestinians that have been attacked by the Kataeb. Téta, one month shy of dying from grief, waits in the car next to the absence of her husband, staring out at the chaos and the lights of Beirut blinking in the distance.

In another time that is the same, darkness falls on the boat pulling away from the harbor and the mountain blinks with light, farther away by the moment. I search for the flashes that signal Uncle Ara's good-bye, and the boat picks up speed but I grip the rail, searching. Then Alaine saw it and pointed, a series of flickers, like a bulb that is almost spent, and perhaps Mummy gazed at it with a hunger greater than mine, as if this frail winking light held the power to bring us back one day. What did I know of the what was coming,

305 ~·

of the yearning, the dreams? My eyes took in these mountains with the edgy casualness of someone used to voyages, and the land receded as was expected, without care, without surprises. Through the silence of the spray, the sea slapping the sides of the boat, the light flickered for the last time then stayed a dim glow so that I lost it among the others, and the shore was farther away with each passing moment that we waited for the signal to come again, although I knew that Uncle Ara would think us too far away.

I left the deck with Alaine, but at the door to the cabin I looked back to find Mummy. She stood facing the way we had come, her legs close together and her hand stretched out to grip the rail, and the boat was lurching beneath us but her body was stiff, unflinching. Her other arm hung along her side, and now and then her hand moved, smoothing her wool skirt. I knew her face, the way it would be, still and resolute, full of that dignified courage people always praised, and I wished I had stayed beside her. I leaned my forehead against the cold, damp wall that smelled of oil, of this voyage and her sadness, of knowing that we were leaving and not coming back.

I sit in the bedroom, leaning my elbow on the windowsill. It is snowing this evening. The flakes floating past the window are big and velvety, filling the sky, obscuring the houses across the street. I can hear Alaine and Daddy discussing their new project, which is insulation. Mummy brings me boots she bought in a thrift store. They are the kind I have always wanted, with fur on the inside. She leaves them next to me still wrapped in a paper bag.

There is the future coming, I feel its wide hands opening around me, the wind like voices, but it is not for here. I put on my new boots and tie the laces, and I go outside into this strange, white world. The snow is quiet and soft, and low broad evergreens bend beneath the snow's weight, their branches forming caves. After I almost died, I felt for weeks a terror that I had been trapped between the living and the dead, that my dreams about home were actually voyages in time and space, and one day soon the two times of my two lives would meet and this almost-death would reveal itself as having really happened. My hands open and close against the cold, throat constricted with tears. I see again and again the light of the door opening, I feel Daddy's hands lifting me, the grief of his voice and face as he begs me not to die, and there is no changing this. But in the silence of this snowfall, so surprising and clean that it hurts, it might be possible to listen carefully, to stare into the whiteness of this late night, and perhaps in the distance on the slope of this foreign road the wings of Saisaban will spread open like milk spilling from a ewer, and his eyes, black as *mazoot*, will gaze with forgiveness on my remembering, and his hooves, sharp as bullets, will pierce the frozen air as he gallops towards me.

Acknowledgments

It was Jerry Badanes, my professor at Sarah Lawrence College, who many years ago gently guided me toward writing about the war, and who read the first pages that came from those efforts. He was my teacher, a second father, a friend. His voice remains with me always.

It has been my great fortune to have many readers along the way; you all have my sincerest thanks. I am particularly grateful to Hanan al-Shaykh, Andrea Barrett, Nicholas Delbanco, and Anton Shammas for your invaluable advice and encouragement over the years; Dan Gutstein, Danny Silverman, and Kit Ward, for your perceptive, critical readings; Nate Flink, for generously obliging my request for a title; Zeina Barakeh, for your beautiful paintings; and of course my family, for your patience and understanding, and my husband Tamer Alamuddin, for teaching me to read in different ways. Matt Bialer, I have come to count on your constant belief in me, and appreciate it more than I can express. Fiona McCrae and Anne Czarniecki at Graywolf, I am profoundly touched and thankful for your sensitive, insightful editing and your faith in my being able to bring this book to completion.

Above all, my deepest gratitude to Jenna D'Alvia for editing every draft with such loving care, and for your precious friendship.

About the Author

PATRICIA SARRAFIAN WARD was born and raised in Beirut, Lebanon, and came to the United States when she was eighteen. She holds a B.A. from Sarah Lawrence College and an M.F.A. from the University of Michigan, where she received Colby and Cowden fellowships and Hopwood awards in Novel and Short Fiction. Since graduate school she has lived in Lebanon and several U.S. states. She currently makes her home in New Jersey.

This book has been set in Apollo, a typeface designed by the prolific type designer Adrian Frutiger, a Swiss immigrant to France. Book design by Wendy Holdman. Typesetting by Stanton Publication Services, St. Paul, Minnesota. Manufactured by Friesens on acid-free paper.

Graywolf Press is a not-for-profit, independent press. The books we publish include poetry, literary fiction, essays, and cultural criticism. We are less interested in best-sellers than in talented writers who display a freshness of voice coupled with a distinct vision. We believe these are the very qualities essential to shape a vital and diverse culture.

Thankfully, many of our readers feel the same way. They have shown this through their desire to buy books by Graywolf writers; they have told us this themselves through their e-mail notes and at author events; and they have reinforced their commitment by contributing financial support, in small amounts and in large amounts, and joining the "Friends of Graywolf."

If you enjoyed this book and wish to learn more about Graywolf Press, we invite you to ask your bookseller or librarian about further Graywolf titles; or to contact us for a free catalog; or to visit our award-winning web site that features information about our forthcoming books.

We would also like to invite you to consider joining the hundreds of individuals who are already "Friends of Graywolf" by contributing to our membership program. Individual donations of any size are significant to us: they tell us that you believe that the kind of publishing we do matters. Our web site gives you many more details about the benefits you will enjoy as a "Friend of Graywolf"; but if you do not have online access, we urge you to contact us for a copy of our membership brochure.

www.graywolfpress.org

Graywolf Press
2402 University Avenue, Suite 203
Saint Paul, MN 55114
Phone: (651) 641-0077
Fax: (651) 641-0036
E-mail: wolves@graywolfpress.org